SLOW POISON

HELEN SLAVIN

D1336260

AGORA BOOKS

ABOUT THE AUTHOR

Helen Slavin was born in Heywood in Lancashire in 1966. She was raised by eccentric parents on a diet of Laurel and Hardy, William Shakespeare and the Blackpool Illuminations. Educated at her local comp her favourite subjects at school were English and Going Home.

After The University of Warwick she worked in many jobs including, plant and access hire, a local government Education department typing pool, and a vasectomy clinic. A job as a television scriptwriter gave her the opportunity to spend all day drinking tea, living in a made-up fantasy world and getting paid for it (sometimes).

Helen has been a professional writer for fifteen years. Her first novel *The Extra Large Medium* was chosen as the winner in the Long Barn Books competition run by Susan Hill.

A paragliding Welsh husband and two children distract her and give her ample opportunity to spend all day drinking tea, nagging about homework and washing pants for England. In the wee small hours she still keeps a bijou flat in that fantasy world of writing. When not working with animals and striving for world peace, Helen enjoys the music of Elbow and baking bread. Her favourite colour is purple and if she had to be stranded on a desert island with someone it would be Ray Mears (alright, George Clooney is very good looking but can he make fire with a stick? No. See?)

She now lives, with her family, in Trowbridge, Wiltshire where, when she's not writing, she's asleep. Or in Tesco.

If you'd like to hear more from Helen, visit her website,
www.helenslavin.com

twitter.com/HelenSlavinBook

SLOW POISON

HELEN SLAVIN

First published in Great Britain in 2018 by Agora Books

Agora Books is a division of Peters Fraser + Dunlop Ltd

55 New Oxford Street, London WC1A 1BS

1

THE VISITOR

Cob Cottage shuddered in the wind, the rain lashing on the windows like tears as the Way sisters stared at the rounded object on the floor at Charlie's feet. It was a head. Definitely, without any doubt, this was a man's head. The wind howled mournfully as Emz looked down at the rather waxen closed eye corpse face, the flesh hanging a bit flaccid just there, where the cheek met the mat, the hair streaked across the forehead where it was brown with blood, but, if she looked for a longer moment she saw the ghost image of his real face, offering her a glimpse of how he had looked when alive. This lost face looked up at her, tired and sad and weary. She knelt beside him, reached to push the hair out of his face, where a strand straggled across his eye and into his slightly open mouth.

Emz touching the head seemed to break a spell that had drifted over them. The waif-like woman, who had carried this burden, darted forward to retrieve her fallen treasure, her small thin fingers pulling the rags around it.

"What are you doing?" she snapped, holding the head tight to her body. Emz held up her hands in a small surrendering gesture.

"Tidying his hair," she said in a quiet voice. This answer wiped the cross expression from the woman's weather bedraggled face and her shoulders dropped slightly before she reached again for her bravado and drew herself up. She was distracted for a moment, stashing the tattered package into her ragged coat. The material, Anna noted, was thin and black and worn and it was torn in places so that she looked as if she had been clawed by wild animals. Anna looked up into her face. Pale. Tired. Strained.

She was breathing hard, her lips pinched as she regarded the three of them.

"This is Cob Cottage?" the woman asked, her eyes darting quick glances at the furniture, the windows. "In Havoc Wood? I'm at the right place?"

Anna's muscle memory kicked her a little.

"Come far?" she asked. The woman backed off a step as if stung, and, Charlie noted, clenched her fist at her side as if in readiness for a fight.

"Where's Hettie Way?" The woman's voice was strong, but Anna could hear the undercurrent of uncertainty, recognised it from her own voice in the last year. Anna's head filled with a smoky image of the boat carrying their grandmother's coffin, burning its way across the lake. She found she couldn't speak for a moment. "You aren't her." The woman asked again, angrier this time, "Where is she?"

"She died." It was Charlie who spoke, brief and to the horrible point. At this the woman looked quite as distraught as the Ways. Her early bravado drained out of her with the rainwater that was puddled on the mat beneath her feet. She had looked skinny before but now she looked ethereal, a pearly grey tone glossed over her skin. Anna was about to say something more welcoming, but their weary guest was crumpling like a paper bag, the head once more rolling from her grasp. Anna stepped forward with a sharp cry, her fingers clutching at the falling woman's sleeve as Charlie lurched to the rescue, arms outstretched.

"Help," Charlie yelped. As Charlie and Emz lifted the slight figure, Anna pulled over the long one-armed sofa. Cushions propped their visitor up as Anna, who by now was shaking, moved to the kitchen to put the kettle on and start to grill a cheese sandwich. There was safety of sorts, in food, for Anna at least.

Emz picked up the severed head and tried to wrap it up in the rags it had been transported in. They were not up to the task, too raggedy and tattered to be of any use at all. Unwilling to throw them away Emz put them to one side and reached for a clean tea towel. That still didn't feel right. To top it all as she put the head down on the table it began to roll slightly once more, as if, scary thought, *don't think the scary thought Emz*, it might still be alive. Emz took her fine wool scarf from the chair by the window and wrapped the head in that before placing it in the crook of the visitor's arm between her and the sofa. Safe.

There was a sudden silence, broken only by the kettle sounds. The Ways looked at each other. Charlie made a face at Anna who shrugged and then they both looked at Emz as if she might have an explanation.

"What are you looking at me for?" Emz asked. Her sisters hesitated for a second.

"It saves having to look at the head," Charlie reasoned.

"What would Grandma do?" Anna's face was creased into a frown as she turned back through the arch as the kettle boiled up. There was the sound of teapot and teabags and chinking of mugs so that life seemed still to be real and happening.

"I don't think Grandma Hettie knew everyone who arrived here," Charlie decided.

"No. Well, obvs. And this is being the Gamekeepers isn't it? Marshalling and patrolling..." Emz cast an anxious glance at the prone figure of their visitor, "and... stuff." Charlie gave a doubtful snort.

"Nothing is easy in Havoc Wood," Anna said as she stepped back through the arch with a tray laden with the leftover scones from yesterday, the freshly melted cheese sandwich and the tea things. The scent of the cheese sandwich seemed to revive their guest in the same manner as a defibrillator. She sat upright, threatened, and at once Emz stepped forward.

"Here," she said, pointing to the scarfed parcel. "He's here. It's alright." The woman grabbed for him, struggled with her burden, the roundness of the head sitting uneasily within the too small confines of her jacket, her knuckles whitening with the effort of holding it to her.

"Would you like something to eat? A drink?" Anna smiled. The woman eyed the food as she took in a deep breath.

"When did Hettie Way pass?" the woman asked. "When was word sent?"

The Way sisters sought each other's gaze before Anna took in a deep breath.

"In July." The brief announcement was all she could manage. The woman began to count back on her fingers and at the conclusion of that she fell deeper into thoughts.

"She was gone before I set off," the woman mused. "Who are you?" she glared at them, the glare sparking against Charlie.

"We're her granddaughters," she declared, folding her arms like a barricade. "We're the Gamekeepers."

The visitor took in this information along with a further deeper breath and Anna asked, in a soft cat's whisker of a voice, "Would you like some tea?" There was a silence, as if she had offered poison; no one moved. With a decisive clearing of her throat, Charlie reached forward and picked up the knife. This action seemed to rattle the visitor and she rose up a little in her seat, defensive, but, rather than stab anyone, Charlie cut the melting, unctuous cheese sandwich into four quarters and took the first one.

"Be careful, it's hot," Anna warned. Charlie gave her an impatient look and blew gently on the hot bread and cheese before popping it into her mouth. Anna and Emz quickly understood and reached for their pieces. The scent of the toastie was deeply savoury, Anna having sprinkled just a pinch of paprika, a hint of cayenne and a smudge of mustard into the buttery, cheesy filling.

The woman flexed her shoulders back to stretch them and reached for her morsel. She nibbled at the edge. Her blonde hair was drying in the warm fug of Cob Cottage and it was beginning to make her look like a dandelion clock, wispy, flyaway. As she nibbled a little more, a little more, Charlie buttered a scone, Emz reached for a triangle of toast and Anna poured a cup of tea.

"So," Anna said as the three sisters unconsciously took up their triangulated positions around the visitor, "come far?"

The visitor took a sip of tea and nodded.

"Far enough."

The exchange of these few words settled something between them. The visitor was not forthcoming with any further information. Charlie was growing impatient with politeness and diplomacy.

"What's your name?" Charlie asked. The visitor took a moment's pause and so Charlie met her half way. "I'm Charlie. Charlotte if you're being formal," she said. Their visitor narrowed her eyes for a second and decided to trust them, a little.

"Ailith." Her voice was soft and low.

"Want to tell us where you started out? How your journey began?" Charlie prompted, her arms unfolded now but leaning forward, elbows on her knees, interrogative.

"Started out a long way away from here." The visitor's breathing was easier, her face less strained. "Back... home." The thought pained her, they all saw it, even Charlie backing off a little in sympathy with this.

"Who's your... who is the...?" Emz nodded to the bulge in Ailith's coat. Their visitor moved her hand once more, protective. The sisters could see where exhaustion and worry were making her drift. Charlie reached for a buttered piece of scone, shuffled it onto a plate for the woman.

"Here," she said. "Eat."

Without asking Emz moved the pot of jam forward.

"Hettie Way made the jam, if that helps," she smiled. "Last autumn. From the blackberries at the edge of the wood." The rain began to drum against the thatch, against the round oak window. Anna felt afraid, as if the door might blow open any moment and Ailith would be lost to them, whisked out into the wind.

"They killed him." Ailith's voice had sunk to a whisper, as if she was talking to herself. "That's where it started. Where they killed him."

Ailith reached up, her hand making measured swipes at her tears. The Way sisters did not move, only their eyes reaching for each other, realising that it was nearly one o'clock and it looked like it was going to be a long night ahead of them.

2

ROLL OUT THE PUMPKINS

Charlie Way sipped at her morning coffee and let her thoughts roll around like dice. She was standing by the sink letting her gaze brush past the garden, which needed a tidy, and on into the trees. Her phone pipped out a couple of times. She glanced down at the several texts from Aron, half reading them before deleting them. She didn't want to think about him and here he was trying to sneak his way into her head. That was the trouble with a text. It was like telepathy, or a whisper. Thoughts of Aron made her edgier still and she drank deeply from her coffee mug, inhaling and wanting the aromas to fog up her head, hide her thoughts.

Her coffee, she noticed, always tasted better at Cob Cottage and she thought it must be the spring water that affected it. This thought mingled with her cogitations regarding the wedding brew she was perfecting and her experiments with a stronger, distilled Blackberry Ferment. She thought she would borrow the Drawbridge van and bring up some of the gallon kegs from work and fill them with spring water to further her experiments.

She was, very effectively, trying not to think about Ailith and the head of the unknown warrior chieftain that she had carried to

Havoc Wood. She was avoiding, with some skill, going over the story of a battle, betrayal and a beheading that they had coaxed from Ailith, a task that had taken until the early hours. If, by accident, Charlie's brain strayed towards those thoughts they did not sit well.

The porch doors opened, and Anna came in from the chill morning.

"Hey," she smiled, and Charlie nodded at the coffee pot and reached for a mug for her sister. Anna had been up very early; Charlie had heard her pottering about in the kitchen and then talking to Emz before she left for a shift at Prickles and, no doubt, some bit of her slightly lax sixth form schedule.

"You off shortly?" Anna asked. Charlie stared at her.

"What?" Charlie asked as Anna reached up to tie her hair. Charlie stared harder. "That's all you're going to say?"

Anna fiddled with her hair some more and did not let her gaze fall from her sister's.

"I don't know what to say," she replied, finally abandoning both ponytail and any pretence at normality.

"Okay, that I can work with. I mean, Ailith has a severed head with her. I didn't dream that did I?" Charlie looked edgy, holding onto her mug like a ceramic life raft, and Anna lifted her own coffee mug, drank deeply to join her. She shook her head.

"No. I saw it. Emz saw it. It is real. It's really a head."

They considered that fact for a moment.

"This isn't like Seren is it?" Charlie said. Anna shook her head.

"Seren walked into Havoc Wood, this woman has walked out of it," Anna said. Charlie took in a deep bright breath and her face lightened. With a quick grin she chinked her sister's mug.

"That's it. That's exactly it." Charlie looked relieved. The feeling did not last long. "What do we do next?" She chewed her lip and waited for her sister to take a fortifying glug of coffee. Anna looked pale today.

"I suggest you go to work as normal," Anna began. Charlie interrupted.

"Normal? Erm... Normal for Havoc Wood you mean?" she gave a slightly manic laugh. It had been a long night. Anna nodded, calm and quiet.

"Yes. I can manage here until lunchtime, but then I'm due at work." Anna's eyes widened as they both hedged around the same thought.

"And then we have to leave her alone here," Charlie stated the small bald fact. They exchanged a glance.

"Yes. I think we do," Anna said. "She doesn't appear to be a threat."

"You think she's more a Visitor than say... a Poacher or Trespasser?" The sisters stared not at each other this time but out through the kitchen window. Their grandmother's ghost pinched out the unruly shoots on the sweet peas.

"Was there ever a time when a Poacher or a Trespasser came into the house?" Anna asked. The two sipped more coffee and remembered. Anna recalled standing at Thinthrough one afternoon as their grandmother saw off two skinny lads and their deadly trap. *"I'll trap you..."* she had warned, and they were gone through the trees.

"Do you remember the man on the bridge?" she looked at Anna, waited for the memory to surface.

The man at the bridge over the Rade, the bright silver fish in his net.

"I caught it to eat it," was his excuse to Grandma Hettie.

"On the Hook Bridge. The fish." Anna laughed.

"She made him eat it. Remember?" Charlie grinned. Anna remembered, vividly.

"Raw," Anna nodded. "Right there." A memory of guts and scales. Charlie tugged them back into the present by refilling their mugs; the coffee splashed onto the table top as Anna considered.

"She was allowed to stay. That must mean something." Anna

sifted her own thoughts and questions and Charlie had a moment of inspiration.

"We *can* leave her here. Cob Cottage will look after itself and her."

"Will it?" Anna waited for the logic. Charlie nodded, certain.

"When Aron came over the place pretty much picked on him. Trapped his fingers, jammed the doors."

Anna looked at Charlie, waiting for a punchline. Charlie nodded. "It's true. If there's something she shouldn't do this place won't let her do it."

The two sisters drank coffee in silence for several moments before Anna spoke.

"We just have to take a leap of faith, don't we?"

And on that decision, Charlie headed into work.

With Charlie gone Anna tidied up the mugs and the breakfast things and realised that Emz had forgotten her lunch. It was still sitting in its plastic box on the countertop by the sink. She put it into the fridge. She was thinking over the story that Ailith had told them of her journey, trying to examine all the pieces of it.

They flickered through her head trying to arrange themselves and could not. Anna gasped to herself. What was going on there?

"Good morning." Ailith's voice cut into Anna's thoughts and made her leap out of her skin. Ailith, Anna noticed, was polite enough to look away. Anna recovered herself and smiled.

"Good morning. Did you sleep well?"

Ailith nodded rather noncommittally.

"Thank you, yes. And you?" she asked. Ailith's thin eyebrows, a very dark brown against the wheaten gold of her hair, were raised in genuine question.

"Yes, yes, I did, thank you."

There was an awkward moment. Ailith's gaze was intense, as if she was trying to work her out and for a few seconds Anna realised they were indeed in a kind of battle, each looking intently, trying to read the other. Anna broke away first.

"So, what about some breakfast?" she offered, and unable to find a smile she looked away, busied herself with the kettle. Ailith cast a searching gaze around the kitchen.

"Shall I fetch eggs? Or I can fry you up some bacon perhaps."

Anna watched their guest's eyes skim over the kitchen as she spoke, taking in the sink, the pans, finding her way around. Anna waited as Ailith's eyes tracked back to her face. Anna realised she was waiting for instruction.

"Oh. No. That's not what I meant at all. You're the guest here, Ailith, I will cook for you." Anna stopped herself. It was a small message, *Servant*. Ailith was used to being the one doing the work. With that filed away for reference Anna was breezier. "I was thinking of making pancakes," Anna offered. "If you'd like? Take a seat?" Anna gestured to a chair. Ailith looked uncertain but after a moment, bent herself into the chair, held herself stiff and uncomfortable.

"Have you lived here long?" Ailith asked as Anna began to reach for the eggs, the bowl, the whisk.

"Not long." Anna's mind was in two places; trying to make small talk was struggling against trying to work out Ailith.

"Of course, no. Your grandmother. Of course." Ailith seemed to be chastising herself mentally. There was a silence. It appeared their guest was no better at making polite conversation. As Anna moved around the kitchen fetching the flour and butter the tension from Ailith was tangible. She wanted, Anna could tell, to be busy and so, as she lit the stove, Anna nodded towards the bowl.

"Ailith, would you like to mix the…" she began. Ailith did not wait to be asked twice; leaping out of the chair she was cracking eggs before Anna finished the sentence. She was more settled with a whisk in her hand.

"You have always lived in the town?" Ailith asked once again. They moved around each other in their joint task.

"Yes. And in Havoc Wood of course, when we stayed with our

grandmother." Anna felt the rush of memory, felt safe within it. The scent from the pan was scorching a little. "Oh, butter..." she turned to reach for the pat in a small dish. Ailith reached, their hands touching briefly, setting off a flickerbook of images in Anna's mind. Ailith pulled her hand back, startled. She stared at Anna. Anna stared back, her heart pounding with what she had seen. She looked down at her hands, recalled the edge of a memory. *"What do you see Anna? I've asked you before... a long time ago when you were little... do you remember?"*

It was like this. It was always like this. Don't be afraid.

Anna reached her hand forwards once again with a gentle nod. After a moment or so Ailith took it. The flickerbook rattled by in seconds. Cliffs. Coastline. Castle. Kitchen. Smoke. Sword. Anna released her hand, looked at Ailith, unsmiling. It was intense, the details blurred and clashed but Anna understood something of what she had been through.

"You're here now, in Havoc. You made it." Anna said. In the pan, the butter burned. Anna turned swiftly to tip it into the sink and to snick another knob into the pan. As it sizzled Ailith asked her question once more.

"Your sisters, do they work in the town?" Ailith reached for cutlery from the pot on the drainer and Anna talked.

IT WAS a good hour later when Anna realised that she had talked a great deal about herself and Ailith had told her almost nothing in return. A little black cloud began to drift over Anna's internal horizon. Hmm. She might have made some sort of small mistake. She felt it, clearly, as she sat across the table from Ailith who was nibbling at the last of the stack of heavily syruped pancakes. She backtracked over all she'd said. Nothing too deep, nothing too serious, but still. She thought she would text Emz and Charlie later and tell them to keep a watch out for this. Anna was not certain, but she felt that she might have been manipulated into her actions as if Ailith had some knack of always turning the conversation onto the track she wanted.

Or was Anna just being paranoid? She watched Ailith, the wary way she ate. This woman had travelled a long way from dangerous times and with a precious, to her at least, package. There was nothing trivial about her.

"I have to head off to work in a while." As she mentioned it Anna watched and was rewarded by sight of the smallest flash of fear in Ailith's face. She was relieved rather than sympathetic.

"You are going out?"

"Yes." Anna waited. Let the track go her way in this conversation. *We are the Ways.* Let Ailith tell her something this time.

"Do I have to go out?" Ailith asked. Anna thought about her grandmother and the idea of asking yourself questions and finding the answer. This seemed like an answer, but she was going to push Ailith.

"I don't know. Do you?" she waited for the response. Ailith's thin lips mashed together for a moment's deep thought.

"No."

"What about your task?" Anna asked. She was aware that last night they had not been given the details of that task. Where, for instance, was Ailith taking the head?

"Today is not the day for that."

There was a moment between Anna and Ailith, their eyes locking. There was the thinnest glimpse of fear from Ailith, as small as the dilation of her pupils but it struck Anna. She was concluding very definitely that Ailith was not a threat or a danger, that she had come to Havoc Wood for help.

That said, as Anna left for work she licked her finger and made the pentacle sign on the door as she headed off.

SHE WAS aware of the looming personal anniversary that October was bringing. Halloween, the anniversary of the accident that had robbed her of husband and baby son. She had thought she was still safe in September, but on arriving at the Castle Inn she noted the red number on the small white square of calendar that sat on the reception desk. 1st October.

Some might think of a season of mist and mellow fruitfulness, some might dig out their favourite boots and scarves and prepare to kick through amber leaves, others might crave a little comfort food, a pudding here, a stew there. Anna Way saw time ticking down into a pit.

To avoid this, she strode on through to the kitchen and snatched at her fresh pinny and began clattering pans about as if the noise might scare away ghosts. *Nothing scares ghosts.* She began to prep for the lunchtime covers. They had a party of Japanese ladies coming in from the Castle, courtesy of a new local tour guide offering bespoke holidays in the Woodcastle area.

"Hey." Lella entered the kitchen wearing her usual little black dress, this one seeming littler than usual; it was slightly too short and rather too tight and Lella looked like a prisoner in it. She had the paper desk diary with her and her tablet, so she meant business.

"Have you got a minute after lunch to sit down and go through the Halloween stuff?" Lella asked. "Only we need to start advertising this week... so any ideas or brainwaves would be welcome..." Anna took in a deep slow breath. She could do this. This was how she could do this, with Cob Cottage and the Castle Inn combining to keep her busy. Of course.

"Yes. Round about 3:00? Lunch will be done by then and Casey can clean down..." Anna gave a beaming smile and, as her face stretched the muscles, she was reminded of Ailith and her wide grin.

"Lella..." Casey's voice had a warning in it. Lella stood in the doorway. "Can I have a word in the bar?" Casey wiped her hands and was pushing Lella out into the bar area. Anna felt a cold little hand of dread on her shoulder. To escape it, she followed her colleagues out. They were already arguing, Casey looking heated and Lella looking hurt and harassed.

"No... I am sorry. I am... I had not 'forgotten'... How could I forget that? Don't be..."

"Then why come in and harp on about Halloween? Hmm?" Casey was arms folded, defensive. Lella was leaning forward, her neck pinking with frustration and embarrassment.

"Seriously... I hadn't. I just didn't put the two together... I had my business head on Case..."

"Your business head? Is that the one full of air freshener? You weren't thinking..." Casey began. Lella had caught sight of Anna's approach and was trying to silence Casey, but Casey was in full flow. "She just doesn't need..."

"What don't I need?" Anna's voice was cool and calm and had the effect on Casey and Lella of a hand on their foreheads; they both took a deep breath and looked at her. "I don't need to think about Halloween festivities because of what happened last Halloween?"

There was a silence. Lella made a sort of popping sound as her mouth opened and closed, unable to find any words. "Wrong." Anna tried to sound reassuring. "I need to do this more than ever. I need to be super busy, the more faff and fuss there is this year the better it will be. I do not need to be sitting around thinking about the past. So, Lella, our meeting at 3:00 still stands... so let's... roll on the pumpkins!" She gave a smile that was glassily bright, but it would do. She touched Casey's shoulder.

"...Casey... breathe..."

Casey let out her breath with a splutter.

LATER, in the quiet of the guests' sitting room Lella talked of her plans for Halloween. They were looking over the posters and flyers for the Crimson Ball.

"The Crimson Ball is more... grown up I suppose? You know, a bit supernatural but in an elegant way."

"Gothic?" Anna suggested. Lella lit up at the suggestion.

"Ooh, yes, oh rats, I wish you'd said that to me before I got the posters printed. Dress code red and Gothic. Vampires. Tuxedos." Lella was daydreaming and enthusiastic and her glee reached into Anna, soothed a little.

"Sounds glamorous. It will make a change from all the orange and black trick or treat stuff," Anna said, fixing the smile on her face. Her mind drifted and she pulled it back, stopped the dark thoughts.

They discussed possible menus with seasonal ingredients for Witch Wednesday lunches and Anna heard herself talking about cakes and pastries and chi-chi puddings that people could lick seductively off spoons at the Crimson Ball.

"Seriously Anna..." Lella was pale faced, her hand stopping swiping at her tablet. "Is this all going to be okay?"

Anna smiled the glassy smile again. It was the facial equivalent of Cinderella's slipper and it might fall off her face at any second and smash on the floor.

"Yes. I mean it. Lots of noise and activity. Full on, full tilt, let's go for it."

Lella paused for a moment and Anna kept the energy level, smiled until her muscles were creaking under the strain. Lella looked down at the screen of her tablet and was swiping away once more.

"Okay. Witch Wednesdays. I had another thought? Get some broomsticks and some hats, not cheap witch hats, I've got a friend in Castle Hill who makes hats, she's got some really stylish ones which we could use as a display? Draw people in. Advertise to groups. Maybe? D'you think?" Lella was full of ideas. Anna smiled, the conversation was interesting. Where before she had been unsettled by the thoughts of Halloween and the anniversary it brought, now she was perturbed by the use of the word 'witch'.

"Okay. So. That's all done and dusted so we can start properly stressing over Woodcastle Apple Day." Lella shuffled some papers.

"We've got the pop-up then?" Anna asked. Lella was nodding.

"And some. All our info is on the website and they've given us a prime space..." Lella pulled up a map of the Apple Day Festival guide, her finger pointing to where in High Market Street their pop-up would be.

"Are you still on to do the hog roast? Or is that just too much to tackle?"

Anna discussed the hog roast plans and preparations with smiling enthusiasm but all she could think about was last year's Apple Day Festival, *wheeling Ethan in his buggy, the sweet of cinnamon, the sour of the cider vinegar.* Anna talked about apple cake and toffee apple flavoured titbits. She could hear herself talking: calm and clear above the rolling images of her memories, and there was a relief in the fact that she could do that.

At afternoon tea, busy today with the Castle Conservation Society Autumnfest, Anna dusted with icing sugar, sprinkled with caster sugar, made things ooze and squodge with cream, but inside she felt raggedy and thin, so much so, that by the time she was heading back to Cob Cottage she expected that the next breath of wind would blow her away.

3

TRESPASSER

Mrs Fyfe was moving at a swift and stealthy pace behind the raggedy girl and they had been travelling together, in a manner of speaking, for some days. Mrs Fyfe was careful not to let her travelling companion become aware of her own presence.

It had been a long dry time of late and she'd been tired out. She was not yet sure what talisman or tool it was that the girl carried. The power that leaked from her was not the kind that Mrs Fyfe could just drink in. Whatever she carried with her it was old magic indeed, the oldest, the kind you had to be very careful with, the kind of power that could own you, could draw you in until there was no way out. It was tempting in the dangerous challenge it offered.

Mrs Fyfe, it must be admitted, was up for a dangerous challenge. If she hadn't stumbled upon the girl sleeping in the hollow of the oak that night then, well, her current circumstances would be rather reduced. You could only live so long on a diet of squirrels.

At first, she had assumed the girl was a wanderer, the kind who was lost. She had tracked her for a few hours and when she was certain that the girl seemed ill at ease in the wooded country

Mrs Fyfe had taken herself by a quicker route to head her off at the crossroads at Five Ways. Mrs Fyfe always managed a mugging or picked up a stray here. She had a particular hiding place in a coppiced hazel where the saplings had grown up into a curve that was a most comfortable seat if you were in need of an hour or two's waiting. Her heart had been pounding at the prospect of this little adventure. One did not often stumble upon such powerful treasure.

Turned out the girl was no wanderer. She was ill at ease because of the burden she carried but she knew her way well enough. When it came to the crossroads she chose her route carefully and, fuelled by disappointment and desperation, Mrs Fyfe had followed and watched. The girl chose her paths with thought; they were not the main routes. These were the side ways and the shortcuts. This girl had been taught well. Damn her.

Mrs Fyfe did not give up. It was worth keeping up with this power. Just the drifts that came from it were invigorating to her. She would follow and, sooner or later, an opportunity to steal it would present itself.

Except that as the days tocked onwards Mrs Fyfe recognised the path and knew where the girl was heading. She took a moment, set her basket beside her on the stile just beyond the boundary and watched the raggedy girl enter Havoc Wood at Top Hundred. It would be easy to let her heart sink, to let the fear get a foothold. Mrs Fyfe was bound out of Havoc, couldn't take one step inside it on pain of, well, one didn't need to finish that sentence.

Mrs Fyfe sat for a few moments longer, her mind stretching itself. She'd come this far, there must be a way. The rain began to lash down, the wind nudged at her. In the distance the crenellations of Woodcastle Castle reached into the storm-tossed sky. Mrs Fyfe smiled to herself and dropped down towards Leap Woods, the mud speckling her neat black boots, the rain settling sparkling diamonds into her once black hair.

4

MARKING TERRITORY

Every time Emz ventured onto school grounds she felt something like the panic a squirrel might be prey to when it attempted to cross a road by running across the tarmac instead of leaping through a tree or two.

This was for two reasons. The whole Logan/Caitlin/Mark scenario was top of the list.

The events of Jess' party, the mad drunk insane moments in the summer house where Emz had been tricked by Mark into being witness to Logan and Caitlin's clumsy sex were not the most emotionally wrenching. Instead, the small moment on the stairs the other day, when Logan had put his hand on her arm as she tried to scoot by. *I'm sorry.* She could feel his heartfelt apology as if it had burned into her arm and it felt dangerous and raw. He might just as well have reached into her ribcage and tugged out her heart. The panic and hurt and desire bubbled upwards from the mental hole she'd dug. Emz rejigged her whole thought process and put Logan Boyle at the very top of her panic list. She panicked if she was going to see him and she panicked if she wasn't. It was emotional DEFCON 1.

Emz had worked out an avoidance strategy and so she skirted

away from the sixth form centre towards the side service road. She planned to avoid just about everyone, use the back door of the Humanities block and sit for a while in the class finishing her essay.

Her thoughts tumbled images of Ailith's face, of the head itself, the weary expression on his real face. Shadowed by thought, she turned the corner of the maths block and barged straight into Logan Boyle's shoulder. He was turned away from her, looming, she saw too late, over Caitlin, his mouth on hers, one hand on her hip, the other... Emz looked away from the other.

"Watch where you're going." Caitlin snapped. Logan shifted his weight, turned his other shoulder now against Caitlin and barred Emz's route.

"Yes. Watch it, Way. Which Way are you going?" Emz tried to sidestep him. "This Way. That Way." He blocked and tripped and trapped her. Emz stopped the sidestepping. She couldn't look into his face, so she looked down at his shoes. He stepped aside and they both laughed. As Emz looked up Logan leaned down to kiss Caitlin, tongues licking like cats. Ugh.

"Seen enough?" Caitlin sneered. Logan's face was obscured as he kissed Caitlin's neck, her hands sliding over Logan's muscled backside. Caitlin blew a sarcastic kiss to Emz. Emz felt fury and tears and jealousy fuse inside her into a hot dark piece of charcoal. In a second, she understood that the white-hot energy of it would not stay within her skin and she grabbed for it, trying to snatch it back. Too late. Panicked she turned away, as the strength of it crashed into the dumpster with a loud 'bong' sound. To the untrained eye it was as though Logan and Caitlin had merely leaned too hard against it. It ground backwards on its scuffed wheels taking Caitlin down with a scream. She scrabbled up from the floor, Logan laughing.

"What the actual fuck?" Caitlin pushed him. "Don't help me then, you dick." Emz was pushing at the door to the Humanities block, watching Logan laughing, reflected in the small rectangle of the window.

What had just happened? *Witch*. That energy came from her. She hadn't been able to stop it. *Witch*. Emz had not slept last night. She'd been tormented by the thought that, as Grandma Hettie had told them, this whole thing was about Strengths, not powers. She needed to recognise that hot charcoal inside her and get a grip. It was about knowing what you were strong in. However, Emz's mind had thrown up the counter argument: what did you do about the things you were weak in? She had thought of the way they had hounded the bullying hard man, Tighe Rourke, through the woods and where justice and right things were. What if it wasn't always so easy to decide?

Witch. Emz understood why Grandma Hettie had never used the word. It carried darkness with it.

More than anything she wanted to put her fears onto the table and sort through them but there was only one person who she could do that with, and that person was dead.

"Emz... Glad I caught you." The voice carried down the corridor towards her. Emz looked up, half hoping to see Grandma Hettie and finding instead it was Mrs King-Winters striding towards her. There was no escape.

There was another reason that school was something of a torment for Emz at the moment. Essentially, she wasn't sure what she was doing with and about her studies any more. She didn't care about A levels or university, that was a fact. She cared about Prickles and she cared about being at Cob Cottage and the whole idea of Gamekeeping seemed to her like a gift, a job she was meant for. A Levels were not. She had been led to believe that A levels were the beginning and the end of the world right now and she was struggling against that.

They were in the process of sorting out their university applications. Mrs King-Winters had asked to speak to her several times regarding progress with her personal statement and each time Emz had dodged it. Emz wished her Witch Way Strengths ran to invisibility. She thought hard. Nothing happened.

"I've been meaning to catch up and we keep missing each other. I'm so glad I caught you." Was there just a twinkle in Mrs King-Winters' eye at that? Did she know that Emz had been evading her? *Of course, Emz.* "How are you today?"

"Fine." Fine was a hopeless answer, try again. "I'm really good and on my way to history." Emz tried to look busy and enthused and feinted moving up the stairs but, with a quick step, Mrs King-Winters blocked her.

"Nothing drastic, I just wondered if there's anything I can help with for the personal statement?" Mrs King-Winters asked with a smile.

"No... it's... okay." Emz had forgotten the statement. There was a half-hearted hundred words sitting in a notebook some-where. Emz was waiting to be dismissed but Mrs King-Winters did not dismiss her.

"I feel you've gone a little adrift lately," she said. Emz felt relieved. She could wriggle out in a moment.

"I'll stop slacking," she confessed, *get this over with.* She shifted her bag onto her shoulder, but Mrs King-Winters made no sign of drawing the chance meeting to a close.

"You're not slacking." She looked directly at Emz. "You're just not... engaged with the process."

Emz had no idea what to say, what was expected of her. Apol-ogy? Promises? With a Canada goose you knew where you were. Emz thought of the flock that had taken up residence at Cooper's Pond late yesterday afternoon.

"Actually, Emz, I think slack is what you might need." Mrs King-Winters enjoyed crossword puzzles and sometimes, as far as Emz was concerned, she spoke like one. Emz's face did not disguise this thought.

"I know that things have been tough this year. All the terrible events surrounding your sister and her family and now losing your grandmother. Perhaps you need some space, time to step back? You've got options you know. You could take a year out for instance."

A hot terror flashed across Emz at this proposal.

"No. No. I'll..."

"I'm not criticising, I'm just letting you know that we're here, I'm here, to help you in any way we can."

"I don't need help. I'm fine."

As she half tripped up the stairs a few moments later Emz thought she'd been a little harsh to Mrs King-Winters but there was no way she could sit and think about the future. Even just thinking the word made her panic more. At the top of the stairs Emz could see the other students milling and seething into the classrooms and she couldn't breathe. She turned on the stair to leave, and, as she did so, she caught sight of Logan and Caitlin pushing in through the doors on the ground floor, their laughter rising up towards her. Emz headed along the corridor, her pace quickening. Instead of turning right into L2 and her waiting History group she turned left and almost slid down the stairs.

By the time she reached the front doors of the humanities block she could barely breathe and she pushed out into the daylight and the fresh air. There was no way, after Logan and Caitlin, after Mrs King-Winters, that she was going to History now, no way she was going anywhere except to Prickles.

5

POINTS ON YOUR COMPASS

One of Ailith's first memories was of her Grandam Orla telling her a tale of Cob Cottage. It was an old memory, tinted golden in her head because they had had candles back then and not the lamps now, that gave a white glow soft as Starlight.

Truth be told, like most of her memories of Grandam Orla, it was a bit scary. Some other memories involving Grandam Orla were raging nightmares filled with pointy sticks and broken teeth; this one at least involved a hot drink and a blanket made of knitted squares.

"... *for all the folks at Cob Cottage*..." Grandam's voice was a bit fuzzy in memory. Loud. Yes. That was its chief characteristic. "... *for them walls were smirched with handprints of them as entered*..." Grandam had leaned close at this point so that Ailith had a close up view of the gap between her two front teeth. "... *and the floors was splattered with the blood of them as didn't*..."

It was a bit intimidating to be sitting on a spindly dining chair by the actual scrubbed table, "... *where Hettie Way wrestled with the creature's gizzards its entrails coiling and roiling round the table legs like laidly worms,*" her Grandam's voice loomed out at her. Thankfully there was no evidence of innards this afternoon, there was just the plate and mug that Ailith had been using for her lunch. That Way sister with the brown hair, Anna, she could cook that one could. Ailith thought it was worth making the journey, all the long days of it, just for the pleasure of tasting Anna Way's food.

This last thought reminded her of the journey and its purpose. It had been a long distance and their setting off point seemed very far away, like, in fact, one of the stories that Grandam Orla might tell. How would that tale start? Because she had to think about what she had told the Way sisters. She needed to give them a tale, that was part of her purpose. No one had said that tale had to be true, had they? Well yes, actually, that had been one of the chief themes of all Grandam Orla's nightmare bedtime tales concerning those who found themselves at Cob Cottage.

She had been thrown by the absence of Hettie Way. Hettie Way was what she had expected, and she was uncertain of these sisters. They seemed too young for this job. Ailith had spent the few hours she was meant to be sleeping going over the details of them. Hettie Way had died. It was only right that her granddaughters inherited Havoc Wood. Yet, still Ailith felt unease, the legacy of all her long travels.

Ailith had edited the story somewhat last night. She could not withhold all the truth, but she needed to keep herself and the Lordship safe. That was the task. She had hoped she would arrive at Havoc Wood, that Hettie Way would know exactly what must be done and she could relinquish her duty.

These girls had not taken charge. She had begun with the blade; she had thought then they might be prompted to take over, to tell her what needed to be done. She'd talked of the castle and the battle. That was true too. There had been the smell of the sea, the saltwater was frittered into the air because of the storm and the only lamp was lightning. There were items that she edited out, of course, little truths that was all, except she was worried about Cob Cottage and how it might judge her for those omissions. So far, it had not, except her mouth felt a little dry.

This morning, it had felt like a sigh when Anna Way touched her hand and reached the memories. She had thought she would be found out then, the truth just sitting there for Anna Way to see. The Gamekeeper had not called her out on it, she'd been kind rather than cruel.

Ailith's mind was doing little dances, finding complicated steps and turns that she had not had to think about before. Ever. For the whole rest of her life so far, she had not been the one doing much thinking. Now everything must be considered. It was one thing to grow up with tales of Cob Cottage and the Game-keeper, but it was quite another to be here and blindly trust folk. She had learnt of late that that was a big mistake.

It occurred to Ailith that the Way sisters, newly come to their Gamekeeping task, might also think it was foolhardy to trust someone. It was possible that the night would bring further questioning. She decided on which pieces of information the Way sisters needed and which she must keep for herself. Having sorted those pieces, she worked up the story she would tell and repeated it, over, over, over until it was like a song to accompany all the little dancing thoughts.

She shifted from the chair and moved to the basket which Anna had given her in which to rest the warrior's head. She looked at it for a moment or two and then unwrapped the scarf.

Ailith had not known what to do and now suddenly, looking over his blank, dead face, she found a task. She looked around for a bowl. There was a big plastic one in the sink but that didn't seem appropriate and then she thought that the sink itself was a bit of a bad idea; he was not, after all, a pot to be washed. She dug a broken comb from amongst her few belongings and she put that into her pocket.

Cob Cottage, as her Grandam Orla had told, understood what she wanted and as she stepped away from the sink feeling despondent, the front doors blew open a little and beyond them the lake water winked in the sunlight.

Ailith carried the basket down to the shore and unwrapped the head. She did not look too closely at the raggedy and bony bits. She concentrated on washing his face with the lake water, letting it clean his waxy dead skin, and then she took out the comb and combed his hair straight, dragging the bits of grass and blood clots and tatters of skin out of it and letting the lake water wash it all away, sink it deep. She dried his face with the teacloth, smoothed his eyebrows, and then she wrapped him carefully up in the scarf once more and took him back inside the cottage.

She had sworn a promise, that she would do what she had to do, and she repeated it to herself. She had repeated it many times over on the journey here and she realised that just saying the words in her head made her feel strong.

She had to be strong too, because after all there were three of the Way sisters and only one of her. She had come all this way and yet, she did not feel quite safe in Havoc Wood.

Ailith had been careful, more careful than ever before in her life, but there might still be those who had followed her. She hoped that her grandam's bedtime stories were true and that Cob Cottage might prove a better fortress than any old clifftop castle had ever been.

6

A BAG WITH SOME CASH

T he phone began ringing out as Emz stepped in through the back door of reception. The microwave was humming to itself, heating up some beans, and there were smoky tendrils rising into the kitchen from the toaster. Emz clicked the toaster off and picked up the phone.

"Prickles Nature Reserve, Emily speaking, how may I help?" Emz rescued the toast and began to butter it as she listened to the woman on the other end. From the corner of her eye she could see Winn heading in from the pens.

"Yep. Yep. Got that. Okay. Yes, I'll let her know. Bye."

Tea brewed. Emz handed Winn a slice of the toast. Winn's taste in toast meant she liked any colour as long as it was black. She took a bite.

"Who was it? They've not spotted that boar again have they?" Winn was not a vain woman and her moustache, while wispy and pale, tended to catch the toast crumbs, little black carbon bits today giving Winn the look of a disgruntled cat.

"No. It was Yolanda from the estate agency. She says she's got a woman interested in leasing Hartfield. Can you go and give her the tour?"

31

Winn made a huffing sound and looked at the clock.

"Do you have to be back in school? Did you say you had history this afternoon?"

Emz took a bigger bite of her toast and shook her head. It was easier to lie if she didn't speak.

"Right. You hold the fort then. Peggy Brunty will be in later for those runaway alpacas... will you manage?"

Emz nodded. Winn looked around for more excuses. There were none. She wiped the rest of the toast off her face onto her sleeve and rummaged around in her pocket for the keys to the Land Rover.

WINN DID NOT CARE at all for this woman, but that was not unusual. If the Sugar Plum Fairy herself had decided to take a short break in Woodcastle it was unlikely Winn would like her and this woman, tallish and thinnish and black haired-ish, was no sugar plum fairy. This woman, with her elegant black clothes and her rounded tortoiseshell glasses, would taste bitter if you got into a fight and had to bite her. The thought of getting into any sort of confrontation with her at all was making Winn's hair prickle, which was very unusual indeed for Winn. Confrontation was her chocolate, her whisky. She prided herself on her twin abilities of being able to give someone a verbal lashing as well as a damn good thrashing, whichever was required.

Clearly her thoughts had wandered a long way. They were standing on the landing at the top of the hewn oak staircase in the east wing and the woman, Mrs Fyfe, was smiling at her.

"Penny for them?" she asked, the smile sliding wider, the blood red lipstick setting off her creamy white teeth.

"I was just trying to recall if there's anything important that might have slipped my mind... I went over the biomass boiler, didn't I?"

"In detail." The smile was starting to remind Winn of the

Cheshire Cat and let's face it, there was one and only one reason that this Mrs Fyfe was being shown around Hartfield Hall: Winn needed the cash from a tenant. Judging by Mrs Fyfe's clothes, and while Winn admitted she was not well up on the fashion world, she knew cashmere when she saw it, this woman had loot. All Winn had to do was make Hartfield Hall seem like home.

"Righty ho… just along here, this is the first of the east wing bedrooms." Winn was trying to remember which of the east wing bedrooms had the indoor waterfall from the guttering when it rained; might be best not to show that one. Mrs Fyfe turned her head and peered down the hallway.

"How many bedrooms?" she enquired. Winn was stumped for a moment. A few. A lot. That tended not to be the number people wanted. They wanted proper maths. She scrambled round her memory.

"Six?" she threw the figure out. Mrs Fyfe nodded and did not question the quantity. Winn worried for a moment; if she'd over-sold the bedrooms then possibly this Mrs Fyfe might require some money back. On the other hand, if she'd undersold, if there turned out to be eight or nine instead of six… well, that would be a bargain. Winn stopped fretting. Actually, there were at least another four bedrooms in the west wing of the house, not to mention all the servants' quarters that haunted the attics.

"Baths at that end and that end…" Winn pointed.

"No en suites?" Mrs Fyfe's wide red mouth narrowed to a kittenish pout.

"No. Hartfield was constructed before bathrooms were invented so they were wedged in where possible at later dates. If you want a bathroom I suggest you choose a bedroom near one. There are two more bathrooms in the west wing near the Chinese bedroom and the airing cupboard if you remember the tour?" Winn was curt. "I thought you said you were intrigued by the period details? The original Crapper on the north corridor?"

"Oh yes. I am." Mrs Fyfe smiled again. It made Winn feel a bit bilious, although that could have been the fact that she had mistakenly put the tin of tuna flavoured cat food onto her toast this morning and then eaten it for breakfast.

"You know, I suppose, that 'en suite' isn't even French? Not proper French… they don't know what you mean when you say 'en suite', or if you say 'c'est la vie' either." Winn thought back to a long-ago holiday in Cholet where she had used both phrases and met with Gallic confusion.

"Ha." Mrs Fyfe gave a rather short, barking laugh. "The French. What are they like?"

They toured the bedrooms. Mrs Fyfe was very impressed with their period details and later, in the kitchen, Winn was very impressed with the large bag of cash she handed over as a deposit and the first month's rental.

"Personally, I don't trust banks. A shoebox and a tea caddy are far more trustworthy." Mrs Fyfe confessed, her eyes looking slightly crossed and googly as she peered at Winn through her spectacles. Winn reconsidered her former opinion of her new tenant.

Winn's real home was a rather sad looking amalgamation of sixties era boxes that called itself a bungalow, squatting in a clearing at the edge of Leap Wood. She swung by on her way back to Prickles to stash some of her rental cash. Some she put in an old coffee tin, still more under the mattress and, safest of all, in a ceramic cooking pot in the oven. No one in their right mind ever looked in Winn's oven, most especially if something was cooking in it.

Almost at once she reached back into the oven, took a few notes from the cooking pot and stuffed them into her jacket pocket. She glanced at the clock and found there was still time to head over to Mole's Farm Goods to pick up the pony pellets she needed.

She had started up the tractor and was half way down the lane before she remembered that it was a bit of a pinch to park the tractor at Mole's and so she rolled down to the crossroads path as that was the only place to do a U-turn and headed back to pick up the Land Rover.

She felt lifted and light. Hartfield Hall was sometimes like a nightmare from which she couldn't awake. Each time she visited her ancestral home there was something dropping off or falling down. The hotel idea had been the worst, of course, and the debts from that haunted her but the few weddings she'd managed to book in at the stables had helped. A little. Diversifying. That was how to explain it to herself, she was simply diversifying.

It would be a different nightmare to be pushed to sell the place, but then, Winn tended not to sleep too much at night so that this nightmare never manifested itself.

Except it did, it tugged at her coat each time a new bill came in or some other workman had to offer up an unearthly quote for rewiring or replastering or generally shoring up. It seemed to Winn, as she pushed the thoughts aside, that it didn't matter how old you were, how much your knees creaked and your hair streaked grey, inside you were still eleven and, still and forever, a disappointment to your father.

WINN BUSTLED in behind the counter at reception and, as Emz sat at the computer and finished the backlog of pro formas for the latest batch of school visits, Winn handed her a wad of notes, possibly about a hundred pounds, Emz wasn't sure.

"Is that the deposit from Rooks Hill Primary?" Emz looked at the crumpled cash.

"It's wages," Winn barked. The thought fluttered for a second in Emz's head and she quickly handed it back.

"No... Winn, no."

"Yes. It's wages," Winn insisted, pushing the money back into Emz's hand. Emz held it out.

"No. I'm a volunteer." Emz reached forward and stuffed it into Winn's pocket.

"You're not actually if you remember? Roughly an aeon ago I took you on as a Saturday girl and I've never bloody paid you... well, there was that Easter egg... but still and all, here." There was a silly and embarrassing hand wrestling between them before the notes burst out and crumpled onto the floor where Emz stooped to pick them up and held them out to Winn.

"Don't. Please, Winn. Spend it on the animals." There was a moment between them and Winn recalled exactly why she'd put up with this girl for all this time and all this time was starting to add up to about three years, possibly even four. Good grief! This couldn't go on. She probably owed Emz Way a tremendous wad of cash. The whole incident, which had started out with Winn feeling generous, was now turning sour and embarrassing for both parties.

"You paid me a couple of weeks ago, remember?" Emz remembered the brief exchange of ten-pound notes after a particularly good day at the visitor centre. Winn had insisted then and Emz had taken it. Now she felt endangered. "That's all I need." There was a continued moment of standoff before Winn shoved the notes into her pocket. She made some grumping noises that were quite usual, but the seed was planted in her head: she needed to consider Emz Way and find a proper way forward. She could not do without her. She put the money into the pocket of Emz's fleece which was hanging off the back of the chair.

"Winn."

But Winn was shaking her head, zipping up the pocket.

"I'm minted, Emz. I rented out the Hall."

7

SOMETHING BORROWED,
SOMETHING BLUE

Mrs Fyfe was settling in very well as Mistress of All She Surveyed. Well, Hartfield at least. She slept, as she should always sleep, in a four-poster bed, one that, judging by the thread-bare drapes, held some history. There was dust here, there were cobwebs there. She had not felt so at home in a long time.

The chequerboard tiling of the hall floor made her think of long ago balls, of sweeping debutante gowns. There was rust, there was mould, there were rats pattering their nervous energy around the wainscoting so that she felt revived. It was like a spa! She loved it here.

Matters needed to be arranged of course, she did not have enough of a supply of the paper stuff to stay here indefinitely, but her mind was humming busily to itself and today, it was humming the Wedding March.

Ah. A wedding. Mrs Fyfe absolutely adored a good wedding.

The fuss had begun yesterday when all the strangers arrived and for just a moment Mrs Fyfe thought that they were going to be staying in the main house. A telephone conversation with the baggage who rented the place out had settled the matter. They were preparing for a wedding in the grounds, in the other half, in the stables and the orangery away from her private garden, her private quarters.

She could watch it all from the corner library windows, being as they were on the first floor and dual aspect. She could look out up the drive and out onto the stables and courtyard. It was a hive of activity, of nervous energy, of anxiety and stress. Men hefted chairs and tables and the young woman with the gadget was mistress of it all. Hmm. Mrs Fyfe brought herself up some tea and observed. It was only a moment or so before the energy tweaked at her from across the town. It was intriguing, the little threads of web from Havoc that twanged and sang by the river. Hmm. Water. Yeast. Hops. Well, she would not be thwarted by a little brewster. Mrs Fyfe finished her tea; it was a simple task to hinder the Havoc witch brew's arrival. She smiled at the thought of drawing first blood on the Witch Ways.

"Vagabonds? What the hell is a Vagabond?" The woman was young and harassed and Mrs Fyfe could not resist stealing a look or two at the silvery tablet she held. Lists. Pictures. All pages turned with a swipe of her finger. A marvel and electrical, Mrs Fyfe assumed, although she was not a great one for gadgets herself.

"Yes. Coming through those big main gates in one of their wagons." Mrs Fyfe pointed into the distance. The young woman looked at the open gates and the tall grass that was growing between them.

"Vagabonds? Wagons?" she said the word over and looked at Mrs Fyfe with some irritation. "Who are you? You're not Miss Hartley-Hartfield? You're not a wedding guest." She was swiping her finger impatiently at the tablet as if the answer might lie within it. Mrs Fyfe swiped her finger on it too. Put a stop to that.

"What are you doing?" The young woman snatched the slim machine away from her. "Can you not?"

Mrs Fyfe held up her hands in surrender, a conciliatory smile upon her face.

"Apologies." She took a step back; the young woman's stress level was rising, and Mrs Fyfe breathed in. At the other side of the courtyard the caterers were unloading tables.

"No... not there... not there." The young woman turned away from Mrs Fyfe.

"Vagabonds," Mrs Fyfe said under her breath. "Lock those gates against them, the tinkers." She smiled again and turned back into the house.

An hour or so later she was enjoying a pot of tea in the corner library, feeling refreshed and relaxed as she watched two of the young men begin the longish trek to the main gates carrying a metal hoop strung with heavy metal keys. She watched as they creaked the gates shut and for good measure, once they had turned their backs, Mrs Fyfe took some of her energy and laid her own locks into the ironwork.

Mrs Fyfe needed to keep a tight ship. She would have to work quickly but that was always fun, skin of the teeth stuff. Hmm. She must prepare herself for the mischief of the wedding. Now, what else did she need? She would need a hat. And where had she left her basket?

8

BLACKBERRY FERMENT

The wedding beer was due a tasting, especially since the wedding itself now loomed large on the Drawbridge Brewery calendar.

"When is the Hillman wedding?" Charlie asked. "Is it the 10th or the 12th?" She was skimming over the diary pages, the diary being an actual paper version that sat on the desk, the cover gathering coffee mug circles until it resembled an over enthusiastic Olympic flag.

"I thought it was the 15th?" Michael looked up from the computer. His face was crumpled into several expressions at once, revealing all his thought processes. Charlie flicked back and forth in the diary. It was a waste of space really as neither of them ever wrote anything in it; most of Charlie's diary dates were on her phone and most of Michael's were written on the back of his hand or on Post-it notes on his fridge at home.

"I've got the 12th in my head. We need to check. D'you want to give them a ring, or shall I?" Charlie asked. Michael's attention was back at the computer. Charlie watched the back of his head for a moment, interested in the way the hair curled around the small bald spot that was encroaching across the crown of his head; she was also interested, no, disturbed might be a better word, in the fact that she was thinking how it might feel to just reach for that hair, to twist her fingers into it and maybe lean her head forward, let its soft curls brush her lips. As she was drifting with this thought her phone pipped out. She glanced down.

"What are you doing?" Aron's message leapt out. Charlie looked at it for a second. He was not inside her head, she knew that, but at odd times in their life together she felt that he was. She deleted the message.

Michael shifted in his seat, reaching for the landline.

"I'll ring them. But I'm pretty sure it's the 15th," he reassured her.

Charlie let his words trail behind her as she headed out into the yard and across to the storeroom.

The wedding brew had been put into casks and racked in readiness. Charlie was going to draw some off today and offer it around the staff to get some feedback. On her way to the cold store she passed by the experimentation shed and checked on the various phials and vats of Blackberry Ferment that she was trying out.

The shed smelt good this morning, a deep, fruity tang, and Charlie moved around the various benches and stills adjusting and tweaking as she went. She liked the colours of the liquids she was brewing; the blackberries had had quite a colour range from a rich almost black liquid that she might take further towards a spirit and the frothier more purply concoctions that she'd brewed and boiled into beer. In the far corner, beside a book she had borrowed from the library about home brewing your own wine, there was, no surprise, a vat containing the first stages of a black-berry wine. She'd harvested more of the Cob Cottage blackberries in the last couple of days and Anna had a couple of baskets that she had made into jam for the afternoon teas and was baking into crumbles for the Castle Inn. As she worked her mind began to drift towards Ailith and her tale.

The trouble was, Charlie knew when someone was lying.

"It's one of your Strengths," Grandma Hettie had told her. Charlie had not thought it was a very good strength because it made life a bit difficult. There was the sense that someone lied, but there was not always a clarification of which bit they were lying about. In Ailith's case it seemed even more complex. Charlie's instinct, Strength, her witch radar, or whatever it was, flagged up the lie, but she also had a sense that the lie had a different angle to it. There were lies that could be told to protect something or someone. The story that Ailith had told last night, with all its blood and guts, was true. That was the difference, Charlie reasoned, the lie was not a lie as such, it was not an untruth, it was more a case of not telling the whole truth. Bits were missing, like the corners of a jigsaw.

It occurred to Charlie, and this was probably because she was inhaling too many ultra-alcoholic Blackberry Ferment fumes, that most of her Strengths, the things that contributed to the whole Pike Lake Havoc Wood Gamekeeper scenario, were twisted and bent. The map reading ability had the possibility to lead you into real trouble. They had, Charlie thought, blundered in with Tighe Rourke and Seren and simply struck lucky in the outcome; nothing had gone to plan. Charlie stepped back from her work for a moment. She was feeling shaky and little alarms of panic were starting to sound in her body.

What they had inherited was danger. The Gamekeeper job or duty or whatever it might be called, carried peril with it. She was still having nightmares about being in the lake, about fruitless searches for Seren, and she woke up gasping for air with her heart racing. How long did that sort of feeling last? How much of a pounding could one heart take?

"It's tomorrow!" Michael's voice barrelled into her head, his physical presence following close behind, almost colliding with her, his hands reaching for her shoulders. His eyes were wild with a mixture of excitement and fear. "Charlie…"

"What?"

"The Hillman wedding! It isn't the 12th, it's the 2nd! It's tomorrow."

To an outsider, it might appear that as Michael Chance's energy crackled and bolted from him it was absorbed neatly into Charlie Way's frame. There was no panic.

"I'll get Jack to load up and I'll take the casks over there myself." She spoke in a quiet voice that brushed delicately at Michael's ears.

"What?" He couldn't quite hear her over the klaxon of his own panic and his hands were still holding her shoulders. Charlie, for several seconds, wanted to hold onto this panic, wanted these two hands to stay on her shoulders and possibly pull her nearer into an embrace. *Honeyed sugar.* There you go, those thoughts sliding again.

"Can we take it down from DEFCON 1? Okay? The beer is brewed. We just need to load it up and deliver it. Now."

Michael took a deep breath in and was acutely aware of his hands on her shoulders. He moved them, his hands falling to his trousers where he wiped them as if her shoulders might be dusty or otherwise grimy. There was an awkward moment and then Charlie stepped away from it towards the cold store.

"Give Jack a yell will you…" she instructed, trying to sound businesslike.

THE HILLMAN WEDDING was going to take place in the grounds at Hartfield Hall. Winn had a licence for wedding ceremonies in the stable block which was cut off from the house by a high stone wall drifted with clematis and pear trees. It was a familiar run for Charlie but today she had let Jack do the driving and was now regretting it. They couldn't seem to take the right road. It was very annoying.

"It was the lane back there on the right." Charlie struggled not to sound terse as Jack reversed into the farm gate and turned them around.

"I know. I know. It's there." He gunned the engine, ground up a gear. "Somebloodywhere."

Charlie watched as they drove past the lane once more and after a second Jack smacked his hand on the wheel.

"Fuck it. I've done it again. What is wrong with me?" He drummed at the wheel and sped up a little. The main gates were just up ahead. "Here. We'll go in the main gates."

He swung the van around at the very last minute, the gates seeming to loom large beside them and then slide away before they had chance to turn. The tyres squealed a little as Jack braked, slammed into reverse and backed up into the gravel entrance.

It was a pointless exercise. The main entrance was blocked by the closed wrought iron gates. It was unusual; Winn very rarely locked the gates and pretty much anyone in Woodcastle could wander at will through the grounds and had, on more than one occasion, been found indulging in a cup of tea in the lovely old kitchen at the back of the house, the door to which stood open in all weathers. Winn did not mind as long as, should she arrive on the doorstep, you weren't stingy with your biscuits. There had always been a tin of teabags on the worktop although most Woodcastle residents knew that these teabags had been there for several years and were tainted by the rustiness of the tin and the general overpowering dampness of Hartfield Hall.

"We can go up by the side of the house..." Jack said driving forward as if he had not noticed the obstacle.

"Except we can't because the gates are closed." Charlie looked at the gates; they were very beautiful, the iron curled into vines and tendrils although the little faces that looked out could pass for cherubs or devils. She felt unsettled by this metallic gang of grinning bullies and was cross with herself when she had to look away. She could see now why Winn kept them wide open and out of sight. Jack was already getting out of the van. Charlie watched through the windscreen as he tried the heavy-duty padlock.

They had to backtrack then and as the small lane loomed into view once more Charlie barked instruction.

"Turn here."

The van lurched into the lane.

The stable block was a buzz of activity. There were several cars parked up and so Jack had to back the van into an awkward space under the trees nearest the house.

They loaded the first of the five casks onto the trolley and trundled it through the arch into the courtyard.

The stables were, it must be admitted, verging on derelict, albeit in an appealing and romantic way. Today they looked rustically festive. There was a sound of hammering and quantities of homemade bunting were being tangled into the trees as Charlie headed inside the large space of the Fore Barn.

The ceremony was to be held in the Owl Barn, the slightly squatter brother to this space and already there had been some confusion about which chairs went where. Men had been drafted in to shift the metal chairs into the Owl Barn for the ceremony and were clashing terribly with the wooden chairs that were destined for the tables in the Fore Barn.

"So where do you want the beer casks?" Charlie asked the harassed looking woman with a reporter's notebook in her hand. The woman, who had not introduced herself, checked her top list and then flicked a few pages back through the notebook.

"Sorry about this, my tablet crashed and it's a total effing nightmare." By the time she had reached the word 'nightmare' her voice was a thin high screech and three men had approached her other side and were asking three separate questions regarding flowers, tablecloths, and Portaloos.

"Wait," she barked, flicking through more pages of the notebook as if it was a novel she had to get to the end of. "Wait."

"Jack, if you unload that just here and then go back for the rest..." Charlie instructed as the woman began to make an odd little keening sound.

"Flowers." She didn't look up from the page. The man asking about the flowers held up his hand, possibly in surrender to the battlefield that was this wedding. "No. First. Beer. Beer. Okay. Can you put the casks in the end of the stable block? Micky and Mike should be there already setting up the bar." She pointed to the last door in the stable block. Charlie moved swiftly to catch up with Jack and they rolled the first two casks across the stable yard and through the doorway.

There was no one in the end stable unless you counted the pigeons in the rafters.

"You sure this is where they want them?" Jack asked. Charlie nodded.

"That's what her reporter's notebook told her. The bar is being set up in here." They headed back to the van, Jack rolling the other casks into the stable block as Charlie approached the hassled woman again for a signature on their paperwork.

"What am I signing for?" she asked as she scribbled a signature.

"The beer. Drawbridge Brewery." Charlie tore off the top copy and handed it to the woman.

In the distance there was a sudden brittle chinking and Charlie glanced up. In the Fore Barn the tower of champagne glasses had toppled over; the woman with the notebook gave a deathly whimper.

Charlie felt sorry for her. Jack tooted the horn impatiently and as the woman stormed off to inspect the damage, Charlie headed back to the van.

THE AFTERNOON TEAS were just finishing as Charlie waded through a large party of tourists who were milling out of the Castle Inn along the pavement towards their waiting coach. There was a greasy smell of diesel from the running engine and it coughed out a black cloud that misted everyone for a moment. Charlie coughed and as she stepped aside to let three of the tourists pass her, cameras clicking at the view above of the castle, she saw, written into the cracks in the pavement, a map of Hartfield Hall, and the stable block blinked into her brain and made her pause. What was it about this map? She glanced over the cracks once more and knew she'd lost it, the map had vanished. It was an irritation to her. She tried once again to recall the brief mental flicker and failed. It had been a long day.

"I need tea. Possibly as much as a bucket," she said to Casey as she took up a seat near the kitchen door.

"Plastic or galvanised?" Casey asked with a poker face. "I'll tell her you're here…" and with a smile she pushed through the doors into the kitchen.

It was relaxing in the Castle Inn. Charlie liked the tea room particularly; it seemed to her that the low beams bounced back the coolness of the white damask table cloths and lent both light and air to the room. It civilised you. She glanced down at the tablecloth where a blob of red jam and a smear of cream sat alongside a roundel of tea stain. Charlie looked at the marks for several moments as if trying to find meaning in them. The conclusion she came to was that she quite fancied a cream tea.

Anna was looking pink-faced as she approached. She'd taken her pinny off and sat down.

"How's it going?" she asked. Charlie shrugged.

"Fine. Bit of wedding beer hassle at Hartfield, nothing drastic." Charlie's expression did not lighten.

"But?" Anna pushed. Charlie took in a deep breath.

"I think we should head home. Talk to Ailith some more." Charlie heard the heaviness in her voice. Anna nodded.

"We were too polite."

"Yeah. Grandma was never too polite. Still, we're learning." Charlie looked lighter already.

"I'm finished here until half five, that gives us a couple of hours." The sisters, decided and united, stood up in unison. As they did so Charlie found the words tumbling out.

"We have no idea what we're doing with this do we?" She looked to her sister for reassurance.

"Nope," Anna smiled. "We just have to busk it."

AT PRICKLES VISITOR CENTRE, Emz was tilling up and looking forward to the walk home when the door to reception opened and Charlie and Anna stepped in.

"Hey." Emz was glad to see them. The edgy feeling she'd had today fell away a little; instead of buzzing at her, it hummed a little.

"Hey. You nearly finished?" Charlie was, Emz could see, in her practical mode, the car keys in her hand and her fleece zipped up. You could sometimes tell how hard Charlie was thinking by how high up her fleece was zipped. Tonight, it was almost all the way to the top. Her left hand fiddled with the zipper toggle.

"Yes. I just have to finish the till." Emz was sorting the coins into little plastic bank bags which were then put into the big red canvas bag. It was very rare that there was anything to put in this bag but this afternoon's school trip had shifted a lot of souvenir pencils and the sweets selection was looking bare.

"We've got a sort of plan," Anna began as she helped bag up the pennies. Charlie stood on the opposite side of the counter, leaned in.

"We thought we'd try and push Ailith a bit tonight. Not back off like we did last night. Go in."

"Go in?" Emz pulled a face. "That sounds harsh."

"Not harsh. But we need to try hard. Or at least harder than last night." Anna said.

"She's got over her trip. Now she has to tell us the truth." Charlie put her hand on the counter as if to seal Ailith's fate. Emz looked up at them both.

"She told us a lot last night." Emz recalled the slightly blood-thirsty story, told in a quiet and weary voice which somehow made it even more horrible. She stopped short of shuddering.

"She told us the circumstances of why she left," Anna said. "She told us almost nothing about herself or why she's come to Havoc."

"It's that head. Got to be about that surely?" Charlie was settled on this. "You don't just wander about with a random bloke's head in your handbag."

"You might do in Havoc," Emz mused as she picked up the big red money bag and nodded to the back door. The three sisters moved into the kitchen.

"Emz is right. Anything is possible," Anna sighed.

"She's here for our help. Isn't she?" Emz shoved the big red bag of change into the microwave and shut the door on it.

"Is she?" Charlie asked with a shrug. "She's a fugitive. I get that. But we can't just blindly trust her."

"Not blindly. Instinctively."

"There's something off about her." Charlie wrinkled her nose as if sniffing a bad smell.

"Fear," Emz stated. "Which is why I think she needs our help."

"Help doing what, Emz?" Anna asked. "D'you think she's here for sanctuary?"

"And if so how long might she stay?" Charlie put in. They were heading out along the back lane. Winn, chugging towards them in the Land Rover, gave a toot on the horn and a breezy wave which they returned as they stood in the ditch to avoid being run over.

"If she's a fugitive maybe someone's chasing her. Maybe someone is after her. After all they chopped off this warrior bloke's head, I mean from what she said last night it sounded like terrorists. What if they want to kill her? What if they show up in Havoc?" Emz stepped back out of the ditch and turned to her sisters. They were staring up at her, Anna looking pale, Charlie rather cross.

"What if they want to kill her because she's the bad guy?" Charlie said.

AILITH HAD enough experience to see that while the Way sisters were preparing food, while they were all chatting to her and smiling, there was a background tension. You could, if you listened at all, hear it, like wires humming above everyone's heads. For most of her life, when Ailith had heard this sort of sound she had been quick to get out of its way. But that was then, and this was now, and now she was in Cob Cottage and they were the Gamekeepers.

Ailith was uncertain of them. She understood their situation, but she also understood her own. She had come to Havoc Wood with good reason. She needed help.

"So. Ailith," Charlie Way began, offering a bowl of green beans that were scented with lemon and some luscious and savoury oil that Ailith had not eaten before. Anna leapt into the conversation before Charlie could continue.

"We hope we didn't give you too terrible a welcome. We were caught a little off guard last night."

"We weren't expecting you." Charlie gave the words weight. Ailith watched her hands as she tore at her hunk of bread. They were working hands, she noted, and that made her feel a connection to this sister. She looked at Anna's hands as they placed a bowl of rosemary scented carrots onto the table and shifted aside some cutlery. Her hands were well worked too and yes, here was the littlest one, slight and slim and her hands looked the most worked of all. She had forgotten what this one did. A scholar was it?

"I am sorry for that. Word was not sent, I know, but there was no chance. No time." Ailith was reminded of the times, few and much treasured, when she had left off her work and sat opposite Lordship at the squares game.

"That's understandable." Anna offered round the herby

chicken and gave Charlie a pointed look. Emz watched them both for a moment.

"Your welcome was kind."

"What are you doing here?" Charlie blurted out. Anna held her breath but Emz watched Ailith.

"I came to bring the warrior home." She tore at the bread a little to give herself time to bring her thoughts together.

"Oh." Charlie thought about it. "Home to Woodcastle? To the castle you mean?"

"Or are you on your way elsewhere after this? Is his home in another place?" Anna prodded with a smile. Ailith's mind recalled the tale she'd told herself to help her keep her dancing thoughts in step.

"The castle. I have brought the warrior home for his Bone Resting."

The sisters relaxed a little. This seemed a simpler matter.

"Bone Resting?" Charlie pulled a puzzled face. Anna furrowed her brow but Emz buzzed with enlightenment.

"Oh! Like a burial you mean... like burying your heart some-where... like Thomas Hardy's heart in a cake tin in Dorset?"

The two other sisters looked at Emz with varying expressions of puzzled amusement.

"They buried him at Westminster Abbey, but they cut his heart out..." Emz tried to explain. Ailith felt a little bit ill at that thought and yet there was all this food. Vegetables scented with the earth they'd just been pulled from. Like home. No, not like home.

"I was sent here for the Bone Resting. To rest him, safe. At the castle. That is the task." Ailith was focusing on the very smallest details and being careful. She thought once more of the squares game, of the movement of the carved pieces, the horse and rider here, the holy man there. Chess. That was the game. Like this. Be mindful, never be cornered.

"Of course. A funeral, that makes sense." Anna's voice softened and Ailith sensed her thoughts drift.

"Is there a particular way you have to do the Bone Resting? Like a church service? A ritual?" Charlie asked. Inside Ailith the worm of worry that she carried chewed a little more, was unceasing. This was the reason she was here, and they knew nothing of it. She cut the food, forked a tasty morsel into her mouth. It tasted like dirt, poisoned with fear.

She retired to bed, no longer hungry.

THE WAYS, wrapped in various blankets and nursing a hot chocolate, a coffee, and a tea respectively, sat out on the porch.

"What do you both think? Is she telling us the truth?" Emz asked and looked at Charlie who blew across her hot chocolate although it was already cooled in the chilly October air. She had watched the way Ailith tore the bread roll into small pieces and then did not eat a single one.

"You're the one who can tell if someone's lying, Charlie," Emz insisted, her gaze not shifting. Anna spoke up.

"She's telling the truth." Anna was serious and formal. "We touched hands by mistake this morning and I was flickerbooked." Anna sipped at her tea as Emz and Charlie stared at her, Charlie's eyebrows rising into her hairline.

"Flickerbooked," Emz said the word over. "You haven't said that in... not since I was..." a smile hovered uncertainly at her mouth, she looked down to hide it.

"Flickerbooked?" Charlie's grip tightened on her mug. Emz took in a pleased breath, put a hand over her mouth now because she couldn't stop the smile. Charlie glared.

"Oh. Right, okay. We're being open about the... the..." Charlie struggled with the word, even when Anna's eyes lifted from her cup and she nodded.

"Magic," Emz whispered the word behind her hand, as if it belonged only to her, a secret, safe.

"Okay. Okay." Charlie held up her hand as if to silence Emz

then took in a deep thoughtful breath as she turned to Anna. "What did you see in the flickerbook moment?"

"The story, pretty much as she told it. More raw if anything." Anna shivered a little, pulled her blanket tighter as the memory of Ailith's flickerbooked memories riffled and shuffled once more. "Something happened to her. She is genuine."

"She's like us, isn't she?" Emz suggested. "Unsure of herself."

Charlie let out a snort of laughter.

"Unsure? Ha. That's one way of putting it." Charlie's voice was raw; only Anna picked up on it where Emz was carried away with the openness.

"It's true. This is all new to us. Only our second job as Game-keepers. It's probs the first time she's done this, you know, couriered a head to Havoc Wood," Emz contributed through a mouthful of marshmallows.

"Yes. That's a good way of seeing it. She's a courier." Anna sipped more tea.

"Or an undertaker," Charlie sealed it.

"Do we have to do the Bone Resting, d'you think?" Emz asked. "I can't remember any time when Grandma Hettie mentioned a Bone Resting."

"Perhaps someone will come. Like a priest." Anna looked out across the lake as if the answers might be there. Charlie gave a grumpy sigh.

"At least she didn't say anyone is coming for vengeance. It sounds like the battle's done. No terrorists." She looked pointedly at Emz. Emz was off on her own tangent, her eyes glittering in the porch light with a keen enthusiasm.

"So, if this is some sort of funeral... then are there going to be other guests? You know, paying their respects?" she asked.

Anna and Charlie looked at each other.

"You don't make this easy, do you?" Charlie was bothered; Anna and Emz could see it in the way she was folded into her blanket, the corners pinned under her legs.

"Emz is right. Let's give it a couple of days, keep a low-level lookout. See who might arrive." Anna was convincing.

Charlie's eyes were skirting the darker edges of Pike Lake, watchful.

"For Pete's sake," she muttered, her hand clenching the handle of her mug so that Emz was convinced she could hear it cracking.

"This is Gamekeeping," Emz suggested, trying to sound light. Charlie put down her mug and tugged her blanket tighter still, her eyes continuing to scan the lakeshore.

"Ha. Well, let's hope someone turns up with instructions on how to do a Bone Resting," she said.

"We did all right for Grandma Hettie," Anna said quietly. The words dandled in the air for a moment, each sister recalling their coffin heist. Charlie released some of the tension on her blanket and stood up. She picked up her mug, looked at Anna and then Emz.

"Yes. We did." She gave a brief smile as she chinked their mugs in a toast.

As they finished up and moved back inside Cob Cottage, the clouds covered over the silver sliver of the new moon and the night grew a little darker. Anna stopped herself from thinking that this was significant in any way. It was just clouds; it was only the weather.

9

INVITATION TO THE WEDDING

Seren Lake had a mouth full of pins and was working very quickly on the last adjustments to the bridal gown. Her new shop was only just open, and this was her first completed commission. She felt on edge, after all she wanted it to be perfect for the bride, and her own uneasiness was mixing with the general wedding nerves of bride, mother and bridesmaids. The room felt hot and small and filled with too many hats and elbows.

It was early, but they had already had a 'breakfast' of Apple Champagne, brought on small silver trays in tall thin flutes. There were several glasses empty already.

"Ooh, have a sip, it's lush," the mother of the bride had offered a glass to Seren who shook her head.

"No thanks. I need steady hands." She had waved her little cushion of pins as the mother of the bride glugged down the fizzing, glittering liquid. She gave a burp.

"Rude," snapped an aunty of some description with a pinched look. The mother of the bride snatched up another glass and raised it.

"Cheers," she said as the liquid sloshed over the rim and splashed the aunty's pale blue dress.

"You clumsy cow," the aunty cursed as she dotted at the stain, others fussing around her with a sound like hissing cats.

"It's a fugly outfit anyway." The mother of the bride reached for more champagne, tipping the fat rounded bottle with its bloody red apple shaped label. The bottle was empty. Tears were shed.

It seemed to Seren that mayhem was going to break loose before most of the guests even arrived.

"I NOW PRONOUNCE you Man and Wife…" the vicar had intoned and the newly made Mr and Mrs Hillman kissed to the accompaniment of a vast cheer. There was ecological confetti and delicious food.

Emptied bottles of cider ranged across the table cloths looking like a glass sculpture. At the nearest table an old man was swilling each green bottle to see if there were any dregs left and sucking them down thirstily before moving to the next table. The chief bridesmaid, Minty, was finishing her third portion of apple pie. Beside her the tall lady with jet black hair and neat little black boots was wearing a dramatic hat. Black silk. Black, black, and some more black on top. Was that a jackdaw? Its wings spread wide as if it might escape at any moment. If only she could carry off an outfit like that. She looked down at her own powder blue dress. She hated powder blue. Oh God, she had been to a lot of weddings lately and always the bridesmaid. Was she ever going to be the bride?

"I doubt it dear. Why not have some more pie?" The woman in the jackdaw hat pushed her own untouched, sugar sprinkled portion towards Minty and reached for a fresh cider bottle, the label a gold edged apple, crimson red. "Here. Wash it down with this."

As Minty swigged the cider from the bottle, the woman in the jackdaw hat raised a glass to her.

Later, the room was swimmy and strange and Minty felt sad when she ought to have felt sick. She needed to go to the bathroom, sprinkle cold water on her hot face.

On her return, feeling a need for further apple pie and possibly a side dish of apple cake, she moved amongst the tables, overheard the snippets of conversation that bubbled from the guests seated around the tables.

"Don't you think Cherry's bottom looks huge? Cherry's chunky cheeks?" sneered a thin lady in a blue suit, her long face lengthening into a cackling laugh as she leaned into the gentleman beside her. He kissed her greedily and she seemed startled by this. Minty wished someone would kiss her like that.

"Because you never think outside the box," the sharp voice sliced across Minty and she stumbled against another table.

"The box you put me in, you controlling bastard."

"Wish I could fit you in a box you fat bitch." The man pinched at the woman's bottom, his fingers like a crab claw. She squealed, tears filling her eyes and still he pinched.

"Squeal piggy, squeal," his face was red and sweating. His other hand moved up to grab the woman's arm, whip her forwards as if in a horrible dance.

"Hungry piggy, eat some cake." The man grabbed the woman's hair, shoved her down onto the table, rubbed her face in the plate of half eaten cake, but she didn't care, began to eat up the smushed crumbs.

Minty sat in her seat. The others from her table were over by the dessert queue having a disagreement. The only person left seated was a man, a stocky older uncle with silvered hair who was smoking a cigar. The woman in the jackdaw hat was seated nearby and breathed at the smoke making it drift towards Minty.

"I don't think you're supposed to smoke in here," Minty coughed. The fellow guest rolled the cigar around in his fingers for a moment and raised his eyebrows.

"You think not?" he sucked in a deep breath. The cigar smoke was not mixing very well with the apple delights. It was making the cake look very brown and dry. The fellow guest blew the smoke over Minty, making elaborate movements with his head to give the smoke maximum swirl. Minty coughed again and her fellow guest laughed. He leaned in close and put the cigar out on her forearm. The pain was so intense Minty could only gasp, the air choking her. The cake fork fell from her hand onto the floor and as she bent down to retrieve it she slid off the chair and hid under the table, beneath the snow-white drape of the cloth, a quiet fortress in which to cry.

10

THE FRIENDS OF WOODCASTLE CASTLE

Ailith was up before dawn, stepping out of Cob Cottage into the almost light of the October morning. It seemed darker to her in the last few days but that might have been the fact that the weather was clouded in, heavy skies of steel grey.

She noted that none of the floorboards creaked and neither did the door as it gave her safe passage out into the wood. She had been cooped up in the house and she needed a breath or two of air.

She was feeling on edge, as if the weight of everything was now starting to bite into her shoulders, strain all her muscles, the mental ones as well as the physical. She had pondered for a long time whether it was wiser to leave His Lordship in the cottage or to keep him with her. She was unsure of the territory, even in Havoc. Her anxiety led her to see shadows where perhaps there were none. At last she decided to leave him within the walls of the cottage. She had no idea what the town was like and Cob Cottage, if Grandam Orla had been right, was a safe haven for now.

She moved in a very few light steps into the cover of the wood. She had her task in mind and was not, under any circumstances, about to go wandering in this wood. She had heard the tales of it from Grandam Orla and she was sensible enough to work out, within her first few footsteps beneath its canopy, that those stories were true. For now, she was respectful and made only the footprints she needed to, keeping the water close by as a guide. She was just at the edges; the wood would understand her situation and grant her safe passage.

BACK HOME, Ailith was nothing, a dandelion seed blown phwip-phwish on the wind, and of no consequence. Except, of course, if a dandelion seed took root in a paving stone then it grew into a plant, a tough rooted guerrilla of a thing that was hard to get rid of. That was how Ailith saw herself, she was ground into the paving stones in the courtyard, a little weed they'd have to dig out.

She kept the dandelion image in her mind. Physically she was strong, always had been, it came with her job, where she was wrapped in a pinny and in charge of an ever increasing pile of dishes. Breakfast dishes were no sooner done than she had to collect up the lunch dishes and then when that sinkful was wiped and dried the castle's inhabitants had dirtied up their dinner dishes and the copper must be boiled once again.

What they didn't know, none of them, was that Ailith was a fast learner, a good observer. Her place was in the kitchen and, in Ailith's view at least, people underestimated the importance of kitchens. The dishes were heavy, so your arms grew muscles, and you learnt of ways to balance them so that you wouldn't have to make so many trips back to the hall and the long table that was made from the tallest oak. A great many people came to sit at that table, visitors and residents. You could learn a lot about someone from how they left their plate, the way they hid their runner beans under their knife, the bits they left on the chicken bones. You learnt to distinguish between the ravenous and the picky.

People gossiped in the kitchen and let their guard down.

Hidden behind the grub and slops of your pinny, you were nothing and therefore you could learn everything.

It would stand her in good stead now for, if the Ways could not help her, she would have to help herself.

There were boundaries where Ailith lived, there were drystone walls and wooden gates knotted with iron but there was nothing like the wires that choked this place. Trying to break out of the edges of Havoc Wood was like being trapped in a snare. Ailith, her hair snarled into brambles, her knitted jerkin nearly unravelling on the thin snake of fence wire, writhed and wriggled her way out of the grip of the wood. With the small triumph of the fence out of the way she skidded and slipped her way down the banking of browning bracken and leaf litter to a straight path.

There was a largish sort of storybook left open by a bridge which Ailith stopped to try to read. Ha. Yes. No one knew she could do that. The pictures were pretty enough and she could make out the words 'industrial revolution', 'railway', and 'disused'. The image looked like a furnace with wheels, everything was odd here. Foreign. Other. There were pictures of a kestrel and a heron however, so she felt connected.

She followed the path and it led into the town itself. It was noisier and more bustling than she had expected and there were carriages that roared by with no horses. She felt adventurous as she looked around, sighted the castle at the top of the hill, and began to walk.

The lady in the castle wall, clearly held there under an enchantment, was asking her for coin she didn't have.

"I need to have a look around the castle, that's all..." Ailith reasoned. "I have come here—" she stopped herself in time, had almost confessed to the Bone Resting. She must not give herself away.

"It'll cost you £4.50 then," the woman insisted and turned her attention to the two women standing behind Ailith. Ailith stepped away and looked sulkily back towards town thinking of a bag of coin she had once had. There was a funny sound, like a bird's brief chirp and the women at the castle wall were all giggly and chattering.

"Oh... this contactless card stuff. Magic money!" The tall woman was waving a card, coloured and carrying a picture of a horse upon it. "Still freaks me out a bit. Where do I...?" She was gazing at a box that the enchanted castle lady was offering, and they were all putting on seeing glasses. Ailith wondered for a moment if she ought to have seeing glasses too, were they like armour or adornment? She couldn't quite work it out. The woman tapped the horsey card at the box and the bird sound Ailith heard seemed to signify that the money magic was worked.

Ailith needed to borrow a little of that magic, just enough to gain entrance to the castle. The enchanted lady was handing out maps and storybooks and the tall woman was absently putting the card into a pocket in her bag. Ailith waited for her moment to reveal itself.

She caught up with them later, standing by another storybook in the Great Hall and Ailith was very careful to slip the horsey card back into the woman's baggage. She understood that borrowing magic was dangerous, almost as dangerous as owning magic, and everything she had done in the last few weeks had been a ridge of danger that she was running and so she did not wish, so near to the completion of her task, to jeopardise it. Once the card was returned she wandered off by herself, trailed in and out of each room and ruinous pile of stones and, finally, took the lichen covered steps to the curtain wall.

CHARLIE WOKE UP WITH A START. She'd been wandering again, trailing her way through a clearing somewhere deep in Havoc, her hands reaching for plants as she did so, putting them into a basket of Grandma Hettie's. It was important, this dream. She had trailed through the wood in several similar dreams in the last few nights, her sleep broken up by these wanderings.

This morning she had put a pad at the side of the bed and she scribbled down a few. She noticed that there were other less legible scribbles from in the night and she was too tired and crabby to try to decipher them now.

She padded into the kitchen in her socks. They were her soft woollen ones and, she noticed as the cold floor touched her feet, there were holes in them. She ought to call into the outdoor shop and replace them. She took the offending sock off; it was, now she looked at it, more hole than sock and she put it down on the table as she turned to the kettle. There was a note on the fridge from Anna regarding their lack of milk and Emz was just exiting the bathroom, dressed for school and carrying a slight scent of toothpaste.

"You need a lift?" Charlie asked. "I'm going into town."

Emz shook her head and opened the fridge.

"Thanks, but no... There's no milk." She waved the empty plastic bottle, plonked it on the sinktop for the recycling. "Shall I get one on my way back?"

"No. I'm going into town so I will. What about our guest?"

"I don't think she can get milk." Emz grinned and Charlie made a mocking 'haha' noise complete with fake beaming smile before the sisters regarded each other properly. "If you're going into town why not take her with you?" Emz suggested.

"Is that against the rules d'you think?" Charlie was trying to remember some of the guests that she had met up with during Grandma Hettie's tour of duty. Emz, clearly, was thinking the same.

"Don't think so. There was that thin woman we took to Leap Woods for a picnic once, remember? And that bloke with the weird rabbit waistcoat, we walked him to the castle really late one afternoon and there was that funny falconry display."

Several memories tumbled forward for both of them. A small album of long-forgotten brief encountered faces.

"Right. Yes. Seems okay. So that's a good plan. I will do that."

"If she wants to go, of course," Emz qualified the plan. Charlie was less sympathetic.

"Well, if she wants breakfast she'd better get up." Charlie spooned coffee into her pot.

Emz headed off and Charlie thought that the house felt very empty and she understood why at once. She took a mug of coffee down the short corridor to the guest rooms and knocked on Ailith's door. When there was no reply she went in.

She stood for several minutes sipping her coffee and looking around the room. The bed didn't look slept in, although the floor did; Ailith's coat was folded into a pillow under the window. The basket containing the head was on the side table, so it seemed that perhaps Ailith hadn't done a bunk as such, unless, of course, she'd decided to abandon the Ways to the task. Charlie reached for the door handle and as she looked away from the room it shifted at the edge of her gaze. She looked back. What had altered? She looked back at her hand poised on the door handle and saw at once.

Ailith's coat was rumpled and folded into a 3D map of the route Ailith had travelled. It encompassed pathways that Charlie had not seen before in Havoc and yet they pinged in her head as if familiar. The trails and tracks turned, revealing to Charlie how careful Ailith had been on her journey. The sensation of travelling, of movement, increased until Charlie was spooked, and she stepped back, pulling the door to behind her. She stood for a moment listening to her heart pound itself back into its usual rhythm. Anna's eyes looked into her head; she saw the moment when Anna had said the word 'flickerbooked'.

It was a long time since her sister had used the term. It was something they said matter of fact when they were younger, when they spent more time in the wood and, Charlie understood, when they were closer to their Strengths. Something deep inside Charlie pushed and she pushed it back, turned to the kitchen.

More coffee, this was definitely a two-mug problem. She toyed with the idea of calling Anna but decided she did not want to appear panicky. It didn't seem to be a rule that Ailith had to stay in the cottage otherwise, Charlie knew, the doors would have shut against her. Charlie felt calmed by this idea, so, where might she be? Taking a walk round Pike Lake perhaps?

A quick scan with the binoculars proved that this wasn't the case. Every second that Charlie looked through the binoculars she understood what she was avoiding looking at. Her fingers were sweating, the pads soft with heat. *Find her.* The word she had used for her own Strength was waiting for her at the back of her head. She would let it wait a little while longer.

It was as she buttered her thinking toast that Charlie happened to glance at her holey sock. She saw the subtle change at once and her mind lurched away from it. Oh. Strength. She glanced at the sock again; the effect was as easy as blinking, the fibres and nubbles of the sock shifting and then, uh-oh, blurring. Wrong. Doing it wrong. She took a deep breath. This was, really, if you thought about it, like riding a bike or learning to drive a car, wasn't it? You could spook yourself if you wanted but you could just accept it as a practical tool. Wasn't that what Anna was doing?

Charlie took in another deep breath and looked down at the sock. Mindful of the way she'd lost the map of Hartfield in the paving stones outside the Castle Inn, she stopped thinking. She did not have to grab at this, that was the key. She looked back. At once the holes combined with the tweedy colours of the wool and the scrubby surface of the table to show her the map, a map quite as clear as the ones she used to see when she was a kid. She looked the sock map over a few times and felt a small fire start up inside her. It was warming and bright as daylight. *The thing about Strengths*, Charlie thought as she scoffed the last of her toast, pulled on her boots and grabbed her keys, *is that they make you feel strong.*

MRS BENTLEY WAS in the kiosk today and there was simply no arguing with her.

"You know, Charlie Way, if everyone didn't pay then very shortly we wouldn't have a castle, you do appreciate that fact?"

Charlie looked at Mrs Bentley's face; the determination seemed hewn out of the same stones as the castle itself. Charlie opened her mouth to speak but as she did so a fierce high-pitched sound struck up and she halted, looked around.

"If the Friends didn't look after it, it would be bought up and turned into luxury flats or a casino," Mrs Bentley continued, her voice lilting around the high-pitched noise before it dipped out again.

"Did you hear that?" Charlie asked and looked around. Faulty electricals somewhere? A noisy drinks cooler?

"Hear what?" Mrs Bentley asked. It was clear from her expression that she thought it was a ruse to avoid payment. Charlie listened for a second longer. The sound had dropped out of hearing. She gathered her thoughts.

"Yes. I get that Mrs Bentley, but it's not a proper visit, I'm just picking someone up." Charlie thought this was reasonable. She knew where Ailith would be because it was all in the weave of the sock, an item that Charlie had stowed in her jacket pocket. Charlie had no intention at this point of mooching round the castle. "I'm not going to be looking round."

Mrs Bentley's mouth pinched into a small prune shape. It struck Charlie that had Mrs Bentley been on the gate in the ancient past this castle would never have been taken; no one, not Edward II or Cromwell and his entire army, would have got past Mrs Bentley.

"Aha, so now you've explained your circumstances, I might be able to help you out." Mrs Bentley smiled in triumph. As she did so the high-pitched sound whined into Charlie once more. What was that? Mrs Bentley didn't hear it. She was still waffling on. What was she saying? Charlie could only focus on the high-pitched and insistent sound.

How she ended up joining The Friends of Woodcastle Castle and finding herself the owner of a Season Ticket, Charlie didn't fully understand but at least now she was inside the castle walls. The sound dipped and became lower, deeper, as if the castle was a bell ringing with its vibration. Charlie halted. She could hear other sounds around it, birdsong, traffic, the beep of the till in the kiosk, which was a good sign surely. That must mean she wasn't going deaf, it wasn't tinnitus, therefore it was outside her. The castle stones relayed the sound for several moments, then it dropped into silence.

Charlie was uneasy for two reasons. The sound, she understood, meant something and it was speaking to her Strength. The fact was she couldn't understand the sound. What was it trying to say? She took a few deep breaths and looked around the castle itself, regarding it the same way she did Havoc Wood when she was on patrol. Nothing stirred, just the grass in the breeze.

The sock map had told her that Ailith would be in the East Tower on the second floor by the fireplace and so Charlie walked over the greensward to the small doorway.

As HER FOOTSTEPS wound their way up the spiral stair the sound wrapped her up, the stones carrying the note of it through her, dark and prickling. Charlie halted half way up the twist and listened hard. The message of it was right at the very edge of her mind. She couldn't reach for it. It was deeply unsettling. Then it faded. Charlie felt compelled to touch the stones, to feel the cold strength of them, her eye drawn out through the arrow slit to the view of the Old Castle Road edge of the motte. The breeze ruffled the grass, the chill clearing Charlie's head for a moment. She gathered her thoughts again. Find Ailith. Upstairs.

She was feeling churlish and out of sorts, keen to escort Ailith back to Cob Cottage and sort out the mystery of Bone Resting and the severed head and stop being afraid. Ha. Yes. She could admit it as she took the last few steps. She was afraid.

As she reached the small stone landing she looked up into the solar. It was a wide high room, the floor above long since fallen through but with a distant ceiling, the cap for the tower. There was a table set with maps which were regularly graffitied or stolen and a couple of goblets nailed to the surface to make it look historic and welcoming and failing on both counts. The hearth was wide and bare and at one side of it Ailith sat on a small wooden stool. She was looking out towards the tall window, a long thin slice of light cutting through the heavy stonework. There was a chilly breeze blowing, wafting at Ailith's wispy hair. She looked small, almost childlike, her arms folded around her knees as if trying to keep warm. The hearth, vast and empty and brushed with leaves that had strayed in from the trees outside looked forlorn, but not as lost and forlorn as Ailith. Charlie felt a twinge in her heart at the sight.

"Hey." She kept her voice quiet, hovered in the arching doorway. Ailith turned and nodded and rose to her feet.

"Is it time to go?" she asked. Charlie shrugged.

"Want to look round?" She wanted to offer Ailith something and had nothing. Ailith gave a brief nod and stepped towards Charlie. As she did so the high-pitched sound strained into Charlie once more, so harsh and hard this time that she took a step back. It was worse if she stood by the stones. What was going on?

"Are you well?" Ailith looked concerned. Charlie nodded and ushered her out.

"Yes. Come on." She could hear the rudeness in her voice, but she couldn't stop it. The whine sank deeper once more and began to toll through the castle stones.

"Can you hear that?" Charlie asked. She was suspicious suddenly; after all, who was Ailith? Should she even be here in town? Was that what the castle was telling her?

Ailith looked flustered.

"Hear?" she looked afraid. "I can hear..." she listened, her head tilting a little, "the breeze. The town. Some birds." She looked to Charlie with a puzzled expression. "What should I listen for?" Charlie was panicking, Ailith picking up on the tension.

"Let's go." Charlie could not find the message. Warning? Signal? Greeting? She had to leave. She took hold of Ailith's arm and bustled her towards the steps. Ailith did not protest, instead moving quickly and quietly down the spiral of stones. Charlie, feeling more uneasy than ever, half bullied Ailith over the grass and out towards the car park.

11

FEARS AND DOUBTS

"What sort of sound?" Anna asked.

"I don't know, what is this, a sound survey?" Charlie was snappish, rising from the table to clear away her plate.

"What sort of sound was it Ailith?" Anna asked, her voice smooth as ever, soft and calm. Ailith looked anxious, looked towards Charlie.

"I..."

"She didn't hear it." Charlie was rubbing her face with her hands, her fingers reaching up to smooth back the tendrils of her hair. "Right. I'm going to say this and it's going to sound mad as a box of frogs."

Anna looked at her; Charlie could see where she was calm as Pike Lake in July, a flat surface glinting, her poker tell that showed she was just as afraid of what Charlie was going to say.

"Okay." Anna gave her the cue.

"The castle was talking to me." Charlie threw the words down. "That's what it felt like. Only it was talking, and I couldn't quite hear the message. Like it was far away or, maybe a bit in French or something so I knew the sound but couldn't catch the words."

Charlie took in a breath, leaned back against the sink, her hands finding the smoothed edges of it and trying to feel grounded.

For several moments Anna said nothing. Charlie pinched her lips together, her thoughts flying around in her head.

"Please say something, Anna," Charlie pleaded at last. "You always do this. You always shut down and I need you to say something."

"The Bone Resting? The castle is calling the warrior home." Anna's voice was low and soft but at the words Charlie seemed to relax a little.

"Oh. Maybe." Charlie breathed easier. The words seemed to have the opposite effect on Ailith. She sat up straighter, her hand resting on the table top, her face questioning and suspicious.

"You have never done a Bone Resting." Ailith stated the fact and neither Way sister denied it.

"This would be a first," Anna nodded. "We only took over from Grandma, from Hettie Way, quite recently."

Charlie cleared her throat at how recently and Ailith looked pained.

"What happened to Hettie Way?" Her tone had a hint of suspicion. Beside her Charlie felt Anna close up a little at the memory and stepped in.

"It was an accident," she gestured towards the porch steps. "She fell down the steps."

"Fell? You didn't decide you would be the Gamekeepers and take her life?" Ailith was steady, her voice strong and her gaze fixed upon the stunned sisters. The breath caught in Charlie's throat as she crushed back a sob. There was a long moment and Anna wiped at her eyes.

"We had no idea what we were going to inherit…" Anna began. Charlie spoke up, angry.

"Don't say anything, Anna."

Charlie could hear her heart pounding and it was no longer

afraid. It was like a drum, one that was psyching her up for a battle.

"You are the one who came to Havoc Wood carrying a severed head," Charlie kept her temper, her voice even. The room was beginning to resonate with her energy, pinning Ailith into her seat.

"I was at the castle with you when it chose to talk to me. Who says it wasn't trying to warn me about you?" Charlie pulled in the resonance of the castle, the deep low sound joining in with her heartbeat to keep her going, feed her Strength. Ailith wavered a little but Charlie did not stop.

"We live here. Havoc Wood is our Wood and we, myself, my sisters, we are the Gamekeepers. You, Traveller, must tell us your tale." Charlie was pointing at Ailith, her finger shaking.

"I have come." Ailith's voice was not strong, it cracked and so she took in a breath. "I have come to rest the warrior, for his Bone Resting." She drew herself up.

"No. Not enough. More. I need more. I'm the Gamekeeper." Charlie's drumming heart began a more settled tattoo, a steady pound that made her feel strong. Within it she could hear the low sound of the castle and could almost hear its message. She focused on Ailith's face and she was rewarded with the merest glimpse of fear, a little teaspoon of confusion dropped into it.

"I must rest the warrior. The Bone Resting." Ailith said it as if they ought to know what she meant. She said it with confidence. "You know this. You are the Gamekeepers."

Charlie knew at once she was lying. Somehow. There it was again, that annoying instinct. She was lying, but there were gradations to the lie. What was the lie? *Not a wrong lie. A right lie.* The words slid through her head.

"You're lying." Charlie stopped pointing, her voice calm. Ailith visibly quailed but shook her head and remained defiant.

"You're lying." Ailith flinched a little as she hurled the accusation, as if tamping down the desire to stamp her foot. "You have not Strengths. You know nothing. Hettie Way would know." The light coming through the window off the lake altered as clouds scudded over the sky and Ailith looked thin and grubby and afraid. That was when Anna spoke up.

"She's not lying, Charlie. It's just she's never done this before either."

Ailith looked at Anna as if she'd hit her; a small thin sound squeaked out of her. Charlie looked at Anna, then at Ailith. Ailith was defensive again.

"You can't help me. This is now made plain. Instead I must help myself." Ailith still looked wan but there was an added sheen of brave.

"We can help you," Anna said. "Sit down."

"You cannot." Ailith was agitated. Anna was nodding her head but Ailith continued.

"You don't have the knowledge. You aren't…"

Anna interrupted.

"We are." Anna's voice was loud. Everyone jumped. "We can help. Charlie…?" Anna turned to her sister. "How did you know where Ailith would be?"

Charlie, feeling the sock suddenly weigh heavily in her pocket, looked alarmed.

"What?"

"You went to the castle to find her. How did you know she would be there?"

Charlie was panicked, she gave Anna a warning look, but Anna pushed.

"Charlie, tell Ailith how you found her."

Charlie felt like a small schoolchild caught out stealing. Anna looked so certain and Charlie wished she felt the same. Sock. Green lentils. Her grandmother's hand on her shoulder, 'Which way Charlie?'

Charlie put the sock on the table where it did not move into any sort of map at all: was just, once more, a mass of holes and frayed wool.

"That is not mine." Ailith took a step back as if it might be a weapon.

"The sock showed me where you were," Charlie said. Ailith looked as if she might run for the door. "The threads. I'm shown a map. If I need it. This morning…" she toyed with the sock, "I needed to know where you were. The sock wove me a map."

Ailith was very thoughtful, her face lightening. She looked at Anna.

"You read into my memories," she said. Anna nodded.

"We can help you," Anna assured her. "If you let us."

AILITH ATE the cake in rushed wedges as Anna and Charlie attempted to formulate plans.

"So. Bone Resting." Charlie poked at her cake with a fork, half hoping that the answer might surface.

"It's obvious that the castle is the place." Anna was certain. "When you think about it." She had not, Charlie noticed, eaten any of the cake; she was chopping at it but not a morsel made it to her lips.

"I hadn't thought about it," Charlie confessed. "I was in too much of a blind panic."

"You've only got to think about how much time we've spent there over the years. With Grandma. Drawn there by ourselves."

"It's a big, old, hub of…" Charlie faltered at the word.

"We're going to have to say this word out loud eventually, Charlie. Make it smaller." Anna was in her biggest sister mood, the one where she was most patronising.

"You say it then," Charlie called her out. Anna fell silent and Charlie felt mean. There was a long moment of silence. Charlie suddenly knew how to redeem herself.

"Let's go back there. See if you can hear it too," she suggested.

ANNA WAY HAD no idea how she and Ailith had ended up joining The Friends of Woodcastle Castle nor how they were now, Ailith in particular, proud possessors of two Season Tickets.

"I wouldn't worry about it," Charlie sympathised as they made their way across the greensward of the yard. "I think Mrs Bentley might have a Strength." The castle, to be fair, looked rather more menacing now as the sky had clouded over considerably. As the three young women headed up the steps onto the walls they could see where a storm was gathering over towards Castlebury.

"Okay. So, what do we do?" Charlie asked.

"Wait," Anna shrugged. Charlie was impatient and watched as Ailith wandered off, trailing her hand along the curtain wall. They waited for a couple of minutes, the breeze snatching at Ailith's hair again making Charlie think about the evenings when Grandma Hettie brushed her hair at Cob Cottage.

"I can't hear anything different," Anna admitted.

"Give it a chance," Charlie nodded towards the East Tower, to where Ailith was about to go in through the doorway. "Let's patrol, shall we?"

They moved up the steps, twisting around the tower, Ailith running on ahead. Charlie reached for Anna's arm, held her back.

"What's her hurry?" Charlie asked with a nod upwards. Anna paused until Ailith had disappeared through the doorway above.

"I think she likes it here," Anna said. Charlie's face creased with puzzlement and Anna continued, "I think she's a long way from home."

Charlie sagged a little.

"How do you do that?"

"Do what?"

"Think like that?" Charlie pushed ahead of her. Anna took a few more steps, peered down from the wall to the dry moat and the banking on the outside of the wall and then continued up towards the Tower room.

They stood by the information board which bore artist's impressions of ladies doing embroidery and knights clashing.

"Is this what it was like back home?" Anna asked Ailith who was standing nearby, looking out of the long thin window. Ailith shook her head and looked sorrowful so that Anna regretted the thoughtless question. Charlie was making a circuit of the room glancing out of each of the arrow slit windows and finally joining Ailith at the broken edge of the tallest window looking out across town.

"Anything out of the ordinary going on in town today?" Charlie wondered as she looked out over the rooftops. "Something that might have made a lot of noise maybe?"

Anna considered for a moment.

"The primary school had a Harvest Festival, there would have been singing," she said. "Was it at all like singing?"

"Not at all," Charlie said, looking thoughtful. "The Hillman Wedding was on."

Anna shrugged.

"And?"

"Maybe the sound was just reverb from the disco or something."

They were neither of them convinced by this. They stood looking out, the wind blowing the sound of a distant siren towards them from the edge of Castlebury.

"Whatever it was, it isn't here now," Anna said. "Shall we have one more flick round the castle and then home?" Anna suggested, trying to chivvy their mood.

They paced the room and headed out through the door to the next set of spiral steps and wandered up to the tower.

It was very windy at the top and so their recce there was brief, and they were pushed down the steps by the gust of wind. They made their way through the tour of the castle, following the little arrows and reading all the information boards.

"Feels like the castle." Anna admitted. "Stony. Ancient."

Charlie nodded agreement.

"Silent," she said and halted on the wooden walkway that gave an elevated view of what had once been the Great Hall. "Grandma always said this place soaked in power. It's a fortress after all."

The others stood for a moment considering.

"I think it was definitely a callout." Anna turned a neat circle, her gaze rising up through the building to where the sky met the broken stones.

"So, what do you think Ailith?" Charlie found the question popping out of her mouth. "Is this where we need to do the Bone Resting?"

Ailith looked around. The old stones were furred here and there with lichen and moss, the colours like jewels to her. The heart had been cut out of it long ago; no fires were lit in the hearth. The kitchen that they had visited was not a hive of potato peeling and hissing goose fat, it was a tumbled down run of stones and the rusted bare metal of the oven door. The homesickness banked inside her. She could not manage to find any words, they lay in a jumble within, like burnt scraps. She nodded and turned down the steps.

1 2

PRICKING THUMBS

It had been a prickly day at Prickles. By the time three o'clock had rolled round both Winn and Emz bore scuff marks and scars and looked as though they had been in a minor war zone.

It had begun just as the school party were making their way up from the clearing. Emz had had a fractious morning with the group of year threes. They had moaned about walking, moaned about being cold, moaned that it was not yet lunchtime, moaned about not having a snack, moaned about the mud. Their constant moaning had, at last, cut into Emz's skin and made her feel edgy and tired.

"Everyone… this way. Follow the lady. In twos." The teacher pointed at Emz.

Emz set off down the path and they moved swiftly on towards the lake.

A keen wind was lashing Cooper's Pond into a ragged blanket. There was chatting, noisy enough to frighten every bird, but as they neared the edge of the water one of the boys piped up.

"There's a monster in this lake."

The teacher touched him on the shoulder, gently.

"No. Sam, there is no monster."

"There is. A monster pike." As he spoke a small group of girls clad in varying shades of pink started shrieking and twitching together. Sam made the classic fisherman's gesture of widening his arms as far as their span. "It's this big and really really really old and it's got loads of really really really sharp teeth and it eats meat and my dad tried catching it once."

The teacher glanced around at the other children, some of whom were too tired by now to continue their previous moaning and were not really paying attention. The cluster of Pink Girls however were shrieking and squeaking and walking, crablike, with too many legs to control, towards the edge of Cooper's Pond.

"There's no monster pike in here," Emz shook her head at Sam. "You've got the wrong body of water. The monster pike is in Pike Lake."

The teacher put her hand over her face in despair as the Pink Girls began screaming in earnest. They were stumbling at the shore line until at last, the weakest, the one with the pinkest wellingtons, lost her footing and fell into the water.

The screams sent every jackdaw, jay, and magpie for a mile and a half radius into the air as Emz trawled into the water after her.

Once that accident had occurred there was no choice but to head back to the visitor centre and their waiting coach. On through the wood they stepped, moving up the path from the clearing towards the car park when there was a sound of breaking branches. Debris began to fall from above them. Emz looked up. Squirrels were fighting, their infuriated 'kackackack' calls cracking around the trunks of the trees as at least ten of them rocketed through the treetops. The first group were skimming down the trunks now, racing along on the path ahead of the school party causing panic. Rabid squirrels! The tide of children stopped moving forward and started to roil and curve back, each stamping on each other, crashing and bumping and crying out. At the last moment a squirrel divebombed the teacher, the small claws tangling in her hair, scratching at her face. Emz had no idea what she should do, torn between the crying mass of children and the distress of the teacher.

"Help… ah… ugh…" the squirrel was scrabbling and scratching, the teacher defending her face, her hands scored with scratches. Emz found instinct taking over as Winn headed down the path towards them.

"You. Here. Now." Winn's voice commanded, the small children shocked into turning to see where the sound was coming from, Winn waving her arms, marshalling the group as Emz pounced on the squirrel.

The second her hand closed around the small furred body she could feel the fear; it ran like shorting electric currents through every muscle, the small heart almost crushing itself in panic, and she reached without thinking. A fingertip here, adjust the ribcage there and the squirrel released its grip on the teacher and bounded from Emz's hands into the nearest tree. A whiplash of bough, a rustle of twigs, and it was gone.

Emz helped the teacher back to the visitor centre where Winn had shepherded all the children. They were sitting cross legged like an assembly on the floor of the education room and Winn was now plying them with sweets and squash. There was an unsettled sound of crunching toffees and hiccupping sobs.

Half an hour or so later, when Winn had been convinced by the teacher that she would not be sued for the incident, Winn and Emz made some fresh tea. As they stood in the kitchen they could hear the squirrels.

"Sounds like they're in gangs," Winn commented as they listened to the footsteps patter across the felted roof. "I've never heard the like…"

Later, possibly an hour later, Emz was hosing out the holding pens when the geese began to land. The first crashed with a thump into the banking just beyond the yard and began to honk and flap its way to the small outbuilding. Emz, her back to the door, was startled as it blundered in and was even more astonished as with a sound like flying flour bags seven more of the Canada geese made emergency landings and followed their comrade into the holding pens. They gathered together in the first one and Emz switched off the hose. What the hell? As Emz tried to leave she was thonked in the head by the wing of a further panicked goose. Once again, she reached without thinking, her hand closing around the fattened breast; at once the wing beats were slow motion and she could sense that electricity once more, crackling and hard. The goose's wing feathers sliced at her face, the beak clonking down at her until she released it into the pen with its flock. Her eye was streaming from where the array of flight feathers had grazed its surface.

She wetted a cloth in the kitchen and dabbed its coolness at her eyelid, blinking at the gritty pain. Tears flooded round her eyeball and her nose started running. Her sight was blurry. What the hell?

"Emz... Emz... Hand! Need one! Emz!" She could hear the sound and wasn't sure what it was at first. Winn? She sounded odd and off balance, not at all like Winn. Emz hurried through to the nursery.

Winn was pinned to the floor by what looked like a raft of giant chestnut burrs. The dozen or so hedgehog casualties that she had carefully fattened were rolled into tight spheres of spikes, the prickles piercing not just Winn's coat but also her hands, pinking into the nape of her neck. Emz tried to pick the first one up and received an electric shock for her trouble. She pulled on the leather gauntlets from the counter top and tried again; the electricity from the hedgehogs buzzed and fizzed through her but she held on. As she hopped and stepped amongst them they rolled and hunkered, the prickles rigid and poking through her socks. They were velcroed together, huddling into Winn for safety.

With the hedgehogs calmed in a vast cardboard box Emz patched up Winn's hands. Winn was very quiet indeed. She was still silent as they took pellets out to the geese who were still holed up in the pens. They were greedy and grateful, fussing around Winn's hiking boots.

As they wandered back to the visitor centre Winn spoke but Emz could not hear her over the clamour of the birds in the trees.

"What did you say?" Emz asked but Winn was halted, looking up into the canopy. The branches above were loaded with corvids, magpies yattering in from one direction, rooks from still another, a great black swooping cloud of them. The trees, almost bare of leaves, were suddenly dark with wings and feathers, the birds flapping and unsettled. Winn said nothing more; she grabbed Emz by the arm and pushed her towards the visitor centre.

Once inside the back door to the kitchen Winn waved a bossy arm at the kettle and the tea mugs and kept watch at the door.

"Never seen anything like," Winn mused. "Never." The bird sounds were lessened by the four walls of the centre but Emz, as she waited for the kettle to boil, stood and watched the shadows on the woodland floor outside the door. They edged and etched, black and light clashing against each other so that it seemed the earth itself was a reflection of the birds above. Emz felt an urge to run, her breath becoming panicky. There was somewhere she needed to be. She did not want to be late.

Winn shut the door so fast she almost trapped Emz's fingers. Emz startled; it was a feeling like waking up. She looked at Winn who was looking concerned.

"You need tea," Winn said. "I need tea. And we need to park our arses on a couple of wooden chairs. Make sure we're earthed."

They sat, a while later, watching the sun wink in through the slightly grubby window above the vast metal sink; it was making the slightly tea stained stainless steel look like burnished pewter and Emz concentrated on that small spectacle.

"Never seen the like," Winn said.

"Panic," Emz contributed, her mind sifting over the images of the morning, of her own feelings.

"Yes. Fear too." Winn dunked another three biscuits into her tea. "Not a bird of prey in sight though… or did you see something? Sparrowhawk perhaps? That'll sometimes do it."

Emz considered. She hadn't seen anything except corvids in the sky. Winn flexed her bandaged, hedgehogged hand.

"Could have been a minor earthquake you know… something we didn't necessarily feel but the animals were aware of… subsonic or something," Winn suggested.

At the edge of Emz's mind was a day at Cob Cottage. She had been there with Grandma Hettie, just the two of them that day. They had been knitting on the porch, Emz, her fingertips sore from pushing the needlepoints through the loops and tangles. Grandma Hettie had been skilled, her needles flying in and out, the scarf reeling off them in quick rows. Funny, gossamer thin grey wool that Grandma had spun herself, and shown Emz how it was done with a little wooden weight and a spindle. The same moments played themselves over and she struggled to reach for the moments around them. Winn's matter of fact voice broke the thoughts.

"Get yourself off home. Might as well. I think we're done for the day."

EMZ WALKED down through Leap Wood, and armed with her binoculars, she found her feet falling into a patrol step, her glance taking in the spaces amongst the trees, her ears listening to the rhythms of the wood outside her own footsteps.

She reached the edge of Havoc and a little prickling feeling started at the back of her neck. The knitting memory was surfacing once more; she recalled that it was a long time since she'd knitted anything and then she realised why the memory had surfaced.

The last thing she had knitted had been a tiny bobble hat for Ethan, something for him to wear to keep him warm in the pushchair. Emz had gone to Castlebury to the designer wool store in New Town, the posh Georgian terraced area where all the indie shops were. The same little hat that the police had found on the riverside later, after everything that happened at Halloween.

Almost a year ago. The sudden grief of it crowded her, a remembrance of the sight of the little hat in a plastic evidence bag. She couldn't breathe, took in air that seemed to blow straight out of her again. She took a few steps into the shadows of Havoc Wood; it was all she could do to stop herself stumbling and so she sat down on a mossed trunk to gather her thoughts.

The tears streamed, and she let them, anxious to be done with this before she headed home, unwilling to bring this to Anna. She wiped at her face. She would need to splash a little of Pike Lake onto her skin later to wash the traces away. She took in a deep breath. The air smelt cold and black and sharp. She shook herself and headed off. She was going to be late. They would worry.

At the edge of Leap Woods Mrs Fyfe leaned against a tree and watched the Gamekeeper wander off into the distance. Interesting. She spat out the bite of apple she had taken, watching its mushed softness curdle into maggots as it hit the floor. The remainder of the blood red fruit in her hand she put into the pocket of her black coat and, with a wry smile, turned back towards Hartfield.

She had work to do.

13

TESTER, TRY ME

M ari had had a trying day at her little shop 'Betty's'. In fact, the shop had seemed very poky indeed this morning. It was clagged up with all the tat and clutter that she stocked, the air inside the small space heavy with roses and vanilla and not even good roses and good vanilla, but rather the kind that some chemist in a white coat had put together from acids and emulsifiers.

That bloody woman. Mari couldn't get her out of her head. That bloody bloody woman.

She had come in several times before. She was small and tubby, rather like a nasty pecking sort of pigeon. She lived, Mari knew, up at one of the few bungalows that clustered round The Crescent. At some point in the 1970s a local developer, Richard Banks, had tried to spread Woodcastle a little wider. He had bought up the rough land north of the castle and paid off the council to obtain the planning permission to try to drag the place into the twentieth century. He'd built the little group of bungalows, stiff and rectangular, and the rule there was that you couldn't have a garden fence, plant a hedge, or have anything that marked a boundary. There were other rules too, no ball games, no cycling, no parking, 'no' just in general, a rule of under the thumb. No pets probably, although a golden lab or a retriever might be beige enough. Oh my God she needed a cup of tea and a Sunshine Muffin from the bakery. And what had she been thinking about in the first place?

That bloody woman. Yes. Always bringing stuff back half used, always moaning that it didn't suit, it smelled bad, it had gone off, it had made her allergic! That was the one this morning.

"I have very sensitive skin," the woman had assured her. Mari pictured the woman's face, the thin lined skin stretched quite tight over the severe cheekbones. Mari had thought she had the skin of a lizard, it might make a nice handbag, possibly the kind of handbag that would pinch at your fingers, or maybe give you a neck ache after it had dangled off your shoulder all morning.

"I have to be very careful… this substance has caused an irritation," and frankly Mari had to agree, it certainly irritated her to have to issue a refund for something that was perfectly good. There was no point that woman coming in and buying anything, it was like an elaborate sort of pass the parcel game between them. Urgh. Mari felt the resentment bubble around inside her. The bell above the door chinged cheerfully and broke Mari out of her thoughts.

There were only two police officers in Woodcastle and one of them was retired.

"Hey." PC John Williamson, his broad shoulders filling out the crisp white of his shirt seemed to crowd the shop. Mari's heart sank.

"Oh no, what have I done now? I parked in the proper space, I'm sure I did." She turned to rummage in her handbag for her car keys.

"Oh. No. No. Nothing whatsoever to do with your vehicle." PC Williamson held up a hand. Mari dreaded what it might be to do with. Just recently it seemed that PC Williamson was waiting around every corner for her. She'd had three parking tickets and been stopped on the Old Castle Road three times for not having a brake light, not indicating at a box junction, and failing to report a stray sheep.

"No. This is… a personal matter. I'm after a gift actually."

Mari's heart bumped a little, ha, after bribes now, was that it? She tried not to look peeved and failed. PC Williamson was put on the backfoot slightly. "It's for my sis… a friend. A woman friend."

Hmm. Did he have a friend? Or had he arrested this woman? Probably holding her hostage in the station. Mari felt a flush suddenly at a brief fantasy of being handcuffed by PC Williamson. He did fill out that shirt. She switched her smile on.

"What sort of gift were you looking for?" she moved around the counter and due to the confined space was instantly beside him.

"Oh. Er. Erm. Birthday. That's the one. Birthday." He looked flustered for a second. It was probably being in a shop that did it. Men were like that. Mari thought of her last boyfriend who could only spend five minutes in a shop before having a meltdown, unless of course that shop sold electrical gadgets, in which case, what a boring afternoon that had been surrounded by HDMI cables and the scent of hot TV screens.

"What sort of thing does she like?" Mari asked with her fingers crossed that his budget would be huge. Oh. What was that thought that just bulged into her head? Her gaze was drawn to his truncheon, resting in a black leather holster at his belt. Mari was feeling a little flustered now.

"What sort of thing?" PC Williamson looked blank.

"Well… is she a girly girl for instance?" Mari asked. "Would she like jewellery? We've got this lovely range." Mari's fingers trickled through the sparkly necklaces draped around a Romanesque bust. "I've got earrings too, does she have pierced ears?" she was enjoying herself now. She had lots of pretty things, things to make people happy if they'd only stop by and take a look. She was not a shop assistant, she was a retail therapist!

"I like your bust," PC Williamson said. Mari stopped mid sales pitch.

"What?" She turned to look at him. PC Williamson was the one to flush this time and he nodded to the Roman statuary.

"The bust. I mean, the statue... er, thingy. Is it Juno or someone?" he was floundering, and Mari let him. He cleared his throat. "These are lovely. Which one would you choose?" he asked, reaching for the necklaces.

"This one..." Mari attempted to untangle the necklaces. They had twisted around each other and it was proving difficult. As she fumbled about another customer came in and the shop seemed filled to bursting. Mari greeted the woman.

"Hello. Welcome to Betty's. If you need any help just ask," before turning back to the necklaces.

"Oh, this is just..." She was getting cross, she could feel herself blushing, and she could feel PC Williamson staring at her and so her fingers were sausages and about as useful.

"That's alright," PC Williamson was squeezing past her, his muscular leg catching at the display table that cluttered up the shop space sending some small stuffed bears onto a cliff dive towards the woman customer. "You're busy. I'll come back again. Later. Thank you," and the bell chimed his exit.

Could today possibly plumb new depths? Mari turned to retrieve the stuffed bears and balanced them back on the table before she took a closer look at her new customer.

"Can I help at all?" Mari beamed a terrible smile. The woman in front of her, dressed entirely in black, was tallish and thinnish and had black hair cut with geometric precision, the fringe of which just brushed the rounded tortoiseshell frames of her glasses. She beamed a smile back at Mari with elegant red lips.

"No thank you, I'm content to look. What a lovely shop." She took a step towards the counter before being momentarily distracted by the display of candles on the rickety dresser. Her elegant black jumper was about to snag on one of the drawer handles. Mari darted from behind the counter.

"Oh... hang on... wait a moment..." Mari reached and rescued the fabric. It was so beautifully soft it must be cashmere. The woman had on tulip shaped trousers in another fabric that looked very tactile; Mari struggled to let go of the hem of the jumper and was envious of the lovely trousers. Even her baggy bottom would look elegant in trousers like that.

"Penny for them?" the woman smiled. Mari felt herself blush slightly.

"Oh... sorry... I didn't want you to catch your jumper... it's *so* beautiful..." Mari realised she was still holding onto the lushly soft fabric, so densely sootily black. The woman smiled wider. Those lips were such a perfect shade of red. "I love your lipstick," Mari ventured.

"Oh, thank you... it's a favourite shade."

"Is it an expensive brand?" Mari suspected it was. She thought of her own rubbishy collection of lipsticks which generally made her look as if she'd been smearing bright pink grease all over her face and usually on her teeth too. The woman was reaching for a neat little black vanity case. Her fingers, the nails painted a matching elegant red, pushed at a sleek silver catch and the case opened. It was lined with red silk and arrayed with a carousel of lipsticks in elegantly glossy black cases.

"No, not at all. In fact, it's my own range." Her fingers trailed over the neat tubes. "I'm in the area on business." Her eyes, Mari noticed as they stared at her, were a very deep blue, just further than navy with a splash of turquoise. "Pardon me saying this but you seem a little stressed." The woman placed a white skinned hand on Mari's arm, and asked "Are you a little down my dear?"

Mari felt a pang go through her. All her thoughts lately were about shutting the shop, about retreating to her uncle's farm and the caravan he offered. She needed, above all else, a change of direction, to get out from under the suffocating floral quilts and frilly hand towels. What she wanted, what she needed, was something crisp and elegant. She looked at the grained black leather of the vanity case, at the lustrous watermarking of the satin inside, like a swirling red sea.

"Let me make you a gift, a little pick me up." The woman's fingers trailed over the tubes once more, Mari found it hard not to follow its course. She could see her face reflected in the black gloss surfaces, *little tiny powerless Mari.*

"Oh no... no you shouldn't do that," Mari said although her fingers longed to curl around the tubes, to smear the lush colour onto her lips and feel lifted, shiny. Glamorous, that is what she would be. "Oh no. I couldn't. Thank you but... no."

"Not at all my dear, it's very good for business. Word of mouth," she smiled. "Which is one of the colours in fact," she laughed, a shrill bird-like sound. "You can tell all your friends where you got your special lip colour."

Later, Mari couldn't recall the whole conversation in her head because the excitement she now felt fizzed around everything and made bubbles where her brain ought to be.

"All the products are natural ingredients, even the preservative... I'm very very keen on Mother Nature and all she has to offer us."

Mari was very keen on the lipsticks; the sun seemed to glint just so from the surface of the tubes and the red silk of the lining, oh, she couldn't stop herself tracing her fingers across its coolness.

"Would you like to look through the lipsticks?" the woman suggested.

The lipsticks were like nothing Mari had ever seen. Oh, this one was lush deep red, like wine: *Goblet,* the gold lettering christened it. She'd spent many a half hour dawdling by the cosmetics counters in the top shops in Castlebury. Oh, those mirrored counters in Milsom's where they only carried designer goods, most of which did not have price tags on them and which were policed by staff so haughty you did not dare ask what that price might be because you knew in your heart they were going to say, 'a kidney'. Ooh, this one was a brighter pinkier red, *Scarlet Fever*, and then this one, this one burst redly into your eyeball, *Bloodshot*. It wasn't just the colours, it was the texture, although Mari had only, so far, tested them out on the back of her hand. She was striped over now and couldn't remember which was her favourite because they all seemed to be her favourite. What was this one? Had she seen this one already? *Vermillionairess*? And the cases were so appealing, the smoothness of the plastic, the surface glossy, and yet somehow you couldn't see your reflection in them, just the way the daylight bounced on and off them and that delectable click they made as you put the lid back.

"Perhaps you'd like to choose one for yourself."

"Oh. Yes." Mari replied. "That would be wonderful... I think... I think this one is..." she picked out a black torpedo and clicked the lid free, twisted up the rich red concoction within, oh my god, she didn't think she'd even seen this one before, this was like red roses, velvet roses. *Petallic*. Oh no though, what about this one like a bead of blood. *Droplet*.

"Oh... No, I think maybe..." she could barely speak with delight and excitement but the elegant woman was reaching a slim finger towards another tube. She pulled it free as if lifting a chocolate from an extravagant box. She revealed it, twisting upwards. A deep red, like church velvet. *Vow*, the gold letters spelled.

"Wear this one," the elegant Mrs Fyfe decreed.

14

STRAIGHT TALKING

The necessity of carrying out the Bone Resting became focused and intense after Emz arrived home and recounted the events of her day, filling them in with the report of crazed squirrels and kamikaze hedgehogs. With all the information gathered the Ways considered.

"All this activity. It's connected to the Bone Resting." Charlie was the first to state what seemed obvious. "You arrive, and this stuff kicks off. There must be a link."

Anna and Emz nodded, their gaze settled on Ailith who looked distinctly ill at ease.

"We're looking at this as if it's a problem. It isn't. We just need to get on with the Bone Resting," Anna hoped she sounded reassuring and knowledgeable. "Once your warrior is rested then, all the..." she too struggled with the obvious word and could not look at Charlie, "... activity, will stop. Yes?" Anna struggled to fake a sense of breezy brightness.

Charlie turned directly to Ailith. "Have you got any clue what we have to do for the Bone Resting?" she asked. Ailith looked anxious.

"You're the Ways. The Gamekeepers. You must know."

"But that's our problem. We don't." Charlie was point blank with her comment. Anna noted that there was an almost imperceptible flinch from Ailith, but she pulled it back.

"Charlie..." Anna had a warning tone. Ailith looked cornered but stood her ground.

"I don't have the knowledge. I was just to bring him here. See him safe to Havoc and Hettie Way."

Charlie could hear that there was truth in the statement but once again there was another layer to what she said. Charlie was infuriated, it was as if she could see the difference, an alteration, but it was in the corner of her eye. She turned, put Ailith into the periphery of her vision. As she did so Ailith seemed thinner once more, tired. Afraid. Charlie felt it, like a spike. What was she afraid of?

There was a silence. The three sisters had never felt their responsibility so heavily. Anna spoke up once more.

"This Bone Resting... it's a funeral service?"

Ailith nodded.

"You must rest him right, that way they can't get him, they can't use him."

"Use him?" Charlie had a sudden inappropriate image of a football match and an unusual ball.

"Use him? How?" Anna asked.

"And who are They?" Emz put in. Ailith took in a deep, sharp breath.

"They? Anyone. His enemies. Your enemies. Whoever as wants the weapon of him." Ailith seemed to think they were simpletons, that she was having to explain something that was blindingly obvious. Charlie leapt on the new fact.

"Weapon? That head is a weapon? You knew this all along?" she stood up. "The place is buzzing with Mag... with, with." Charlie was struggling with her temper and fear, no wonder Ailith had been afraid. Anna tried to calm her.

"Charlie."

Charlie was not to be calmed.

"No Anna." Charlie flashed a look at her sister. Anna backed down. Charlie focused on Ailith. "All along you knew this, that his head can be a weapon? And you kept that from us?"

Ailith was silent, her face losing all colour, her breathing fast and shallow. Charlie watched her and again that uncertainty about Ailith flashed up. What was going on?

"Why wouldn't she?" Emz said in a voice soft as a whisker so that everyone turned.

"What?" Charlie's mind was glad of the reprieve. She was filtering and sifting. There was a nugget within all this. What was it?

"First off, she thought we knew about it." Emz was cool, calm. "She's not from here. She's come from far enough and expects that the Gamekeepers at Havoc Wood will know what to do. It's their job." She let that thought settle amongst them. Again, the tension in the room dipped a little.

"So. She arrives, and we haven't got a clue." Emz continued.

"Emz is right, Charlie..." Anna agreed with a nod. "That's our fault, not hers."

"And why would she tell us? We're not Hettie Way. We're just three weirdos who don't know what they're doing." Emz was reasoned and certain. "She can say it now because she's got to know us."

Charlie relented. She did not sit back down but her hands dug themselves deep into her sweatshirt pockets.

"Fair point."

Ailith remained tense. Charlie watched her, thoughtful, but less aggressively so. That was the wrong angle. She recalled the image of their guest sitting in the solar at the castle, small, defenceless, lost. Ailith was not an enemy.

"The weapon of him?" Anna asked; her mind was sifting memories now, a swift, efficient search for any information and suddenly it burst into her mind. She gave a gasp. "Oh. You mean like in the legends… like the Head of Bran?"

The other Way sisters turned to look at her. Ailith, for her part, looked relieved. She seemed to draw herself up taller.

"It is so… you do know."

Charlie and Emz looked at Anna.

As Charlie made fresh tea, Anna made bacon sandwiches and Emz pulled the copy of the *Mabinogion* from the bookshelf and they all glanced over the story, Ailith viewing the book as if it was an artefact, her eyes drawn to the colourful cover.

"The belief is…" Anna began, "that there was power in someone's skull. That all their soul and spirit resided there and if you took their head after a battle you could use that power."

"Weaponising someone's head?" Charlie concluded. Emz reached down another couple of colourful volumes.

"We know about this, Charlie." She was riffling through the books. "If I show you you'll remember. The Celts… Look." She flicked through the book, shoved it towards Charlie. Charlie was flooded with memory of the colourful knotwork art in the old volume. She remembered how often she'd followed the mazes of these patterns, losing herself. A strand or two of tension untwanged themselves as Anna continued.

"They believed the soul resided in your head. If you took your enemy's head you owned them. You'd stop them resting in peace at the very least," Anna said.

"The Green Knight," Charlie said almost to herself. "I'd forgotten." The Way sisters flicked through the books and the memories were flicking with greater clarity. As they stood beside Ailith they were also in the past, sitting on the baggy old sofa with Grandma Hettie, this book open and the tale of the Green Knight, of Bran, being woven into them with the wood smoke scent of the fire in the hearth of Cob Cottage.

"Everyone always thinks stuff is in your heart, but your head is where it all is." Emz sounded almost as though she was talking to herself. "Everything is going on up here..." she tapped her own temple. "All your memories and movements, all the electricity zapping and sparking, your own personal lightning storm."

This image resonated with all of them.

"It makes sense of what's been going on. It's because he's here at last, perhaps. It's Havoc's influence on his head." Charlie chewed over the thoughts.

"Because he's near to the end, there's like a funerary plume of Mag..." Emz felt Charlie tense at the approach of the word and altered course. "Of Strength. His Strength," Emz suggested. The air in the room seemed to lighten, the sunlight streaming in off the lake making sparkles of the dust motes.

"Maybe that's what the sound was in the castle. Maybe it's calling to him," Charlie rolled the thought around her head. "Like the Last Post on Remembrance Day."

The Ways tried to recall anything that their grandmother had ever said about deaths, funeral rites, and burials, other than her own burning of boats approach. Clearly that was not the way to go here.

"I can't see Mrs Bentley letting us build a pyre of any description in the castle grounds, can you?" Emz asked with a quizzical look.

"Let's face facts. I can't see Mrs Bentley letting us dig a hole and bury him," Anna was trying not to sound defeated.

"I don't suppose we can just put him in a shoebox and tell her he's a cat?" Charlie pondered. It was not the most sensible solution, but it was, at least, doable. She had an intense uneasiness and wanted the whole business, Ailith included, dealt with, fast. Anna gave her a withering look.

"I'm sorry, Ailith," Anna apologised and offered a newly opened tin stocked with half a pistachio and lemon curd meringue roulade that she had brought home from work. "We're a bit new at this."

"All well and good." Ailith smiled. Once again Charlie heard a wrong note. She played it back in her head as Anna got organised.

"Anyway. We can get this Bone Resting sorted and then you can be on your way." Anna smiled. Ailith's eyes flickered up to her face, distracted from the glistening sugared surface of the meringue for a moment or two. Her smile widened and as Emz watched she was struck by the sudden appearance of the young woman's raw real face. Where before Emz had thought it scary and off-putting now she seemed to see it with different eyes; the face was raw indeed, but raw with long held fear and it was stretched with tiredness, distorted out of its usual placings. Emz wanted to reach out for Ailith and as her arm flinched slightly with the movement it was Ailith who moved out of reach, standing up suddenly.

"I am very tired. It is time I slept," she smiled briefly and then she seemed to vanish behind the bedroom door.

The Way sisters exchanged a glance. Anna looked directly at Emz.

"What did you see?" she asked. Emz looked back over the memory of Ailith's face.

"Tired. Scared." Emz offered.

"Join the club," Charlie confessed. Anna reached out her hands; Emz took one, Charlie the other and, triangulated for a moment or so, they let the feeling of bedtime stories, of Grandma Hettie, of home, settle into them.

"Anyone feel like a quick patrol of Havoc?" Anna asked.

"Yes. Check for guests and visitors that might be headed this way." Charlie was already reaching for her jacket.

"They'll be mourners, won't they? Since it's a funeral," Emz said as they trooped out.

"Good point. Well made," Anna said as they shut the door.

Ailith standing in the room, her ear to the door, tried to hear what was being said. She was tensed, like an animal waiting and then, at the last moment as the Witch Ways headed out, she scuttled down to the little nest of duvet she had made beneath the window.

15

LIPSTICK ON A PIG

The Craft Club were meeting tonight, not at The Sisters at the foot of Horse Hill but at Roz's house, a semi-detached Victorian villa at the Castlebury end of town. Villiers House, as it was grandly titled, had a wooden porch that ran around the front of the house to a set of steps at the front door and a cellar beneath which had recently been tanked out and made into what Roz titled 'a garden room'. The garden was a tangled mess of shrubs and odd sculptures and wind chimes. Inside, the house was painted with a palette of gloomy earth tones and furnished with junk shop finds; it was a masterpiece of Gothic majesty.

The women had gathered in the Withdrawing Room, high ceilinged and continuing the Gothic theme with blue black walls and bronze coloured ceiling. There was a vast dining table set up with candles and wine goblets. Above them an antique chandelier shimmered with light.

Tonight, it was Fliss' turn to open their gathering by casting their banishing spell. Each member of the Craft Club had their own personal style of their 'practice' as they called it. Fliss' involved what appeared to be advanced yoga moves.

"We reach for the cobwebs and corners." Fliss' arms were flung very wide at this point. Roz had watched this banishing before and always thought that cobwebs and corners were the most interesting part of any room. This evening she was struggling to think at all. The more Fliss waved her arms and asked the beneficence of the Spirit Goddess, the more Roz Woodhill yawned. Fliss was not unaware but rather than confront Roz's rudeness she threw her banishing moves more vigorously towards her.

"We dash the darkness from the corners." Fliss folded herself forwards and flung herself upwards, arms raised, head tilted back, "We throw the shadows from the edges." Her arms were flinging in each compass direction now. There was a lot of hand flicking, Fliss' compass including all the South South Easts and South South Wests, rather than the basic four points.

"We push the darkness..." Fliss' voice had raised itself by several screechy decibels and just as Roz thought she ought to intervene in this tedious display, Mari stood up from the table and pushed her way past Fliss and her banishing.

"'Scuse me... thanks..." Mari moved to the French doors and opened them; she was fanning at her face. "Phew... is it just me or is it hot in here?"

Everyone, it appeared, was relieved to be saved from the banishing spell. Roz was slightly miffed; she did not, as a rule, tend to relinquish control of the Craft Club.

"If you don't mind?" Fliss' voice was hard and plastic. She glared at Mari.

"If I don't mind what?" Mari took neat little breaths, wafted a hand at her face. "So stuffy in here..." she made a pointed glance at Fliss.

"If you don't mind, Mari, I was in the middle of our banishing spell." Fliss was holding herself very stiffly. Roz could only hope she'd pranged a neck muscle with that last handwaving.

"Oh, I think we were done, don't you? You've banished all the cobwebs," Mari looked to the others, "and I think my interest is just about banished too." She sat back down. For several seconds no one spoke as if they were all replaying what she had just said to pick out the meanness of it. It was unlike Mari. With a little uncertainty Kirstie sat forward and the meeting began.

It was Fliss, once again, who started to cause ructions. She had been talking for some time about the necessity of seeing each other's Book of Shadows. No one agreed with her on this point. Each of the members of the Craft Club kept their Book of Shadows very much to themselves and each had their own personal style. Kirstie's book, for example, was mostly filled with textile squares that she'd sewn and created herself and called 'spells'. It was, and Kirstie knew this, more a workbook for her sewing ambitions than a grimoire.

"My Book of Shadows is private," Kirstie insisted. "Sorry but that's how I roll." She was pulling a face, her hand waving like a policewoman stopping traffic. Several other club members were nodding agreement. Fliss was looking irritated.

"The trouble is we need to keep to a grammar of process." Everyone looked puzzled at this but Fliss ploughed on. "If we want to progress we need to be a team, to share. I thought that's what being part of a group was about."

"Coven," Mari spoke up, a sharp little bark, her fingers tapping on the table. Fliss looked around.

"What?"

"Coven." The word was one the Craft Club liked. To them it smacked of their united witchy community, of shared power and togetherness but, suddenly, from Mari's blood red lipsticked lips it was like a tiny piece of darkness. Something altered in the room. Roz Woodhill felt it sharply. She glanced around the table. There were several Craft Club members who appeared unaffected. What was that?

"Coven." Mari said it again.

"Will you stop saying that?" Fliss rolled her shoulders "How is that relevant to anything? Why can't we share our thoughts? Hmm? It doesn't seem unreasonable and that way..." As Fliss talked there was a slimy slugness about her lips. She licked at her lips as she struggled onwards. "We all learn from each other. We shouldn't be selfish..." The lip gloss was gluing her lips, it was bright pink and, Roz thought, clashed so horribly with everything else about her. It was lip gloss for fairies; by rights Fliss should have been wearing something flouncy and a little pink ballet wrap cardigan made of angora. Instead she wore her usual office casual. Fliss looked, at all times, like someone who was about to take an audit."Yes. We should. I don't want you sharing my secrets." Mari was confident and relaxed. "Your trouble is you're trying to make witchcraft into the boy scouts."

The flashing truth of this halted Fliss for just a moment, but only a moment. Fliss continued with her diatribe. "We need to standardise how we do things otherwise how will we learn from our mistakes?"

"Standardise?" Hannah looked unconvinced and turned her gaze on her closest Craft Club friend, Kirstie, who was already shaking her head.

"No. That's not what my magic is about." Kirstie shook her head more vehemently. "I work from the heart, from the three wisdoms... I'm definitely more touchy-feely in my practice."

Fliss' tongue licked at her lips a little; they were looking sticky now and as she spoke up to defend her theory the effect was clear.

"We all need to know what we are each doing." She moved her mouth harder as little spittles of gloss stretched and gooed, not too much, just enough to make it awkward, to make it repulsive. Around the table several of the Craft Club members were trying different methods of reacting. Kirstie and Hannah were looking directly at Fliss, their eyes locked on the slimy lips. Jill and Alice looked at the table top and Bobbi was making a terrible gurning face at everyone as if to ask, *"Can you see this? What is wrong with her mouth?"*

"We need to know... what we are all doing so we can learn from each other." Fliss wiped her mouth with a tissue; it didn't help, little pocks of paper caught in the general mucousy goop. Mari was shaking her head, determined.

"We need secrets. We need darkness. Be selfish with your knowledge so others can't steal it," Mari continued, her fingers drumming on the table.

Fliss looked at the horrid pink in her hand, her mouth making little spitty sounds.

"What? Sorry, what?" Fliss was flustered; the slimy goop was finishing, the lip gloss cleaned off her face.

"Thief." Mari's word was small and spiteful. Fliss put a hand to her mouth for a second, as if she might be sick.

"Let's move on, shall we..." Roz attempted to steer the meeting back to, well, she wasn't sure where. She felt odd and rattled and what she really needed was a good cry.

"Okay. I'm okay." Fliss recovered herself; she consulted her tablet, swiping at the screen so she did not have to look up into Mari's unflinching stare.

"I think we can hazard a guess that Fliss' Book of Shadows is mostly spreadsheet." Mari piped up. Everyone stared. Fliss looked bewildered, a new look for her and not one that suited her thin face.

"What?"

Mari licked her lips. Roz noted that there was a slight waft in the air as she did so, something sweet and sickly like rotting fruit.

"You're obsessed with rules, Fliss. With regulations. Don't you understand?" Mari leaned forward conspiratorially. "There are no rules for this stuff. This is... power. Raw. Unfettered." Mari flung her arms up. The effect this time was very different, sensuous and free. "We fanny about, traipsing all the way up to The Sisters once in a full moon when really, what's to stop us running stark naked round the garden on a starlit evening?" She began to peel at the edges of her waterfall cardigan; her large bosom was only just contained within her soft satiny shirt as her fingers fumbled at the tiny pearly buttons. "Look at the night... It's time to release the Goddess." She kicked off her shoes and stepped out through the window. Rain was pattering. She paused, shivered a little in the chill damp.

"Ah, stuff it, it's pissing down." She turned back looking disconsolate, her lipstick streaked slightly across her face, spotting her teeth. "I don't know about you lot but I'm about gagging for some cake and a bottle of wine." And she began to pad towards the kitchen.

Grateful for the interlude, Kirstie, Jill, Bobbi, and Alice almost ran towards the kitchen.

Roz's kitchen, dominated by a range vast enough to roast a deer in, was a masterpiece of hand-carved craftsmanship. With so many shelves packed with so many jars it would be a revelation to most people that there was no hint of chicken stock or teabags.

As the tea was brewed and cups found and put out there was an unveiling of cakes in their black, Craft Club tins. There were some black cakes which looked quite chic. Liquorice. Treacle. Beetroot and treacle. Treacle and liquorice.

Except tonight even the cakes caused argument.

"Lemon?" Fliss looked at the epic beauty of Mari's cake.

"What's wrong with lemon? It's straight from the Earth Goddess." Mari was sullen at the verdict on her efforts. Roz looked at her. There was something distinctly different about Mari this evening. Roz struggled to pinpoint it. She certainly had not washed her hair. Ah, it was the lipstick, some new colour making her lips look bloodied and venomous. Roz saw where it had left little crimson smudges on two or three of the other women's cheeks where they had greeted each other with a hug on arrival.

"I love lemon," said Kirstie. Mari blew her a smoochy kiss, the red lipstick rubbing off on her teeth. Roz, slightly repulsed by this, looked away and revived her spirits by giving Kirstie a withering look.

"Lemon isn't very Wicca is it?"

"It's bloody delicious though," Kirstie confirmed through a mouthful of buttercream icing. As she did so two of the other Craft Club women reached in and took greedy slices, their hands sticky with buttercream and a heavy scent of lemon suffocating the kitchen.

"Its quality isn't in question."

Bobbi and Alice were smearing cake into their mouths now.

"No, it isn't. This is lush." Bobbi's voice was thick with sponge and lemon curd. Roz did not notice, choosing instead to continue her lecture.

"It is just that if we are going to meet and make ceremony then I think we need to have a few ground rules and personally I don't think 'lemon' is going to add to our craft," Roz decreed. Her attempt to doom the luscious looking lemon cake was failing. The Craft Club women were reaching for more, dispensing with slices now and clawing at the cake.

"Lemon sours," put in Fliss. This appeared to be the final judgement as at that point a greedy scuffle broke out between Bobbi and Alice over the last slice and finally Roz's husband, Matt, had to come in from the games room and pick the two women apart.

"I THOUGHT YOU'D GONE OUT," Roz could barely talk, her head was ringing, she felt quite ill. Matt had mopped the floor and there was a crisp scent of lemon and floor cleaner that was not helping.

"Not tonight," he confessed.

"You do usually when the Craft Club come round." Roz wanted very much to reach for him, but he seemed to be standing so far away she hadn't the energy.

"Yeah. I dunno. Tonight I just… didn't feel like it." He leaned the mop against the worktop and moved to touch her hair. He kissed the top of her head and closed his arms around her. The relief she felt was huge, as if a wall had tumbled down around her. Lovely. Lovely. She loved him so much, how could she forget how much?

16

AFTERTASTE

M ichael was not the best of passengers, especially when Charlie was driving. As they neared the roundabout at the Castlebury turn off his foot pumped out into the footwell. Charlie was used to this.

"Thanks for the emergency imaginary braking there, Michael, always effective." As she spoke she was careening onto the roundabout, sliding the van in behind a small runabout car. Michael clutched at the door handle.

"Assume the bracing position," Charlie joked as they rolled around the roundabout. "Emergency exits are here... here... and here." She waved her arms about, never taking both from the wheel, but the dramatic effect was very amusing as Michael winced and braced in the passenger seat.

"I am not a good passenger," he admitted, as he always admitted whenever she drove. Charlie did another lap of the roundabout for a laugh, pipping the horn for good measure. "Alright, alright," he protested. "You made your point."

They were on their way to pick up the empty barrels from the Hillman wedding at Hartfield Hall. This time there was no mix up over the entrance as Charlie took the proper turn off and they drove straight to the stable block.

It looked like a battlefield. At the far end the windows to the orangery were a series of shards in splintered frames. Inside the tables were knocked over and at the far end, stacked up like a barricade as if against a battle.

"Okay. Somebody had a party." Michael's feet crunched over broken glass. He lifted a chair out of Charlie's path and a bottle rolled towards them. Charlie picked it up.

"What is this?" She looked over the fat green bottle. It was not one of theirs. It bore a gilded red apple shaped label with dark green lettering, 'True Brew'. She looked up at Michael. He shrugged.

"Don't know it. Guests might have brought it."

Charlie took a sniff at it and drew back, the acrid sharp scent stinging at her, making her think of thorns.

"Doesn't travel." They moved towards the centre of the stables where the organisation had been. There was no one around.

"Let's just get the kegs and go." Michael gave an involuntary shiver and stepped towards the far end of the stable block. As they did so there were other kegs strewn around, emptied, all bearing the gilded red and green label of 'True Brew'.

"How much did they drink?" Charlie asked as they entered the stable block. Michael turned to her.

"Not nearly enough apparently." He stepped aside to reveal to Charlie the Drawbridge kegs, neatly stacked exactly as she and Jack had left them. A small spider was sitting in its neat web between the top two barrels. They were silent for a few seconds.

"But I... I don't under..." Charlie was stunned. She looked back outside into the detritus of the wedding. "What happened? Why didn't they drink it?" She looked back and forth, back and forth, even though no resolution offered itself.

"Maybe there's something wrong with it." Michael approached the stack, began to examine the kegs for damage or leakage.

"Everything looks okay. They don't look touched. At all. Not one drop."

It was very puzzling.

Charlie and Michael loaded the van together.

"I'm not sure what's happened... or where this leaves us."

"You mean we can't charge them for beer they didn't drink?" Charlie reasoned. Michael nodded.

"Effectively. I mean... they paid the deposit for the brewing... but no one drank any of the beer."

They were pondering the situation and arguing about who was going to drive back to Drawbridge when a thin, precise voice cut into their thoughts.

"What is happening here?" Michael jumped, and, as he did so, he revealed a tallish woman dressed entirely in black with a severely geometric haircut standing behind him. It was rather creepy in Charlie's book, the way that she had, well, crept up on them.

"We're collecting the barrels from the wedding yesterday." Charlie informed her. Her glasses were very round and magnified her eyes. Charlie, who always looked everyone in the eye, was unnerved by the directness of this woman's stare.

"Ah. Yes. That small disaster." The woman raised a thin white hand in a supplicating gesture. It was made thinner and whiter by the intense blackness of her sweater.

"What?" Michael blurted.

"Yes," the thinnish, blackish figure smiled a thinnish, smallish smile. Her lips, Charlie noted, were very red, the lipstick a glossy colour that made Charlie think of roadkill innards.

"Yes?" Michael asked with a puzzled frown.

"Police were called in the end. It was very ugly." The magnified eyes looked away from Michael towards Charlie. Charlie felt a compulsion to look away and fought it. Who was this old bat?

"Is Winn around?" Charlie asked. The thinnish smile thinned

out further until, combined with the smear of lipstick, it looked like an opened vein.

"Indeed."

Charlie was not the most patient of people which combined well with Michael's burning desire to be the Politest Man in Britain.

"Well, we don't need to trouble…" he began.

"Who are you?" Charlie asked outright. This woman might, for all they knew, be trespassing and although Charlie was aware of the lax rulings regarding wandering into Hartfield, there was something about this woman that rankled her. Charlie knew that Winn would take an instant dislike and that would, most likely, result in an incident involving a twelve-bore shotgun. Charlie doubted this woman could outrun or outwit Winn Hartley-Hartfield.

"I'm so very sorry to have disturbed you," Michael began, as he was taking a step back towards the van. "We do have permission. We are from the Drawbridge Brewery and it is just a simple task we're engaged upon, to retrieve the barrels… we will be gone in a mere moment."

Charlie stopped staring at the thinnish woman and stared at Michael. What was wrong with him? He was smarming so hard he was going to leave a slug trail. In fact, was he bowing? As he moved back towards the driving seat, he was, yes, distinctly dipping from the waist. What on earth was wrong with him?

"Good. All of this debris needs to be cleared. These barrels, those bottles…" she pointed out a stack of the *'True Brew'* bottles that tipped from and rolled underneath the horse troughs.

"Yes. Yes, of course, it won't take us…" Michael was already rolling up a sleeve and gathering the bottles to himself, the last dregs of some dripping out onto his arm, down his trousers. Charlie stepped in.

"No. We won't be moving any of that. Those bottles are not ours and neither are the kegs. They are the property of another brewery and nothing to do with Drawbridge. We won't touch them."

Michael rolled his sleeve down and then licking his finger rubbed at the cider stain on his trouser, making it worse. There was a waft of sickly, stale cider.

"You will take them away." The voice was cold and hard and sharp. Once more Charlie thought she could see thorns waving in the breeze at the edges of the stable yard but she didn't move her gaze.

"We will not. They are not our property. There has been a mix-up. We will take our property and we will leave." Charlie was pleased that all her temper was funnelling into the timbre of her voice.

"You will take them away." The thinnish, tallish black clad woman's voice sank a little lower, her gaze unblinking. Charlie unblinked back. Those eyes stared out from the glasses and Charlie had a not very pleasant glimpse of the veins that crackled around the eyeballs. Ugh. It was like a map in there, the red veins like roads or paths. As she stared harder the woman blinked.

"Penny for them?" the woman's voice was unpleasant. Charlie had a sensation as if an unwelcome dog had licked her.

"Who *are* you?" she asked. The thinnish woman stared at her, very hard, as if this was not the answer she required. Charlie pushed onwards. "Does Winn know you're here?" Charlie realised she could not keep the threat out of her voice. The googly eyes wobbled just slightly and Charlie's own gaze held them, rigid.

"I'm the new tenant." The woman seemed to have to squeeze out the information. Charlie doubted it for a second and then recalled a passing comment from Emz about Winn letting the house.

"Well… it was delightful to make your acquaintance." Michael was fawning his way back along the van, still bowing very slightly and now, it seemed, offering his hand. The thinnish woman offered her thin, white claw in an elegant gesture.

"Charmed," she smiled, and Charlie let her gaze fall, turned to close up the van with a heavy bang. The sound seemed to wake Michael out of his charm offensive.

"I'm driving," Michael insisted and getting inside he gunned the engine so hard that Charlie had to jump in and had no further time to quiz Winn's horrid tenant.

IT WAS NOT funny when he pranged the van on the fence post at the end of the drive at Hartfield. They both got out to examine the damage; the front wing was crimped slightly at the bumper.

"The paint's scrawked. That's all." Charlie played it down. "It's cosmetic… look." She pulled at the mangled bumper and pushed it back into its rightful place. "Not a problem."

"You should drive." Michael raised his hands in surrender. "Seriously, I don't know what I was thinking." He looked a bit green.

"You feeling alright?"

"Bit sick." He was definitely a lovely shade of celadon, but Charlie was cruel.

"Nope. Back on the horse." She pushed him into the driving seat. He wound down the window and took a deep breath.

Back at the brewery Charlie made her rounds of the brew-house but the small tweaks and tasks could not distract her from the memory of the map of veins in the woman's eyes. At the foot of the office stairs she took a moment, closed her eyes to concentrate on the mental image. It was pushed out of her head by the sound of raised voices above. Charlie took the steps two at a time.

Mr Hillman, father of the bride, was berating Michael. Mr Hillman was red-faced with little flecks of spittle spuming at the corner of his mouth.

"Well I don't know Mr Chance, you brewed the beer, you must be able to find out how it was contaminated or… I don't know… tampered with."

Michael tried to cut in to the diatribe.

"Mr Hillman that's my point. All our barrels are full. Untouched. No one drank any of the Drawbridge wedding beer."

Mr Hillman was not listening.

"...and if you think I won't be putting out the word of mouth about this, this, debacle, well, then you are a deluded and sorry individual." Mr Hillman's finger was pointing now, quite as jabby and dangerous as a spear. Michael stood his ground, although the blush rising up his neck gave away his true feelings.

"Deluded? No... I don't think you heard me Mr Hillman... no one drank any of our beer, all our kegs are still full and untouched. I have no idea what beer you did drink."

Mr Hillman's redness gave off a heat and Charlie could see the veins in his eyeballs like thin red wires of anger. She was reminded of the veins in the screechy woman's eyes. Mr Hillman's eyes had an odd look, grey, tinny.

"Cider. We drank your cider. I am going to my solicitor today to find out what further action can be taken against your company."

"None." Charlie's voice cut like a blade across the conversation. Mr Hillman was silenced, his head turning to look at her, his finger still threatening Michael started to waver a little and he looked more uncertain of his territory. "Whatever happened it wasn't our beer. I'm sorry Mr Hillman but..."

"No. No, I don't understand. It was bad... the beer... our guests..." his voice halted, and he began to cry. "It was terrible. So terrible."

Charlie was swift to move a chair under him as his legs gave way, his head falling into his hands. He looked as if he might faint. Charlie darted to her desk and poured a shot of Blackberry Ferment.

"Oh, no, no I couldn't." Mr Hillman looked at the small shot glass.

"For medicinal purposes," Charlie suggested. Mr Hillman

breathed out and took the glass. He sipped at the alcohol and looked up at Charlie before knocking it back and leaning back into the chair with a sigh. Mr Hillman looked pink and deflated suddenly; sweat was breaking out on his forehead and he looked very tired. He ran a shaking hand through his hair as he gave a heavy sigh.

"Oh. Oh my. Oh goodness me... I," he looked tearful and a little bewildered. Michael was conciliatory.

"I am sorry, Mr Hillman. I don't know what happened yesterday, perhaps the caterers brought the other alcohol, the cider and champagne?"

Mr Hillman looked flushed.

"Oh. I do apologise, Mr Chance." His voice was breathy and faint. "I don't know what on earth has come over me."

Michael offered him a glass of water to chase the Ferment. He sipped at it, the colour coming back into his face, his eyes brightening.

"Never again," he said, tearfully. "I'd never go through that again."

He wiped at his eyes and it was some time later before he was recovered enough to let Michael run him home.

17

WITCH WEDNESDAY

The idea of Lella's 'Witch Wednesday' had been to promote chic Halloween fun and the consumption of cakes but the Historical Society group that had arrived were not into fun or cakes or fancy dress. Dressed in a scruffy selection of jeans, hiking trousers, and sweatshirts, they were currently engaged in a discussion of Cromwell and the siege of Woodcastle Castle and the role played by Lady Antonia Hartfield in said siege.

"Lady Antonia faced down Cromwell himself. I've been in the archive... I've read the documentation," one stern-faced woman insisted, the palm of her hand coming down on the white cloth draped table with a certainty that rattled every piece of crockery.

"Documentation? A poxy little pamphlet written ten years after the event," one of her colleagues argued. There were other grumbling noises which were difficult to interpret. Anna wasn't sure if the other women were agreeing, disagreeing or hedging their bets.

"By a witness." The stern-faced lady lifted her hand once again, once again brought it down with a chinkle of trembling china.

"A witness? Piffle." Again, there were the rumblings and grunts from the rest of the group. "And what was Cromwell doing in Woodcastle? Hmm?"

The grumblings and rumblings grew more intense, but the stern-faced woman simply smiled and presented her case.

"His horse threw a shoe and he was forced to call in at the smithy."

This crowd of ladies were not interested in the Halloween and witch themed cakes and dainties on offer, nor in trying on the velvet cloaks and pointed hats that Lella had provided. It was an odd scene, Anna thought, all the stern ladies intent upon their history surrounded by, and ignoring, the trappings of witchcraft.

Anna was feeling uneasy. She had never paid much attention to witches' hats and werewolf masks on previous Halloweens other than to be mildly annoyed by the fuss created. Today, the pointed hats that Lella had provided were screaming out at her; she thought them trite and stupid and they made her feel uneasy. Twice she had come into the dining room with a stand of sand-wiches and felt the hats were a message of some kind, like pointy black pennants. They seemed to lurk behind the guests as if they were distant peaked hills in a magical landscape that the women had no idea they were sitting in.

It grew worse as the afternoon moved on and the Historical Society left, determined on moving their squabble to the actual Castle grounds, and were replaced by the local book club.

These women were more Halloween minded and had come dressed; most wore black dresses and striped tights, and several had bought besoms from the local hardware shop. As their event progressed they passed Lella's elegant black hats around their circle and participants could only speak if they were wearing one of the pointed hats.

"Oooh, these are beautifully made," one lady admired the workmanship and Lella handed her a card from her milliner friend.

"Hats by Hollie, ladies. I've got to have one. That one I think."

She pointed to one with a tall slender crown. "Or maybe that one actually." She picked off another with a more flattened crown and a larger curved brim which she began to model. "I can't go into her shop with my credit card." Lella sold hard but was charming. "Oh, that looks fab on you," she pointed to the last hat, the one with the widest brim and a twisting point. "Did I tell you she did trilbies for my brother and Dad for a Sinatra stag do?" As Lella posed and passed around more hats even the most reluctant head was eventually adorned. "And she did these amazing fascinators for me and my girlfriends for Ascot this year." She pulled out her tablet, "I've got pics somewhere." With a couple of swipes the hat pictures were revealed, racked up and ready. Everyone began to crowd round the tablet and little cooing noises filled the room as Lella held court, giving directions to the chi-chi hat boutique. Several ladies were planning visits as there were a lot of weddings in the offing and with that turn in the conversation Lella began handing out wedding brochures too. Anna liked to watch Lella in action sometimes, it was as though she switched on a different self, a twinkling fairy with the skill of offering you a good bargain.

But the hats loomed, worse still, in their progress around the heads of the group, moving and shifting each time Anna glanced up. It gave them animus, and, what seemed very significant to Anna on this particular Wednesday, there were three of them.

Anna had an hour for her break and, to get away from the hats as much as anything, she took a walk up Dark Gate Street. At the corner she was pleased to see Seren putting out the street sign that declared her new shop was 'Now Open'.

"Hey." Seren hugged her. "How's it going?"

"Fine. Good. You look busy." Anna turned to distract herself with the shopfront. The display was stunning, three mannequins, elegant in linen and wood and displaying three of the most beautiful red ball gowns that Anna had ever seen.

"Wow." It was the only word she could find; she was choked with emotion. She looked back at Seren and was pleased to see how bright and happy she looked. Her face lit up at Anna's reaction.

"Come in for a minute." It was not a question, it was a kind command and Seren's hand tugged lightly at Anna's sleeve.

Inside, the main body of the shop had plain wood floors and a gilded velvet junk shop sofa for 'clients', as Seren called them, to sit upon. At the back was the work room, the bones of it showing clearly, machines and fabrics making an appealing jumble of craftsmanship and skill. There was a single rack beside the stairs that led up to the floor above. This rack held a collection of dresses. Silk. Satin. Pearls. Silver. Ruffles. Elegant. Frivolous. Chic.

"You've been busy."

"I certainly have. Villette sent a whole van of my things from home but it's still been mad." Seren laughed, "I love it. I can't seem to sew enough."

Anna felt the shop held a warmth and a cool pleasing scent of fabrics.

"Time for some tea?" Seren asked moving towards the small sink at the side of the workroom. Anna sat on the chaise.

"I have. What about you?"

"I think I can squeeze you into my schedule." Seren laughed as she took two mugs and some teabags from a small cupboard.

"No champagne then for your opening day?" Anna asked. Seren shook her head.

"I wish. I've been so busy this week it doesn't feel like an opening." She laughed again and raised her eyes to the sky. "Although after yesterday at the wedding... Trust me, champagne cocktails for breakfast are a no-go."

Seren offered Anna a biscuit, one of the ones from the local baker's pop up market stall, Anna was pleased to note.

"I'll remember that advice." Anna chinked her tea mug to Seren's.

"I just have my fingers crossed I stay busy." Seren looked a little uncertain for the first time and Anna rushed to reassure her.

"Well, if Cinderella is stuck she knows where to come," Anna joked. Seren pointed to the window.

"That's what inspired the window. Lella mentioned the idea of a Crimson Ball the other day and I just... went mad!"

The dresses were three differing shades of red, a rich deep velvet, a lighter crimson lace, and the final one, almost black blood red.

"I have so much to thank you for," Seren began tearing up a little. "So much." She reached for Anna's hand. "You and your sisters, you're like my fairy godmothers."

And for the first time in a while Anna laughed.

Taking her leave of Seren, she wandered back towards the Castle Inn the long way round and found herself at the foot of Top Lane looking towards the old chapel.

The 'SOLD' sign was still in evidence but so was a large skip, parked in the lane that ran up the side of the chapel. The doors and windows stood open; plaster dust and radio music filtered out into the cool October air with the sound of hammering and rending wood. Anna paused on the opposite side of the road to watch the activity. She thought, briefly, of her own long-gone plans for the place and she wished that whoever had bought the place would treat it kindly. She had a sudden dread that it might be converted into flats. There was a planning notice flapping against the lamp post outside and with a glance to the traffic, she crossed.

"Renovation not demolition," the voice was low and serious, "... if you were worried?"

Anna looked away from the planning notice. Matt Woodhill was covered in grime and plaster dust and was scratching his nose with his wrist, his hands hindered by thick leather work gloves.

"I was," she confessed. "Not being converted into flats I see."

"Was that what you were hoping for?" he asked.

"No. Not at all. The opposite actually."

He nodded and looked back at the building for a moment, considering.

"You religious?" he asked.

"No," Anna confessed. "I just like the building. Didn't want to see it spoiled."

He nodded agreement and then made a sweeping gesture with his gloved hand.

"Want to take a look? See what we're doing?"

Anna hesitated. She had been with Calum the last time she had been inside the chapel. The memory prickled at her, bringing the desire to remember, to hold him close and not forget, tainted with the deep black well of grief she was struggling not to fall into.

For a moment she thought it would be a bad idea to enter the chapel, that it might be as dangerous as walking over the ill-fated and newly repaired Knightstone Bridge. Then she saw the witches' hats in her head, saw Ailith smiling, recalled the warrior's head rolling onto the rug, and thought it might be a moment for some exorcism.

She noticed, as they walked up the path, that the grass had been cut around the gravestones.

Inside, the building was filled with light, yellow and gold and white, and the loftier panes of the stained-glass cast carousels of colour onto the floor. Two young men worked on a scaffold platform chipping at plaster.

"We're stripping out the rotten stuff ready to replace with like for like..." Matt Woodhill indicated the bare patches of plaster stripped back to the wooden lath. "It's a history lesson," he smiled. There were dust sheets over some of the pews; plaster dust lay everywhere, *like icing sugar*, Anna thought. She felt light inside. Matt was observing her. She found her smile stretching a little, making her face ache. He nodded and as he did she felt her face relax.

"Do you approve then?" he asked.

Anna was troubled momentarily by a torrent of memory and

she felt unsteady on her feet. Speech seemed just too much to cope with, so she smiled again, less frantically, and nodded. This was going to be very embarrassing. She was going to faint. Or cry. Maybe both. She took in a shallow little breath. Black butterflies crowded at once. Matt offered his gloved hand.

"Sorry, but I've forgotten which Way you are. Charlie?" he smiled, and Anna found they were shaking hands, the glove rough and textured, his grip strong so that their hands were almost bouncing up and down with the energy of it. The energy spooked the black butterflies and her heart rate steadied itself.

"I'm Anna," Anna replied.

"Anna — at the Castle Inn, right?" he gave a nod and Anna smiled.

"Thanks for the tour."

"Any time." Matt gave a wave as he turned back to his workbench.

Outside, Anna stopped and turned part way up the path. It was going to be safe. She suffered a fleeting second of a sense of loss, an edge of grief that grazed at her before she saw Matt Woodhill appear up a ladder, perched against the windows. Inside the building someone began whistling.

18

JOB DONE

It appeared to Emz, as she sat in a fug of equations, that the world was split into two spaces. There was the general and crowded space of the sixth form centre where noise ran like water, a constant and a comfort. This space expanded into the studious hum of M2 where Mrs Kumar was imparting her knowledge of mathematical theorems. This space was lit with electricity and the reflection of the white board on Mrs Kumar's almost perfect skin and her long and incredibly shiny black hair. Mrs Kumar, although somewhere in her forties, was universally admired and looked up to by the sixth form because she was clever and extremely beautiful. She was also stylish. Rumour had it that she had, once upon a time, been a runway model in Paris. Into this space clicked the numbers and the denominators and the vectors and factors and all the machinery of Mathematics. Everyone moved around this space with energy and speed and a brightness of eye.

Bounded by this space was the miniature universe that contained Emily Way and Logan Boyle. The only noise in this space was of hidden thoughts, of thudding heartbeats and shallow breaths. Right at this moment, for example, Logan Boyle was existing in the two spaces, his hand moving quickly across his notebook making mathematical markings, but, as Emz watched him, she could see the real edges of him, where he pushed out into Logan Space where his chair was angled so that he could watch her from the corners of his vision. This Logan Space lifted from the chair now and walked towards her, his hand, the one that was not marking out mathematics, was at her neck, her head was tilting towards his face and his mouth was—

"Emz?" Mrs Kumar's voice warped Logan Space. "What have you got?" she looked expectant. Emz looked at the page in front of her, the rough jumble of symbols. Mrs Kumar's perfectly groomed eyebrows wrinkled elegantly with impatience.

"Erm." Emz considered busking it. She looked up to the front. She could just pull this together from a standing start. She could hear her voice intoning the terms and she could see the maths in her head as it engineered itself. Mrs Kumar nodded and enthused and pulled up more slides from the presentation. Emz retrieved herself from Logan Space and concentrated.

At lunchtime she avoided all human contact and took herself off to sit under the pagoda shelter listening to her stomach rumbling and rueing the fact that she'd rushed out on Ailith this morning and in her haste to get away had neglected to bring either lunch or money. It was going to be a long afternoon of History and English. She rummaged in her bag for the copy of *Wuthering Heights* that the English group were currently intent upon.

As she moved through the chapter there was a scent of ham and cheese and then she was hallucinating that a hand was offering her a torn half of supermarket bap. The edges revealed a slice of Emmental, a thickly sliced wodge of off-the-bone ham, a shining glint of mustard. Emz did not look up at Logan Boyle.

"Aren't you having lunch with Caitlin today?" Emz stared at her book. Emily Bronte, it appeared, had written in gibberish, the words a jumble.

"She doesn't eat lunch." Logan waggled the torn bap at Emily. She was trying to play it cool but her aggrieved stomach was having other, growlier ideas. Logan smirked and sat beside her. Emz took the offering. His other hand lifted the twin half of the torn bap to his lips and began to chew. Emz took a small bite, fighting the urge to cram the whole delicious concoction into her mouth at once and then ask where the doughnuts were. Instead she thought she might push the obvious Caitlin point.

"Where's Caitlin then?" Emz was conflicted, the question seemed both mealy-mouthed and confrontational. She wanted to retract it at once. Logan ignored the question and ate in an easy silence for some moments. He wiped his hands on his jeans and reached into his bag.

"Impressive bit of busking you did for Kumar," he mused as he dredged, no, it couldn't be, a packet of supermarket doughnuts from the depths of his rucksack. Sugar snowed onto his jeans, frosted itself over Emz's own leggings. "How did you pull that off?"

"Skills," was all Emz managed. She bit into the doughnut, sugar crusting her face and a creamy burst of chocolate making her stomach rumble ever more greedily.

"Fucking not." His laugh was brief, and he didn't look at her; his stern gaze roamed across the empty space of the pagoda shelter surroundings, the wildlife pond, the balding grassland that bordered the back of the maths block. "Kumar was one bracket away from owning you..." Again he watched her from the corner of his eye. Emz gave her own brief and carefree laugh. At least that is what she aimed for, what came out was a sort of snort, a cross between an amused goat and a horse sneezing. There was a pause for more munching of doughnuts, Logan offering the bag for further pickings.

"She's going to take you down at the Parents' Consultation Evening," he predicted. Emz almost choked.

"What?"

"Well she is… you don't show up… you don't do the…"

"Parents' Consultation Evening?"

"Yeah. Week Thursday?"

Emz recalled very dimly the slip of paper she'd been given, two, or possibly three, weeks ago requiring her to organise herself and her parent into attending the consultation evening. What had she done with it? Whatever. It didn't matter. She could come alone. Her mother did not have to know anything about the event and would no doubt be splitting an atom or something that night. Panic over. Panic over. Panic.

Logan was looking directly at her now and Logan Space expanded and eclipsed all other space in the entire universe so that Emz was hyper aware of his smell, the colours of each strand of his hair, the pen mark on his sleeve. He had come to find her. Hadn't he? He leaned towards her and she waited for the kiss. His teeth, neat and white, bit into the doughnut in her hand before he rose up and stepped away from her.

"Whenever," was his farewell.

EMZ MANAGED to force herself to participate in the English lesson but History defeated her and once again it was a mere half an hour or so before she was pulling on her hiking trousers and tugging her Prickles sweatshirt over her head. The second her arms filled the sleeves she felt better and more in control.

The infirmary was free of hedgehogs this afternoon, Winn having just returned from an extensive release programme in the farthest reaches of Leap Woods. Emz cleaned out all the cages and pens in the infirmary itself and in the yard beyond. Their only occupants this afternoon were a selection of pheasants who had strayed into a garden in town and been retrieved by Winn.

"Why isn't the kettle on?" Winn grumped as she moved into the kitchen. "There's bugger all else for you to be getting on with."

Winn was always edgy when there was a lull and she was not required to relocate a badger's kneecap or resuscitate a vole.

Emz stood in the kitchen with the back door open. She looked out into the wood as the kettle rattled on the worktop. Today the squirrels were all calm and going about their business. She needed to refill the bird feeders at the front of reception too. Emz made a mental note and wondered if she had time before the kettle boiled. She put the teabags in the pot.

Sunlight slanted through the trees as Emz funnelled seed into the largest holder. There were three bird feeder stations at the front of the reception shed and they attracted a wide variety of local birds. She put the lid back on the feeder and looped it over its hook. As she lifted off the peanut holder she saw something move through the trees on the path to Cooper's Pond. The movement was not an animal and it was evasive. Emz thought of the vandalism they'd suffered to the hides in recent months and set off down the path in pursuit.

A biting breeze blew through the wood; she could see where the breeze wafted the leaves further into the wood. As the hairs on the back of her neck prickled the word *Trespassing* printed itself onto her brain and the breeze chilled further. The sensation was strong. She could see Grandma Hettie at the edge of her vision. Trust your gut.

She made her way quickly through the wood, following the twitching branches that the breeze snapped through the wood. As she moved further and deeper into Leap Woods Emz felt anger burble up inside like indigestion. Who was this?

"Ailith?" She called out the name and at once knew it was wrong. The trees seemed to know it too, catching her voice and softening it so that the name did not ring out, was muffled and pushed down into the leaves. The hairs on Emz's neck prickled further.

"You're trespassing," she announced. There was a moment when the air stilled completely. Emz felt the anger's heat fizz and build to a fierce, prickling spark that pushed out of her, rattled the leaves. Wait. Stop. What had they talked about last night? Mourners and guests.

"Oh. No. Wait." Emz lifted her hand in a wave. "Hang on. Are you a Guest?" There was no response. Emz took a breath, thinking of what to do next; she recalled the mental feeling of pushing Tighe Rourke through Havoc Wood and she tried that out too, shoving hard, mentally, into the space in front of her.

In the near distance a small branch broke free of the limb of a tree and thudded earthwards. Emz's gaze scanned every inch of her landscape, her feet moving her at speed through the undergrowth, off the paths, towards the small act of violence.

"Hey." She gave chase, her feet pounding and the earth springing away from her. "Hey!" Her voice was snatched at by the wind which whipped a branch into her face.

"YOU NEED TO BE CAREFUL." Winn patched up her scratches with a dab or two of witch hazel and a restorative cup of tea.

"It was just a branch," Emz grumbled. "I was stupid."

"I meant the vandals. Be careful."

The witch hazel began to pinch at her small wounds and she felt grumpy and out of sorts. Winn half pushed her off the chair.

"You'll do. Now get home," she instructed.

EMZ STUCK to the path that wound away from the back of reception down to Cooper's Pond. Usually she did not walk the paths, she had her own ways and means through the wood, but today she wanted to walk a boundary. Each footstep she planted firmly, and was aware of her breath which was, currently, shallow and sharp with anger. She made a conscious effort to look at the anger, to breathe it out in the continued little blasts and by the time she was at the shore of Cooper's Pond she was smiling to herself at the image she had in her head of small bright orange flames scorching from her lips.

The cool steel of the water quenched her at last as she looked out across the surface. She drank in the bright lemon of the late afternoon autumn sunlight and breathed in the distant darkness of a storm rising above the other side of Castlebury. The sky was a deep and attractive shade of grey, one that made Emz feel very much better. There was a breeze rising now, one that carried the scent of rain.

She could shake off the anger, but she could not shake the sensation that there was still someone else in the wood. *Other.* The word printed clearly and Emz's gaze picked its way through the trees. It was not impossible for some guest or mourner to have wandered into Leap Woods; there was the rush of the River Rade, of course, but that was not uncrossable and there were other boundaries of bogland and scrubby ground that separated the two entities. Leap Woods was, as Emz had been taught, the younger sister of Havoc Wood, the frilled and tilled edge. There were more paths through Leap Woods because more people entered it but, very early in her life, Emz had walked the boundaries of those paths and learnt the parts of Leap Woods that few others ventured into. In the main the townsfolk of Woodcastle did not stray from paths. They closed gates and kept their dogs on leashes.

Emz walked the wood. She wove her way along the trodden tracks and then began to criss and cross the landscape taking herself up to the edges where Leap Woods just shied away from joining with Havoc Wood. Here and there branches reached and connected with each other forming green lanes between the two parcels of land and Emz walked each familiar one of them.

In each place she felt the *Other* watching her. Except this time she was not the watched, she was, rather, keeping them in her sight, however much she could not see them. She had the new sensation that she was pursuing them and that whoever this was they were on edge, they had overplayed their hand, and now she was aware. It was interesting to Emz that each time she thought of *Other*, the advantage seemed to thin a little, the breeze that was not a breeze blew up a little swifter, rattled a tree, or pushed at her shoulder. When this nagged at her and she substituted the thought *Trespasser* she felt an energy pull back into her making her feel stronger. It was a mental tussle. She was standing in the easternmost firebreak road when this revelation occurred to her and as a consequence she walked the wood once more, crissing and crossing her paths and with each footprint pressing the word *Trespasser* into the earth.

By the time she turned out of Leap Woods and headed into Havoc she was tired to the bone and let the soft golden light of Cob Cottage reel her homewards.

AT THE EDGE of Hartfield Hall Mrs Fyfe stumbled out of the woods. There were twigs in her hair and she was breathing heavily. She crossed the lawn at a swift pace looking nowhere and as she entered the building the door slammed to behind her.

That girl. That girl. If she only knew her own Strength. What a tussle. Mrs Fyfe felt drained, the altercation taking a chunk out of the reserves she had gleaned from the wedding. That girl. Mrs Fyfe needed to regroup. Her work had been interrupted and now she must continue into the night.

A cat, one-eyed and malevolent looking, was sitting on a chair watching her. Its tongue licked out, interested, thoughtful. Mrs Fyfe's tongue licked out too.

"Here Puss…" she reached out a hand. The cat, old and wise, lashed out a set of claws and drew blood.

He was sorry, during his last moments on earth.

19

MY KINGDOM FOR A HEAD

The Way sisters were ranged around the table at Cob Cottage, none seated, standing in an unconsciously formed triangle. By the window Ailith was standing looking out with the basket, containing the wrapped warrior's head, at her feet. The room was filled with a smooth and rich scent of honey and wood smoke.

"Does it matter that this Trespasser or whatever was in Leap Woods and not Havoc?" Charlie had chewed over Emz's thoughts about the wood and possible visitors. Anna shrugged and looked at Emz.

"What do you think?"

"I think it's like Grandma taught us, Leap is the edge, the boundary. Whoever it was might have been lost or off track." Emz suggested.

"If you thought Trespasser then whoever it is shouldn't have been there," Anna said. This thought settled onto the table between them.

"Well, we patrolled and there's no one and nothing around," Charlie said. "I'd say the coast is clear."

"Yeah. No one's up to pay their last respects," Emz said.

"Or steal him?" Charlie was on edge "That's still a possibility. We need to make him safe. Maybe Emz's Trespasser was just on a recce."

There was a long silence. Anna blew out a long anxious breath.

"We need to do the Bone Resting…" Anna began.

"Tonight," Charlie said without preamble and the other sisters nodded. As they turned from the table Ailith had already lifted the basket from the floor and the handle was looped over her arm.

"Do we have a plan?" Anna asked as they pulled on jackets and laced up walking boots.

"A plan?" Charlie asked.

"To get in. It's a castle after all," Anna reasoned. Charlie shrugged.

"It's old. We'll climb in through a window or something."

Except of course, breaking into a castle was rather a tall order. Mrs Bentley, it transpired, used all the ancient security measures that had been fitted over the years. While the original drawbridge was no longer functional there was a portcullis and the doors, hewn from oak some centuries ago, were firmly locked. Charlie could look in through the giant-sized iron keyhole and see the tantalising vision of moonlit greensward within.

"Moonlit?" Emz looked up, the sky was clouded over.

"It isn't even a full moon…" Anna chipped in, pushing Charlie out of the way so she could have a look. "That's not the moon, that's a security light." She could see the fox who had triggered it strolling across the lawns with some sort of morsel in its jaws. "There's a fox…" she pointed it out. Charlie looked once more. There were a few moments of silence during which Anna walked a few paces up and down the nearest stretch of curtain wall.

"Think we could climb this door?" Charlie asked Emz. "Maybe use the rivets as footholds? We could get in through those murder holes at the top? D'you think?"

Charlie had several goes. She reached almost the top of the gate only to realise that the murder holes that looked out from above were not nearly wide enough to squeeze through having been fashioned large enough only to drizzle through boiled oil. With several grazes and splinters she slid and bumped back to earth as Anna returned and beckoned them into the shadows.

"This way... the old gate!" They walked with some purpose up towards High Market Street.

"The old gate?" Emz puzzled. "Is there one?" She couldn't remember ever seeing a gate at the back end of the castle.

"You won't remember. You were too small." Anna strode onwards not noticing that Emz looked a little hurt at this. Charlie shook her head, held up her hands.

"Was I too small?" she asked Emz. "I don't remember."

Emz laughed.

The group walked uphill along Keep Rows to the high banking until Anna halted. Above them the wall rose up and at the base of its perimeter was something resembling a doorway.

"This is an exit?" Charlie looked up. Anna was already starting to push her way through the thicket of brambles and buddleia.

"Yes. Don't you remember getting trapped in the turnstile when you were six?" her voice trailed into the undergrowth as Charlie struggled to recall the incident.

"Er. No. Clearly traumatised."

After a few moments the flora flexed and bent, twigs snapped, and Anna hauled herself back up into view, balancing on the thin path along the perimeter wall. The group watched from below as she disappeared into the ivy choked rectangle cut into the thickness of the wall. There was a creaking and squeaking sound and then a deep metallic groan that seemed to echo from the houses opposite. A light switched on at the end of the driveway to Whyre House and Major, the Great Dane, could be heard barking.

"It's a process of elimination," Anna persuaded them when she rejoined them, picking thorns out of her hands. "Let's do a circuit and see what we can find. There was that little wooden door in the north wall, remember?"

Charlie grimaced again and shook her head and the party followed Anna further along the road, turning sharply into The Bend, a small and nondescript lane. Their progress was hampered by a high wire fence circling the partially demolished cottage which went by the name of Old Bend Hide. There were signs of renovation, a pile of breeze blocks, a stack of wooden joists, and the carefully recovered original stones, marked and set in piles. There was no way they could get through the small building site.

"Plus, the door's blocked off... look," Emz pointed upwards to where the small wooden door had been bolted over with a heavy and slightly rusted-in metal one.

They returned to the front of the castle and there was a grim silence lasting several minutes until Emz, who had been deep in thought, said, "How did the fox get in?"

CLEARLY, the fox did not get in over the curtain wall but, with a beech tree for an accomplice, the Ways and Ailith managed to clamber into branches and transfer themselves onto stones. There was a chill breeze blowing as they mustered at the top of the wall leading into the North Tower.

"Where's the basket?" Emz asked and the sisters turned this way and that in an effort to locate the precious burden before Ailith lifted herself back into the tree branches once more. The Ways leaned over the wall to assist and watch as she skinned back down the tree with some agility and lifted the basket from the slightly hummocky patch of ground where she had left it. There was just a moment's pause in the inner heart of the boughs as a lone dog walker strolled past, the dog running ahead and sniffing at the base of the tree. It jumped up, resting its paws on the trunk, and began barking.

"Shush. Wilfred, shush up," the owner hissed before hooking

the dog back onto a leash and strolling off up the dark and empty street.

The church clock tolled the half hour and Anna became anxious.

"It's half eleven," she whispered.

"So?" Charlie shrugged. "What does that signify?"

"We've only got half an hour until midnight," Emz pointed out. Charlie gave a quick groan.

One of the many things that their Grandma Hettie had taught them was the importance of midnight. Many had been the nights at Cob Cottage when the sisters had been staying and had been allowed, in fact, encouraged, to stay up until midnight and very often beyond.

"Are you thinking of the midnight picnic?" Charlie asked her sisters. They looked at her and nodded. Charlie was beginning to think that there was more method than madness in their Grandma's teaching methods. She had, by some strange process of love and curiosity, managed to imprint a lot of things into her granddaughters.

"Get a feel for the small hours," Grandma Hettie had whispered as they sat at a clearing in Thinthrough with a basket recently emptied of its cargo of scones, jam, and cream. "They're the longest and darkest sometimes."

As one they remembered this snippet of conversation and saw it anew: it was advice. They all took heart.

"We've got time. We've timed it just right." Anna tried to sound reassuring and then they realised that the Bone Resting might be hampered by the fact that they had not brought even a trowel with them.

Charlie headed towards the kiosk and the small potting shed wedged into a dark meeting place between barbican and curtain wall. This shed was not locked and it was a simple matter to find the necessary tools.

It was not such a simple matter to work out where the head needed to be bone-rested.

"Should it be in the chapel bit?" Charlie theorised. The sisters looked at Ailith.

"Was he a Christian, Ailith?"

"No. We stayed with the old gods." Ailith looked wary.

"There's got to be some significance to the resting place," Emz said. "So how are we going to work that out?"

"Bran was like a security guard, guarding a gate. Should we be nearer to the gate?" Anna suggested. They looked at Ailith. She was standing to one side, the basket held tight in her hands. She looked distracted, a glazed look over her face, and she was staring up at the velvet blue sky, heavy with rain clouds.

"Eh?" She was aware she was being looked at.

"You got any ideas about where exactly we need to dig?" Charlie asked with not much hope. Ailith began to shrug and then halted; her glazed look intensified a little and her mouth made a concentrated line, the teeth behind pinching it tight as if to stop the thoughts from being lost.

Charlie, ever impatient, was about to chivvy her but Anna held her back with a shake of the head. Ailith was tensing by the second, searching for the thought. Something important, something far back, at journey's beginning.

"Rest me," she began the phrase, halted, her mouth pinched tighter, her gaze intent on the basket. "Rest me..." She put the basket down of a sudden and knelt beside it, folded back the tea cloth.

The Ways were surprised at the condition of the head, that the skin looked pale and waxen, that there was no livid blueness or deathly dryness. His hair had been combed and he looked very much as if he was sleeping. Anna felt tears prickle in her eyes and Charlie let out a small gasp.

So did Emz as his eyes opened only for her and he looked directly into her face, his gaze soft and intent.

"Rest me..." Ailith struggled for the phrasing. Emz did not, reciting it to them as the warrior recited it in her mind.

"Rest me by herepath and ridgewayed rampart... Make me at last the watchman of the western gate."

His smile was wistful as he turned his real face to the earth and his eyes closed.

The first logistical problem was the cutting into turf.

"If we do this it's going to show. Mrs Bentley will spot it through the oak door at one hundred paces with her eyes shut..." Charlie warned as she balanced her foot on the spade.

"What if we cut a square of turf to recover it?" Anna suggested. Charlie considered and shook her head.

"She'll notice," Emz agreed. As they were staring at the blade of the spade Charlie spotted the large square stones wedged into the ground slightly to the left of where she was about to dig.

They levered up the middle stone and Charlie dug quickly into the soft earth beneath. With the small hollow readied, Ailith stepped forward. She handed the basket to Anna. Anna wouldn't take it.

"No. It's your task," she smiled. There was something off kilter about Ailith tonight. She seemed thinner, slighter, more ghostly. It occurred to Anna then to wonder what might happen to Ailith after this task was done.

"No. My task was to bring him. Your task is to rest him." Ailith's small thin face was etched with seriousness and, with some small ceremony, Anna took the basket from her. Ailith took one step back, her hands coming to rest in front of her, ceremonial and solemn.

Anna lifted the head from the wrappings. It was not the unpleasant experience she had anticipated but she was swift now to lay it in the hollow they'd made. She could almost hear the church clock ticking down the seconds.

"Wait..." Emz hissed as Anna leaned downwards. Emz scooted

to one side, and, in the darkness, there was the sound of tearing plants before Emz scuttled back bringing a scent of sap and leaf and dropped a handful of dandelion leaves and the desiccated heads and stems of cow parsley and feverfew from the rough edge by the wall. "It's a resting, isn't it? Got to give him something to rest on."

With the vegetation in place Anna settled the head, at first on the back of the skull so that he was looking upwards, and then, remembering the words that Emz had spoken, tilting it vertical so that the raggedy, dried up meat of the spine and severed vertebrae were downmost, the head, for all intents, looking out towards the gate instead of up towards the sky.

"We should say a few words," Charlie reminded them. She looked at Emz. "What was the phrase you said?"

"Rest me by herepath and ridgewayed rampart, make me at last the watchman of the western gate," Emz said in respectful tones.

"Rest me by... Okay... got it?" Anna looked at Charlie and Emz.

"Rest me by herepath..." Charlie intoned and reached for her sisters' hands; the three joined together, making their triangle, and as they did each felt the burst of energy, a crackle of static between them and their voices raised slightly.

"Rest me by herepath and ridgewayed rampart. Make me at last the watchman of the western gate." They repeated it together and then each dropped to the ground to scuffle the earth back over the head. Anna, ever the gardener, made certain the hollow was backfilled, just as Grandma Hettie had taught them, slicing her hand down in front of the face, the nose catching against her palm as she filled in the earth.

With the hole filled, Charlie slid the stone back into place and they did their level best to push back the weeds and wildflowers that skirted its edge. By the light of Anna's torch, it seemed like a passable job.

"Yep. Seamless. Mrs Bentley won't notice," Charlie concluded, wiping her hands on her jeans. She touched the stone.

"Rest your bones beneath this stone," she said. There was a moment then, when the breeze blew up a little and the leaves left on the branches of the beech tree that had assisted in the Bone Resting rattled wildly, anticipating that it would now be an accomplice in their escape.

THERE WERE some twigs and leaves to be picked out of hair and necklines back at Cob Cottage along with several scuffs and scratches and a comparison of bruises. Anna made a pot of tea because, in spite of the evening's exertions, no one was particularly tired, indeed there was a crackling of energy in the air in the kitchen.

"Ow," Charlie said as the wooden chairback spat static at her. She looked at her hand, her face a crumpled puzzle. "Can you get static off a wooden chair?" she asked but no one was really listening. Anna was humming and bustling about the kitchen, managing to hunt in every drawer and cupboard for something that she couldn't remember she was looking for. Jam? Tea? Stock cubes?

Ailith stood in the living area and watched the activity. Her heart was a titmouse caught in a box, battering itself to death, waiting for the moment, and finally the moment arrived.

"Ailith," Anna Way smiled. Charlie Way pulled out a chair and made an ushering gesture before she put down a plate and a silver knife and a crisp white napkin.

"Come and sit down." Charlie said. The Way sisters began taking up their triangle of places at the table, set now with tea and mugs and the hearty cake for the condemned. Ailith's throat was closing up with the effort of trying to breathe, of trying not to think. Her face, try as she might, would not pull on the mask of her smile, all that was gone from her now. She did not make a move. She watched the sisters pour tea, milk, Charlie licking jam from her finger.

"So, Ailith, where will you go now?" Emz asked.

The simple question unmade her at last and, after all her journeying, after all her adventure and bravery, inside Ailith snapped, like a winter twig.

20

FINDING A WAY

"It's wrong," Ailith's voice was like a wild high wind, piercing to listen to. "I shouldn't be here." The Ways watched her struggle with her breath, with her composure, they saw the way she drew up the last little dregs of the strength that had got her here. "And now on a cause of that I have no place. There is nowhere for me." The Ways could see how tensely she held herself.

Charlie, in licking the jam from her finger, had glanced up at Ailith and seen something like a distress flare go off in her face. A reminder pinked in Charlie's head, her mind flashing up the moment when Ailith had confessed about the head being a possible weapon, when she had thought that there was another layer to what Ailith said. Now, she understood what Ailith had hidden. For the first time since her arrival Charlie felt, not afraid of Ailith and her motives, but afraid for her. She glanced at her sisters to be sure that they had clocked this change. Ailith was shaking and her eyes were very wide and bright.

"Ailith..." Anna stepped forward, her voice soft and comforting. "Why don't you sit..." but before she could finish the distress was white hot in Ailith's face. Anna wanted to back away. It was Charlie who stepped forward.

"But you are here," Charlie said. "There's something in that, Ailith."

Ailith was shaking her head.

"It's wrong. It's wrong."

"No, Ailith, it's not wrong." Charlie was certain. "Havoc let you through."

The others looked at her. Ailith looked startled.

"But... It wasn't meant to be me that did it. It was Tiercel who was meant. He was gifted the task."

"Why didn't he do it?" Emz asked.

"They killed him too." Charlie could feel Emz and Anna bristle beside her. Ailith seemed to thin out, it was almost possible to see the lake outside through her skin. The skinny weed of her hair crackled with static. As Emz looked into her real face, she could see the sea storming in her eyes. Anna stepped forward and took Ailith's shaking hand. At once the flickerbook began, this time the images more forceful and clear. Anna almost backed off, afraid of intruding into this woman's mind, but as the pictures flowed she understood they carried something else with them. The despair and fear flooded out of Ailith, dragging with it homesickness, a sense of loss. Faster and faster the flickerbook moved, blurring into one last image, of Ailith coming over the stile at Top Hundred.

"You've come far, Ailith, all the way here to Havoc. You took on the task. We can help you find your way."

Ailith opened her mouth and began to speak and this time the words flowed like the sea, unstoppable.

AILITH WAS NEVER OUT of a pinny; a leather one for the outdoors work, for the fetching and carrying across the courtyard, for the horse work, for the waggon work, for the hauling of firewood; a linen one almost waxed with the fat from a thousand dishes she'd sloshed the scraps from.

She raised the bucket from well and sinkhole dependent upon what the water was required for. And while they all thought she was good only for the scullery, Ailith learnt fast. She could cook the dinner for the Feast Hall when the cook was too pissed on spirit. No one knew. She could doctor and heal the horses after Lordship took umbrage against Mother Whitmore. She could doctor and heal the castle inhabitants too. She moved invisible through every room and walkway. Look twice and learn, that was what Grandam Orla had always said. No one looked twice or cared once for Ailith.

Not even Ladyship. And yet there was only one reason for the fact that she was sitting sewing in the solar, one sole reason she had that boy at her feet playing with his wooded soldiers, because Mother Whitmore took her dislike and put the word down and when that boy was struggling out into the world none would venture. None would go against Mother Whitmore.

Except Ailith. She had been there every time. Every birth. Mother Whitmore ordering her about and not caring what she saw, and she had seen the lot. Every time. Legs and heads and twisted cords and Ailith sharpening the knife and fetching fire and scissors.

She understood. Ailith did not grudge it. She knew that Ladyship was out of her sort, and besides that, Ailith didn't want thanks, didn't need it. She just wanted to do the stuff. To feel useful, as practical a thing in that castle as the machinery that drew up the drawbridge.

That time, with Ladyship, she'd used all the knowledge she'd ever stolen. She kept Death on the other side of the drawbridge the night of that boy's birth and so, she knew, she understood, she owed him twice, a debt in her left-hand pocket and her right.

Lordship was not away at war. This time the war come up the beach below instead. Climbed the cliffs. Dropped out of the pine trees at the wall. The war come for him and him alone and down in the kitchen they bolted the doors.

Only Ailith was not there. Ailith was straining and stretching herself up the blackwood ladder in the smokehouse hooking up the fish she'd filleted. And she heard the racket and stayed up the ladder, moving higher, up and up into the rafters like a fillet, melting herself into that smoke and it was choking her, snaking into her, and she saw them then as she aimed to breathe, pushed her nose against the slat in the roof where the turf had dried loose.

"The time is here, Tiercel, your task is at hand." Lordship was sweated out, his skin shiny as armour, patches seeped out on his jerkin, more sweat to cure the leather of it over time. "When they lop it off, you must take my head and run," Lordship instructed.

"I know it Lordship." Tiercel was cooled and calmed as still water even though they could hear the slicing swords and there was smoke curling up in towers and Ailith thought of that boy in the solar. That boy, she would learn later, that boy, they carved up for meat.

"Rest me..." Lordship paused, breathless at the sound of rending wood, like a forest toppling from above. "Rest me by herepath and ridgewayed rampart. Make me at last the watchman of the western gate."

"Lordship."

Tiercel, with his courtier bow.

"You know where? How to travel there?"

Tiercel, he had that map written into his head by his father and grandfather before him.

"By Havoc Wood." Tiercel's confirmation sealed by a hand-shake and then they were out of her sight, into the smoke and fray.

Ailith breathed through the slat in the roof, the smoke rising around her, disguising and deterring warriors from entering except to snaffle and snatch at the smoked fish with greedy hands and ravenous mouths. Ailith, above them, barely breathing.

She never saw a sword carved with symbols. That had been a

tale told for the Ways. She was not witness, not brave. She had stayed in the smokery until the pipes and drums began, the drums sending a rumble through her they were so loud, so hard, the sound knocking at the castle walls. What Ailith witnessed was the pennants set aflame, the smoke curling away into the sky, telling all the news of the end of their world.

It was dark and quieted when she crept down out of the rafters and wondered where she could go. The castle, her home since she didn't know when, a home no more. A thought struck her that she must go with Tiercel, go to Havoc Wood because Grandam Orla had knitted the tales of it into her head and maybe there was a meaning in that now. She could help. She could cook and sew and skivvy for him on his journey. She could trap rabbits and fetch water and perhaps find, somewhere on the other side of Havoc Wood, a new life.

She knew the quiet ways of the castle, how to move through like a mouse so no one saw or cared. She used that now.

Under the ribs and joints of the castle she moved, wandering because she had no notion where Tiercel might be. Might be long gone from here. But her feet led her to the masters in the Great Hall.

There was a strong smell of ale, the air fuggy with it, breathed out from the snoring nostrils, farted out from the slumped arses, drooled out through the drunken mouths of the sleeping soldiers who littered the room.

The smell of burning meat that was Tiercel, his fat spitting in the dying fire.

Somewhere distant there was shouting, singing, bawdy noises, so Ailith hid herself under the table, crouching. Afraid. From this shelter she saw where the Lordship was, a makeshift crown on his head now, the head on a pike at the top end of the hall above the chair where his body sat, the bones out, an eagle made out of him.

She looked at the Lordship's face a long time, her thoughts a ravel. Only when a soldier stirred and pissed did she understand that it was more dangerous to hide under the table and do naught. She didn't think then, she just did. Her feet moving up onto the dais, taking the pike down, the head sliding into her hands, and she reached for the tatters of Lordship's battle shirt and wrapped the head like a loaf of bread. An errand, that was all. She was the errand girl.

She did not have Tiercel's map in her head. The paths she followed to and through Havoc Wood were the back lanes and the greenways that her Grandam Orla told her of, and as Grandam Orla had always said, she kept eyes in the back of her head for the rogues and cutpurses that come after.

21

APPLE DAY

Charlie did not have any qualms about Ailith being hired for the Castle Inn Apple Day pop-up stall. Since the Bone Resting they had been trying to work out where Ailith could go and what she might be able to do. With Seren the answer had been obvious: she was a seamstress, a dressmaker. Ailith's possible future career was proving more trying. For one thing, Ailith had come out of Havoc Wood and, the sisters suspected, might be subject to different rules. As yet the wood had not offered up any solution for them and so Ailith remained a guest at Cob Cottage.

The Ways were happy to have her company, but it was clear to them all that Ailith needed something more. At mealtimes she picked at the food, hardly eating. She was quick to excuse herself in an evening, refusing an offer of hot chocolate and leaving the Ways sitting on the porch night after night, pondering.

"She's on the edges," Emz said, pulling her blanket a little tighter around. All their conversation had been about Ailith, their hot chocolate going cold in the chill air. "She keeps herself to one side of us."

Charlie was aware that Ailith did not sleep in the bed in the guest room, she slept in the little recess by the windowsill in a sort of nest made of the feather pillow and the duvet.

"It's not home," Charlie mused, thinking of her own former flat and how it had felt to finally move into Cob Cottage, to come home. "That's what she needs."

"She needs a future," Anna said. "It's up to us to help her find one."

The week of the Apple Day dawned, and it was Anna who found a small solution to Ailith's problems. She needed some assistance at the Castle Inn pop-up and after all, Ailith had the skillset.

"It will just be helping to serve food and drink. Clearing up, collecting rubbish."

Ailith was pleased at the offer.

"Yes. Thank you." Her face took on a little more colour, her eyes brightened.

At the table at Cob Cottage that evening they all noticed Ailith's improved appetite.

APPLE DAY DAWNED. The weather looked good as Charlie, Anna, and Ailith headed out at the crack of dawn to their respective tasks.

At Drawbridge Michael and Charlie had selected several kegs for the event alongside a special barrel of Charlie's Blackberry Ferment for a random taste test. So far, those at the brewery who had tasted the first decoction of it had loved it. Better than vodka, had been Kevin the maltster's view and his girlfriend, Lola, who had come in one afternoon thought it was 'lush'.

When Charlie parked up, Michael and Jack were loading up the wedding apple beer that had been left behind at Hartfield.

"Should we be doing that?" Charlie queried. "I mean... aren't they going to come back about it? Claim it or something?"

Michael shook his head.

"Is it sorted?" As Charlie said the words she was struck by the authority in her voice and the fact that, for once in their professional life, Michael Chance did not prevaricate or walk around the centre of the story.

"Yes. I've written it off." Michael opened the van door. "The way I see it the Hillmans had a terrible wedding and we can step back from it."

Charlie agreed.

"We can always sell the wedding beer," Michael said as they rolled out the first keg. "They, unfortunately, can't rewind their wedding day."

There was a moment then, a pause where Michael seemed deep in thought as he looked at her. Charlie looked into his eyes. *Honeyed sugar.* The rattle of Jack and the forklift heading across the yard broke her thoughts.

"I feel sorry for them," she said, Michael nodding.

"Yep. Anyway. This stuff," he patted the keg at his feet, "is one of your best concoctions so we should make a mint at Apple Day."

They were not destined to make any kind of mint as it turned out. The next keg rolled off the forklift and down into the river. As Jack and a couple of the work experience lads attempted to retrieve it Michael and Charlie loaded up the next two. They loaded the ordinary brew and their other bits of kit and attached the trailer with the gazebo and trestle table folded into it.

The van blew a tyre before they were out of the brewery car park.

"We've got time to change it. I'll tow the trailer into town and set up while you and Jack sort the van… okay?"

As Charlie unhitched the trailer from the van and re-hitched it to the rusting tow bar on her own car Michael made several attempts to release the spare tyre from the van.

"It's like it's welded." His face was purpling with strain. Charlie tried with her slightly smaller fingers and was sliced in the process. Jack brought the WD40 and sprayed the clip liberally so that Charlie left him and Michael coughing in a cloud of vaporised grease.

In town Charlie drove to their appointed pitch and began to set up the gazebo. She'd done it a hundred and one times before, and she had a system now that was failsafe and foolproof. With a bit of luck and a following wind here she might actually be able to set up the pop-up and then head over to the Castle Inn to scrounge a bacon butty off Anna.

The gazebo had transformed itself into a Chinese puzzle. Where usually the struts would clip and click into place and the top slide itself over the corners, today nothing would fit. Charlie examined all the poles which had been jumbled into a crazed order. One or two seemed bent and she was struggling to remember the last time they'd used the gazebo. She'd put it away herself according to her system. What on earth had happened to it? As she unfolded the canopy there was a pitiful tearing sound and a frayed slash appeared along the central seam.

"You can't set up here, Charlotte." It was Mr Bolton, the Chair of the Apple Day committee. Charlie looked bewildered, firstly by being addressed by her given name of Charlotte and secondly by being told she couldn't set up.

"Oh? Why not?" She was wary now. Mr Bolton was already turning his tablet to a landscape orientation and swiping at the screen. While he dressed in tweeds and a waistcoat and had a handlebar moustache to rival any Victorian gentleman, Mr Bolton was a gadgeteer. As she looked at his face she saw the Bluetooth headset clipped into his ear. His wrist bore a Fitbit; he was training for a multi-marathon.

"No, look... here's the orientation map. You — Drawbridge that is — need to be much further down, right at the end up there, by Poppy Cottage and the old garage... See?" He was tapping at the screen showing her the map in such minute detail she could see what the residents of Poppy Cottage had had for breakfast.

"But at the orientation meeting this was our spot." Charlie was foxed, the map on the screen seemed fuzzy and bewildering and as she watched it appeared to adjust itself into another map entirely, somewhere familiar, little red roads spreading out, where was that? It blurred and vanished. It must have been something to do with the screen resolution, or possibly this bright sunlight she was now having to squint into. "We were… here, at this corner with Laundry Lane." She looked about her. Yes. This was where they had agreed to be.

"I don't recall that meeting. You can't just alter your pitch to suit, months of planning goes into this, Charlotte, months, to get the right balance of food, drink, and craftsmen. I don't just sit down with the map and a load of little flags you know. This is all paced out for maximising footfall according to a retail software programme I've been developing…"

Mr Bolton owned three antique furniture shops in Castlebury, Woodhill, and Kingham, not to mention having a share in the teashops in Knightstone and a new one opening at Tower Gardens in Kingham.

"Well, where have you put us?" Charlie could not disguise her impatience. Mr Bolton pointed.

"Down there," he said. Charlie looked down Laundry Lane to where it met Red Hat Lane and the dead-end junction of Smithy Row. Poppy Cottage sat on the corner of Smithy Row. Who else was setting up down there? There was some activity. Oh. Just the postman with his trolley.

Mr Bolton gave her a hand with the faulty gazebo and her other bits of kit. As they passed down Laundry Lane other stall holders were already up and busy: bakery, jam makers, cheese merchant, everyone had their shelter or waggon, their signage, their tables and chairs even. The activity thinned out the further they walked. Finally, as Mr Bolton strode off to harass another stallholder, Charlie looked around. It was very quiet at Smithy Row. There were cars parked the length of Red Hat Lane and she watched as the people currently parking there locked up and then headed straight back up Red Hat Lane to join the main drag of town at the corner of Dark Gate Street. No one was even getting lost down Red Hat Lane. She set up their table, and, as she did so, her mind wandered once again, flashing images of that lost map of Hartfield, spilling itself into the paving stones beside Castle Inn. It was distracting. Charlie began to feel a little bouncing ball of panic start to thump inside her.

The Castle Inn pop-up was positioned on the main street and they had a range of foldaway tables and umbrellas that Casey and Ailith were putting out. As Charlie approached she could see Anna, already busy with the hog roast sited to the side, her hands stuffing herbs and sliced apples under the skin of the pig as the heat of the charcoal beneath flushed her face. Already the roasting pork smelt savoury and delicious.

"You started early," Charlie commented. Anna didn't turn, she was adjusting the spit.

"Casey started cooking last night," Anna turned, wiping her hands on a cloth. "She's done a wonderful job." Anna smiled. "What do you want?"

"Emergency rescue," Charlie confessed. "My gazebo's bust. I wondered if you'd got any spare umbrellas?"

Anna was already nodding and moving towards her stash of equipment. "Ailith can help you with them... Ailith?"

Charlie found Ailith useful and practical as they abandoned all hope of sorting out the gazebo and instead arranged a delightful sheltered spot with the borrowed umbrellas. It proved a two-woman job to set up the trestle tables, Charlie feeling like a fumbling buffoon.

"This is such a load of bollocks," she half said to herself. "What is wrong with everything today?" She held up a spare bolt. Should there be a spare? Charlie hunkered down to try to find the spot where the fixing bolt should go and saw it at once. She slotted the metal into place, almost pinching her fingers before the trestle table gave a slight easing creak. As she stood up Ailith was looking at her.

"You alright?" Charlie asked. She wasn't sure what the expression was on Ailith's face and didn't trust her own judgement today since everything felt so out of kilter.

"Yes." Ailith looked charged up, her face bright. "Lots of people. Their energy." She smiled. "It is good to be busy."

"Yes. It's Apple Day. It's always like this. Brace yourself." Charlie joked as her phone buzzed into life and Ailith was called back to the Castle Inn marquee.

The phone died as soon as Charlie heard Michael's voice, but she had enough instinct to know that it was probably time to get back into the car and head up to Drawbridge once again and solve whatever new problem had popped into the vacuum left by the last one.

The suspension on her car would not take the weight of more than two kegs at a time. She was going to have to run a short relay back and forth while Michael took the van for a new spare. The current spare wheel, once it had bounced free of the clip, proved to have a nail in it.

By nine o'clock Charlie had improvised a new set up for the Drawbridge pop-up, asking Michael to bring the bunting. Despite the early hour she poured a couple of samples into the shot glasses and tried not to look as if she was waiting for the first of the Apple Dayers. She could see most of them, walking by in the distance at the far end of Laundry Lane.

"Why did you move us?" Michael asked as he pulled up in Smithy Row. "No bugger is going to wander down here." He looked up and down the two lanes.

"We were reassigned by Mr Bolton," Charlie told him. "So don't blame me."

There was activity in the distance towards the main streets. "I just don't understand why we're here..." He looked miserable and Charlie did not have any patience with him.

"Look. You man the fort. I'm going to hand out some freebies and tell people we're in a lovely shady spot down Smithy Row. I'll get them down here if I have to kidnap them." She poured a tray of shots and headed off up Laundry Lane.

The weather was being exceptionally kind; the warm autumnal sunshine burnished Woodcastle town centre with a lush golden early morning light. The air was sweetened with the scent of apples. The Two Hills Farm orchard had pyramids of apples arranged around a central table where the venerated senior owner of Two Hills Orchards, Mr Welbeck, was waiting ready to identify anyone's apples from their garden tree. The signs around him declared 'Huxton's Pippet', 'Woodcastle Russet', 'Knightstone Blusher': the three heritage varieties only grown in their orchard.

Other stalls offered apple sauce on pancakes, apple speckled muffins redolent with cinnamon and sultanas. There were dried apple pomanders and potpourri. Apple conserved, preserved, brewed, decocted, pickled, dried.

Actually, if Charlie was being honest, the general sweetness of the scent was starting to make her feel a bit sick. There was something underlying it all, a sourness, as if the only apples that had been picked were the windfalls and the wormy.

The feeling grew worse and worse, the tray of Blackberry Ferment shots grew heavier and heavier. No one was interested. She paused for a moment, rested the leaden tray on a garden wall. She took in a deep breath; the thick apple scent rushed her but it was cut with the aroma of Blackberry Ferment. If she was being honest, there was nothing she wanted more now than a shot of that Ferment. It must be the sunshine. With a shaking hand she reached for the nearest shot glass. Oh. The cooling sensation in her mouth, a crisp green of leaves, a prickling of thorns, and the bright blackberry itself. It carried quite an alcoholic kick. Charlie felt better, but still the Ferment tickled at her nose. She swigged a second shot and the effect was even more pleasurable. It tasted of summer and of sunlight and earth and... oh. She stood for a few minutes recovering her composure. She had been feeling stressed lately. Oh, what the hell. She took a third shot and then, since no one was interested at all in her boozy wares, she gave up and headed back for the shade of the borrowed umbrellas at Smithy Row.

BY LUNCHTIME ANNA was thoroughly smoked, her face flushed red with the heat from the hog roast. It had been a task to cook the beast, Casey and Anna working in shifts, but it had been worth it: the Castle Inn pop-up was proving a great success. At the moment she could hear loud voices from within the marquee itself, voices raised in conversation, and a lot of laughing. She basted the meat a few more times, enjoying the scent of it and feeling that she was, in fact, rather hungry, before she rolled the lid back down on the roaster and looked about her.

The street was crowded, and Anna could see other people jostling down the side streets which sometimes, especially if the weather was bad, were sidestepped. In past years there had been bad feeling about the jockeying for position and the best pitches but that seemed to have evaporated this year. There was music from Dark Gate Street. The shadow of last year started to stretch itself across the day. *She'd wheeled Ethan up Laundry Lane and it had been really bitingly cold...*

"Another pork cob roll," a rude voice spoke behind Anna. She turned from her unwanted thoughts and plugged in a smile.

"Yes, and would you like apple sauce or stuffing?" Anna was slicing the tender morsels of meat, the flesh stripping off the carcass now with a juicy unctuousness that, Anna thought, even the most diehard veggie would be hard pressed to resist. Oh my God, was the woman licking her lips?

She was; her tongue, small and pink and reminding Anna of a cat, was licking her top lip with speedy and rather odd little movements.

"Both. And mustard." She gestured to the pot of English mustard and then looked greedily at the chutney. "Is this apple chutney?" the woman asked, as she leaned forward to sniff at the opened pot.

"It is. Apple and caramelised onion and... this one..." Anna was about to give her the full tour when the woman simply lifted the spoon from the apple chutney into her open mouth. Anna had no idea what to do and stood, mesmerised, as the woman wolfed in another few mouthfuls, the chutney beginning to spill out of her mouth and down her chin. The woman made a beckoning gesture, her greedy eyes on the pork cob.

"Gimme."

Anna handed it over, the woman shoving a sticky fiver into her hand in return.

"Thank you," Anna called after her, trying to banish the urge to throw down her cooking utensils and head to the castle. Ugh. This Apple Day was horrible; it was her mood, the shadow hovering beside her mind, and she was struggling to stay a step ahead of it.

WHEN IT WAS time for her break Anna sat in a rather wobbly deck chair at the back of the marquee with a pork filled cob. In spite of the mood of the day she was hungry and already the rich aroma of pork and apple was making her stomach gurgle. The intense Hog Roasting duty rota had meant she'd skipped breakfast this morning, which Anna always felt was a bad idea. As she took a bite she could see through the tent flap to where the people were crowding, and the three Saturday girls were waiting at tables. From this angle Anna could watch Casey making a better job than she did of slicing and pulling the hog roast and, it was clear, dealing with the rather boisterous customers. Again, the conversation inside the marquee was ramped up and noisy. It clanged a little inside her head. She took another succulent mouthful of the pork cob.

Nearby was a pitcher of apple juice, some slices of apple bobbing on the surface. Thirsty, Anna reached for a plastic glass and poured herself some.

She was obviously very thirsty indeed, the juice delicious, with its bronzy hue and heady scent of tree and blossom and honey, and what else was in there? She glugged down the glassful. Oh. No. She was drinking from the jug, how had that happened? Who cared? It was lush. The idea of a summer's day lingered on her tongue, shone bronze light right through her. She reached for the pitcher again, but it tumbled from the worktable, the apples that had been sliced into it browning quickly on the cobbled floor.

"Rats…" Anna put down her lunch and attempted to pick up the pieces of apple. She wasn't going to eat them, just a little lick. Ailith pushed her aside.

"Don't…" She reached for the pieces with a pair of barbecue tongs and flung the scraps into the bin bag she was filling with paper plates and abandoned plastic glasses. "It's turned."

"It's not bad… just brown, it's been in the juice. I wasn't going to eat it." Anna could hear a small and peevish voice utterly unlike her own. "What do you think I am? An animal? Grazing crappy apple scraps off the floor?" Ailith looked at her, her face thinned with emotions that Anna was struggling to read. Ailith reached for the slightly chewed pork cob roll with the barbecue tongs and put it into the bin bag.

"I hadn't finished that…" Anna reared up, felt her teeth baring in anger and Ailith, her face not blinking, stepped back.

"Might well step back you little stray." Oh. No. God. It was like a horrible belch of nastiness from within her. She put her hand over her mouth and looked at Ailith. Ailith looked very still and serious.

Anna wanted to apologise: the words queued up in her head, but she understood that if she tried to say them they would be corrupted into insults and meanness. Ailith was still watching her. Their eyes met and exchanged a long and anxious glance before

Ailith moved on her way picking up bits of apple, of pie, of cake, of toffee apple shards and throwing them into the bin bag. Anna sat down. The light was brighter still, headachy yellow.

"You sure you're alright?" Casey asked. "Only you look a bit flushed…" She looked, as always, concerned. Anna could see the words she wanted to say in her head, but they were overwritten.

"*Stop fussing you annoying bitch*," were the words cued up in her mouth. Anna pressed her lips tight closed and nodded to Casey.

"You sure?"

Another nod, it was as much as Anna could manage. The delicious aftertaste of the pork and the apple juice had soured leaving a dry tinny tang in her mouth. Inside her head her interior monologue was watching itself make spiteful "*blah-di-blah-di-bitch*" sounds at Casey. Anna had to keep them in. The apple juice must have been cider, must have had alcohol in it. Anna reacted badly to alcohol, it made her morose. She nodded vehemently and shooed Casey away from the roaster.

The heat from the coals began to make her feel irritable, she couldn't get away from this. The fat spat at her and several people began to hassle her for pork cobs. Their voices were demanding, short tempered.

"For Christ's sake how long does it take to pull some bloody pork?" one man bellowed as others jostled up behind him. Several lewd comments regarding the pulling of pork ensued. Spit. Laughter. Teeth. Ugh. Anna was repulsed.

"Hoi Pushy! Get back. I'm next, waiting here, like a lemon." A woman grabbed for the shoulder of a small old lady who was elbowing into the queue. Anna wanted to wade in, to tell the woman not to be rude, to offer some comfort to the old lady but she found she couldn't. A long list of short sharp swearwords were cued in her mouth. They were pushing hard to come out and she pinched her lips together. The day had lost its sunshine, there seemed to be clouds lowering overhead, and the air was heavy with the promise of rain. She watched as the man shouted at her some more, the sound rasping against her mind, and then the old lady helped herself to a bun and some pork and Anna was pushed aside and the rest of the queue began to do the same. Scrabbling. Greedy. *Pigs at a trough*. Anna stepped back, and back, and back. She sank to her haunches by the edge of the marquee and watched the customers take what they liked. She was too hot and too tired and enough was enough.

It was half an hour or so later when the uproar began in the Castle Inn marquee. There was a loud male voice yelling objection and then other male voices joined in and then there was the smashing of glass and the rumble of foldaway tables being toppled. Anna, still sitting beside the now emptied pork roaster could hear the uproar and she felt afraid. Her eyes were blurry with tears as she tried to lift herself onto her feet.

Inside the marquee she thought Lella might be trying to take charge but in fact Lella was the ringleader. She was yelling at Ailith who was standing, defiant, with a bin bag filled with the remains of the roasted hog and her tongs.

Anna couldn't translate all the words, there was just the rawness of the sounds as it hammered against the smooth surface of Ailith.

"What have you done?" Anna grabbed at Ailith's shirt front. Ailith didn't soften or give, her face was set hard.

"What must be done. It's bad and it has you. All of you. The meat has turned." As she responded there was a man snaffling at the bin bag trying to retrieve some of the lost pork. Ailith snatched the bag tighter to her and as he swung for Ailith his fist connected with Anna. She saw Ailith reaching out for her. Anna's bones creaked, her cheek slid against her teeth, the skin inside leeching blood; her skull echoed with the sound of the thump it made.

The world in the marquee was a broken mirror of arms and legs, of roaring faces and bared teeth. Ailith vanished into the storm of it, her face pushed back into the crowd. Here and there random shoes cluttered the floor and flew through the air as smaller fights broke out. Anna felt the sourness of the apple sauce, the apple juice, the greasiness of the meat in her mouth and throat, and she felt the salty grief of her tears because she just couldn't do this anymore. The man had done her a favour, he had punched some sense into her.

All in a moment she knew where she had to go and what she must do, something she should have done a year ago.

22

TWITCHER

E mz had spent most of Apple Day trying to appear studious
in the sixth form centre. She had managed to book in her
Parents' Consultation Evening appointments and now she was
looking for a moment in which to escape to Prickles. The
windows were open on account of the glorious autumn sunshine
and, above the garage grind of music playing from the common
room, Emz Way could hear a woodpecker. The sound, a tiny frag-
ment in the vast technological soundscape of the secondary
school, was calling her out. There was the general white noise of
electricity, the subsonic and ultrasonic frequencies of everything
from Wi-Fi to the communications of the elephants who were
resident at Castlebury Zoo. Emz, her mind filled with leaves and a
small dark pond of cool dark water, wondered what those
elephants might be saying to each other. She had read that
elephants could communicate over vast distances, obvious really,
since Africa and Asia were vast continents. Now she was struggling to think where the nearest elephants might be and what
conversation might be taking place. Also, where was that small
dark pond of cool dark water? That looked familiar, but she was
struggling to place it, it was teasing at her, tugging at her memory.

It dodged in and out from behind the herd of elephants. Two. Two probably wasn't a herd. Were they lonely? Elephants were gregarious, weren't they?

Her train of thought was derailed by the arrival of Mark Catton with his new entourage of Wes and Harry. Before Emz could look away Caitlin and Logan appeared, Caitlin draped around him like a snake. Before she could look down into her book and hide she saw Logan's eyes lock onto her for a brief second and the aftermath was a prolonged kiss for Caitlin. *Showing off*. Emz's inner voice sneered even as her heart creaked.

She flicked through to the middle of 'Wildwood' so that she looked busy and kept the little group in the very corner of her eye. She had her earphones in although her iPod had run out of battery half an hour ago.

There was a soured sharp scent of dry cider and apples in the air. Emz wrinkled her nose a little. Cider was not her favourite drink, too sweet or too sour and usually too fizzy. A slop of apple sauce flicked past her, a spot landing on her book, most of it landing on the floor beside her. She looked up. Mark Catton and his friends were involved in a food fight; they had clearly stopped off at Apple Day on their way back from town at lunchtime. Piecrust and frazzles of sponge cake pitted with apple were littering the room and being picked out of hair. The cider, in long thin brown bottles, was being passed around, the glass chinking into a discordant music. As it passed to Logan Boyle he shook his head, his fingers toying with the bottle in his hand, untouched. He watched Caitlin for a minute or two as she threw back her hair and launched into a snaking dance with Wes and Harry. It was then that he looked over at Emz. Out of the corner of her eye she watched him, watching her. Emz felt paralysed, an urge to run coupled with an urge to turn her head, to match his gaze. What was this? What was going on with him?

When Caitlin kicked Wes and Harry onto all fours and began riding them around yelling *"Faster my Man Beasts!"* Emz thought it might be time to leave. She headed down the staircase where Ellie was puking over the bannisters, the waterfall of thick rich apple-dappled vomit landing with a splat on the floor below.

WINN WAS NOT in a good mood. She hated Apple Day. Winn preferred cauliflower cheese.

"Apple Day? How delightfully rural, and where does Apple Day take place?" Her tenant seemed inclined to small talk. Winn was not, balanced as she was up a ladder fixing a swan neck fitting which had worked loose on the guttering above the kitchen window. It was annoying the tenant and so the tenant, Mrs Forster or Foote or whatever the hell her stupid name was, was annoying Winn by insisting on an immediate repair. The phrasing she had used on the telephone was 'detrimental to the fabric of your building' and Winn had, for a moment, heard her father's voice on the telephone line, not that he had ever believed in tele-phones. He thought they were a contraption that people would soon tire of. Plus, he could shout very loudly and therefore didn't need one.

"Hmm?" Mrs Whojit Fielding looked up the ladder. Winn had half-forgotten the gist of their conversation and her attention was focused on the new hole she'd had to drill with the masonry bit. She rummaged in her waxed jacket pocket for her screwdriver. Twist and twist and yep, that was tightening, that would hold. The wall might tumble down but the swan neck downpipe would remain secured to it.

"Is it going to be held here? Like the wedding?"

Winn clambered down the ladder.

"Is what going to be held here?"

There was just a glimmer of anger about Mrs Fiddle Faddle. Winn was adept at recognising such glimmers, a skill learnt from her father. His temper had been like an open gas tap and Winn's very existence a lighted match.

"Apple Day." Mrs Eff Whatsit, Winn thought, was not being so charming now, pinching those red lips together. Yuk. That red lipstick was a bit gory really, like a hound that had just rent apart a fox.

"Where is this Apple Day and why aren't you there?" Mrs Faffy Fyfe was looking a little less... Ah. That was it, her name was Fyfe. Mrs Fyfe, ha, she was looking a little less patronising and a lot more peeved.

"I prefer cauliflower cheese," Winn shrugged.

"What?" The red licky lips pursed and behind the black framed glasses Mrs Fyfe's small black eyes widened.

"I don't like apples. I don't go to Apple Day. It's not compulsory. It's just in town. If you like cider and apple pie and people telling you about the folklore of pips then knock yourself out, otherwise I wouldn't bother. Although there is sometimes some nice cheese, obviously, to go with the apples." Winn raised her eyes to the sky. Mrs Fyfe stared very hard. Her eyes, through the thick lenses of the black glasses, looked like glass balls and were unblinking.

"You'd rather have a Cauliflower Cheese Day?" she asked, the too-red-by-far lips thinned.

"No," Winn shook her head. "I don't tend to bother with 'events' and such. I don't go in much for enforced jollity."

Winn didn't think Mrs Fyfe looked like a woman for any kind of jollity whatsoever. Mrs Fyfe was lost in thought for a moment or two, her eyes staring at Winn in a manner which reminded Winn of her Labrador, Napoleon, when he wanted her to give him a share of her sausage.

"After all your exertions the least I can do is make you a cup of tea." Mrs Fyfe's rare-steak-red smile curled up into her face. It was alarming actually, and Winn found herself stepping back.

"Oh... er... no that..." Winn wanted to get away, plus it was highly likely that some bit of equipment might go wrong in the kitchen and she'd be forced to dig the socket set out of the back of the Land Rover or have to remember where she'd put that length of copper piping.

"Of course… of course… you must come in." Mrs Fyfe made an ushering movement towards the kitchen door. Winn hesitated. A cup of tea was always a good idea. But it was a better idea if it was brewed at Prickles and enjoyed with no company. Or Emz Way's company. Those, Winn realised, were her social limits.

"Actually no… I think I…"

Mrs Fyfe's face grew shadowed: the effect was of little storm clouds racing across the lenses of her glasses. Winn drew back once again.

"I've already made the tea. You are being rude." Mrs Fyfe spoke in a hard, little voice and Winn recognised it, it was the kind of voice her father had often used to make you do something you didn't want to do. Like castrate a pig for instance.

The tea, Winn thought, was horrid sharp fruit stuff, not proper tea at all and so she only sipped a little of it. It was an insipid golden colour like cat's piss tasting of sour apples and served without any milk and what was far worse, without any cake or biscuit.

"Would you care for some cake?" Mrs Fyfe turned from the countertop with an elaborate vintage cake plate. It was gilt edged, and Winn thought she recognised it from the Spode cabinet in the Top Hall.

Winn did not mind apples if they were disguised as cake, so she ate three pieces.

EMZ WAS SURPRISED to find that Prickles was deserted. The reception area was open but empty and there was no sign of Winn or the Land Rover. A hasty note had been scribbled on the desk in chalk: 'GONE TO HARTFIELD. REPAIR.'

They were not due any school trips this afternoon and since Apple Day was in full swing it was unlikely anyone would drop by. Emz, relishing the unexpected solitude, changed into her hiking gear and, armed with her binoculars, headed down to Cooper's Pond.

She had not walked a hundred yards when the sensation of prickling began at her neck. She was not giving it her full attention, her eye drawn in fact to a set of distinct deer tracks which she followed. At first, she scratched at it, thinking it was an insect biting but once she was in the thick of the trees of Leap Woods the leaves began to rattle a little in a cold sharp breeze and Emz halted. This was the Trespasser feeling.

She wove her way through the trees to come out at the rear of the hide at Cooper's Pond. As she stepped out onto the path a fox crawled out from beneath the hide. Emz saw the umbrous red of its coat and her uneasiness shifted. It was a wonderful autumn afternoon; the chill of winter was hinted at in the bright gold of the light.

The fox stood sniffing for a moment or so and then turned to look at her. Emz stood very still and with almost a shrug, the fox trotted off into the trees. He kept up an easy pace so that Emz did not have to run or chase him, in and out of the trees he wove on his particular path. She only half realised when they had strayed into the edges of Havoc Wood because the territory was so familiar. She was lost in no thoughts, just the burnished red of the fox's pelt like a beacon lighting ahead of her, the black edging to his fur, the stark white of his underbelly, she was focusing on matching her steps to the rhythm of his. Sky. Earth. Bark. Leaf.

She took a step forward. It was like grabbing an electric fence, the zap went straight through her making her fingers ache. She stepped back, looked at the ground as if she might have stepped on some gadget or gizmo that some idiot had dropped. The zap became a low-level buzz as if, in the near distance, she could hear someone using a power tool, an insistent electrical whine.

She looked out across the trees to where a few rooftops of town could be seen. Maybe there was a power surge or an outage or something. She could hear noises, offkey and jolting. Was that smoke? It was a thin snake of black and now it was thickening. Something was on fire in town. Emz turned and ran.

Back at reception Winn had returned and was loading the shotgun.

"What's happening?" Emz asked. Winn looked up at her.

"It's all kicked off in town. Some loon set fire to the Castle Inn marquee... there's been a bit of a punch up and Mrs Bentley's been forced to shut up the castle." Winn's hands were not shaking but the fingers were white with clinging to the barrel of the gun.

"What are you doing?" Emz felt shaken. Winn broke the gun over her arm.

"Well, after all this Apple Day malarkey I thought we'd shut the gates. Just as a precaution."

They wandered down the lane. Loud music could be heard drifting up from town; it might have been a festival except for the thick black smoke. The gates had not been closed in forever and so it took a moment for Emz and Winn to scrabble the weeds from its path. There was a sharp scent to the air from the smoke in town.

"Right. Done. You need to get yourself home, Emz." Winn waved her back towards the kitchen. "Don't go via town. There's traffic mayhem according to Barbara. Go through the wood." Winn set off along the thin track to her bungalow.

"I'll see you tomorrow," she called out with a weary wave.

23

DOWNHILL FAST

To Charlie, Apple Day was Apple Disaster Day. When Michael at last arrived with the final keg and they were set up not one person walked by their pop-up. Not. One. The only creatures they saw all morning were a succession of cats from the mad cat woman's house on Cordwainer Street.

Now she could see Michael coming back down Laundry Lane scrunching a napkin and wiping his mouth. He waved at her.

"Long lunch?" Charlie asked. She was feeling hot and out of sorts because today she'd had to sit under a stupid umbrella in some godforsaken corner of Woodcastle instead of brewing beer.

"I am the boss," Michael responded, his voice slightly harsh. "I own Drawbridge Brewery." He tipped his head in a childish manner and leaned in too close. "You, Charlie Way, are just my humble employeeeeeeeeee."

Despite the fact that they worked in the brewing industry Charlie had never seen Michael Chance drunk. Not once. She stared at him.

"You've been doing some market research then? Checking out the competition?" she asked, keeping the anger out of her voice. She was very hot and her eyes felt tired. Michael looked at her; his eyes looked odd, had an unpleasant tinny shine to them. She was worried. "Michael, what have you been drinking?"

"Tea," he said licking his fingers.

"Tea. Not cider or beer or wine?"

"Tea. Lovely apple tea."

Charlie struggled to register this.

"You hate herbal teas."

"Ha. This was different… this was a delicious Tisane," he over pronounced the silly word.

"So, you didn't check out what the alcoholic Apple Day competition is?" she asked, with a quick glance towards the far end of Laundry Lane where there seemed to be some sort of commotion beginning: voices were being raised.

"Nope," he wiped his sticky fingers on his jeans and looked at her. "It's the usual cider and apple cake and same boring old Apple Day apple shit."

Charlie didn't speak for a few seconds. She watched her boss mooch about their stall, flinging a few plastic glasses back into a cardboard box.

"We should just fucking bin this lot, I tell you, what a fucking washout."

She had never heard Michael swear before and it surprised her how the words were like little razor blades. She watched him opening and closing his mouth, sticking his tongue out like a cat about to cough up a furball.

"Yuk. That cake… bleugh… there's a reason they give this bollocks away fucking free."

"Okay. Stop talking now. Sit down," she pushed him into the deck chair and turned away from him. She wanted him to stop talking because the more he said the more edgy and raw she felt. As he sat, burping to himself, she began to pack up. With the glasses stacked in their cardboard box she moved to the trolley to roll the first keg towards the van.

"What are you doing?" Michael asked, watching from the chair.

"Loading up. We can't leave the kegs here…" As she rolled the keg Michael got up and headed to the back of the van. She thought he was going to help her lift them inside; instead he reached for the tyre iron. With a strong lashing movement, he broke the taps off the kegs and the beer made a small fast flowing river down into the nearest drain. When the first was empty Michael rolled it a little to get the dregs out and then threw it, with ease, into the back of the van.

"What did you do that for?" she asked. He shrugged.

"Fucking felt like it. I'm the boss. Remember?"

Charlie finished loading the van. It was clear that Michael could not drive; he was, probably, possibly, drunk. He seemed drunk, if only in a quiet and rather hostile manner. Charlie got into the driving seat.

"Fuck that. Get out." Michael stood at the door gesturing for her to leave the driving seat.

"Will you stop swearing please and get in." Charlie's voice was very quiet. She was struggling with several emotions, but she understood that chief amongst them was fear, intense and scorching. She started the engine, it roared inside her. What was wrong? The air seemed metallic. At once Charlie understood she was thinking too much and she stopped, took a deep breath.

As she did so the windscreen shattered outwards like a silver constellation. Charlie let out a scream, her arms raising. She could not work out this terrible feeling of dread. She looked out at Michael, looking at the tyre iron in his hand as if he had just woken from a trance before sitting down on the kerb's edge, his head lolling forward like a rag doll.

The air was charged, like standing under a pylon. Charlie got out of the van. Michael was snivelling a little now, his nose running.

"Oh… I can't do this… I can't…"

Charlie heaved at Michael's limp body, flung his arm around her shoulder.

"Yes, you can. One, two..." Charlie tugged at him, he was heavy as a sandbag and crying.

"It's all passed me by. Love. Life. All too late."

Charlie felt a jolt of fear and fury combine. She kicked Michael. He yowled like a child and folded over.

"Get up," she pulled at him. "Get. Up."

Michael wiped his snotty nose and stood up, his head bowed, meek.

"Get in the van," Charlie shepherded him to the van and as he lolled back in the seat sobbing a little, she fastened his seatbelt.

Charlie gunned the van's engine, punched out the windscreen and drove off.

At the end of Laundry Lane Charlie saw her mistake. Where there had been an access route for Apple Day Traders there was now a fire engine. Smoke billowed away towards Ridge Hill and the nearby stalls were partially burnt with stall holders clearing up the blackened bits. A woman with black marks swiped onto her face was coming towards them waving a half-singed flag from Woodcastle Castle and singing in an operatic voice.

"Is that from Les Mis?" Charlie asked Michael. Other people massed behind her, stacking the broken and battered stalls into a barricade and singing along.

More music clashed against them, a tinny beat. On a flatbed truck several men were fighting over the wiring for a set of vast black speakers. There was a rush of bodies and sound, a sudden hail of brown and rotting apples rained down through the smashed windscreen, landing hard on Michael and making him cry more. Charlie attempted to reverse the van, the gears protesting but finally grinding into place, the van squealing backwards.

It took half an hour to drive the long way around by Old Castle Road and back to Drawbridge via the Woodhill side of town. By the time they pulled in at the car park Michael was calmer, his eyes red, but he was capable of being helped out of the van.

"Where are your keys?" Charlie asked. Michael's hands wandered in and out of his jeans pockets and he shrugged. There was a gnome by the door to Michael's small cottage and Charlie looked under it. As she did so Michael seemed to fail, his body sagging against hers, his face, snotty and tearstained, nuzzling into her neck. He inhaled the scent of her very deeply.

"Oh, Charlie is my darling…" he sing-songed into her ear, his lips brushing at her skin, his hands at her waist as if he might dance her away somewhere. There was no escaping his hands, sliding round her waist now, pulling her closer. "Charlie is my… darling," he whispered as he leaned in to kiss her. The charge ran through her hips, snatched her breath as his mouth moved soft and tender and meant, on hers. Then Charlie breathed in: the metallic feel of the air was in Michael's kiss, like a taint. She pushed him away, wiped at her mouth and, with a burst of energy, twisted round, lifting him, in a martial arts style move, across her shoulders. He gave a weary groan but did not fight her. Stumbling like this, she half dragged Michael through the door and tipped him onto the sofa where he began to snore.

There was only one place she needed to be right now but her car was still parked at Laundry Lane. She looked down towards town; the noise had risen and the flames from the fire could be seen, the smoke thick and black and choking. Charlie shrugged deeper into her jacket and cutting across the road began to walk across the darkening field to the edge of Havoc Wood.

24

THE BEST LAID PLANS

I t had been a long walk back to Cob Cottage, but Charlie did not care. Each footstep had lent a rhythm to her thoughts, clearing her head. Leaving the cover of trees at the far end of the lake, Charlie saw one of their boats slithering back and forth against the shore with the lap of the water. She climbed in and rowed herself quickly across the lake's surface to Cob Cottage, tying up on the jetty.

The situation was eating at Charlie and as Emz opened the door and stepped onto the porch she spoke up.

"Where's Ailith?" Charlie felt suspicion rise through her like bile. Emz shrugged and shook her head.

"I don't know. She would have been down in town with Anna. She was helping out at the pop-up remember?"

Charlie remembered, and the two facts seemed to weld themselves together into a nut and bolt of certainty.

"Helping out isn't what I would call this," Charlie had decided. Nothing had been quite right since the door to Cob Cottage had blown open and allowed in Ailith and the severed head.

"You feel it too?" Emz asked, the prickling electrical sensation she had picked up in Leap Woods starting to make her neck tense and give her a headache, a dull singing pain starting just over her left eye.

"Feel it? Town is mayhem. They're all bladdered or something."

Emz looked at her hands, flexed her fingers stiffly.

"What?" Charlie watched her sister as she reached up to her neck and massaged at the tensed muscles, rolled her head around.

"I've had this feeling... like electricity, really horrible. Painful almost." Charlie noticed how pale Emz looked. She knew that if she looked in the mirror she'd look exactly the same.

"There's a tinny feel to the air," Charlie said.

"Is it like the sound you heard at the castle?" Emz asked. "Can you hear that?"

Charlie shook her head.

"No. But something is up." The words squatted in her head and Emz picked them out.

"It's magic."

Charlie tensed at the word.

"You can't not say it, Charlie. Something is going on. Something bad."

"Power then." Charlie wrestled with herself. "Strength." She was beginning to understand why their Grandmother had always named it Strength.

"Something's gone wrong. We've done something wrong," Emz said.

"Or Someone is wrong. It's got to be Ailith." Charlie was decisive.

"Got to be? But she hasn't done anything. Why has it got to be?" Emz reasoned. Charlie was positive in her pessimism.

"Because she came OUT of Havoc Wood. We should have taken better care."

"It's something we've not done right... or even not done at all? For Ailith, for the warrior?" Emz suggested. "Something that we missed—"

"Or maybe we did exactly what she needed." Charlie felt better sharing the theory. "Maybe we weaponised that head."

She watched the idea of it sink through Emz like a stone.

"No. It... Oh." Emz began but her thoughts jammed. She looked up at Charlie, stricken. "Because we don't know what we're doing."

"So, neither of them are here then?" Charlie cast a cursory glance through the window. Emz shook her head.

"I've been waiting here an hour, maybe longer. No sign."

"We need to find them both."

Charlie felt the panic subside as a plan pushed forward. Do something, yes, make a move.

"Where will we find them?" Emz asked. It was a sensible but annoying question and as Charlie looked across Pike Lake towards town where there was a thin tower of flame burning beneath a smoked black sky, she dreaded the answer.

2 5

DOUBLE TWISTING PIKE

Seren Lake's head was filled with seams and darts and she was, she realised, humming a tune to herself, something she'd heard on the radio this morning. The late afternoon was autumnal and golden, and she was a little afraid of how happy she felt.

She'd spent the day at Kingham Gardens with a small theatre company who wanted to commission some costumes for their upcoming Christmas Shakespeare season. It was exciting. So exciting that for part of her day Seren had struggled to breathe or to stop smiling, or indeed to stop drawing her ideas for the company. Possibly she was still asleep in bed and just dreaming.

The Knightstone Bridge hove into view. The newly renovated towers poked up through the trees, guiding her onwards. There were gilded weathervanes glinting in the afternoon sunlight which, Seren thought, gave no hint of the sad history of last Halloween.

The sweep of the suspension cables made a graceful cobweb across the wide expanse of river. Everything had to paddle hard along that river, cormorants glided across the surface, not daring to land in the fast-flowing current. Seren was brought sharply out of her daydreams as the cars ahead pipped wildly, a woman darting across the roadway, almost being hit.

The traffic flowed onwards, and no one noticed the woman lift herself up onto the handrail.

Seren gaped. What? Where was she going? What was she doing? Wait. Wait. Seren knew her. Oh my God.

She pulled the car up onto the kerb and began to hurry towards Anna Way. What was she doing? Taking her shoes off. *Oh my god. Oh my god.* Seren's heart pounded with her feet as she watched Anna begin to scramble with some agility onto the handrail.

"HEY!" Seren shouted, the word cannoning from her mouth. "HEY!" She was closing the distance, there had to be time.

"Anna." Seren, breathless and afraid, looked up. The wind blew at Anna's hair and she leaned into the brief gust, her hand still gripping the cable support so that she looked like a figurehead, sailing the bridge.

"ANNA." Seren made her voice boom. Anna glanced sideways at her. Her eyes, Seren noticed, had a bleak tinny sheen to them. Seren's heart was a stone inside her. She reached for Anna's ankle, managed a high, sharp laugh. "Hey there." Words would not come to her mind, just the sense of the empty air and the rushing river waiting beneath. Seren reached up a hand.

"Take my hand." Anna did not respond. Seren stepped up onto the base of the railing, straining to reach Anna. "Take my hand, Anna."

"Down." Anna said and looked down into the water. Seren flinched grasping for words. "Anna. Anna." If she could say it often enough she could hold her there. Anna's ankle felt cold. Seren gripped it tighter, strained further upwards, her fingers snatching at the hem of Anna's top.

"Take my hand. Take it." Seren felt Anna's body weight shift. If she jumped there was nothing Seren could do other than follow her. She let go of her ankle, panic washing over her as she began to lift herself up higher onto the rail. Her left hand's knuckles were white, gripping the wire beside her, and she reached with her right hand and gripped Anna's waistband. It might not be scientific, but it felt strong. Yes. A plan formed for Seren. Crazy plan.

Anna leaned forwards into the wind and Seren felt her muscles strain in holding her.

"Where are you going?" Seren asked the mad question, the dangerous option, the catalyst.

"Down." Anna's voice tumbled down like a stone, her gaze falling with it and Seren took her cue.

"Yes." Seren said and with a sudden lunge pushed Anna backwards onto the deck of the bridge.

They landed heavily, and Anna was limp and lifeless. Seren checked her pulse. It was there, a slow drumbeat, and as Seren tried to shift her body Anna gave a sorrowful moan. No one had stopped. The few cars rolling towards Woodcastle seemed not to care. Seren looked back at her car. She could do this. With all her strength she pushed herself under Anna's arm and with an inelegant but effective clean and jerk move she lifted her to her feet. Their progress was rapid, Seren using the momentum of Anna falling to drag her quickly towards the car. She folded her into the back seat and strapped the seatbelt around her prone body just in case.

There was only one place to take her and Seren knew the way. She was burning with adrenalin as they pulled along Bridge Road into town. With the window open Seren heard the wails of discordant music over a public-address system and remembered it was the Apple Day event.

There was no traffic; instead the road was blocked by barriers and by the crowd that swirled the length of Dark Gate Street. On a flatbed truck drawn across the junction at Barbican Steep men were struggling with speakers, the speakers screeling with feedback with a sound like wild beasts. Around them the town seemed to be arranged into groups like a military tattoo. There were scruffy flags and banners and flaming torches and lots of singing. Apple Day looked like the French Revolution.

Seren turned at the castle towards Long Gate Street trying to get to Old Castle Road by the longer route. The light was fading now. As Seren ground through her gears, pushing the car up the steep hill, an empty bottle dinged off the bonnet. Seren glanced at the group of women running into the path of the car, hurling abuse and more empty bottles: one cracked the windscreen, another clipped the wing mirror. Ahead of them a car burst into flame. There was no way through town, no way she could get Anna to Cob Cottage. Seren turned the wheel, bounced up onto the pavement, aware of the women in the rear view gaining on them; another bottle whirled through the air as she gunned the engine, the little car squealing along its escape route.

26

HELL AND A HANDBASKET

Charlie had never seen Woodcastle in this light; that is, firelight. A dramatic haze of black smoke drifted through town.

It appeared that this year's Apple Day finale was a re-enactment of the English Civil War and the 1815 Woodcastle Sausage Riot. Flickering beacons guarded the barricades and fiery torches were held aloft by various cohorts and battalions of Woodcastle residents. The castle walls were glimmering with the reflected light of the torches of the massed band of Roundheads, their helmets plundered from the castle before Mrs Bentley had time to lockdown. Residents had upcycled the rags and remnants of the disastrous Apple Day fire into motley costumes and banners and were singing and marching their way along Dark Gate Street.

Beyond them, at the traffic lights by the junction with Long Gate Street, was, well, what was that? This crowd had piled up a barricade of Apple Day stalls and were waving vast flags, looking for all the world as if they were defending the castle. A cannon was being rolled down Barbican Steep with some difficulty, the wheels sending it careering in different directions and at lumbering speed.

There was that song again. It was familiar to Charlie from earlier in the day. The voices grew and clashed, each singing off against the other. Loudspeakers mounted on a flatbed truck were ranged around like Stonehenge and with an intense whistle they burst into life. Drums, violins, and brass. The drunken residents' chorus and banners battled it out.

"What the...?" Charlie could only stare at the spectacle. The cannon was being rolled into position.

"*Do You Hear the People Sing?*' Isn't that from *Les Mis?*" Emz asked; Charlie nodded. As they stood at the edge of Old Castle Road looking down Emz could see the shiny apple-cheeked faces.

"I am Jean Valjean!" it was a defiant cry from the butcher, Owen Greene, as he clambered up onto the nearest barricade, the tattered flag cracking behind him.

"He's got a... is it a sword?" Charlie and Emz stared at the weapon he was waving. It was wooden. Beside him several women were banging other wooden swords on small wooden shields bearing the Woodcastle Castle arms.

"It's from the Castle shop." Charlie looked out over the crowd; other swords were being waved. Some, she could see, were metal and being wielded by the opposite faction; clearly Mrs Bentley hadn't managed to lockdown the armoury exhibition fast enough. From this group the local plumber, Rich Hardiman, jumped forward with a roar.

"NO! I am Jean Valjean!" The two tribes were rumbling and roiling behind their leaders, swords waving, the weight of bodies pressing forward with shouts and whistles. The song was rising, throats scratching with the effort of singing louder, louder. Drums rattled from nearby just as PC Williamson leapt up onto the bus shelter.

"I AM SPARTACUS," and with that all hell broke loose. There was a sudden clatter of hooves from behind them, Charlie and Emz stepping aside as the riding school, swords waving above their heads, made a cavalry charge, disappearing with a roar down

High Market Place towards the Moot Hall, and the Spartacus vs Valjean melee surged and seethed like a tide.

"We need to find Anna," Charlie said, and the sisters began to move into the fray.

They dodged peashooters, catapults, the debris of apple cores and bits of doughnut, of shards of crackling that were flying through the air, a pig's head shot from the cannon and all the time, scarier than anything else, the vast wave of choral sound carried on a tide of drums, rattling out of the speakers and into the combatants.

The Ways moved quickly, keeping together. In the tension of the situation Emz's real face instinct kicked in and she was surprised at what was revealed. While people sang their lungs out, mouths wide, throats wobbling, cheeks red with firelight and energy, their real faces seemed asleep. Emz could not work it out and as the crowd moved and seethed around them she was distracted as she tried to keep her feet.

She followed Charlie to the smoking remnants of the Castle Inn marquee. There were twisted and melted poles and struts, charred and ashen textile, chairs and tables were like abstract sculptures of themselves. In a corner several of the residents warmed themselves by the remains of the hog roast, flames licking weakly, splashing hot fat.

Where was Anna?

The Castle Inn itself was dark and locked up and although Charlie hammered on the door there was no reply.

"We could go round the back, to the kitchen door," Emz suggested and the two climbed over the side gate and dodged through into the beer garden.

"Hoi... You're trespassing!" a voice screamed from the depths of the long fish pond. Emz turned to see Lella skinny dipping in the water. She was standing now, the water only coming up to her waist and Emz could see she was shivering, her skin turning blue.

"Charlie," Emz gave a short bark and her sister stopped, clocked Lella.

"Let's get her out of there…" Charlie said, as she and Emz backtracked to the pond. Lella was stock still, her chin juddering with cold.

"Lovely… water… water… lovely…" She reached and with graceful movements draped herself in more cold water.

"Lella, come on, time to get out," Emz reached. Lella remained, her face now framed with blue as it encroached from her neck. Her skin was hard with goose pimples so that she looked almost amphibian.

"Time to swim…" she slid beneath the surface. Charlie was straight into the water after her, her arms under Lella's arms and dragging her onto the side as Emz found her clothing, abandoned by the picnic tables, and wrapped her soft blue waterfall cardigan around her.

Charlie kicked the door in as Emz supported Lella. There was no electricity, so they stumbled and fumbled their way into the lounge. Lella was shivering and as Emz half dragged her to a couch Charlie went into the dining room and pulled the cloths off the table. Glasses shattered, cutlery scattered with a sound like clashing swords.

"Should I get some tinfoil?" Emz suggested. "You know, like runners after a marathon?"

Charlie was smoothing back Lella's weed draggled hair. Lella appeared to be snoring softly.

"No. No, I think she's okay."

Lella did not look too bad, swaddled in tablecloths.

"She looks like a silver service mummy," Charlie commented as she wedged a cushion behind Lella's now definitely snoring head.

"Anna isn't here," Emz said. Charlie shook her head.

"Probably waiting back at home. Probably missed each

other..." Charlie hoped. When they were certain that Lella was warming and asleep they left.

Outside, the Apple Day party was winding down. The fires were mostly out, and people were rolling homewards with a few sharp words and the odd scuffle and a sword-fighting duel. One or two traipsing down from the Moot Hall shouted lairy and incomprehensible slogans, waved their flag with a defiant yawn. Dark Gate Street looked like a war zone, the air stringent with the scent of burnt tyres and melted gazebo. At Long Gate Street the riding school horses, abandoned, snickered and grouped, restless, their hooves churning up the grass banking below the castle wall.

Back at Cob Cottage there was still no Anna. The Way sisters waited in silence, neither taking up a seat, both taking up a sentinel post at the window to Pike Lake. Their thoughts were scurrying.

"You think something bad has happened to them?" Emz asked in a small voice. Charlie had to take a moment to answer.

"I don't know. If we've done something wrong maybe. If Ailith's tricked us into making a weapon out of that head, releasing power. Maybe she's got Anna hostage. Maybe she needs her for something." Charlie's mind was churning. She needed Anna to be here, for Anna to talk sense.

"Or maybe they're out there, together, trying to sort it out." Emz sounded determined.

Charlie considered this, her face was hard and pinched.

"That's a possibility. Yes. Okay. That could be it." She was mentally crossing her fingers. Let it be that. Did their branch of witchcraft run to three wishes? I wish. I wish. I wish.

"Can't you find them?" Emz asked.

"What?" Charlie was sharp.

"Can't you look for them?"

"Oh great. Push it on me." Charlie snapped. Emz flinched at Charlie's flinty look but she continued with her own theory.

"I mean use your Strength, maybe it will show you where they are?

THE JAR of green lentils proved tricky to open, Charlie's fingers fumbling at it. She stepped back from the jar, the table and took a deep breath.

"Are you alright?" Emz asked.

"No," Charlie snarled. "It's too much," Charlie's voice had a crack in it; Emz blenched at the sound of it, "and I don't know what to do." Charlie was crushing down her emotion, her voice thin and tight. Emz folded deeper into silence, her lips pressed together so she wouldn't cry.

"But Charlie, we have to..."

Charlie gave an impassioned grunt as she struggled with the jar.

"What? What do we have to do?" She was tugging at the wire fastening on the lid, her fingers whitening as she tried to pull the loop upwards. She knocked against the table sending Ailith's breakfast cup and plate crashing to the ground.

"NO." Charlie slammed the lentils down on the table, her hands resting on the table top, her head bowed. "For Pete's sake."

"You alright?" Emz's voice was small and uncertain. Charlie shook her head. Then, glancing down at the smashed crockery, she nodded her head.

"Charlie?"

Charlie held up her hand for Emz to be quiet and then took in a deep breath. She could do this. It was, she knew, like riding a very old and rusty bike.

The map was pieced out in bits of china. Where was that path? There was no path? And yet lots of paths? And a border? What the...? She saw at once that it was Cob Cottage, the back garden, the criss-crossed meanderings of the permaculture that was Grandma Hettie's veg patch. She shot to the door, Emz following.

Ailith was in the farthest corner of Grandma Hettie's shed and when Charlie pulled back the tarpaulin she shot across the space like a cornered rat.

"Where's Anna?" Charlie burst out. "Why isn't she here? What have you done with Anna?" Charlie demanded.

"Charlie...?" Emz's voice was small, she was hovering nearer the doorway.

"Stay by the door so she can't get out." Charlie snarled. Ailith was flattening herself against the old cedar lap of the wall as if she could press herself out into the night and flee.

"Ailith... what have you done with our sister?" Charlie demanded, her voice really loud in the confined wooden space.

"Charlie. No." Emz took a step forward, touched Charlie's elbow. Charlie shrugged it off but Emz pushed forwards. "You're wrong, Charlie. Look at her." She dragged Charlie backwards, out of the way. "I mean it." Emz stepped forward.

"Ailith. Come with us. It will be alright." Her voice was very small and soft like a mouse. Ailith flinched again, her fingers scrabbling at the wood, her mouth letting out the most pitiful whimper either Way sister had ever heard. Emz picked her way through the gardening tools and bric-a-brac; there seemed to be a vast collection of small brown earthenware teapots and galvanised watering cans.

"Ailith..." Emz's voice was even smaller, the velvet twitch of a mouse whisker and, at its sound, Charlie felt her anger and her fear wind themselves onto a small bobbin in her head so she could control them. She took a deep breath as Emz reached a hand to Ailith's shoulder; Charlie tensed, anticipating Ailith's flight, but at Emz's touch she seemed to rise up, as if letting go of wings, before she turned, folded away from the shed wall towards Emz who took her hand, held her elbow as she negotiated her way out from behind the wheelbarrow.

Charlie gasped to see her face in the light from Cob Cottage, her face a mass of bruises, her nose bloodied, her thin hair matted with dirt.

Inside the cottage Emz was already running a bath as Charlie cleaned up Ailith's wounds. She said nothing until there was a small pile of grubby cotton wool and she was fixing a small plaster to the cut on Ailith's cheekbone.

"What happened?"

Ailith shook her head.

"The people… they were drunk. The meat was turned. Everything went to the bad."

Charlie looked into Ailith's face.

"This isn't our doing? You didn't trick us?" Charlie sounded more certain than she felt, but she could not hold onto the suspicion. Ailith was firm.

"I did not trick you."

She didn't have Emz's skill at seeing real faces but now, she felt, she was being shown Ailith's true face and it was kind and concerned and frightened and, she understood, loyal.

"I'm convinced it's the head," Charlie said. "What else is there?"

"It could be by accident," Emz offered. "You know, if we haven't rested it properly. Maybe it's set something off, like an alarm?"

Charlie considered and nodded.

"The charged feeling in the air. The resonance." Charlie was thinking aloud. "I wonder if it's linked to the way the castle was sounding out?"

"Yes. This time whatever was working was stronger, more current in the circuit."

"Could be. That day at the castle Ailith had only just arrived. The head was still inside Havoc Wood." Charlie's mind had stopped seething with sound and tinny prickling sensations and confusion. Instead the thoughts began to separate and clarify themselves. "That could be the difference. Anna said it before, it's the difference between what walks into Havoc Wood and what walks out."

Ailith sat in silence.

"No offence Ailith," Charlie looked at her. Emz was chewing her lip.

"Maybe we've switched it on by mistake?" Emz suggested. Ailith looked uncertain but Charlie was willing to take anything.

"I can run with that." Charlie took in a deep breath. It seemed plausible. This incident was proving to be a steep learning curve; nothing was simple. Charlie had a sudden vision of the future where nothing was simple ever again. Guess. Second guess. Still get it wrong.

"We can work out the details later. First. Ailith, when did you last see Anna?" Charlie asked. That was top of their to-do list. "She was still at the hog roast? You were clearing up?" Charlie was chief interrogator, she was reaching into the drawer for a pencil: there was always an old pencil in the top sink drawer.

"Everywhere. Everyone. It was all turned and bad. I tried to stop it, to clear away the bad meat, but there was too much. People were fighting. Then the man punched her."

Charlie stopped scribbling her notes.

"What?" Emz looked wobbly. "Someone punched Anna?"

"In the fighting. The man punched your sister."

The two sisters let this sink in. Neither could look at the other for fear of giving away their own vulnerability.

"Punched her." Charlie and Emz held their breath. Charlie could not speak.

"She fell," Ailith said. "They overpowered me. I could see her, where she got up and walked away. But I could not break free of them in time to catch her." Ailith's head dropped forward, contrite.

Charlie and Emz were at a loss. Anna's workplace was not on their search list today; they'd been to the Castle Inn. Her old home at Keep Rows was now occupied by Seren Lake.

"She could be at Keep Rows," Emz reasoned. "Maybe. Possibly?"

"Mum's maybe," Charlie said and grabbed her keys. Emz looked at her.

"Strength." Emz stated.

Charlie gave a deep sigh and Emz did not back down.

"I'm right, Charlie, we're wasting time trotting over to Keep Rows and Mum's house if Anna isn't there."

"Keep Rows is a good shout," Charlie was holding onto the car keys as if they might help. "Seren is there. She might have gone to Seren."

"She might have gone anywhere. We need to know." Emz was exasperated. "Why can't you just use your Strength?"

Emz could be so reasonable when it didn't involve her having to find someone and be completely responsible. The jar of green lentils seemed to look particularly muddy and green as it sat on the table.

"Charlie!" Emz was wild-eyed. "You just DID it. You found Ailith. Now find Anna."

"Oh... for Pete's sake." Charlie slammed down the car keys and snatched up the jar. Her fingers struggled with the metal catch, the snap mechanism unwilling to let her in. A whisper, very deep inside her, became as annoying and as reasoned as Emz. She let go of the green lentils. Instead she walked to Anna's jacket which was hanging on the wall in the corridor.

"Charlie, why are you wasting time?" Emz was fizzing. Charlie reached into the pockets. Inside was some loose change, a couple of receipts, a small length of kitchen string, and, for who knew what chef-type reason, some black peppercorns. Charlie turned to Emz, her fist raised.

Ailith and Emz watched as Charlie strewed the items on the table. The coins rolled off the edge, Ailith stooping to pick them up. The receipts were scrunched paper. The kitchen string, however, was a snaking map of Woodcastle, showing Top Lane and the little streets and roads that ran off it, but the black peppercorns had formed themselves into a little square just stepped back from the Moot Hall. Where was that? Charlie felt the map slipping under the cloak of her own doubts. *Get a grip. Pull back.* She took a deep breath, closed her eyes for a moment and looked again. She could see at once where Dark Gate Street curled away down the string and, at once, she knew where her sister was.

"You…" Charlie pointed at Ailith. "Stay here." She heard the severity in her tone and qualified it at once, "The cottage will keep you safe," and she was rewarded with Ailith's grateful smile. Emz was already opening the cottage door.

When, a little later, Ailith thought she might step out onto the porch it appeared Cob Cottage would not let her: the door stayed shut. Ailith, remembering something Grandam Orla had told her once, thought that that was a good thing and feeling safe, perhaps for the first time in her entire life, she curled up on the floor and fell asleep.

27

SAP

Apple Day. Quaint, traditional, and perfect, rather like Mrs Fyfe. Her exterior might be sleek and contemporary, black was her colour after all, but her interior was antique, genuine ancient monument stuff. Those round glasses gave the perfect looking glass view of the world, a little distortion here and there to keep things interesting. She had wandered through the Apple Day stalls and drunk it all in.

All the bad energy, all the darkness from within, all the hurts and resentments, all the sorrows and griefs, pride and arrogance, all the words bitten into tongues, insults, bitching, fighting, squabbles, oh The Gods, was there anything more perfect and delicious than a squabble? Squabbles and pettiness, the carrot and onion in the stockpot of slow poison.

She had felt invigorated as a result of all the surly minded argy-bargy and a closer inspection of town revealed several small treats.

"Penny for them?" she asked the black-haired young woman who was biting into a pastry that she, Mrs Fyfe, had watched her buy at the bakery stall.

"Mm?" the young woman turned sharp eyes upon her. "I was

just looking at the quality. Usually there's better fare on offer. This is greasy."

Mrs Fyfe rootled around in the woman's head for a few moments and found white robes, a crown made of skulls, rituals at a stone circle. Mrs Fyfe wanted to squeak with glee. She would mark this young woman well. A young woman who liked meddling in magic of which they had no true knowledge was always useful. Oh, Woodcastle was filled with treasures.

"Isn't that the trouble with these kinds of market? Everything looks so good except they put the best ones at the front and pick the bad ones from the back... see..." Mrs Fyfe's voice was almost musical, but a kind of dissonant music that got inside your head. As Roz turned, the woman at the bakery stall reached into a basket on a trestle table at the rear and filled out the order that had just been shouted to her. Roz looked outraged, she looked into the grim and greasy bag and then up at Mrs Fyfe.

"Allow me..." Mrs Fyfe reached for a pastry. It was more golden, more crisp than any other pastry Roz Woodhill had ever seen. "You should get what you have paid for." Mrs Fyfe smiled and moved on.

Her marker was set in the young woman. If all went well she might need a familiar later and that young woman would be the perfect conduit. Ah. What a day. With that small magical task completed she moved on towards her more pressing magical priorities. She stepped through the crowd, unnoticed.

She had needed some short time to replenish her strength. There had been no point in seeking out the raggedy girl and her precious cargo before this. This morning she was ready and began her hunt in earnest. She was starting to feel a low thrum in her head and as she neared the castle it became more penetrating. It felt as if the ancient source was close, was not cloaked in the leaves and bark of Havoc Wood at all. Could she be this fortunate? What had that messenger girl couriered here? It could not be this simple. Mrs Fyfe's rusted heart gave a creaking patter. If she could only hunt it down, whatever it was, take the measure of it, use it. She had a revenge list written in blood in her head. She'd see Havoc Wood burn.

As she moved onwards she drew in the silted black energy of the Apple Day crowd, letting it soak in to her, electrified with the power surge that was slow poison.

Oh my stars, this was fun. There was a delicious self-pitying gravy just oozing off this young woman. Penny for them.

"I'm thirty this year you know..." the young woman was pleading with a disinterested looking young man who was sucking at a cider bottle as if it was a cow teat. "Thirty. We need to get married. I want a baby. I want triplets."

Mrs Fyfe was grateful for the knowledge and set ideas of biological clocks ticking in the poor woman's head. And remember the damp patch in the front bedroom and don't forget the little mushrooms growing in the toilet under the cistern where it dripped and of course the paint peeling off the windows and that guttering that leaked. Mrs Fyfe liked the small domestic worries best because they were very easy to maintain, an endless supply of snacks. She looked hard to see what else might be inside this woman; a crust of self-pity always thickened the general emotional stew. Mrs Fyfe rootled around a little, drew out more shadows with which to sustain herself.

At last, she turned her gaze to the castle. The building loomed, casting a strong shadow in the bright morning sun and Mrs Fyfe noted that it was exactly the shape and shade it should be, it was not affected by her slow poison of the town. This, she knew, was the hiding place.

She walked around the castle walls, looking up at the fortress, for despite its venerable age it still was such. She found her way around the entire boundary, heading up the banking at Bend Lane and walking along the earthworks. The stones ground against her so it was clear that they had seen her kind before. Never mind, she liked a challenge, so she finished her circuit of the walls and headed back to the main gate.

Mrs Fyfe trudged up Barbican Steep and found that it lived up to its name, the cobbles that greeted you after the car park ought to have been renamed hobbles after she turned first this ankle and then that. She paused for a moment. Hmm. These stones really didn't like her.

Having fought her way footstep by footstep to the edge of the wooden walkway she paused for several moments to drink in the energy from the woman in the kiosk who was quaffing apple juice from a jug. Her shadows were rich in all the disappointments, the hurts, the self-pity, a delicious bourguignon of bitterness, and it was just the pick-me-up required. Mrs Fyfe felt ready to brave the old magic. There was no mistaking its presence, the castle was alive with it. The sensation sank far deeper than the blood and battle and toil soaked into the stones. These Way women were very careless to leave a power like this just waiting to be taken. Mrs Fyfe took a step into the castle. The air bristled. The old magic did not care for her.

Neither did Mrs Bentley. Throwing aside her poisoned drink, she exited the ticket office at some speed, snatching up a halberd from the display as she did so. She had the tinny glazed eyes that showed Mrs Fyfe she was slow poisoned.

"Halt... who goes there? Friend or foe?" Mrs Bentley menaced Mrs Fyfe with the halberd, the unwieldy weapon looking deadly in the skilled hands of the castle's custodian.

"Why, Friend, of course." Mrs Fyfe was amused. Mrs Bentley was unyielding. She lunged forward; the spiked blade of the halberd sliced through the air in front of Mrs Fyfe's face and halted just shy of her skin.

"Halt. Foe." Mrs Bentley's tin glazed eyes glinted with fierce anger. To Mrs Fyfe it was like a glass of single malt but in a large measure, too much to be consumed at a sitting.

"Friend," Mrs Fyfe reiterated, her voice commanding, trying to push a little at Mrs Bentley's edges.

Mrs Bentley raised the tip of the pikestaff until it jabbed, very delicately, into the underneath of Mrs Fyfe's chin.

"Why then do the stones shriek Foe?"

Hah, that challenge stepped matters up a gear. Mrs Fyfe licked her lips and sipped a little of the single malt of this woman's fury. Then she had a rootle about in Mrs Bentley's head to find what she needed.

"Is it possible to buy a season ticket? As I said, I'd like to be a Friend of Woodcastle Castle…" Mrs Fyfe's smile was small and ingratiating. Mrs Bentley stood the halberd down.

"Come Friend…" and she set off towards the kiosk.

Mrs Fyfe put her season ticket and her Friends of Woodcastle Castle membership into her pocket. These times were interesting; the people inhabiting them had different magic. Armed with her talismans she continued up through the drawbridge arch and out into the wide greensward of the castle yard.

The old magic trailed like smoke. Wood smoke and… Mrs Fyfe drew in a deep breath, honey. Oh. It had been so very long since that particular perfume had breathed its life into her. It reached out, bringing golden memories of home and long ago and once upon a time. It wound itself around her, a wisp of old smoke smudged across a long forgotten blue sky. She had found all that she had lost. For just a moment, fleeting and poignant, Mrs Fyfe thought she might cry. It was only a moment; as her throat constricted with the charm of it she stepped back. No. You don't trick me. She pushed back, lengthened the shadows around her, a dark protective circle in which to walk.

She hunted, tracking and sniffing for the old magic, for whatever talisman or weapon that raggedy girl had hidden here, a talisman or a weapon that she could steal and make her own.

2 8

ON THE RIDGE

It was a dream, Anna understood that, because she was blurred at the edges but after the tight feelings of grief that had bound her lately, the wind here at Yarl Hill was very soothing. The breeze ruffled at her hair and rustled through the long grass making a sighing sound that matched her own.

"*Hey.*" The familiar voice made Anna turn. Emz, eight and wearing that favourite white sweater and the shoes she'd had with the lights in them. "*Race you.*" Charlie, nearly fifteen, running, her sweatshirt hood flapping behind her and Emz, her legs pounding. "*Waaaaaaaait.*" Her small eight-year-old voice echoing. Anna turned; Grandma Hettie, her black waxed raincoat cracking slightly in the breeze, smiled and started up the slope.

It was a winding path that zig-zagged up to the ridge at Yarl Hill. They had walked this route many times. The sunlight was soft and warm and very comforting, and the wind was at their backs whichever direction they turned so that their steps were light. From here Anna could look down on Woodcastle, the castle in the distance, the towers rising up, the curtain walls curving around, protective, and beyond them the spill of buildings and gardens, streets and junctions that made up her home. She liked the way the houses jaggered and straddled the valley sides, thinning out gradually until there were just the few bigger properties peeking out from the curtain of trees. At Hartfield Hall the sunlight winked on the windows, so they looked like gold. There was Leap Wood, the soldier formations of the planted pines guarding the more deciduous heart of the place. The river wound like a metal ribbon through the valley and on the opposite bank was the edge of Havoc Wood, rising and sweeping up the other ridges and hilltops, only clearing a space for Pike Lake. From here, in this lovely dream, Anna thought Pike Lake looked like a round shield, laid down on the soft earth after a battle.

"*Southern.*" Grandma Hettie turning in a circle as the girls raced off, Emz in the wrong direction, Anna tugging her back, laughing, Charlie ahead, Charlie winning but before they reached the southern edge, Grandma Hettie's voice sang out.

"*Northern.*" The sisters running screaming and breathless to the back edge, nearest to Havoc, the edge with the barrows, but before they could reach the barrows Grandma Hettie's voice called out once more.

"*Eastern.*" Grandma Hettie standing in the centre of the earthwork, her arms waving, the Way sisters running, racing to the raised banking, and just before they crested the summit Grandma Hettie turning into the wind, her arms stretched wide.

"*Western.*" They were giddy with effort now, rosy cheeked, Charlie hanging back because Emz was getting tired but not letting Emz know it. Anna strolling, letting the breeze cool her skin. At the western gate they sank into the grass and Grandma Hettie pulled out her red-spotted handkerchief, unfolded the picnic of sausage rolls and hard-boiled eggs. Anna let herself sink into the earth. The grass whispered, "stay".

Anna thought she would. Forever. A shadow fell across her, cooling and soothing. Grandma Hettie's hand reaching for her, helping her to her feet.

"*You've work to do.*"

The wind got up, snatched at Grandma's black raincoat so that it cracked like lightning and as it did, Anna woke up.

Adrenalin was not the best wake-up call but it surged through Anna as she sat up in a strange bed. Stranger than strange, it wasn't a bed at all. It was an odd little sofa, in a tiny tiny room filled with sewing and needles.

"Hey," Seren's voice was soft and wary. "How're you feeling?" Seren leaned down offering a mug and a nervous smile. A second helping of adrenalin washed through Anna along with something darker, a sense of loss, a sliding of the earth from under her accompanied by a vision of Calum and Ethan, waiting for her on the bridge. She lurched upwards, her head swimming.

"I have to go to the bridge…" She heard the words coming out of her mouth as if they were spoken by a stranger and somewhere deep inside her there was a very tiny warning voice shouting something to her.

"No. You don't." Seren Lake blocked her way to the small door. "You need to drink some tea."

"I have to go to the bridge." Anna took a stride forwards; Seren blocked her. It was such a little door. She must go through. She pushed past Seren. The door was locked. She rattled at it. She had things to do.

"The bridge. Go to the bridge."

Seren pushed in front of her, one hand reaching to push her gently back towards the sofa, the other offering a mug of tea.

"Yes. Yes, we will go. But first we need to drink some tea. Okay? It's cold on the bridge. A mug of tea will bolster you up a bit. Okay? Okay."

Anna dashed the mug from her hands, pushed Seren out of the way. The key. There.

"No." Seren made a grab for it, the door opening just a crack, revealing the shop beyond. The darkness outside. Anna shoved Seren once more but Seren bounded back, threw her body weight against the door.

"No. Anna, you are staying here." Seren's smile was edgy, sad. Anna tugged at the door but no matter how hard she tugged at it, it would not open. She felt her anger subside into a terrible seething sadness; it filled every part of her. It was just so hopeless. Her life was a wasteland, a desert of loss. She leaned her head against the surface of the door. Seren reached a hand to her shoulder. At her touch she slumped further forward, crushing herself against the grain of the wood. Oh, it just wasn't bearable. The grief washed like a tide, it pushed at her, it pulled her down. She shrugged Seren's hand away, squirmed against the door.

"Let me out…" Her hand flapped feebly at the old grain and her voice was a whisper. "Let me out." Anna slumped again with a moan. At once there was a knocking at the back door. Seren looked up through the kitchen door. Emz was banging on the window.

"Key!" Seren gestured. "Under the gnome!" She did not dare to leave Anna's side. In a few seconds Emz and Charlie were with her.

"What happened?" Charlie asked as she dropped to the floor beside her sister.

"She was on the bridge. Going to jump." Seren felt the tension in her start to give a little and shift towards shock. "The phones were dead. No signal… couldn't call you… she was going to…"

Without warning Anna rose from the floor, lurching towards the open back door. Charlie, Emz, and Seren all made a grab for her, the three of them struggling to halt her progress.

"LET ME GO." Her voice was harsh, little ballbearings of spittle landing on Emz's face, Emz's feet sliding across the floor behind the relentless push of her eldest sister."No. It's me… It's Emz, Anna… what is wrong with you?"

Charlie was being kicked, the blows severe and the expression on Anna's face so sorrowful and harsh that it was distressing Emz.

"Let me *go*." The wail from Anna was heartrending. Seren was struggling with Anna's writhing form as Charlie took hold of Anna, very firmly, by the wrist.

"We'll take you to the bridge now," she said, nodding at Emz. Anna moaned, a thin, sorrowful sound. Emz took Anna by the other hand.

"Yes. Yes. We're going now." Emz held her tight. Charlie looked at Seren.

"We're parked in the lane at the back. When we leave, you need to lock the doors."

Seren did not doubt it.

It took two seatbelts to restrain Anna in the back of Charlie's car, and, even then, she was clawing at the windows.

"Let me go, I have to go to the bridge, I must go, don't stop me..." It was horrible, the waves of grief and desolation were rolling off Anna and were being concentrated in the confines of the car.

"Look, just sit in the back with her and we'll get back as fast as we can." Charlie had faith that getting Anna back to Cob Cottage would help; however, they had only moved a few feet along the lane when Anna broke free of the belts, lashed out at Emz so that her head knocked so hard against the side window both almost cracked. Charlie jabbed at the central locking and sealed the exits.

"What are we going to do?" Emz was visibly distressed. Charlie's mind ticked and whirred reaching, as it always did, for the solution. It was sitting in a plastic crate in the back of her car.

The opened bottle of Blackberry Ferment smelt heavenly, of summer days and turned earth.

"Blackberry Ferment? You want to get her drunk?" Emz asked. Charlie shook her head. Anna was less fighty now, more limp and maudlin.

"It'll slow her down a bit at least. One should do it... she's usually a lightweight." Charlie reached for the last bin bag of discarded shot glasses from the Apple Day disaster pop-up and poured a hefty shot.

Anna drank the first shot of Blackberry Ferment as if it was nectar.

"Oh, it's so beautiful... so delicious... so... so... so..."

Emz looked at Charlie.

"Has she been drinking already d'you think? At Apple Day maybe?" Emz asked. Charlie shrugged.

"She doesn't usually."

"Take me to the bridge. Take me now, before it's too late to go." Anna was more sensible now which made the plea all the more upsetting.

"We will..." Emz lied.

"After we've had one more toast to the bridge... yes?" Charlie faked enthusiasm, her eyes watching Anna. Anna nodded, her face crumpling into tears. She drank the second shot and began to soften, the tears melting out.

"They're gone," she whispered. "They're gone, aren't they?"

Emz looked at Charlie, her face stricken with an expression of sadness and realisation so raw that it made Emz look about seven. "And I have to follow them..." Anna whispered as her head lolled backward and she gave a low keening howl. Emz juddered with emotion, her arms throwing themselves around Anna's neck.

"You have us. You have us. Please don't go." Emz's voice was little and small. Charlie rammed herself into the driving seat and turned the ignition. Action. Do it.

By the time they arrived at Cob Cottage Anna was unconscious and the Way sisters, shaken by events, were struggling with the logistics of getting her out of Charlie's tiny car. As they fumbled about, Anna slumping down or folding up, Ailith came out through the door. She stepped between the sisters.

With a strong, deft movement she reached into the car and picked Anna up in her arms.

"Inside with you," she ordered the Way sisters. "Quick sharp."

Ailith rested Anna on the long sofa and, as Emz and Charlie, one sniffily, one red-faced, looked on, Ailith gathered the blanket and the cushion and made the elder Way sister comfortable.

"You..." Ailith pointed at Emz, "sit you down here... and you..." she pushed Charlie into the other chair. The two looked forlornly on their sibling, her face less pale now as it looked over the top of the blanket. As they sat in silence the clock chimed midnight.

"There you go... 'tis your time now, the small hours have come," and she gave a little bow as she moved out of their way into the kitchen where, for the next half an hour, Ailith carried on a bustle of activity, of kettle boiling and tea steeping and griddle cake flipping.

In the living area the Way sisters sat, the sofa and two chairs making a corner each of their triangle, and they tried to puzzle out what was happening and how they might stop it.

"HIS HEAD IS RESTING in the wrong place." Anna's pale face loomed into Charlie's as she woke up. There was a scent of tea and maple syrup and Emz was already seated at the table with Ailith, eating pancakes.

"Who? What?" Charlie scrabbled up towards them from her morning fug. It had always been like that, Emz and Anna were cheery morning people and Charlie was a grumpy morning person, a trait she had shared with Grandma Hettie.

"That is why the Stuff has been buzzing town," Emz said through a mouthful of maple syrup-soaked pancake. "All this mess and hoo-ha. We sussed it last night. Anna had a dream. Remember when we used to play Battle with Grandma Hettie, up on Yarl Hill?"

"Rest me by herepath and ridgewayed rampart..." Anna began. Charlie looked at her.

"I'm sorry, the Stuff?"

"You know...the 'Stuff'." Emz made speech marks in the air.

"I think we can say 'Magic,'" Charlie barked. Emz looked shocked.

"I thought you wanted to dodge the word?" she said. Charlie gave a heavy sigh.

"It doesn't work. Not saying the word doesn't make it go away. We're just giving it power by not saying it. Magic. The warrior's head is leaking Magic because we buried it wrong. Call a spade a spade."

"Or a witch a witch," Emz said. Charlie grunted, gave a decisive nod.

"Owned," she conceded. "So... we did it wrong first time... how do we get it right the second time?"

"Well..." Anna handed her a plate of pancakes and a fork. "First... we have to go back to the castle and dig up the head."

Charlie grimaced, let out a resigned but weary breath.

"I'm going to need bacon first."

29

PARENTS' CONSULTATION

The fly in the ointment of the Witch Ways' Bone Resting Part II in 3D was the Parents' Consultation Evening for the sixth form. Emz had managed to cram all three of her appointments into the first hour and a half so although there was going to be some hanging about waiting to see Mr Mill, the evening's horror would be over by half past eight at the latest. She had assumed that she would be able, in the circumstances, to skip the whole event.

"The Bone Resting is more important," she had insisted to Anna, and Charlie had laughed out loud.

"If you don't show at the parents' thing you will be in real trouble. It's going to be bad enough when Mum finds out you didn't tell her it was on."

Anna nodded.

"That was a bad move. You know what Mum's like..."

Emz made her argument.

"Yes. Camped out at De Quincey Langport R&D mostly. What she doesn't know won't..." Emz could not say it wouldn't hurt her, she knew absolutely how hurt her mother would be. "Whatever. It won't make a difference. I am eighteen."

Charlie laughed again.

"Will you stop laughing?"

"I will if you stop saying stupid things."

Anna gave Charlie a flashing look. "Don't give me that look… she knows what I mean."

Emz did know and was adamant.

"You will not do the Bone Resting without me." She was getting red faced with indignation. Charlie and Anna looked at her.

"We can't do it without you," Charlie reasoned. "End of."

They were making plans for a return visit to the castle. The moon was waning, but that couldn't be helped, and the Way sisters had talked it out and decided that actually some things just had to be tackled and couldn't wait for new, old, or any other kind of moon.

"So, you'll definitely be done by half eight?" Charlie was checking the details.

"Check." Emz was certain. She was certain because she was not going to be delayed or detoured.

"We just have to get up to the castle ready for witching hour." Anna reassured her sister. Charlie looked puzzled.

"The head is a head. It's buried under the stone. If we could find a way to distract Mrs Bentley that didn't involve a small cupboard and a handful of Quiet Life tablets we could do this anytime."

Anna nodded. "You're right. Okay. So, we're a go. I'll give you a lift, Emz, I've got to call in at the Castle Inn anyway about tomorrow's shifts."

Emz grabbed her bag and Anna her keys. She opened the door and was startled to find someone already standing there.

"Ready to go?" said Vanessa on the doorstep. There was a silence in Cob Cottage broken only by Charlie stifling a shocked laugh. Emz looked at Anna who shrugged.

VANESSA AND EMZ sat at the traffic lights at the top of Old Castle Road, lights which seemed, to Emz, to be forever red.

"How did you find out?" she asked at last as her mother took the car out of gear.

"I'm a scientist. I have my ways." Vanessa's tone was not harsh or upset although she didn't appear to be able to look at Emz. She felt guilty now, for having done this to her mother.

"I assumed you'd be busy."

"I've never missed a parents' evening." Vanessa threw down the gauntlet of information and Emz knew it to be true. The lights stayed resolutely red. Vanessa shifted back into gear for something to do.

"Sorry."

"Don't be," she said, and the lights turned green.

THE SCHOOL SEEMED ORGANISED and usual but Emz was aware, the moment they stepped into the entrance hall, of that prickling electrical feeling she had had the day before at Prickles and later in town. She was nervous of outcomes this evening and bolstered herself with the knowledge that, in a few hours, she and her sisters would have sorted out the problem.

"I think we're seeing Mrs King-Winters first..." Vanessa consulted her phone. As she did so Mrs King-Winters was moving to greet them. Emz looked into her eyes; they were a bright and deep shade of blue.

"Good evening Mrs Way... Emz." She was all smiles. Emz's mind poked at her. By contrast Mrs Wilson, the drama teacher sitting at a small table close by, was tinny eyed and exuding sadness. It almost curled off her like smoke. As Mrs King-Winters and her mother exchanged a few pleasantries Emz could see sadness, despair, resentment, jealousy, revenge, rolling around the room, each emotion an incipient smoke clagging the air. Deep inside her an instinct was growling and it was, at once, both powerful and frightening. She had an urgent need to take action but before she could turn on her heels and head back to Cob Cottage Mrs King-Winters was ushering them along the staff corridor, away from the assembly hall.

Mrs King-Winters had been very clever and arranged a kind of ambush. Where the other students had to brazen it out in the full glare of the assembly hall, Mrs King-Winters, Emz's first and, Emz anticipated, most troublesome appointment, ushered them into a side office on the staff corridor.

"If you'll just bear with me…"

Within minutes Emz and her mother were sitting in the too small office with Mrs King-Winters, Mr Mill, Mrs Kumar, and Miss Beaton, who was responsible for sixth form pastoral care. As Vanessa was filled in on Emz's current pick and mix attitude to attendance, Emz took in the spectacle of her teachers. Mrs King-Winters, still fine. Mr Mill, tinny eyes, thin smoky trail of resentment. Mrs Kumar, still fine.

Miss Beaton. Tinny eyes and her real face peeked out, unbidden. It was a sleeping face, but the kind of sleep that comes from anaesthesia or a drug; it was a deep sleep.

Vanessa wanted to ascertain the facts about Emz's misdemeanours.

"Has she missed many deadlines?" Vanessa asked with interest. "I mean, if there are essays and things that she could catch up on…"

"Well. Er…" Mrs King-Winters seemed to be struggling. Mr Mill filled the void.

"She does the work. She just can't be bothered to turn up. When others, teachers, her elders and betters, they have to be bothered. These kids have no idea. They are so entitled…"

Vanessa looked at him in the same way she looked at mice involved in intelligence tests.

"So... the fact is that Emily has not missed any work deadlines? Is that the case?"

"The case. The facts. You are such a scientist, aren't you..." Mr Mill peered at her through peevish eyes. Mrs King-Winters looked uncomfortable.

"Well... I think, I mean it is clear that Emily is a very capable student..." she gave an ameliorating smile to Vanessa who, Emz noted, did not smile back.

"Shall we hear the evidence from Mathematics?" Vanessa's voice was very cold and Emz wasn't sure she didn't see Mrs King-Winters shiver.

"Mrs Kumar?" Mrs King-Winters prompted, hoping that Mrs Kumar would have some fresh ammunition.

"Emz is a gifted mathematician." Mrs Kumar smiled directly at Emz and so Emz braced herself. "She just does not attend lessons. Which is a problem."

"Is it though?" Miss Beaton's voice was thin and sad. "I mean... they're young, we push them so hard and for what? For what in the end? So, they can trot off to university, run up a massive debt and get their hearts broken by Brent The Bastard Williams."

Mrs King-Winters and Mrs Kumar stared at their colleague. She stared back.

A tear could be seen dropping from her face onto her lap and Mrs Kumar reached into her bag and handed Miss Beaton a tissue. Miss Beaton was pitiful and grateful.

"I think..." Mrs King-Winters moved to take the reins, "that Emily is, we all agree, a gifted student with a bright academic future."

"I agree," Vanessa stated. Emz dared to look at her mother. Still fine. No tinny eyes. She did not very often look at her mother's real face; she was always distracted by the fact that Vanessa was her mother, it was as if her real face didn't matter in the same way, she was simply Mum. Now Emz looked. Vanessa's real face was turned away, was looking out through the office window, dream-like and thoughtful. At the nape of her neck, just below her hair-line, Emz could see small black marks tattooed into the skin, angular, like writing. Emz gasped and her mother turned to give her a sharp look.

"So. Can we agree on a way forward for her?" Vanessa concluded. Mrs King-Winters jumped in.

"Your family has been through such a lot in the last year, Mrs Way. Such a lot. I think that any forward planning for Emz needs to take all that emotional upheaval into account."

"Go on." Vanessa did not sound encouraging. Emz was panicking.

"It is a small matter to defer a year and take the exams next time around… there are options here and we're here to help." Mrs King-Winters was the ringleader, Emz could tell, but Mrs Kumar attempted a coup.

"I'd be happy to offer one-to-one tutoring out of hours," Mrs Kumar smiled. "If you wanted to defer then we could work together at keeping your knowledge ticking over… if that would be useful in your decision making."

"If you keep slacking here Emz…" Mr Mill chipped in. "You will fail in the summer and when you fail, I fail. You make the school fail. Is that fair?"

Mrs King-Winters cast him a cold look. Emz could see his real face, his mouth slightly open and drooly. She looked into his eyes. That tinny effect was very strange, like a contact lens made of the sheen of diesel. Emz stared hard, her instinct once again drawing in information, readying itself for action.

"I think what we are advising is…" Mrs King-Winters took charge, leaning forward, smiling at Vanessa, who, without allowing her to finish, turned to Emz, took her by the elbow and began to move them both towards the door.

"Okay. Well. Great meeting. Lots to think about. We'll let you know." Vanessa bustled them both out into the corridor. "Bye," she called as they hurried towards the door, her mother half shoving, half carrying her.

Emz was waiting for the storm, the blasting, the ultimatum. They walked across the car park and they got into the car.

Her mother started the engine.

They drove out of the car park.

They drove, still with not one word spoken, out onto Horse Hill Road and ran along the length of it, the only sound the creak of the suspension as they passed over the sleeping policeman at the junction with Hartfield Road. They drove on towards town and Emz was surprised that they did not turn onto Old Castle Road. Instead they turned back onto Ham Street and out towards Leap Woods. As they ran past the trees Emz found her thoughts tumbling down into the paths and snickelways. There was the brief ticktick of the indicator and they were bumping along the drive into Prickles.

Winn already had the kettle on and had invested in a box of cakes from the bakery. She was snaffling down a vanilla slice as they arrived and Emz was aware that clearly Mrs King-Winters was not the only one with a strategy. Emz's real face radar scanned Winn. No tinny eyes and Winn's real face, a rosy cheeked young woman. Emz liked Winn's real face, it was, by far, one of the best faces she had ever seen. With no tinny eyes or sleeping real faces, and the shotgun safely out of sight, Emz felt less geared up and turned her full attention to whatever battle these two had planned.

They sat around the Formica topped table in the kitchen. Winn had got out the best mugs, the really big ones from the local pottery that were a stormy blue and green. Vanessa opened the box of cakes.

"Ooh, religieuses, Winn, you remembered." Winn nodded through her mouthful of vanilla custard and handed out plates. Emz's mother picked out a fat choux pastry affair swizzled with chocolate. "Oh lush... the mocha ones."

Emz did not choose a cake. She sat down in the chair that was offered, Winn licking her fingers as she poured the tea. Emz could not pick up the mug, although she wanted to, she wanted to feel its rounded warmth, to look into the storm of blue and green of the glaze. She was shaking. Time was ticking. Town was poisoned, what was more important than dealing with that? She knew the true word for what was going on, it was lurking in the shadow of her head but she couldn't use it just yet. *Stuff. Yes. Okay. Deep breath, Emz.*

"Eat the cake before I do," Winn warned and pushed the box closer. Emz's shaking hand just about managed to pick out a bakewell tart criss-crossed with pastry and sparkling with caster sugar. She put it on the plate but did not eat it.

"So. That was… quite an experience," Vanessa began. "They're offering you a chance to defer your exams. What do you reckon?"

Emz did not like the prospect; it would just put off the fact for another year and then she'd still be in the same boat. There was a passing thought of Logan Boyle, but it did just that, passed along the staircase of her mind.

"I don't want to do that." Emz thought she could see where this was heading, that Winn was here as backup, to make the threat, do your exams or don't do Prickles, but then Winn spoke up.

"Do you want a job here as a wildlife ranger?" she asked and reached for a large square of chocolate cake. Emz looked at her mother. Her mother waited for the response.

"Yes. Obviously. You know that."

She waited for the threat, *come on, bring it.*

"I've got funding from the WildWood Society, that bunch of townie loons in Castlebury. Do you want the job?"

Emz looked at her mother, who picked up the remainder of her religieuse and ate it in one creamy squodge.

"Yes."

"Then you have to finish your A levels." Winn was definite about this. *There it was. What a scam.*

"But if I..." she looked at her mother. Vanessa sipped some tea before speaking.

"That's the bargain, Emily. Take the job but finish your exams. Do it this year. Get them done and dusted." She sounded reasonable but the use of Emz's full name indicated her intent.

"I don't need A levels. I don't want to go to university." Emz wanted to make her feelings clear, felt relieved at having been forced to say it out loud.

"I know. Not a problem," Vanessa said.

"Then why bother with my exams? Why not just take up the ranger job now?"

"You can't," Winn looked grumpy. "I don't give a squirrel's arse about it myself but it's out of my hands. It's part of the rules of the funding, the WildWood people want A levels. Minimum requirements."

There was a moment of silence and thought. Emz looked at her mother. Vanessa smiled sympathetically and gave a small shrug.

"Yes. Please. I'll do it," Emz said in a quiet voice.

"Sorted," Vanessa said and winked, a gesture that was so filled with Grandma Hettie that Emz could not stop herself from crying.

3 0

FOXED

It was dark by the time Anna, Charlie, Emz, and Ailith had walked through Havoc Wood and out into town to the castle. They had come up from the river path through the quieter streets of town.

Even here the effects of the leaking magic seemed apparent. There was loud music blaring from one house, the heavy drum bass beat pounding at the air. Elsewhere there were raised voices. At another the women could hear someone crying. Here and there was the mini blast of a door slamming. Harsh words. Somewhere in the distance a cat screeched, a dog howled.

The group walked up onto the banking below the curtain wall and one by one made their less than elegant progress up the tree and over the wall, Emz tearing her sweatshirt on a stray jag of branch. With everyone safe on the wall they processed down to the greensward.

"Are we sure it was this stone?" Anna asked Charlie as they upended the heavy slab they had used to hide the warrior's head and found nothing but an empty hole beneath. Charlie looked into the disturbed earth.

"Yes. Look." She picked out the last draggles of the flowers they had lined the spot with.

"I'm looking. I was just trying to put off the panic," Anna admitted. "The head is definitely not there."

They all peered into the void. Ailith looked stricken.

"Someone has taken him?" Her voice was a tiny moan. She began to look around. Her shoulders were tight.

The Way sisters looked at Ailith, then at each other. Charlie spoke up first.

"I can hear the stones again. Low level. Like a deep drone. Not as fierce this time."

The other sisters listened and heard nothing. "What does that mean, d'you think?"

"Residual magic." Anna suggested.

"Like leftovers?" Emz looked pale. "So, you think someone has taken him?"

Anna shrugged.

"They want to use the power," Anna said, and the three sisters seemed to shrink a little at the thought.

"We just handed it over. As if the castle was a drop-off point," Charlie's voice was as heavy as the stones; she stepped forward. Unconsciously they had formed their triangle, Ailith central to it, protected. There were several moments of silence.

Anna shook her head.

"No. Nothing from Havoc is that easy," Anna's voice was cool and calm and made Charlie even tenser as a result. She dug her hands deep into her sweatshirt pockets.

"This is what I'm talking about. We don't know anything do we? There's no user's manual for all this." The tension trilled between them.

"And who wants it?" Emz asked. Anna looked severe, glanced at Charlie.

"Who knows about him except us?" Charlie reasoned. Ailith flinched slightly and, witnessing it, Charlie asked, "What is it?"

The sisters turned to Ailith.

"On the journey. At the split oak, I slept."

The Witch Ways were none the wiser and waited for Ailith to continue. She looked stricken as she continued.

"The woman. I was safe in the oak but... perhaps she followed."

"Trespasser." Charlie said the word with no emotion, flat, factual.

"Oh my God. The Trespasser." Emz was hopping back and forth on her back foot at the thought, put her hands over her face. Anna started to nod.

"Everything kicked off yesterday, that means the head was still here, still leaking its magic..."

"Oh God, yes. Like an alarm. Like we said. A big massive smoke signal of magic."

Charlie nodded, her train of thought chugging decisively forwards.

"Yep. This woman, still on Ailith's trail maybe, hanging around Havoc on the off chance..."

"... and picked up the trail." Anna finished the thought.

"Boom." Charlie said with a nod.

"She could still be within the bounds of Havoc. They might not have got out yet." Anna picked out the small splinter of hope.

"Let's go." Charlie began to make her way across the greensward with Ailith at her side and Anna a step or two behind. Behind her, Emz was side-tracked by a sudden movement by the far wall. She halted. *There. Something moving steadily. There by the wall. Waiting now. Watching for them.*

Charlie, Anna, and Emz were part way up the steps to the cobbled yard when Anna looked back and noticed Emz was missing.

"Emz? Where's Emz?" The party looked around. There was no sign of their sister. If they felt panicked at the loss of the head, the panic now spiralled to critical mass. Charlie leapt off the steps onto the sward. They all began looking for her.

"Emz?" Their whispered calls were growing hoarser and then, suddenly, she was there.

"Hey," her voice called out. Anna, Charlie, and Ailith spun around. Emz was striding towards them from the dark shadows by the potting shed. "This way," and as quickly as she had appeared she vanished again.

The three streamed towards the potting shed, Charlie just in time to see Emz's booted foot as it disappeared behind the shed.

"What the…"

At the back of the shed the wall curved into the bottom of the keep tower and, if followed round, the curve ended in what looked like a drain gulley, a thin rill of stone set back. One step into the rill revealed the hidden stairway. Emz was already down there; the others could follow the small glow of light from her phone.

"What is this?" Anna asked as they stood in the tunnel. It was dank and mossy and smelt powerfully of fox.

"It's the siege tunnel," Emz was matter of fact, "from the Civil War. Remember, when Cromwell threw a shoe and Lady Hartfield didn't surrender? This is how they survived."

Charlie was less than impressed.

"We're on a clock here, Emz. We need to hunt down the head thief and you're giving us a history lesson?"

Emz stood her ground.

"Remember the last time we were here, and I saw the fox through the gate? I said, 'how did the fox get in?' only we didn't bother, even I didn't pay attention to it, it's a fox. We were distracted. But this…" she made a sweeping gesture at the dank darkness before them, "…is how the fox gets in." Emz seemed excited by the discovery.

"Well, great, but how does this help us?" Anna asked looking puzzled and feeling the heat rise out of Charlie. Emz inhaled deeply.

"Breathe in. Smell."

They all breathed in; Ailith's face lightened.

"Honey and wood smoke." Charlie understood the implication.

"The head was carried through here. It's left a scent."

Ailith took several steps forward, halting where the darkness deepened.

"Where does it go?" Charlie asked. Anna stepped forward and placed her hand on Charlie's shoulder.

"As Grandma Hettie used to say..." Anna began. Charlie nodded.

"I know, I know... 'Which way Charlie?'" Her expression was gruff but inside she felt her Strength glimmer. *Like riding that rusty old bike.*

Charlie cleared her throat and looked down into the darkness of the tunnel. At first all she could see was the darkness because, as usual, she was overthinking it. *Don't push.* She let the idea of a task slip from her mind and she thought of the fox. At once the mossy dankness revealed a green cushioned path off into the distance that broke out into Leap Woods. A hillock, stranded over with ivy and clogged with bramble, the rot of an old door colonised by fungus.

"Leap Woods. Just up on the far side of Cooper's Pond." She felt uplifted by this small new piece of knowledge and as she didn't think about it she could see the track the fox took, the small paws printing into her head, trees towering above before the fox looked back at her.

At once Charlie set off along the tunnel.

"Charlie?" Anna's voice was muffled against the damp moss of the walls as her sister disappeared into the darkness. The others followed, Emz holding up her phone, the soft white light illuminating their way, catching at the edges of Charlie as she hurried forwards.

After some minutes they scrambled out of the raggedy exit into the tangle and stumble of Leap Woods and Charlie was still running onwards down the rise of the banking.

"Here." She stopped. There was a hole dug into the ground, a fox's earth. Charlie hunkered down and took a glance inside. The earth seemed to be unoccupied.

"There. The fox saved him," Ailith pointed and the Way sisters looked up to where the fox was sitting a short distance above them, watching. Charlie reached inside the hole, her arm flailing at nothing and yet, there was something.

"I can't reach." She pulled out, brushing the dirt and draggle of dead roots off her arm. "Emz, can you fit down there?"

She took a step forward.

"It should be Ailith. Not any of us. It has to be her, she's the guardian." Emz stood aside, nodded to Ailith.

The head, although slightly bedraggled, had not suffered overmuch from its adventure.

"It's not chewed… much." Anna brushed some earth from the socket of the eye as Ailith cradled the head. He still looked as though he were sleeping very heavily.

"Right. We'd better make tracks."

IT TOOK them almost an hour to walk through Leap Woods into the edges of Havoc Wood and from there up towards Knightstone and the almost hidden curve of Yarl Hill. It marked, Anna realised, a boundary for Havoc Wood itself, a boundary she recalled walking, that long-ago day, with Grandma Hettie, her black waxed coat cracking in the whipping summer breeze. *Herepath. Ridge-wayed rampart.* As they began the steep pull out of the trees she saw at once the manmade curves of the hillfort:

"The lookout line."

Grandma Hettie's face, wrinkled against the intense sunshine, the strong summer breeze whipping her hair as they had walked the perimeter of the place. So long ago.

At the top, the views were astonishing. As they all stood on the zig-zag path to catch their breath, Ailith cradling her precious bundle, they looked back across Woodcastle and on towards Castlebury itself and Woodhill and Kingham, lit up like twinkling beacons. The trees of Leap Woods and Havoc Woods clothed the slopes and valleys, the River Rade itself flashing into view just here, over there.

"Which is the western gate?" Emz asked as they clambered up onto the base of the hillfort. "Should have brought a compass?"

"No need," Charlie said from up ahead.

"Of course… your Strength…" Anna puffed to meet her sister. Charlie shook her head and pointed.

On the far side of the hillfort a group of seven horses cropped the grass. They were saddled up and the riders were waiting by the scooped-out rampart. The Ways looked at each other, then at Ailith.

"Do you know them?" Anna asked. Ailith shook her head, folded the warrior's head deeper into her tattered coat, stood straighter. Anna took in a deep breath.

"Alright," Anna's voice was low, conspiratorial. "We can think this through. If they were here to attack…"

"They'd have done it by now," Emz suggested.

"Yep. When we were down there on the slope, wrong-footed and easy pickings," Charlie concluded. The riders looked unhurried; they were moving now, grouping themselves but in the way of people waiting to greet guests, not enemies.

"They're here to pay their respects," Emz said. She couldn't see faces clearly in the deep bronze darkness. "They don't feel bad." It was a very clear sensation. They felt, if anything, slightly chilled and weary. They had, Emz could tell, come a long way.

"Seven horses," Emz said. "But only six riders."

Charlie and Anna nodded.

"Let's do this." Anna took the lead.

The small Bone Resting party made its way over to the riders. As they did so they became aware of a small circle of glowing flames, small unearthly tea lights, set into the grass that covered the western gate.

"Welcome, Wanderers." The words came out of Anna's mouth without her having to think about them, it was as if the wind blew them into her. The riders gave small bows and in the light the Ways took them in.

There were, indeed, six of them, and, it appeared, they were all women. Dressed to ride they wore leather breeches draped with what Anna could only think of as kilts, the fabric woven with earthen colours, one woman in tones of umber, another in greens, like, Anna thought, a badge of colour. Their jackets were protective, leather moulded to their forms and strengthened here and there with metal plate that had been etched and scratched at in equal measure. Raggedy looking shirts straggled and frayed from beneath a further layer of warm looking coloured woollen jerkin.

"We thank you, Witch Way, for your greeting," and the chief amongst them, wearing a penannular brooch that pinned a frazzle of black wool to her shoulder, gave a courtly bow that Anna felt compelled to return. Behind her, Ailith, Charlie, and Emz did the same. The sense that the riders gave was of the oldest of friends. "We give our sorrow at your grandam's passing." At this all the riders gave a deeper bow and with the movement the women gave off a combined scent of sweat and horse, of leather and wormwood.

"Bring the warrior rest." One of the riders stepped forward, her voice soft, her arm stretched out to Ailith. "Let the glims light his way."

Ailith stepped forward; already, in the circle of glims, there was a hole dug, neat and deep. Ailith stepped into the light of the glims and as she did so they burned higher and brighter and the riders began to speak.

"Rest him by herepath…"

The Ways joined in at once, the words rising together in the soft night quiet of Yarl Hill,

"...and ridgewayed rampart, that he might be, at last, the Watchman at the Western Gate."

The flames burnt brighter, whiter, and the chief of the riders stepped forward and touched Ailith on the shoulder. Ailith knelt, and placed the head into the hole, the face outwards, watching, forever, the landscape beyond.

"Be wakeful, Watcher." The chief rider threw a handful of earth onto the head, the others followed, and then the Ways. The chief rider left Ailith until last. Ailith's handful of dirt scattered as if alive, rolling and compacting itself and the grass knitted back so that the small Bone Resting place was not visible. The glims lowered.

Anna watched Ailith's face, the tears that she was wiping away, and she stepped forward, put her hand on her arm.

"We can find a way for you, Ailith, don't worry," she reassured her. Ailith looked at her, her face stark and raw with fear.

"Her way lies with us," the chief rider said. Anna's hand did not leave Ailith's arm; if necessary there would be a tug of war. Anna felt protective. The chief rider smiled.

"We are the TaskMistresses, we ride and do whatever must be done. In the taking on of this task that she was not set, Ailith has proved she is one of our number."

Ailith looked uncertainly from the rider to Anna.

"This... this is my way?" Ailith asked. Anna looked at the chief rider, looked around at the others. One was already reaching into the saddle bag of the seventh horse and pulling out a woollen jerkin, a leather jacket, leather breeches, and a kilt, woven in a golden autumn yellow. Anna turned to Emz and Charlie. Charlie nodded.

"Seven horses..." Emz said.

"Six riders," said Charlie.

Ailith was already scrambling out of her own rags and into the leather breeches.

It was a cold walk back to Cob Cottage. Charlie, hands deep in pockets, frog marched ahead of them.

"The Lookout Line. How could I forget?" Anna was angry with herself and not a little anxious. "And Yarl Hill fort? How much time did we spend here as kids?" She looked to Charlie's back. Her sister did not turn.

"Loads of time but how could you remember it all?" Emz chimed in, trudging beside her. "There's so much to remember. We can't do it all."

Charlie halted.

"We can. We have to."

Emz and Anna looked crestfallen, but Charlie was harsh.

"We have made a mistake. A big one. We can't afford to be this careless. Ever."

They could not see her face clearly, but they could hear the edge of tears in her voice and when she turned away from them and began to stride once more towards Cob Cottage, Emz and Anna did not chase her.

It felt dark. It felt cold. Nothing would ever be the same.

31

NO REST WITH THE WICKED

After a successful Bone Resting and a wayfinding for Ailith, the Way sisters might have expected, hoped even, that the next day would be blue skies and blueberry muffins all round; instead it was burnt toast and bad dreams.

Anna had been up within a few hours of going to bed as she was on breakfast duty this morning. Emz was putting the finishing touches to a history essay and burning some toast, as, instead of her alarm, Charlie found herself being woken by a bad dream.

It had been the same dream all week. She had made her way out of the garden and the Wood and was in a rather elaborate greenhouse, something cobbled together out of what looked like driftwood trees. She was surrounded by pots of herbs and beyond the windows there were other beds and potagers that seemed to whisper in the wind.

It was the same sensation as in the castle. The herbage was trying to convey something. She glanced down at the lists she had made and began to shuffle them like playing cards; the lists blanked and refilled until she had one list and just as she was about to read it the wind caught it, slapped it against the window of the greenhouse so that it couldn't be peeled away. She understood at last what had to go onto the list and reached for a pencil. As she leaned on the paper to write the last herb on the list the pane cracked and at the sound she awoke.

Charlie sat with the list she had compiled at her bedside. It was by now several pages of crossing out and scribbling in and she turned the page sideways to fill a fresh space at the edge of the page. The pen hovered with her thought: what was that last herb? How had she seen it in the dream? There had been a scent. Charlie always dreamt in scents. Damn, she should have concentrated on remembering that. There was no use for it, she was too wired to try to drop back into the dream now.

WITH HIGH LEVELS of adrenalin white-water rafting themselves through her bloodstream Charlie offered Emz a lift and they left Cob Cottage.

It felt like a relief to be away from the cottage and in the relative normalcy of the brewhouse at Drawbridge. Even before she had pulled in at the car park Charlie had wound the window down to let the first scent of the brewhouse drift towards her. She breathed in deep, letting the breeze rustle at her rather untidy hair. Nothing. A vague whiff from the sewage works possibly, over in Castlebury. She grew uneasy.

At the brewery Michael's car was parked up alongside Jack's motorbike and the Morris Minor Traveller that Ryan borrowed from his gran when he'd pranged his Nissan. Charlie was surprised at the lack of visible brewery activity.

In the office Michael was sitting at the computer, his head balanced on his hand so that his cheek was crumpled up. He was staring at the screen, clicking idly at a game.

"What are you doing?" Charlie was harsh. What was going on today? She glanced down into the yard at the rear to see Jack and

Ryan squabbling, the squabble reaching the point of pointing fingers and heads jabbed forward.

"Losing." Michael's voice was low and sleepy. Charlie reached over and clicked the screen out of the game. Michael slumped sideways slightly. "You might as well shut it down, I'm shit at it."

"Get out of the chair and get the kettle on. Brew us some coffee. I'm going down to the brewhouse to see what isn't going on there..."

"We've got kegs and kegs of beer..." Michael smiled. "We don't need any more."

Charlie gave him a pinched look.

"This is a brewery, Michael. People drink the beer, we brew more." Charlie felt unsteady as she looked at him. There was something wrong about him, and she couldn't pinpoint it. Not simply his mood, something more.

"You have no idea how beautiful you are." He sounded mournful. Charlie felt a sudden spiking feeling in her chest, recalling the Apple Day fiasco and the way that Michael had nuzzled into her neck *"Charlie is my darling"*, blushing at the words, the kiss, his voice singing in her head. The blush seared over her face and she folded her arms, drew herself up taller.

"Have you been drinking?"

"No. I have been thinking. Much more poisonous." He gave a despairing sigh and stared at her. His eyes, usually *honeyed sugar*, were not honeyed sugar this morning. They looked blank and tinny. Clearly, he was suffering one hell of a hangover.

"Okay, well, you keep doing that and I'll run the brewery today." She was too tired to handle the emotions, her heart and mind lit with lightning bolts of confusion and desire. Busy. She needed to sort things out. She turned off down the stairs.

"When are you going to realise you love me?" His voice was only slightly raised, just enough for her to hear. The spike in her chest stabbed very hard and she did not look back.

As she entered the yard the squabble was about to become a

fight and so she stepped in and caught Ryan's fist as it flew towards Jack. Ryan's face was a dog's, snarling, bared. He pushed hard at her but Charlie, geed up with her own emotions, pushed harder, Ryan tripping over his own foot and stumbling backwards.

"What's going on?"

"Him... he's what's going on... Didn't put the kettle on for break. Ate the last effing BISCUIT." Ryan was spitting little dobs of white saliva in his fury. Charlie turned to see Jack sitting on his haunches crying softly.

"You. I want you up in the storeroom getting those kegs down for the pickup this afternoon." She pointed at Jack; at once he was happy, puppy-like as he jumped to his feet.

"Yes... yes... course... yeah... course... brilliant," and he headed off. Ryan was sweating anger.

"It's a biscuit, Ryan, get over it. In fact..." She had a brainwave, the solution to all the problems currently brewing, ha, in her tired head, pulled out a tenner from her jeans pocket, "...get over to Trim's Corner and buy us all some biscuits. And get more teabags and some milk while you're at it."

Ryan's face looked less red and more pink as he calmed and nodded. He gave her a sage look.

"You talk sense. For a woman."

Charlie gave a disapproving grunt and was glad to see the back of him as he climbed up into the cab of the Drawbridge van.

In the brewhouse she hung up her jacket and, to settle her mind, took a look at the paperwork she had on the anteroom table. Her lists leapt out at her, crossings-out and scribblings-in combined. She assembled them and took a look. She could see where the old gentleman in the dream had reproduced the notes from her head. Her instinct suggested that something was brewing here, something that was worth pursuing if she could just extract it from her brain. It was still, however, something of a puzzle to her and one she felt she would tackle better if she got today's normal everyday brewing under way.

Within a few hours Charlie was siphoning the sweet wort into the copper and sparging the mash tun. The air was filled with her favourite aromas and her mind swirled and steamed with the brew and was refreshed and clear after the last few days events. She had been relieved that Ailith had found her way, supposing that another option, a less Stuff option, would have been a job at the Castle Inn with Anna, bussing tables or washing dishes perhaps. Charlie scolded herself for trying to ignore the fact that she had shied away from the Word; after she had told her sisters off for calling it Stuff, now she was at it. She had said that not saying the word gave it power.

It had power. That was its whole purpose. She was afraid that in some small way her own blurting out of that word 'Magic', when they had discussed the head, had set something in train. She had released the power simply by saying the word. She knew it was not so in her brain, but in her heart and in her gut, she was unsure.

That was why the word was difficult to say once you had slept a few nights in Cob Cottage. Those Craft Club twats who were friendly with Roz Woodhill, fannying round the woods, skyclad and in their birds' nest tiaras, had no idea of the danger. They were running with scissors.

As Charlie cleared out the mash, she cleared out these thoughts. Then she grabbed up her lists and headed through to the smaller brewhouse where she had all her Blackberry Ferment experimentations stewing and distilling.

The scent in the small brewhouse was thick and summery and like hot fresh earth. She drained off a little of the Blackberry Bitter she was brewing. The liquor looked better than she'd hoped, the slightly brownish quality of the wort she'd fermented had begun to deepen to a rich and jewel-like purple. She held the glass up to the light from the high mill window and the sunlight shafted in. The scent was good too; just the right amount of sharpness, she thought. She was thinking that the Blackberry Ferment itself might end up too sickly sweet. She thought she'd tap some of that too, to taste what a further day had done to it and reached for another glass. The Blackberry Ferment was not sickly. The colour, once again, was rich and earthy and the liquid had come clear, no sediment floating or sinking. The scent was clean and wild and made her think of Cob Cottage, of the garden, of newly lifted potatoes. As she watched the sunlight shafted through this glass too and she noticed the small rainbow that splashed onto the workbench through the prism of the liquor. She put the Blackberry Ferment spirit beside the Bitter. The prism effect was beautiful.

She toyed for an hour or more, stirring, decanting, and taking more of the blackberries from the small freezer and starting another recipe, this time using the lists. It seemed to her that all the lists might end up being one recipe; there were reasons why she'd crossed out and scribbled in and now, looking over the five or six different versions, she took the remainders from each list. All the herbs she'd thought of combining were growing in Grandma Hettie's garden. If she got the wort boiling now she could leave it over lunchtime and pop back to Grandma Hettie's garden. Except that it wasn't Grandma's any longer, was it? *It's yours.*

Dragon. Without warning the word banged into her head, so loudly that she thought someone was behind her and spun round. She was alone. Dragon? What the...? Then she recalled the breaking of the pane of glass in her dream hothouse. The scents drifted across her memory. Her thoughts tumbled and rolled for a moment and then she wrote the words 'dragon' and 'wormwood' on her hand to remind her when she popped back to Cob Cottage at lunchtime.

Except that she didn't get back to Cob Cottage because at lunchtime when she headed into the car park, Aron was waiting.

He was leaning against the boot of his car wearing what looked like a new leather jacket.

"How's it going?" he asked. Charlie recalled their last encounter at Cob Cottage and the myriad texts that she had ignored. He checked his watch. "Got time for a bite of lunch?" and he opened the car door with a smile. Charlie hesitated.

"You should have texted," she said. Aron's face twisted into a wry smile.

"Surprise," he said with no surprise. "I know you love surprises." A wink because he knew, of course, that she did not. "I should have come naked, wrapped in a big red bow," he joked, his smile stretching across his face and across time, to the first moment she had ever seen that smile.

"Not if you don't want me to puke up the lunch." Charlie made no move to step into the car.

"I've forgotten about the whole Haunted Hell Cottage fight by the way," he mentioned, his voice casual, his face glancing at the interior of the car. Charlie looked at him. His eyes were a pale-ish blue underneath the glossily black-brown hair that he always wore slightly foppish and got away with.

"So not forgotten then?" she rallied. It was not going to be as easy as opening a door. He gave her an assessing look, shut the door and approached her.

"Hey. Round One. Ding, Ding…" He reached to brush her hair back from her face which made her remember that she'd slept in her pony tail and it was probably a Turk's head knot of hair by now. "What do you want to wrestle me for today?" He stood very, very close but he didn't kiss her, and she did not kiss him. Their kiss and make up standoffs were a matter of personal pride. He wanted to kiss her, she could see it in those pale-ish blue eyes and in the way he was pressing his lips together, trying to look serious. She moved close to him as she reached for the car door and reopened it. She climbed in.

"Wrestle you for who is buying lunch."

They drove off, at speed, Charlie trying not to see Michael standing in the office window, watching.

She tried not to see Michael, but the image of him, his arm leaning up against the curved top of the window, stayed in her head and was joined by the feeling of his nuzzling at her neck, his arms around her as she struggled to get him into the van. She was so busy trying to shove all of this aside that she did not see the car pulling out of Smallbridge Road until it was crushing into the side of Aron's car. The noise, the jolting motion that whipped her almost out of the seat, the world turned sideways very slowly and then stopped very quickly as the airbags punched them.

Aron was concerned for her, his hand reaching for her.

"You o…" but he got no further; the door was ripped open and the other driver, a stocky man, reached for Aron, wrenching him out of the car. The seatbelt stretched and twisted at his throat as Aron struggled with his assailant.

"No." Charlie yelled but the man would not let go. Charlie undid her own belt and lunged across, the airbags suffocating pillows. "No." Charlie could hear the fear in her own voice and the man now giving up on the notion of freeing Aron from the car, pushing him down, punching him.

"NO." Charlie was scrabbling forwards, leaping from her seat as the belt snapped back, "NO." Her voice was heavy as a door and as she spoke the door slammed forward into the attacker's back, knocking the wind out of him. He staggered back, punching at the metal and plastic assailant, before turning his feet to Aron, his left leg kicking. Hard.

"NO." Charlie's voice was like a sonic boom and the door slammed hard, closing out the driver. She reached for Aron, dragging him to her. His face was a bloody mess, but he smiled at her.

"I'm good… I'm good…" A tooth dribbled out.

THEY WERE some time with the police before Charlie rang the

insurance company and a courtesy car was sent, and they were some time longer before they finally rolled into the designated parking space at the marina complex.

Charlie helped Aron into the lift and he kept his arm around her shoulders. As the lift door closed Charlie did not feel very strong any longer; something gave inside her like a deep breath and she was going to fall.

"I've got you," Aron whispered into her hair, his arms knotting around her waist, holding her close.

ONCE AGAIN, the pane of glass broke in the hothouse and so she awoke beside the snoring Aron with the tinny silver light of the marina winking in through the windows. It unnerved her, reminded her of something, and with a jolt it appeared in her head, the look in Michael Chance's eyes. *Not honeyed sugar.* Tinny, diesel sheen grey.

These thoughts pushed her out of bed and she began to sneak about picking up her discarded things. Her other shoe must be in the living space. She tiptoed out through the sliding bedroom door.

"Where you going?" Aron's voice made her startle; she turned. He was standing naked, his hands on his hips. "It's the middle of the night, Chaz."

"Home," she replied. It was true.

"How? You walking there?" He tried to look nonchalant, tugged at his nose as he sniffed. "It's a long way back to your Mum's."

"Cob Cottage. Remember?" Charlie turned the handle of the front door. Behind her she heard Aron reach for his jeans and tug them on.

"Christ... you can't... look, let me find my shoes..." He grabbed a trainer from behind the chair.

"It's alright. I need some air."

He pulled on the other trainer from in front of the TV.

"Seriously Chaz... just wait until morning. We can go and have breakfast at the Boathook and I can run you back... or run you to the brewery..." She could tell from the way that he was concentrating on tying up his shoes that he was upset, on edge.

"No. That's alright." She turned to the door again.

"It's just a couple more hours," Aron said. "Come back to bed."

Charlie wanted to run. Fast. Far. She faced the door.

"Scrambled eggs," he said. "That weird sourdough toast you like. Big mug of Boathook special roast coffee."

Charlie couldn't speak. She rested her head against the door. Aron stepped up behind her. He didn't touch her, he leaned in close.

"I get it," he said, his voice soft and low and sounding so like Old Aron that it pained her even more. "I do." He brushed her hair back off her shoulder. "You and yours... you've been through shit this year. Through hell. I get it."

Charlie nodded.

"I just need to get home." She couldn't stop the tears. Aron pulled a little at her shoulder; she turned to face him. With his thumb he wiped at her tears, but he did not try to hold her.

"I just need you to know... I get it." He was reassuring and his eyes, she noticed for the first time in a long time, were glacial blue, light. They were eyes that she had looked into for a long time, forever almost, the eyes that saw who she was. She nodded so that more tears tipped out. Aron tugged on a sweatshirt and reached for his keys.

32

BEHIND YOU

Anna turned off the hotplate and considered the fact that there was no cleaning down to do. The bacon and eggs were untouched in their packaging in the fridge, the toaster was cold. No one had come down for breakfast. No one had wandered in off the street. She had never witnessed a morning like it.

Casey was away for a couple of days visiting her aunt in Kingham so there wasn't even anyone to share this with. Anna felt befuddled by it, considered texting Casey to ask what she thought, when Lella wandered into the kitchen.

It was nearly eleven o'clock but, far from being dressed in her usual hotel manager outfit, Lella was wearing her Hello Kitty pyjamas and a baggy old jumper. She was barefoot, her toenail polish chipped.

"Good morning," Anna said, watching Lella very carefully.

"Is it?" Lella asked, opening the fridge. "This place is buzzing as usual." She made a dismissive gesture in the general direction of the empty restaurant. Lella helped herself to some cheese by simply biting off a chunk from the wedge that was on the shelf.

"You alright?" Anna asked. Lella gnawed at some more cheese and picked out some cold ham as she nodded.

"Yeah. You?" Lella gave Anna an odd look. "Oh no… course not." She gave a pitying laugh. Anna did not ask any more questions. She stood in silence and watched Lella forage her way around the kitchen.

"I'm going to watch Jeremy Kyle, want to come?" Lella was part way through the door to the lounge, wedging it open with her body so that she could balance her snacks. Anna could hear the twangy music of daytime TV advertising. "You could go on that show, you know. With all that happened to you."

Anna tamped down the flinch inside her, managed a smile.

"I'll take a rain check," Anna said. Lella glared at her.

"Does it not get tiring? You lost everything. How can you try to be alright about it?" Lella asked, licking her fingers free of some chilli sauce. Anna did not reply. Lella waited a moment before giving a shrug and heading out into the lounge.

As she left, Anna turned the sign to 'Closed' and locked the front door to the inn. It seemed the best thing to do in the circumstances.

What were the circumstances? Lella was having a breakdown perhaps? Hence the PJs? Anna walked away from the inn.

At first glance Woodcastle seemed to be fine; that is, if you gave it the kind of cursory glance you might give through a car window when you were only half concentrating and had a map open in your lap. If you were a resident, then Woodcastle looked bad. Bits of homemade flag were snatched on the breeze and blown about.

The most obvious fault was the lack of traffic, due, probably, to the fact that the makeshift barricades were still in place. Although, this morning they looked less like a barricade and more like a load that had fallen off a skip lorry. As Anna thought it, a skip lorry began to reverse down Dark Gate Street, its warning alarm sounding mournful.

Things did not improve on High Market Place. Doors were

open, but the shops looked abandoned or looted; there was an emptiness about the place.

"Why aren't you coming in here? Why aren't you supporting your local shops? Hmm?" The butcher, Owen Greene, was standing in a bloodied apron haranguing a young woman with a pushchair. The sight of the pushchair alone was prickling at Anna but she pushed her own emotions to the side for a moment. Owen looked pale and desperate.

"I'll tell you why… you can get it all cheap at the supermarket. Yeah. Really cheap. This is my skill. My livelihood. You are a robber and a thief…" He was waving a knife at the woman who was reaching into her bag and crying, pulling out her purse and scrabbling around for coins.

"Look… look, I'm a vegetarian," she was repeating the phrase. The baby was mewling and miserable and was, Anna noticed, sticky looking. She took a step nearer. The child's face looked as if it had not been washed and there was a strong poo smell that was sickly and sweet.

"Get away from there," the woman swiped at Anna. "Get away from my baby," and she rattled the pushchair away.

The few people who were out were miserable looking, tearful, or arguing, even with themselves. At the bakery people were wandering inside and taking what they liked. Anna turned down onto Church Lane. The few shops were closed. Mimosa the florist had a window display of thorns; there was nothing to disguise them, no gypsophila to soften the effect, the window was crossed and tangled with leafless branches bearing barbs. It looked oddly safe to Anna as if it might be a good idea to push the door open and hide inside but the door was locked.

Next door Mari was having what can only be described as a jumble sale.

"What's going on, Mari?" Anna asked as she looked around at the almost bare shelving. Two women were squabbling over a quilt.

"Hang on..." Mari shoved a stolen pain au raisin into her mouth and reached for the big black dressmaking scissors she kept at the counter. It took three snips and then some rending of fabric to divide the quilt into two and as each woman scrabbled for her tattered portion and ran out, Mari turned back to Anna.

"Closing down sale. I'm off to that caravan. I'm going to work at the farm shop for my uncle. He's going all rustic chic..." Mari's gestures were wild and a little bit drunk as she drew the picture of her future. She leaned down to the counter for another pastry. "Going to open an organic farm café and all that. Quids in. And I'll get out of this dump."

Anna was quiet.

"God Anna, how do you even get out of bed in a morning? If I'd lost what you lost I'd be... I'd be..." Mari struggled to think what she might be and then she looked to Anna for an answer. "Aren't you just broken?" She peered closer, genuinely interested. "I mean... you must be, right?"

Anna held herself together with small shallow breaths.

"I'll see you around," Anna said and headed out.

"At the farm... remember!" Mari shouted.

As Anna walked through town she felt the metallic tang once again, the vibration of the air like a charge. She took one circuit of the castle walls and finding herself at the top of Long Gate Street she kept walking until she came to the gate that led to Havoc Wood.

Once inside she kept walking and kept walking and the lost wheels of Ethan's pushchair squeaked in her head.

"UGH. THAT BLOODY FYFE WOMAN." Winn shoved her phone into her pocket and grimaced. "If it's not one thing it's another." Winn looked tired. They were about to set off on a recce of the badger sett at Ridge Hill after Winn had had a tip off about possible badger baiting.

"What is it?" Emz asked, zipping up her daypack. Winn gave a big sigh.

"There's a dead bird wedged in the troughing." Winn was thoughtful, tapping her foot as she thought it out. "Right. We'll get over to Hartfield and sort that bloody Fyfe woman out and then we're free and clear to focus on the badgers."

As they headed out Winn put the twelve-bore in the back of the Defender.

THREE QUARTERS of an hour later and Emz was holding the ladder very tightly, not least because Winn was balanced right on the very top rung, the ladder leaning against the single storey scullery. Winn's safety was not what was bothering Emz, it was Mrs Fyfe.

The second that she had stepped out of the kitchen to greet them Emz had struggled. There was no disguise to this woman's real face, it leered out at Emz without her even trying to look for it. Angular and direct, the bones stretched against the skin of it but in a way that suggested strength rather than starvation or illness. Her eyes goggled behind the glasses but that was just the fake face, the joke eyes, the real eyes were intensely observant, unsmiling, cold as stones rimed with frost. Emz felt a compulsion to turn and run but she would not leave Winn with this woman. Her instincts screamed and growled. She needed to help Winn do this task and then they had to get out of there, quite fast.

"Oh. You have a companion today." Mrs Fyfe greeted them, evidently displeased at Emz's presence. Those eyes dissected Emz Way. Emz struggled for a second and then, unwilling to appear cowed or shaken, she pulled on her own brand of fakeness. She gave a wave that was so cheery her wrist hurt.

"Hey there… I'm Emz." On a sudden sharp impulse, she dared to offer her hand to be shaken but Mrs Fyfe looked at the hand as if it was tainted so Emz withdrew it with a bouncy giggle. Emz was channelling Caitlin very hard, keeping her face vapid and smiley. Her mind was pulling down the visor on an imaginary steel helmet, the kind that a welder might use rather than a knight. "Don't mind me... I'm just here to hold the ladder." She gave another giggle which thankfully Winn did not have to witness as she was busy wrestling the stepladder out of the coal shed.

With a clank and a clang Winn swung the ladder out, narrowly missing putting it through the kitchen window.

"Oh bugger." Winn cursed.

"I could go up there, Winn..." Emz offered, but Winn was already half way up, showing remarkable agility for a woman of her age and tweed attire.

"No problem. Just hold it steady." She motored up to the guttering to confront the clag of moss and dead leaves and rainwater.

"I need a bucket." Winn looked down, pointed to the bucket by the coal shed door, and Emz abandoned her post for just a second to fetch it.

As Winn slopped out debris Mrs Fyfe watched Emz. Her direct stare was making the hair on Emz's neck prickle to the point of pain.

"So... 'Emz' is it?" Mrs Fyfe took a step closer. Emz looked up towards Winn but kept her voice breezy.

"Yeah. Emz, with a 'zed'. You alright, Winn?" she called up. Winn barked something and some hideous black gloop splotted into the bucket.

"Emz. Is that short for something?" Mrs Fyfe enquired. Emz was feeling off, she had the sensation that someone was pulling at her hair and she wanted for all the world to pull back against it.

"You are some kind of assistant at Prickles then I presume? Miss Winn's servant." Mrs Fyfe left the name issue alone for a moment.

"Ooh yes. I love it there. Animals are so cute." Emz notched up the cheerleader cheeriness and glanced at Mrs Fyfe. The angular face gave a flashing grin of grim delight.

"So what is 'Emz' short for then?" Mrs Fyfe was, it seemed, obsessed with finding out her name. "Is it Emma?" Mrs Fyfe persisted. "Is it Eleanor? Elouise perhaps?" It was only going to be a few seconds before she reached for 'Rumpelstiltskin'. Emz kept her silence and watched the face for a moment, challenged the direct look, and as she did so there was a single blink from Mrs Fyfe. It seemed like a sign, a tell perhaps; at once the cheerleader insincerity vanished from Emz and with a mental flourish the visor flipped up sharply on the heavy welder's helmet.

"My name is Emily Way." Emz heard the confidence in her voice, felt the Strength behind it and, it was very obvious, so did Mrs Fyfe. The angular face backed away behind its white skin and googly glasses in an instant. Emz was taken aback at the reaction.

"Got the bugger." Winn waved a dead jackdaw from the top of the ladder. As she descended the smell came with her. The small corpse was draggled with rainwater and riddled with maggots. "This poor chap can go in the bin."

At the slightly cracked Belfast sink in the sunny corner of the kitchen Winn had got the worst of the grime from her hands and sleeves.

"Right. A lick and a promise will do me." She wiped at her hands with a rather grubby looking teacloth. Emz did not want to mention the freckles of mud that peppered her cheeks and forehead and neither, it seemed, did Mrs Fyfe.

"Oh, you must stay and have some tea," Mrs Fyfe offered. On the range a kettle was coming up to the boil, a hard, rattly sound that pittered at Emz.

"Oh no, we mustn't." Winn was flustered, the teacloth flapping in her hands. "We've got badgers to…" Winn struggled for the words "… to attend to and those hedgehogs are… rioting."

Emz had never seen Winn like this. Mrs Fyfe seemed to enjoy Winn's discomfiture. Emz did not.

"You must have tea… and also apple cake." She waved a hand at a dismal looking wedge of cake on a chipped plate on the table. The dry looking sponge was pitted with brown bits of apple and, as Emz looked at it, she could only see the jackdaw in her head, the maggots writhing in its breast.

Winn did not disguise her reaction, her tongue licking out in disgust.

"Oh no thank you… no offence but that last lot gave me appalling wind." Winn was grabbing at Emz's sleeve; Emz needed no prompting to move towards the door.

"Oh, but the kettle is boiling…" As Mrs Fyfe spoke the kettle began to whistle, low and insistent; the hair at the back of Emz's neck began to prickle like pins. Winn was holding onto Emz now.

"Please, take tea and cake… as a lovely thank you." Mrs Fyfe's smile, sickly and red with lipstick.

"No thank you." Winn's voice was suddenly strong and had the same impact on Mrs Fyfe that being hit with a shovel might. She looked aghast, took a slightly stumbling step back and Winn and Emz made their getaway.

They were pretty much running for the doors of the Defender, Winn driving off before Emz had got the door properly shut.

"Saints preserve us from Mrs Fyfe's cake." Winn spat the word. "Absolutely appalling stuff." Winn's face gurned through several degrees of repulsion.

"When did you have cake with her?" Emz braced herself against the swerve of the tight angle Winn was taking round the curve of the driveway.

"Oh God. The other day. Bloody Apple Day when I'd fixed the swan neck."

"The swan neck?" Emz had an image of Winn performing the Heimlich manoeuvre on a flapping water bird.

"Yes. That ruddy drainpipe thing over the kitchen. She INSISTED. Forced me." Winn grimaced. "I only ate it to take away the taste of the dreadful tea."

As they handbrake-turned out of the gates a familiar voice in Emz's head whispered *"Poison"*.

33

SLOW POISON

That night the patrol of Havoc Wood that the Way sisters undertook was not a pleasurable experience. An unspoken decision to stick together had been taken and almost the instant they left Cob Cottage things felt wrong. There was a terrible quiet as if the leaves themselves were holding still.

"Can you taste it? Smell it?" Emz halted as they stepped into the clearing on Ridge Hill.

"It's making me feel sick." Anna confessed. "Like carsick, that rattled and bumped feeling…"

Emz halted, her face losing colour, Charlie turning back a step or two to face them, her face bright with revelation.

"Poison." Emz and Charlie spoke in sync. Anna looked at them both.

"What do you mean?"

Charlie stepped up onto a fallen trunk, gesticulating.

"I mean, I said before we made a mistake. Well, that mistake was much bigger than we thought."

"Mistake? This isn't about the warrior's head then?" Anna looked to each of her sisters. Charlie was shaking her head.

"This is about Apple Day." Charlie was digging her hands into her sweatshirt again, her fists showing through the fabric straining at the seam. "Remember how Ailith said the meat had turned? That it was off?"

Anna nodded.

"This is about poison." Emz said. Charlie was nodding. Anna was looking at her sisters and trying to remain calm.

"Poison."

"Remember the Hillman wedding? How that all kicked off?"

"I thought we'd decided it was all due to the warrior's head?" Anna played devil's advocate.

"We were looking at something shiny. That was the day the castle called out and it was this stuff starting up. This poison." Charlie said, decisive. "The castle was sounding the alarm because we let a Trespasser into Woodcastle."

Emz's voice was very quiet.

"Mrs Fyfe."

Her sisters looked round.

"Who?"

"Winn's new tenant."

Charlie took in a gasp of recognition.

"Black hair. Goggly glasses?"

Emz nodded.

"You think she's the woman who followed Ailith? The one from the split oak?" Anna picked up the thread of logic. Emz nodded. Without another word Charlie hared off through the trees.

"Charlie?... Charlie?" Anna called out as she and Emz chased after.

As Anna and Emz emerged from the trees, Charlie, fizzing with energy, was already in Grandma Hettie's shed throwing out every carton, container, and watering can she could find. As her sisters approached, she took up the secateurs from the hook on the shed door and began barking instructions.

"We need all the blackberries we can pick and every water bottle we can lay our hands on."

"Isn't it a bit late to pick them? Didn't Grandma Hettie always say that after September they were touched or tainted or something?"

"Exactly the point. Get picking." Charlie chucked the wooden trugs at Emz and lobbed a selection of water containers into a nearby wheelbarrow.

"Anna, take all these inside and fill them, tap's easier than the stream, it's all Havoc water." She turned away to make her sweep of the garden, stooping suddenly into a patch near the shelter of the shed to snip at this herb, because this herb was tarragon, except that Grandma had always called it Dragon. She sliced at this plant too, taking a sprig or three, yes, that was right, oh how the wormwood had been nagging at her. She put them carefully into a small trug, the handle of which had been darkened over the years by Grandma Hettie's hands.

"Are you going to work out the poison?" Emz asked. Charlie shook her head.

"No. This is the antidote." She was moving methodically, cutting more of this, less of that. "This is what I've been dreaming about. I've been letting my mind wander over the herb garden and not listening to myself."

Inside the cottage Anna worked at filling the containers with Cob Cottage water and within an hour they were turning in at the Drawbridge Brewery.

Emz and Anna were roped in as assistants and as the copper heated the scent of the brew filled the brewhouse. It was a heady mix: as soon as one aroma entered your nose another was tickling at the back of your throat. Charlie was mixing and decocting the old matured Ferment with the new stuff. The scent intensified.

"I feel really thirsty," Anna confessed. Charlie stopped working for a moment and Emz offered her some water. Charlie watched her drink it. Anna's face was pale again and she looked tired.

"Here." Charlie poured her a shot of Blackberry Ferment. Anna looked at the small glass.

"I'll stick with the water," Anna said, but she looked at the glass with licked lips. Charlie pushed the glass forward.

"Humour me as they say." Charlie poured one for herself and one for Emz. The shot glasses chinked and with a look to each other the sisters knocked it back. It was rich and sharp. At once Anna felt her thirst and her fuzzy headed feeling dissipate. She looked at Charlie.

"It's like Mag..." Anna held back from the word.

"Yes." Charlie nodded. "That morning at Seren's, I gave you the Blackberry Ferment to knock you out." She looked at her sister.

"It's the antidote." Anna looked at the last glimmer of purple in the bottom of the shot glass. The Blackberry Ferment was delicious in the extreme.

"I think so. I gave some to Mr Hillman too after the wedding. It's the eyes. He had funny eyes."

"What did you eat or drink at the Apple Day?" Emz asked. Anna thought back. She'd gone hungry most of the day, not had an appetite and then...

"Pork."

Charlie looked uncertain. Anna held the thought. "With apple sauce. Drank some juice..." Anna's mind replayed the day. "Which actually I thought must have been cider because I reacted to it." It was so obvious from this angle.

"Definitely the apples." Charlie chimed in as she turned back to her brewing.

"There was apple in everything, in every shape and form..." Emz said.

"Cider at the Hillman wedding," Charlie chimed in, and then with wide-eyed realisation "and on Apple Day Michael said he'd had an 'apple tisane.'"

"Mrs Fyfe poisoned the apples."

"Why? What would she have to gain from it?" Anna asked.

Charlie gave a snorting laugh.

"You missed the full-on Cromwell meets the Sausage Riot on Apple Day." Charlie did not pause in her tasks. "She did it for a laugh maybe? An evil laugh? Who knows?"

Emz was looking very thoughtful.

"Power."

"Power?" Anna's mind was troubled by memories of how she'd felt on Apple Day. The sensation was a dark shadow sitting inside her, too close.

"She's like Nan Withers," Emz said, taking in a deep breath, "Remember?"

And, just like that, like a plug pulling out, they did.

THE DAY HAD BEEN SUNNY, and the Way sisters had been spending the week with their grandmother. Their mother, during that particular summer, had been in the Arctic on a research and development project.

Pike Lake looked like molten metal beneath the heat shimmer as they set off, Grandma Hettie carrying her red spotted handkerchief tied around a wedge of cheese slivered into slices, some tomatoes from the pint-sized Cob Cottage greenhouse, and a cottage loaf that Anna had baked this morning. It was high summer, and they had walked along the shore and into the shade of the trees, on through to the river, strolling by its rushing waters feeling the cool of it waft up through the forest of hogweed that towered even over Grandma Hettie.

Their intention was to head up to Frog Pond to go swimming. They had been up there each day for the last three and although the walk was long the reward of cold, clear water at the end was worth it.

On this day they did not reach the pond. Part way through the wood the air turned heavy and there was a metallic taste in the air.

"Thunder?" Anna said. "A storm's coming." The sisters were watching their grandmother, her sudden alert stance and thoughtful, distant look. Anna recalled that at moments like this her grandmother resembled a gun dog.

"Storm of sorts," Grandma Hettie said. The girls understood that now was not the time for chit-chat and they waited, holding their breath. The metallic taste was worse, the crooked daylight, showing through the trees, darkened perceptibly and a breeze began to blow through the trunks, tugging at their clothes. Anna felt dread, sapping down through her body making her feel heavy. It was as though she could see her energy being drained into the ground. Emz was wiping hot tears from her face and making no sound as Charlie gave an angry shout, picked up a fallen branch.

"Charlie…" Grandma Hettie turned, her hand offering a hank of the cottage loaf. "Here. Need to keep your strength up if you fancy a fight." Charlie snatched at the bread, snaffling it down. Grandma touched Emz on the shoulder; Emz's face was red with the effort of the stinging tears.

"Here. Soak up the tears, sweetheart." Emz nibbling the bread before Grandma Hettie turned to Anna. Anna sinking to the ground.

"Anna, take it." Anna's arms felt heavy; she could not lift them any higher, it was only the soft scent of the loaf, wafting to her nostrils, carrying an idea of home, of her baking this morning, that made her reach, take it. It tasted delicious. She began to feel better. Emz stopped crying. Charlie did not let go of the branch, but she did not wield it.

"Now, Charlie, you come up front with me and your branch." Charlie stepped forward with energy. As she stepped forward the old woman stepped out of the trees.

She was scrawny and thin, but her face was flushed. She smiled, a thin wide smile, and looked greedily at the girls.

"Quite a crop you got there, Hettie Way," she said, her voice breathless and high, the sound unpleasant. "Perks of being a Gamekeeper I imagine."

"On your way, Nan Withers." Grandma Hettie's voice, by contrast, was strong and familiar.

"Oh, don't mind me. I'm only passing through, only passing through." She took a few doddery steps closer and sniffed at Charlie. Charlie flinched a little, but Grandma Hettie put her hand on her shoulder.

"It's alright, Charlie. Nan Withers is on her way." The words were clipped-sounding and as Grandma Hettie spoke them Nan Withers gave what Emz could only remember as being a growl. Anna moved closer to Emz, put a hand on her shoulder. Nan Withers gave a disgruntled sigh.

"Yes. That's right. You Ways stick together. Yer big army," she sneered and leaned in close, grabbing at Anna's free arm. In the instant that she did so Anna was battered with images, of fighting, women weeping, of destruction, a wild storm of disaster threaded with the small and petty, resentment, jealousy, greed. As Anna thought she was going to fall into the nightmare Nan Withers pulled away, sharp. She looked at Anna and then at Grandma Hettie.

"This 'un," she pointed. Anna did not like the way the woman's finger felt, jabbing into the air in front of her, but before she could react Emz had stuck her finger out, was pointing it at Nan Withers, her tear smudged face fixed and angry.

"It's rude to point," and with that Nan Withers stumbled back. Grandma Hettie was smiling.

"That 'un," she said to Nan Withers and then, reaching her other hand onto Charlie's shoulders, safe, secure, she said, "And this 'un 'an all." Nan Withers made an outraged gasping noise.

"Would you like us to see you on your Way?" Grandma Hettie said, her voice heavy with threat. Nan Withers, with a shuffle and a stumble and a curse word or two, made her own way out through Havoc Wood.

"Change of plan," Grandma Hettie said as Nan Withers vanished from their sight. They turned off at Thornwicket, making their way through a sea of frothing cow parsley to a tiny tumbledown house.

Mrs Massey was the wrinkliest person that Emz had ever seen, her skin lined like a drawing, but her eyes were the sparkliest that Charlie had ever seen and as she wrenched open the door to greet them, her smile was the warmest and friendliest that Anna had ever seen.

"I need to get the plane on that, smooth it. It's been sticking in this heat," she said by way of greeting. "Come in, I've got the tea brewed. We can sit in the garden."

They sat in the garden and refuelled with scones and jam and small sandwiches which Anna helped Mrs Massey to make from the remains of the cottage loaf. The warmth in her garden was just right and the girls lolled in the grass and dabbled their feet in the small pond by the wall as Grandma Hettie and Mrs Massey caught up on gossip.

Later, as they walked home through a twilit Havoc Wood it was Emz who asked the question.

"Who was that Nan Withers lady?"

"Just a wanderer," Grandma Hettie said. "She goes around, makes people feel bad so she can feel good."

The Way sisters took in this information. Charlie thought of one of the girls at school.

"Like Jilly Watford?" Charlie thought that Nan Withers and Jilly Watford would get on very well together.

"Yes. Exactly like. Some people are drains, they need the bad energy, the bad thoughts…" she hopped across the stepping stones at Trickle Brook. "Then, there are other people who just radiate, want to make people feel happy. Kind people."

"Like Mrs Massey," Emz said, the sweet aftertaste of Mrs

Massey's strawberry jam lingering in her mouth, making her feel like skipping, so she did.

She slipped, her foot skimming the stone's edge so that she fell knee deep into Trickle Brook, her grandmother's hand shooting out to save her from falling headfirst, but everyone laughed anyway.

Their laughter rang out, pushed at the back of Nan Withers. Pushed her out of Havoc Wood.

THE WITCH WAYS took in a simultaneous breath and felt energy bump into them. Charlie smiled.

"Exactly. Like Nan Withers."

Anna thought of the nightmare images she'd been given that day and tallied them with the feeling of dread and sorrow she'd felt. Out of that negative there was a positive, a resolution.

"She's a drain." Anna thought of the heavy sadness of her grief amplified by the poison.

"She poisoned everyone and now she's feeding off the negative energy," Emz finished.

"But we can put a stop to her." Charlie waved her wooden spoon as though it was a wand.

34

THE CRIMSON BALL

"What do you think?" Charlie was staring into Lella's eyes. They had a distinct and tinny glaze to them.

"Why don't you take a picture? It'll last longer?" Lella was remarkably fighty for someone in Hello Kitty pyjamas. Anna watched her.

"I think she could do with a shot."

"It's that tinny look. Like diesel contact lenses," Emz chipped in. "I think that's what we've got to look for."

Charlie was pouring a shot from the rather cumbersome plastic flagon of Blackberry Ferment. As the liquid slipped into the tiny glass the light from the window caught in it. Even though it was rather grey and overcast the Ferment seemed to intensify the light and Lella stared at it.

"Pretty." She reached for it. Anna stopped Charlie handing it over.

"Is this okay? I mean… should we be doing this?"

Charlie and Emz looked at Anna.

"It's Magic. Poison magic. We're here to police it. I think it's more that we have to do it, it's our job," Charlie said.

"We're the Gamekeepers… remember?" Emz's face was a

frown. Anna nodded. Charlie offered Lella the glass and the shot vanished in a moment, Lella licking her lips in a rather fox-like manner, her teeth briefly stained blackberry pink. She held out the shot glass.

"Hit me," she demanded. Charlie poured another shot.

"Her left eye is not as tinny looking..." Emz declared, leaning into Lella's face. Lella's fighty mood was visibly softening. Her face took on a slight blackberry pink tinge as if she was flushed from exertion and then the flush faded, and her eyes were filling with tears. Charlie handed over the second shot.

"Bottoms up," Charlie smiled. Lella drank the shot, her tongue licking at the glass.

"Oh my god... that stuff is delicious." She began to cry. "It tastes of summer and happiness and oh... I feel so tired." The Way sisters made no attempt to conceal their observations of Lella's face.

"Yep. Her eyes are clear," Anna confirmed, and the Way sisters exchanged a look. Lella was wilting a little.

"I need a nap..." she yawned, and Anna helped her to the big saggy sofa in the guest lounge.

The sisters cleared up the worst of the mess that had been made as they waited to check that Lella was, indeed, fine.

"She's snoring," Emz said as the sound of Lella's snores drifted towards them. "That should be a good sign?"

The Way sisters' hopes struggled under a high tide of fear and uncertainty. Charlie held up her crossed fingers.

HALF AN HOUR later and Anna had made a pot of tea and scrambled some eggs and Emz was in charge at the toaster. Lella joined them in the kitchen and was, to all intents and purposes, completely recovered.

"That was one hell of a hangover," was her only comment and the Way sisters did not elaborate further.

There was one more experiment to conduct before they went public with the Ferment.

AT THE DRAWBRIDGE Brewery Michael Chance lived in the small cottage at the back end of the yard. The tiny garden backed onto the stream.

Charlie had knocked on the door several times and there was no answer. She looked up at the windows, no sign of life.

"You stay here, I'll go and recce round the back, see if he's there," Charlie offered as Anna knocked on the door once more and Emz peered in through the side window. Charlie opened the small squeaky wooden gate and brushed her way past the over-grown clematis that was swamping the side lane. The earth smelt good in the shadow it created, cool and scented with rain and sap.

Michael Chance was sprawled face down under a blanket on the wooden lounger. At first, Charlie wasn't sure if he was even breathing. He seemed too still, and her heart was beating so hard she couldn't hear anything else except for the insistent alarm call of a great tit. His skin looked too pale, almost grey, and his arm, draped down onto the floor, looked cold.

"Michael?" Charlie whispered, not wanting to startle him. She could hear the shake in her voice. Was he breathing? She watched the blanket; it didn't seem to rise and fall. She couldn't remember whether the night had been chilly or not. Had he been here all night?

"Michael?" Charlie's heart was a V8 engine of anxiety now. She looked at the back of his head where his hair was matted with leaves and clots of dirt. What had he been doing? She was hoping that the third time would be the charm.

"Michael?" At the sound of her voice his body rolled, his arm shot out, the muscles in his forearm tensing as his hand grasped her leg and pulled her down towards the blanket. As he did so Charlie was unbalanced and, as the blanket raised, and she saw he was naked, her mind ranged in two different directions, trying and failing to recover itself. His body folded around hers, his bad morning breath breathing at her as his hand smoothed over her shoulders, down across her hips to settle in the small of her back.

"Charlie is my darling..." He was holding her too tight, his mouth at her neck, the words mixing with kisses that were sending electrical currents down through Charlie. "When are you going to work it out? Too late when we're dead." His voice was mournful, the words cutting at her. "I want you, Charlie. No one else, but you look away." For just a moment Charlie let Michael Chance's hands roam across the surface of her, greedy and tender both. His hand clamped at her jaw and turned her face to his.

"Charlie," his mouth on hers, her fingers in his hair, feeling his breath, his chest move against hers, his heart, she could hear, pounding like a drum meant only for her to hear. She pulled away, Michael snatching at her as she reached for the plastic flagon and the shot glass from her pocket.

"Drink," she said, trying to wrestle an arm free. He grabbed, he clutched, and she let him. She wanted those handprints on her skin, even as the Ferment poured. He was looking directly into her eyes, his own tinny glazed and unsettling.

"I don't need one." Michael rose up, the blanket falling back from his naked body. Charlie gave a gasp and swigged the Ferment as he took a step towards her, pulled her a step back towards him.

"I need you." As Michael's mouth opened on hers she released the Ferment into his mouth, he swallowed and kissed her more hungrily. For a breath. Two. Three.

He coughed and spluttered, and Charlie stepped away from him, reached for the blanket and wrapped him in it.

"What? What the...?" Michael looked around at the garden, realised his lack of clothes and tugged the blanket tighter. "What the hell?" Charlie poured another shot.

"Drink," she commanded. He looked at the shot glass and a thought shadowed his face.

"Hair of the dog that bit you. Drink it," Charlie insisted. He looked at her, direct and ashamed. Charlie did not blink, stood strong as she watched the tinny glaze begin to drift from his eyes to be replaced with their familiar honeyed sugar brown. She offered the shot glass more urgently, pushing it at his chest so that a little tear or two of it spilled down the blanket. Michael looked at the glass for a second and then drank it as if it might be poison.

"Feeling okay?" Charlie asked. Michael was quiet, he gave her a long look and then nodded.

"You'll need a nap. Maybe not out here though." Charlie smiled. "I'll see you later," and without further farewell she headed back around the side of the cottage.

Michael felt the Ferment smooth and zing over his tongue, heightening and strengthening the taste of Charlie Way. He sat down on the lounger and hunched into the warmth of the blanket for a minute to try to gather his thoughts.

THEY WERE SATISFIED that the Blackberry Ferment was the key. Thus, the Way sisters raided the Drawbridge van for the stack of plastic shot glasses that Charlie had left over from Apple Day and headed into Woodcastle, three women with a definite plan.

A group of pensioners had gathered with shopping trolleys stocked with paint-filled balloons. As the Ways watched, an old gentleman bowled a balloon towards a passing car. Cheers and whistles went up at the pop and splatter of the white paint as it obliterated the windscreen.

Those who had partaken of the Apple Day delights were coming in from other parts of town to take part and to join in the general mood of road rage that was building. Voices were raised, swear words sparked in the air. Spittle gathered claggy and white in the corners of angry mouths.

The first bomb splattered onto Charlie's windscreen as the Way sisters rolled the car to the roadside, Charlie manhandling the flagon of Ferment out of the passenger seat and Emz and Anna dividing the stack of plastic shot glasses. It was no small matter to dodge the barrage of flying water balloons as they approached the group.

"Hey," Charlie challenged. "What the hell do you think you're doing?" A balding gentleman with a tartan trolley gave her the finger as another bent slowly to the trolley bag to pull out a missile. Emz deflected it as it lobbed towards Anna.

"Letting loose!" one old woman yelled and with a small crouching movement let rip a vast and trumpeting fart. Some laughed raucously, others were infuriated, little sparks and crackles of anger filtered into the air like a storm.

"Hey. Who wants a drink?" Charlie offered as she filled a shot glass with the Ferment. There were no takers. The pensioners jeered and as the woman in the brown cardigan and jeans started to punch a tall moustachioed gentleman in a garish golf jumper all attention filtered away from the Way sisters and their flagon of Ferment. The pensioners began a raucous chant of *"Bring it on. Bring it on!"* and headed off down High Market Place to menace some depressed looking teenagers.

A couple bickered past. Charlie blocked their progress.

"Free sample?" she said, the shot glass sloshing slightly onto the man's trainers. His face was at once a snarl, shoving at Charlie so that the shot glass fell, gave a flimsy crack on the paving stone, the liquid draining away making a stain on the paving slab.

"Hey." Anna stepped in between the man and her sister. "Back off." Her voice took on that deep timbre that Emz and Charlie recognised from the crematorium on the day of their Grandmother's funeral. The man backed off with an unintelligible string of swear words and he and his partner resumed their bickering.

"I want a baby and I'm going to have one." She was jabbing at his shoulder; he shrugged her off.

Charlie sat for a moment on the edge of the pavement.

"Well. No one said it was going to be easy." She looked at the Blackberry Ferment, sticky on her hand, and licked it off, felt better. "Okay." Charlie's confidence drained out into the paving stones. "Plan B anyone?"

"Yes." Anna was staring at the stain on the paving stone, the rich velvet berry red of it. Charlie and Emz looked at her. "Plan B, for Ball."

THE CRIMSON BALL was Lella's brainchild and the Moot Hall had been booked out. Tickets had been available for the last few weeks, but sales were disappointingly low.

"Thirteen." Lella looked despondent as she tapped at her tablet. "That's all. Not even a round number. An unlucky number! I should cancel. No one is interested." Charlie, standing behind Lella, Anna, standing at her side, and Emz, standing without thinking at the other side, looked across their triangle at each other.

"We're going to make them interested," Charlie said.

"How?" Lella looked unimpressed.

THREE HOURS later the Way sisters were spread through town handing out the crimson flyers declaring that the Crimson Ball was 'Tonight'. Prominent black letters informed all takers that there was a 'FREE BAR'.

"Crimson Ball tonight at the Moot Hall." Charlie's voice was commanding people taking her flyers "Be there, or miss out you losers," so that people snatched them from her.

Down at the bottom of Barbican Steep Anna was being more polite.

"Would you like to come to the Crimson Ball this evening?"

"No, I wouldn't. Crimson Ball off," said a skinny old lady in a polka dot dress. Anna, who had been drilled by Charlie before they left the Castle Inn, smiled and said,

"There's a free bar." At that news another woman grabbed the flyer from her.

"I look good in red," she said, with a sneer at the lady in polka dots: "Spotty."

The polka dot lady gave an outraged roar and a small scuffle broke out.

"What are they fighting about?"

Anna felt a jab in the back; she turned to see an old man poking his walking stick at her. "You a troublemaker?"

"They're fighting about the Crimson Ball. It's on tonight. Free bar and fisticuffs for anyone that wants to bring it." Anna was channelling her sister. "Come on to the Moot Hall if you think you're hard enough, Creaky." Anna kicked at his walking stick. The man gave a shout, his face reddening in fury. Anna walked off without handing him a flyer.

"Hoi. Gimme one. Come back here you effing bitch." He was waving the stick, attracting considerable attention. Anna could see where others were being drawn to the energy of the confrontation. What had Grandma Hettie always said about kindling a fire? Stack it, let the air breathe through it, breathe out flame.

"Can't have one."

She walked, not fast enough to lose him, just fast enough to annoy him. With each wave of his stick more people came, more people took the flyers.

"Oi, I know you, you're that effing cook at the effing pub!" As the Crimson Ball flyers flew from her hands, Anna felt like the Pied Piper.

Emz pinned the flyers on school noticeboards and put them onto seats in assembly. They were stuffed in pigeonholes in the staff room and slid through the doors of lockers.

At Prickles late in the afternoon she offered one to Winn.

"Come to the Crimson Ball?" Emz offered. She was looking at Winn; her eyes were their usual twinkling brown, a relief to Emz.

"Oh. Er. No thanks. Not my kind of thing."

"It's free and there's a free bar." Emz watched Winn, her eyes were definitely alright and the way she had been bustling about suggested that she was her own curmudgeonly self.

"You didn't go to Apple Day then?" Emz asked as they began the task of tagging the Canada geese at Cooper's Pond.

"Lord no. I did go once. When I was quite small and they still had the whole burning the effigy of the Apple Daughter thing."

"Apple Daughter?" Emz did not recognise this bit of local folk-lore. Grandma Hettie had never mentioned it. Winn winced a little and grimaced.

"Yes. Bit of a fiasco really. No one could find the matches and then it started raining. What you might call a damp squib." Winn gave a short barking laugh, "Ha, which is why they started calling a bad apple harvest, a damp squib. When the apples are all wizened."

Emz felt a little fizz of nervous energy at the idea of apples, wizened.

THE WITCH WAYS met back at Cob Cottage to make final preparations. Charlie had been troubled by the quantities of Blackberry Ferment and, since the latest batch had no chance at all to ferment and was therefore more of a strong cordial, she was now filling baskets of even more blackberries with Anna to take to the Crimson Ball sprinkled with sugar from Grandma Hettie's pantry. The kitchen smelt of earth and sunlight and sweetness.

Lella was already at the Moot Hall and Anna had said they would be no later than six o'clock.

"We can ship this lot down to the kitchen at the Moot Hall and you can make the crumble top. I can skim down to Drawbridge, pick up the Ferment. We need to not leave that unattended. Mrs

Fyfe managed to drive the Drawbridge wedding beer into a hidden corner at the Hillman wedding. I'm sure she'll be looking to stop us getting the Ferment down everyone's necks."

"Remember to bring some of the new Ferment, I can reduce it to syrup, pop it in the crumbles," Anna said, looking flushed and edgy "A top up? Yeah?" Charlie nodded.

"We haven't got anything red to wear," Emz said as they began to bundle up the sugared blackberry mess into tubs and plastic cake boxes. Charlie shrugged.

"Does it matter?"

Anna stopped in her tracks, looked across at Emz.

"Yes," they both said at once. Charlie took a frustrated step back from the blackberries, wiped the back of her juice-soaked hand across her forehead.

"Yes. Us not dressed for the ball leaves a gap, something incomplete. This is a spell. It must be right." She slopped some blackberries across the table. As she did so there was a knock at the door. The Way sisters halted.

"Mrs Fyfe?" Charlie mouthed to her sisters, grabbing up a handful of blackberries and lifting her hand as if they were a weapon as Anna gave a panicked shrug. The door creaked open a little and Seren Lake stepped inside.

"Hello? Hey. I'm glad I caught you..." she smiled. "I've got something for you."

THE WAYS ARRIVED at the Moot Hall less than an hour later, Charlie last of all, bringing up the rear with her cargo of Blackberry Ferment. She looked nothing less than regal in her sweeping ball gown, the rich red velvet embellished with blood red beading. The bodice, tight laced, showed off her figure and Charlie had to admit that she liked the swish of the skirt.

Emz, in light crimson lace, the dress slim and layered so that the effect was as if Emz was walking through a burst of red autumn leaves, was helping Lella with the dishes for the apple crumble which Anna was baking in the back kitchen.

Anna, a pinny over the black blood red shot silk of her bustled dress, the neckline high, culminating in a tall lace collar, pricked with garnet coloured beads. The scent of the blackberry crumbles baking in the vast stainless steel oven was rich and enticing and Anna moved to the fold back doors that led from the kitchen into the main hall. She unhooked the panels and opened up the space: a blackberry scented cloud wafted into the Moot Hall.

Outside there was the rumble and raised voices of the citizens of Woodcastle.

"I'll take a look..." Emz hitched her ball gown up and clattered up the wooden stairs at the side of the room that led to the minstrel's gallery and the rows of leaded windows. She stood up on tiptoe to look out.

The street was swarmed with people, a tomato soup seethe of fighting, shoving, pushing, and singing, the protest like a round, layered over each other, chanting and wild.

"Why are we waiting...?" came a clapping chorus, feet stamping, "Wh-y are we waiting?"

"I think everyone's here." Emz said nervously "And I mean everyone." She hurried down the stairs, hovered by the door. "What do you think?"

Charlie looked up from her bar preparations. Anna took off her pinny.

"Let them in," she said to Lella.

THE SHOT GLASSES glinted like stars, Charlie and Emz barely keeping up with the demand. At the kitchen trestles the crumbles were being snicked away, some people eating them straight from the bowl without bothering with a spoon. The evening wore on; the squabbles and tears began to dissipate as the antidote took effect. The music grew softer and slower, couples moving together to dance, kissing and making up. Children running about, skidding across the shiny wooden floor of the Moot Hall before everyone began to feel rather more tired than they'd felt before in their life and, taking hands, saying neighbourly farewells, making plans to meet for coffee tomorrow, to swap the Book Club latest, the people of Woodcastle headed home.

35

BONE MAGIC

Winn had rolled up at Hartfield in the Defender and was unwilling to leave the vehicle. She sat in it for several minutes as the rain deluged down, blurring the view she had of Hartfield Hall's grand entrance. She had not used that entrance overmuch in her life; generally, as a child she had used the back door in the kitchen, spending much of her time with the house-keeper Mrs Walters.

Her annoying tenant, Mrs Fyfe, had telephoned again this evening, this time concerned about an intruder in the garden. Winn had listened to her talk about the stranger and the prowler and the invader though she was not personally convinced.

"Are you sure it wasn't Leo on his round?" Winn had been determined to pursue all leads before actually having to head to Hartfield. Why hadn't the blasted woman gone to the Crimson Ball with everyone else?

"Leo? No. It was not the postman. Or a delivery man. Or a reli-gious maniac. It was an interloper, an outlaw," Mrs Fyfe insisted. She was getting quite heated. So, with all possibilities eliminated Winn felt duty bound to head over to her ancestral home and check it out. Winn felt she might take an opportunity to inform Mrs Fyfe that really there were very few trespassers at Hartfield and the ones that did wander in were generally just enjoying the view rather than casing the joint. Everyone knew that there was nothing to steal at Hartfield unless you were keen to expand your national collection of moulds and fungus.

Winn did not like her tenant. It wasn't just an irritation at the being called out for every tiny inconvenience, it was the woman herself. Sitting in the Defender listening to the rain Winn understood that she was afraid of Mrs Fyfe.

She could see the front door opening and so, unable to put off the moment any longer, she gathered her coat around her and reached to let herself out of the car. As she did so the little leather pouch she always had slung around her neck was squidged into the slightly crepey skin of her chest. It gave off a small amount of bodily warmth and a delicate whiff of old leather that was, at once, comforting. Winn resolved to tackle Mrs Fyfe, see off any intruders, and head back to Prickles for a cup of tea, soon as.

It didn't help that as soon as Winn stepped from the vehicle there was an almighty sky-rending crack of thunder.

"What dreadful weather," Mrs Fyfe said as Winn dashed over the threshold of the hall. Despite it being only a few feet from car to door Winn was dripping sheets of storm water from her raincoat. "Here... let me take your coat." Mrs Fyfe reached for Winn, but Winn pulled away.

"Not necessary. I'll be off out again in a moment to hunt down your mystery guest." Winn wiped the rain from her fringe, flicked the water onto the parquet floor. "So. Where did you see this... erm... miscreant?"

"In the grounds." Mrs Fyfe's eyes were particularly googly today. In fact, as Winn looked they seemed to be wandering a little, one in one direction and the other, ugh, trailing off in the opposite, like stray marbles.

"There's fifteen or more acres including the woodland, you're going to have to be more specific." Winn was feeling slightly chilled; the rainwater had found its way in through the shoulder seam of her coat where it was worn through.

"It was in the wood, at the edge. They were skulking." Mrs Fyfe relished the word. The thunder pounded once again. This time Winn thought that it sounded scared. Mrs Fyfe reached to a nearby hall chair and pulled on a black leather cape. "I can show you." She pulled up the hood, her face disappearing at once into its darkness as the storm outside began to shut off the light inside the hall. Mrs Fyfe opened the door.

"Shall we go?"

The rain hammered, and Winn was wishing she had brought the twelve-bore from the back of the Defender as they made their way across the lawns to the edge of the wood. Leap Woods simply ended where the mowing began, the trees never shifting forwards, no stray saplings ever having dared to disobey her father's rules. The wood was the wood and this was its boundary, beyond that was horticulture and formal bedding. As she thought of her father she realised that she was leading the way and turned to Mrs Fyfe.

"You know where you saw them, shouldn't you be leading the way?" she suggested and Mrs Fyfe, sunk deep into her leathery hood, halted.

"You know the way." Mrs Fyfe's voice curled out of the darkness of the hood and she didn't move forward. Winn stood her ground. The rain was now a small tributary coursing down her neck and she was quite enjoying the feeling of it.

"But you know where you saw the trespasser." Winn was losing the little thread of patience that had been spun by the bag of cash Mrs Fyfe had stumped up at the beginning of her tenancy. Mrs Fyfe stood her ground.

"You lead. You know the way." Her voice was small but cold and hard and unpleasant. Winn gave a little shiver, on account of the cold rain.

"I didn't see where the trespasser went," Winn insisted. The rain had flattened her hair completely and was now starting to form a curtain of water down her face. She wiped at her eyes again.

"You know the way through the wood," Mrs Fyfe pressed. Winn took in an impatient breath and was rewarded with a small shot of rainwater, cold and bright tasting. She spluttered a little and had a sudden moment of clarity.

"Is it Wednesday?" Winn asked. Mrs Fyfe looked furious.

"What?" She made the 'wh' sound like a small whip, lashing at the air.

"It is. Ha. Mystery solved. They weren't strangers or trespassers. It would be the Rambling club. They have permission to come through the wood on their Wednesday Wander… Ha." Winn's laugh echoed back into Leap Wood, knocking against the trees like a woodpecker. Of course, why hadn't she thought of that sooner? She took one step back towards the house.

"No. Look. There." Mrs Fyfe pointed with some energy into the trees. Winn looked and saw nothing.

"I don't see anyone…" she peered; she didn't have her glasses on so that might be a factor.

"Look. There." Mrs Fyfe's finger was very pointy and commanding. Winn was torn for a few moments. If she headed off now Mrs Fyfe would only call her back later. This had to be locked down, didn't it? Winn took a deep and resigned breath and moved a few steps into the trees. Beneath the thinning autumn canopy the rain pattered and sounded anxious. Winn tramped further into the wood, thinking that it might serve Mrs Fyfe right if she led her on a little hike. The woman was hardly dressed for it, what with the leather cape and the black dress and those funny little black boots she had, like Victorian boots, thin and useless. Winn tried to think of a good route through the woods that she would enjoy and which might tire Mrs Fyfe out. Ha. Yes. Up towards the back end of Cooper's Pond should do it.

"Up this way..." Winn turned to direct Mrs Fyfe. "Mrs Fyfe?" The woman had vanished. Winn stared for a moment at the spot where Mrs Fyfe had been standing. The rain pattered a little harder, a little more anxious. "Oh for Heaven's sake." Winn looked back towards the lawns, hoping to see a retreating figure heading towards the mostly dry shelter of the hall. There was no sign of anyone. The thunder rattled once more; it felt to Winn as if it was shaking at her shoulder, trying to get her attention.

"How rude." Winn licked some rain off the end of her nose and turned back to the woods. She could see Mrs Fyfe scurrying through the trees further down. "What on earth?" Winn watched her for a moment. Mrs Fyfe turned to glance back and disappeared deeper into Leap Woods.

"Mrs Fyfe?" Winn hesitated. She was not really up for this sort of shenanigans. She took a step back towards civilisation, thinking of the dry of the Defender and of the twelve-bore in the back. Plus, there was half a packet of chocolate HobNobs in the mapbox. However, it was starting to get dark and if Mrs Fyfe came to grief it would be Winn who was sued. Winn had a vision of her tenant chewed by foxes. Bugger the woman.

The wood was muddy and draggled but Winn found her way, surefooted. Deeper and deeper they were going, right off the usual path into the old heart of Leap Wood. Part of Winn was enjoying the hike: the rain made the earth smell particularly, well, earthy. There was nowhere really that Winn felt more at home than in Leap Woods. On and on she tramped; ahead of her twigs snapped or branches whiplashed and waved to show where Mrs Fyfe had passed before her.

All at once she could see Mrs Fyfe ahead, still glancing back every few steps as if to make certain that Winn was sticking with her and that was the moment that Winn knew. It was such an old, old sensation, she was whizzed backwards, back to being nine. What had Mrs Walters always said? Keep to the path; and where was Winn? She'd done it again, worse than all those years ago.

With a startled breath Winn reprimanded herself and turned. As she did so the bough came smashing through the air with the power of a steam piston.

There were stars, a galaxy of them sparkling in the leaves of Leap Woods; it was very beautiful and distracting. Winn could not be distracted because now there were two or even three of Mrs Fyfe and they were all carrying a heavy bough as if it was a club. She was standing over her, the bough lifting, trying to fit itself back into the dead tree from which it had fallen and Mrs Fyfe was trying to help it, wasn't she?

At the last second energy pulsed through the floppy and semi-conscious Winn and rolled her out of the path of the blow. The heft behind it sank the bough six inches into the soft woodland leaf litter and its dead bark burst into the air like welding sparks.

"I pin you." Mrs Fyfe was spitting the words, hard, as she brought the bough down, this side, that side, each time Winn's limp body rolled or spun out of the way. "I pin you," but Winn would not be pinned. With a wild growl Mrs Fyfe abandoned the bough and stepping her black booted foot forward she pinned Winn's right wrist beneath it. Mrs Fyfe's face leaned down into Winn's.

"I. Pin. You." Her other foot stamped on Winn's left wrist, the sound of bone cracking could be heard all through Leap Woods as if every tree had snapped in two, the sound ripping and tearing through the wood, on, skimming itself over Cooper's Pond, on, renting the air apart as it rushed onwards, forwards, rattling the ground.

Mrs Fyfe gave a scream of agony and stumbled back. Winn, her head aching but her vision restored a little, could see only one of her now, but that one woman had an ankle that was broken so cleanly the foot was now turned the other way. Mrs Fyfe screamed but the sound could not be heard beneath the after-shock of the bone cracking.

"YOU." The sound from Mrs Fyfe was like the wind rattling

and it blew back the hood, her face staring at Winn with fury, her skin white as snow as she reached for the bough once more. Winn lifted her arms to protect herself, but the blow did not come. When she found the courage to put her arms down, Mrs Fyfe was gone.

36

AFTERSHOCK

The Witch Ways had changed out of their ballgowns and, tired and uncertain, came out onto the porch at Cob Cottage, Anna handing out coffee.

"It seemed to go well," she ventured. Charlie nodded, her face giving nothing away.

"Seemed to. We just have to wait and see." They shared an anxious glance. With an anxious gasp Emz stepped forward, her mug dropping from her hand, bouncing and cracking down the steps.

"What's wro...?" Charlie began and was halted as the wave hit them, a sound tearing across town, screaming across bark and along bough, rattling leaves, the surface of Pike Lake suddenly dipping deep, a concave grey mirror that swirled, the water no longer sloshing at the shore but skidding like a blade.

Beneath them the deck creaked, and the ground rumbled, the vibration growing more intense until it became another sound, harsher, that pierced in through ears and needled into bones. Charlie gave a pained gasp as she stood up, Anna's skin paling to a shade of green that flushed out of her and left her looking ashen, her lips blue lined.

They looked at each other, standing in their triangle, Emz at the apex this time, standing at the front of the deck, and Charlie and Anna making up the lower corners. The sound kept travelling and, they could see, it made its way into the deep pewter bowl of the lake where in an instant, it was swallowed. The lake water settled, the trees seemed undisturbed, the ground was still.

A quick glance to Woodcastle showed only streetlights, no panic or wakefulness or sirens wailing.

"What the hell?" Charlie whispered.

"Where did that come from?" Anna asked. "Did you spot which direction?" Anna glanced back into the wood at the rear of Cob Cottage. The trees there seemed undisturbed even where, a moment before, they had been echoing with the sound. "Has it left a trail d'you think?"

Emz was already stepping off the porch.

"Hartfield," was all she said before she began running. "Mrs Fyfe." She was ploughing down to the shore, swerving towards the trees. Charlie thundered after her. On the edge of Charlie's vision, a path had winked into view. Quicksilver bright. She dragged at Anna.

"What's wrong?" Anna struggled to keep up.

"Wait." Charlie bellowed after Emz who blundered onwards. Charlie dug deep, her stride lengthening, her arm reaching to snatch at her sister's sleeve. Emz shrugged her sister off.

"No time. We have to get to Winn." She was distressed, staggered forward. Charlie caught her, shoved her and Anna towards the left.

"This is the way."

The path was thin as a fox trail, the girls racing along it in single file, Charlie ahead of them never missing a step.

As Charlie burst out of the trees at full speed Winn Hartley-Hartfield toppled backwards in surprise and landed, not heavily, on a large bank of moss that had once, about a hundred years ago, been a fallen elm. She was shaken and jolted, all the breath kicking out of her, and she thought of weaponry as she turned to see who or what had exploded at her out of the wood.

"Emz?" Winn's heart fluttered back into a reasonable time signature, something like a waltz as opposed to the fandango it had been embarking upon. Emz leapt into her personal space, her hands reaching for Winn as Anna and Charlie checked for the presence of Mrs Fyfe.

"You okay?" Emz spoke in a hushed voice. "What happened?" Emz did not try to make Winn stand up, rather she held onto her arm and sat beside her, her eyes tracking over her friend and employer looking for signs of damage. She looked a little greenish and there were some twigs in her hair but realistically, there were always twigs in Winn's hair.

Winn was struggling with the memories of the evening. There was one version that was a blurry nightmare. As she tried to pull focus on that Winn felt the small leather pouch around her neck generate a little breath of heat and she felt safe. This was Emz Way she was talking to. This was Hettie Way's granddaughter.

"Mrs Fyfe, that's what happened," although Winn could not recall details. "She… was rambling out in the garden… she…"

Emz had noticed the bump on Winn's forehead.

"That's okay. Don't worry about it. We need to get you back home." Emz looked at the bump on Winn's forehead and, concerned, she reached up to examine it. She touched it delicately, her fingertips brushing at the broken and inflamed skin. As she did so she saw the bough rise in the air, saw the black boots, the white face leaning "*I pin you*" and then the searing shock, the twisted foot. Emz saved all this information and set it aside for a moment to concentrate on the wound, it was clean and *if she just moved this and cleared at that.* Winn gave a deep, relaxed sigh and her face took on a pinker hue.

The Defender was parked at the hall and so that was where Emz and Winn headed. As they reached it, Charlie and Anna were already there looking winded and red-faced from their travels.

"Winn? Everything okay?" Anna reached for Winn's arm to steady her. Winn leaned into her. As she did so Anna's mind was fluttered through with black butterflies leading a procession of images. *Black boots. A bough. A cape. I pin you.* She stopped herself reacting in time and Winn escaped her grasp, stepping closer to the vehicle, her hand, Anna could now see, shaking visibly.

"Winn?" Anna was concerned. She looked to Emz for reassurance. Emz nodded. Charlie stepped in to help Winn as the key scraped along the paintwork.

"Whoa... hang on, let me..." Charlie took the key from Winn. In the second she did so there was a rewind of memory, *black boots, a bough, I pin you.* She did not glance at her sisters, instead she concentrated on the vehicle. *Black boots. Bough. Pin.*

Charlie held onto the keys. "We should get you inside the house, take a look at that cut," she pointed to Winn's temple. Winn snatched at the keys and got into the car.

"I'm not going into Hartfield. I'm going home." She started the engine. Anna opened the back and climbed in, Charlie following suit with Emz strapping herself into the passenger seat.

"Good idea," Anna said.

"You okay to drive, Winn?" Charlie asked. Winn gunned the engine.

"Probably not," she said, and they shot off down the driveway.

IT WAS CARRIE, the vet, who was called out to check on Winn's head injury and pronounce her fit.

"She's the only medic I trust," Winn had insisted and, since Winn could be very insistent, the Way sisters were only too happy to contact Carrie. Carrie, as it turned out, was content to make a house call for her sole two-legged patient.

"So, what happened?" Carrie asked as the Way sisters made tea and watched Carrie put a couple of stitches into Winn's forehead. "Did the badger win?" she joked.

"I tripped in the woods," Winn blustered. "Bloody stupid oaf of a woman. I ought to know better. Going out in a thunderstorm for a start!" Winn gave out a withering bray. "And I hadn't even had a snifter."

"What made you go out into the woods?" Anna asked. Winn looked less certain, her eyes holding Anna's gaze as if the answer might be in her face.

"Not sure really…"

"The Defender was parked at the hall." Charlie offered the information "So you must have gone there first, not just wandered into the woods from here."

Emz was keeping very quiet. In her mind she was flicking through the small images that had burst into her mind when she touched the bump on Winn's head. *The boots. The bough. I pin you.* When she looked up Anna looked away.

Winn's expression crumpled into thought and she made her usual harrumphing sound. "That's a point… Ha. Now I recall. That bloody Mrs Fyfe woman had called me out on some stupid landlord errand." Winn clapped her hands on her thighs and reared up a little in the seat so that Carrie had to adjust her stitching a little.

"Steady on there, Winn," she said, reaching to snip the suture.

"Yes. That was it, a load of nonsense she was talking, and I was feeling miffed and so I thought… what did I think?" Her gaze settled on the floor this time, on the Persian rug which was worth in excess of ten thousand pounds, but which Winn used for drying the dog. "Ha. Yes. Thought I'd take a wander up to Cooper's Pond, work off the… you know… the thing… the stress." She waved her hand; her face had taken on a little more of its usual reddish glow. "Am I done?" she turned to Carrie who nodded. "Not going to slip me a worm tablet?" she joked as Anna handed round mugs of tea. Carrie shook her head.

"I've given up trying, Winn. That and the flea collar."

Emz was not freaking out. That was another small side

thought that nudged forwards now that she had gone over the important details. She was not freaking out because as she revisited the images in her head that she'd sifted out of Winn she saw that Winn was wearing, in the memory, Grandma Hettie's black waxed raincoat.

It was an hour or more later that the Way sisters made their way swiftly and with distinct purpose back through Leap Woods to Hartfield Hall.

"We did this." Emz was shaken.

"You didn't hurt her. Mrs Fyfe did." Charlie turned to Emz, shutting her down swiftly.

"Mrs Fyfe was here all the time and we didn't see." Anna did not need to remind them. Charlie glared.

"Yes. We're idiots."

"No. We made a rookie mistake that we won't make again," Anna insisted. Their mistake loomed too large. "Think she's still here?" Anna asked as they yomped up over the tumbledown drystone wall that draggled and ranged at the most distant edge of Cooper's Pond.

"We'll find out soon enough," Charlie said, and as they began to climb in earnest up through the plantation towards Hartfield they grew silent.

They came over the boundary at the raggedy edge of Leap Woods near the back door of Hartfield Hall because, without them exchanging this information, they all remembered that this was the route Grandma Hettie always took.

They left the heavy cover of the wood for the gone to seed tangle of the former walled garden, stepping in through the mass of moss and rot that had once been a gate, the only remnant of its past history a rusted latch and thin strip of blue paint that had been colonised by lichen.

The walled garden was pungent and knotted with plants and

shrubs left to return to the wild. The Way sisters, once again with muscle memory flexing deep inside, trod only the path already trodden by the fox so that, at a glance, no one would know that anyone had walked through there.

At the far end of the walled garden they would have to climb through the small gap in the tumbledown bricks by the arched black gate.

"Listen. When Winn handed me the keys... I thought I saw a... like a flashback?" Charlie said. Anna turned.

"The black boots and the twisted ankle?" she asked with a grimace. Charlie nodded.

"I pin you," Emz whispered. They all took a breath. "Mrs Fyfe," Emz continued. "Trying to kill Winn." The words whispered into the dark and were scrambled into the desiccated stalks of the nearby fennel.

"We cut off her power in town," Anna said.

"So, she went for Winn as her nearest available backup." Charlie was shaking her head at the thought.

"Well, it backfired. Whatever it was she was doing." Anna tried to sound positive but her mind was drinking in fear and darkness.

"How do we know that?" Emz looked uncertain.

"Her twisted foot," Anna said. "My guess is the bone that was supposed to break was Winn's."

Charlie nodded.

"Okay. Right. So, we know what we're up against."

"Do we?" Emz asked.

There was a brief moment before Charlie blurted out.

"No. But we'll learn," and was first to edge out through the gap in the wall.

THE BACK DOOR was open and the rain had come in and made itself very at home on the kitchen floor. There was, the Way sisters noted at once, a very strong scent of rotting apples.

Charlie reached for the light switch. It clicked but darkness remained.

"Power's out."

Anna gave a small, scared laugh.

"Of course! Duh!"

"Torch." Emz was relieved to see it hanging on a hook above the drainer. She clicked that on, a beam of white LED light illuminating the space.

A quick tour of the house showed that no one was home, but the strong scent of apples lingered everywhere.

"That apple pong is strong isn't it? Think she's left any behind?" Anna sniffed deeply. Charlie nodded. They were all three sniffing now, trying to locate where the smell was emanating from.

"It was strong in the kitchen," Emz suggested when a trawl of the cellar, the billiard room, library, and sun parlour had revealed nothing.

The basket of apples was in the larder.

"First place we ought to have looked really," Charlie suggested as the white LED torchlight shone onto the blood red skin of the apples.

"We're new at this," Anna excused them. Charlie grunted.

"What? Food storage 101?"

Emz was feeling sick. The apples seemed to be giving off a black smoke.

"Are they on fire?" she asked, taking one small step towards the larder door. There seemed to be nothing to breathe but apple air.

"On fire?" Charlie asked peering at the apples, leaning as close as she could without actually touching them. "No. Why?"

"They look like there are wisps of black smoke threading out of them." Charlie backed away from the basket and she and Anna exchanged a look.

"You're the brewer, what are you getting?" Anna asked. Charlie, she had noticed, was breathing in very shallow breaths.

"All sorts. Like a fungal smell. Layered up with..." she took a sniff "... blood I think, metallic and rotten tasting in the back of your throat. Must. Fowst. Really old smell that I don't recognise."

"How do you know it's old?" Emz asked, taking another half step towards the haven of the kitchen.

"It tells me. Very dry." Charlie was stepping away from the basket. "I have to get out of here." She pushed past Emz and took in a gasping breath in the kitchen.

Anna looked at the apples. She smelled almost nothing other than rotting, slightly sweet apple and the skins were, to her eyes, black, a dense velvet black that she did not want to look into because, she knew, it looked back.

"What do we do?" Charlie asked.

"She isn't here." Anna ought to sound relieved but she did not feel it.

"She's not here at the minute," Emz said.

"The incident with Winn, the bone thing going wrong, back-firing. That's the signifier. We're rid of her." Anna made the suggestion. "I'd run if that happened, wouldn't you?"

"Fingers crossed," Charlie reasoned. "She might hobble back at some point for the apples though."

They all looked at the larder door which seemed to creak a little wider open.

"We could use the apples as bait then," Emz suggested. "Trap her." Charlie and Anna looked at their sister.

"And do what with her?" Anna asked. Emz thought for a moment and then shrugged.

"I hadn't taken the plan that far," she confessed.

"But it is something we need to think about," Charlie said. "In case she does come back."

Anna considered for a long time.

"We can't feel the magic any longer. Can we?" Anna looked at her sisters. They focused on their feelings and their surroundings. They took several moments about it.

"Apart from the whiff of the apples I think it's an All Clear." Charlie gave a deep sigh.

Charlie, Anna, and Emz walked back across the yard to the walled garden and, snitching themselves back through the tumbledown wall, felt better. They walked with confidence and in silence up through the walled garden and back into the edge of Leap Woods where their feet automatically turned left as they traced the edge of the trees until Leap Woods began to leak into the edge of Havoc Wood. They crossed the stream by the fallen stone, the old lion face carved in the edge of it, just nosing above the waterline so that it didn't wear out.

They were silent for a long time, each sister in her own thoughts. Their footsteps ranged up towards Top Ridge and walked along for some distance. Through the trees the moon glinted on the windows of the rear of Hartfield Hall making it look like a doll's house.

They walked without speaking, each locked on their own thoughts about events. Emz found her mind rewinding back, over and over, recalling the picture she had gained from Winn.

"She was wearing Grandma's coat," Emz said. The Ways halted.

"Who was?" Her sisters looked at her, their voices once again ringing against the wood. The sound was a good one, it bounced back at them.

"When I touched Winn's head... I saw the boots, the pinning, all that... but in that mental image she was wearing Grandma's coat."

THEY HURRIED BACK to Cob Cottage and found the old black waxed raincoat hanging on the back of the door where Emz had left it.

"I don't know why we're surprised," Charlie said. "We knew the coat was here. We knew Winn was wearing her own coat. We saw her in it."

"But what we were shown must mean something," Anna insisted. Charlie nodded.

"Probably. But what? Does it matter now?" Charlie asked.

"We cut off Mrs Fyfe's magic power supply." Emz dug her hands deep into her Prickles fleece, inhaled the scent of wood and pond water that it misted up to her.

"And she's gone. End of." Anna said.

An image of Mrs Fyfe's snapped ankle haunted all their minds.

37

SAFE HARBOUR

Mrs Fyfe felt the magic stifle her own and it was a head rush, violent, sickening, and unpleasant. She was in the garden at Hartfield when it happened, her hand just around the neck of the squirrel. She let it quiver for a moment, the tiny source of fear bolstering the drain she now felt on her main resource.

Oh. It had been such delight, to be strong and unfettered and now, each minute that ticked away, a little of her strength sapped, first one grey hair and then another and another striping their miserable way through her lustrous black locks. Oh. It had been so easy here and now someone, she could well guess who, was robbing her of that.

She had not come this way through Havoc Wood for many years, too many for anyone to count and even back then it was a Way who had tripped her, a Way who had barred and bound her.

She needed enough strength for these last few steps. She would finish them. Make no mistake.

The squirrel's heart gave out in her hand and since it was no longer any use she threw the furry corpse onto the grass. She didn't have to think about what she was going to do next, this drain on her resources was simply the fanfare for battle. It was time.

THERE HAD BEEN something off about this Winn woman from the very first day. Mrs Fyfe had noted an edge that she couldn't quite fathom and it interested her greatly that the woman herself was oblivious to whatever this edge was. Apple Day had sealed the woman's fate. She had eaten three goodly slices of the apple cake that Mrs Fyfe had baked and yet she had been unaffected by the slow poison. For anyone to withstand this magic there must be something, something powerful and talismanic inside them that was worth obtaining. Mrs Fyfe prided herself on her resourcefulness and now she was going to use that resource. Winn Hartley-Hartfield was going to be her backup generator.

There was no magical summoning required, there was simply the request over the phone. She had dragged the woman to Hartfield on several occasions already in order to poke and prod at her edge.

So it was very vexing this time to have her request denied.

"It's an interloper. An outlaw," she insisted. Mrs Fyfe was standing in the main hall and was aware of the fact that this central part of the building held nothing for this woman. She had reached for the connection several times and found it thin but there had been two or three occasions where the lure of the place was stronger. Where had she been? Was it in the garden? That had quite a draw but no. Where else had she summoned her to?

Mrs Fyfe took the phone into the kitchen and at once the lure worked, the intriguing and edgy Winn woman was on her way and Mrs Fyfe would triumph.

The charm or the curse or whatever it was revealed itself in the woods after the first blow with the bough. Mrs Fyfe couldn't recognise it, knew only that she was powerless against it and that its source was outside Winn Hartley-Hartfield. It infuriated her but she pressed ahead anyway; the bone magic would strip it, would deny it.

"I pin you." The smell of marrow was twitching at her as her boot pressed into the first wrist, the bone of holding, and then her other foot stepping down hard on the bone of cracking.

The charm was strong, twisting her magic back on herself. The pain sapped everything out of her, her own foot twisting as surely as if a hand had reached for it, Winn lying prone but unharmed, the protection fierce, sounding the bone magic back and out so that the air was alive with it, the strength and power dissipating at once into the wind, the trees, the sky, taking everything she was with it, signalling to her enemies like a distress flare. How could she have made such a mistake? How could she have done this? Desperate, she knew there was only one way to survive her error and, holding that hope, Mrs Fyfe twisted herself up.

MATT WOODHILL WAS out this evening. He had been called out for a quote on the edge of Kingham. Tilda Mitton was a rather posh lady who had over the years added little bits and buildings to her rather lovely home and regarded Matt, quite rightly, as something of a craftsperson. Roz had, in the past, harboured an idea that if Tilda ever decided to move then she and Matt would buy the house from her. She had, in point of fact, openly admitted as much to Tilda on several occasions.

Matt had been keen for her to come with him.

"You get on great with Tills and you could have a good nosey round," he had suggested. "You've had a crap day at the gallery, why not cheer yourself up?" He had a point but there was also the matter of the financial housekeeping for the upcoming gallery committee meeting. She'd been putting it off for too long.

"No. I'd love to. But seriously, Matt, I have to do the accounts," and he had been reluctantly understanding.

But now she'd finished catching up on the accounts for the gallery and was disappointed when she looked at the clock. She could have gone to Kingham after all. She opted to assuage her disappointment with a pot of her favourite tea.

As she reached for the tea caddy she was sure she heard the letterbox go in the hall and she pushed through the kitchen door. There was no free newspaper on the mat, no flyers for the curry house in Castle Hill or the pizza delivery service from Castlebury, and although these small facts shouldn't have bothered Roz, they did. A cold panic rose inside her and when the doorbell chimed out she walked back into the kitchen and shut the door. For good measure she put one of the chairs up against the handle and sat on it.

At the edge of her mind a thought was telling her she should run across the lawn right now. She should clamber over the back fence and keep running until she reached the Sisters. It was a prickly thought, like panic.

The doorbell chimed once more. Was she imagining it or did the sound lengthen strangely, as if it was in slow motion? The cold panic chilled a little more and she moved to the French doors that led into the conservatory.

She found that she was not opening them to make her escape. Instead she locked them and then her feet, unbidden, carried her back towards the kitchen door and into the hall. It was a sensation like hands pushing at her shoulders. Roz Woodhill was too scared to cry.

The letterbox rattled more, louder, longer, the hands pressed harder until Roz had to slump forwards. She felt as though she was being crushed. Her heart was booming in her head, a boom that began to match the rattle of the letterbox until she was joined to it, the rattle becoming her heartbeat and then her hands reached to open the door.

The woman stood on the porch; her hair was striped unevenly black and white and her face had a white pinched look.

"Invite me inside."

Roz felt her jaw creak and spasm, the ball and socket of it grinding against the unwelcome words.

"Enter, please," her voice cracked, and she took a step back, her arm lifting unbidden, ushering the guest inside; the woman's ankle, Roz noted, was horribly twisted, dragged in a trail of rain. The door shut of its own volition. The woman stood in her thin black boots, her leather cape sodden and sending up a scent of old sweat.

"By the hair on my chinny chin chin, you will let me in," grinned the woman, and everything was dark and sweat and skin.

38

THE POWER WE HAVE

In the bare white palace of an apartment at the marina, Charlie made it clear that this was the last place on earth she wanted to be. Aron stood looking peeved and, to Charlie's critical gaze, childish.

"Why? Why can't Anna and Emz just cope without you?"

He wanted to go to the opening of a new club in Castlebury. The occasion meant something as the place was owned by one of his friends, but Charlie didn't care. They had parties every week. It was just another club.

"I want to take you out and show you off. I've made plans." He had got very frustrated. "It's Halloween for Christ's sake." The word Halloween was like a spell, sparking itself off the surface of Charlie but leaving Aron untouched.

"Hey, remember last year?" His face lit, Charlie paused in her judgement of him. "We were VIP at Pandaemonium? Shit. That was mad. We should go back there. We could do that. Let's do that."

Charlie said nothing, did not react, waited. She watched Aron as he stood up straighter, smoothed his hand through his hair. It was clear he did not, right at this moment, remember the tragic significance that Halloween might have to the Way sisters.

"Remember last year," she said.

"Oh. Right. Bring that up." He was angry. Charlie felt a flare of fury, took a mental step back until she realised what he was angry about.

"You gambled away your car." Charlie had no mercy this evening, at least not for Aron.

"A car is just a car. Scrap metal." He was trying to shrug it off, he was good at that. There was still no recollection of the much bigger tragedy that had occurred. Charlie felt her mouth sealing. His face stretched into his best sexy Aron smile, the one he used to get upgrades at the airport.

"You know, Chaz, there are other girls who would kill for my attention." The sentence, usually, would have seemed a silly Aronism, something he said to push her buttons. This time it carried threat; Charlie heard it very clearly and, in the hyper state that she'd existed within lately, she would not suffer it.

"You don't owe me a thing." She heard the bleakness of her tone. Aron flinched, just a glimmer and no more, before resuming his cocky persona.

"What?" His stance was edgy and strutting, his head shaking as if she was a question mark and a nuisance. "What are you on about? Are we going out for Halloween or not?" There, that spell again and still he did not realise. Instead he raised his eyebrows, the look he gave her when he expected her to comply. Charlie could not find that easy going, eager to please Charlie, that part of her was slumped inside like a cast-off slip dress. Flimsy. Crumpled. The idea shook her, her chest compressed, and she thought she might cry.

"I have to work tonight. And tomorrow," she had said and reached for her jacket. He had persuaded her to come out for 'just one drink' tonight and she felt sickened by the liquor. She could taste factory grease, chlorine bleach, a beer brewed without heart in an industrial laboratory.

"Work?" Aron gave a snort. "How is hanging out with your sisters in Havoc Wood work? What are you? A fucking crack team of Girl Guides?" His face twisted into his most arrogant sneer, the one that signified he was most afraid. Charlie was shaking as she reached for the door. She had to go. Now. Aron came up behind her, slammed the door shut and leaned in close.

"How is that crap 'work'?"

Charlie looked into his eyes. If she looked hard enough perhaps she could see all their memories together, all their life, and it might rescue her. Might. She thought of Ethan the first time she ever saw him, of Calum busy at the stove in Cob Cottage last year making a curry for Anna's birthday. She knew then what she would say to Aron.

"I'm a Gamekeeper," she said. His face tensed for a second or two, his eyes took their gaze from hers before he gave a snide laugh and reached to open the door for her.

CHARLIE ARRIVED at Cob Cottage just as her sisters were stepping off the porch.

"Hey. Wait up." She hurried to meet them. Anna handed her a torch and they said nothing further, settling into each other's space as they headed out towards the edge of Pike Lake.

As on all the nights since the aftershock had hit, the Witch Ways' evening patrol had become something more than a straightforward Gamekeeping task. They were all aware of the anniversary that was looming and, without voicing the plan, Charlie and Emz were a cordon around their sister and Havoc Wood was their safe place.

Each evening as Halloween drew closer, they seemed to set out earlier and wander farther. They did not talk, allowing the sounds of the wood to siphon into them, the leaves rustling and beginning to fall, more each day as the autumn breezes intensified.

"We're making little checkpoints, have you noticed?" Charlie said as they pushed up the short rise that they knew as Hazzard's Pass. The path here was wider and the trees thinner and more graceful, the ground beneath them a thick carpet of moss, deep and green and, to Emz Way at that moment, inviting enough to drop down and sleep upon.

"Each night we've been out... there's been a pattern to it," she commented. "Don't you think?"

Anna nodded.

"Birch Stripes, Lull's Step, Top Hundred, Troop Edging, Hazzard's Pass..." Emz taking a striding step over Trickle Brook.

"... Quill's Gate, Thinthrough..." Charlie chimed in.

"... Thornwicket, Knoll," they all finished together, the names reeling from their tongues in time with their footsteps.

"We're marking our territory," Emz said with a smile.

"What did Grandma Hettie call it?" Charlie was energised with the memory.

"Beating the bounds." Anna said with a sad smile and, as they walked back down to Cob Cottage, their path was marked by the memory of Grandma Hettie's weatherbeaten black boots, their chunky soles surefooted through the rough and tumble of Havoc Wood.

At the porch Charlie hesitated.

"You all desperate for some hot chocolate then?" she quizzed, zipping her fleece high enough to catch her chin. Emz shrugged.

"Why?" Anna asked, dreading Charlie's answer, some instinct that was shouting danger, a warning sign somewhere? She looked around.

"It isn't that late. Half nine? There's a band on at the Highwayman, Karma and her boyfriend and his brother doing their stuff. Fiddle. Drum. Singing. Sort of." She was doing a little shoulder shuffly shimmy and waving her hands to try to sell it, her face animated and wide-eyed.

"Like the jazz hands," Emz laughed.

"Seriously. They're good. They can actually play." Charlie settled down. "First round's on me?"

"You never have any cash," Anna grinned. Charlie pulled a tenner out of her pocket.

"Abracadabra," she joked.

THE PUB WAS CROWDED but in a 'hail fellow well met and have a pint on me' mood. It appeared that after its recent trauma Woodcastle was attempting to get over itself and The Banshees were doing their best to assist.

"Shit, I'd forgotten their name," Charlie said to Emz as they struggled back from the bar with the drinks. "I was hoping this would distract her from—"

"Halloween." Emz prompted. She nodded to where their sister waited, clapping in time to the music and singing along. "I think you've succeeded."

"For a few hours anyway." Charlie conceded.

"YOU DREAMT WHAT?" Emz and Anna were a couple of pints of cider in and their faces were softened and warmed, their smiles easy.

"She was wearing that bird skull crown hat thing." Charlie made a whirling bird gesture around her head, gave a little burp into her hand. "You remember. Quite fancy one for myself. Now I'm a witch."

"No wait…" Anna was bright with laughter. "No, that wasn't the bit I found mad. I can handle you dreaming about Roz and about her wearing the bird skull crown. I get that. Queen of the Craft Club… Fine. Done." Anna was struggling to speak through her amusement. "What I can't... I don't get... Wha..." she dissolved into giggles.

"It's the toffee apple." Emz said, attempting to be serious and then bursting into laughter, shaking her head at Anna. "What the hell is she doing with a toffee apple?"

"Was it organic?"

They spoke together in a high shriek that made the couple next to them turn around.

"She was sort of looming over me with it. Waving it a bit. Like this." Charlie waved her hand in mimicry of her dream and her sisters dissolved into yet more laughter. Emz was slapping at the table, Anna was making a whooping sound, her eyes streaming, leaning into Emz. Charlie watched them for a few moments.

"I'll get some more drinks," she said. As she pushed her way through to the bar she was secretly pleased. She had not seen Anna laugh so hard in a very long time.

At the bar she waited, and, as she did so, the music started up again. A rollicking drum beat that seemed to send a sharp sting up her arms as if she'd touched an electric fence. She stood back from the bar. What the hell? She touched the bar rail: the electricity was not coming from it. It was pricking into her from the air. Around her the bar was thronging and beneath it all, a thin hum. There must be a feedback issue with the amp. Ow. Charlie took the drinks and headed back. As the three sisters sat, triangulated around the table, the electrified inkling had a power surge and Charlie could tell instantly that her sisters felt it too.

"What the hell?" Charlie was shouting above the music. Anna and Emz were looking over her shoulder. Charlie turned.

Roz Woodhill had come through the door with her husband, Matt. The Way sisters watched as she made her way to the bar on a broken looking ankle. As she turned her gaze upon them her tinny eyes were obvious. Anna stood up at once, all smiles.

"Roz?" She stepped out from behind their table, touching Charlie on the shoulder as she did so. "Roz, how are you?"

Roz looked threatened, Anna casting a beaming smile at Matt as she reached to hug Roz.

"Roz. It is so good to see you." She wrapped her arms fully around Roz. The power surged, pushing her away but Anna held tight and let the flickerbook images rush her. The real Roz in the kitchen at Villiers House and the letterbox clattering. *Invite me inside.* More, "*I pin you I pin you I pin you*", all the bones that had been broken down centuries, the power, the darkness, and finally a white bite taken from a blood red apple. The surge of it was almost too much; just as Anna felt her own darkness begin to cloud in, billowing and smothering velvet black, she let go. At once the electrified zap lowered to a cracking tick. There was a faint diesel glimmer of blue and purple to the tin glaze of Roz's eyes before they settled back to their grey dullness.

Anna was afraid, a thin, sharp fear. She did not cut it off, let it seep towards Roz and observed the glimmer in those tinny eyes.

"Hey Anna... can we get you a drink? Join you perhaps?" Matt looked tired and desperate and it was all Anna could do not to react.

"Oh, no, that's okay... we're just..." Anna fumbled for an excuse and Matt nodded as Charlie and Emz bustled up behind.

"Hey Roz." Charlie glanced casually at Roz Woodhill. "Anna, time we were off..." She tapped at her watchless wrist.

"Oh yes, yes." Anna faked. Emz faked a smile and a small wave at Roz. Anna made a calling gesture with her hand.

"Another time, Matt. Roz, call me about Craft Club. I haven't been for ages. Or I'll speak to Mari. See you around."

Roz glared at her and then, turning, hobbled on her mangled ankle towards the bar.

The Way sisters were hurrying down the street and not talking. They were part way up Long Gate Street when Charlie said,

"Are we not going to say it out loud?"

Anna was striding.

"Halloween," she said. Charlie increased her pace.

"That wasn't what I meant."

"You meant, Mrs Fyfe is possessing the body of Roz Wood-hill?" Emz slotted the thought in.

"Halloween," Anna said again, sounding more breathless as they headed uphill. Emz and Charlie kept pace.

"Tinny eyes. Broken looking ankle. It's a no brainer. What happened when you hugged her?" Charlie asked Anna. At last she halted, her breath coming in heavy gulps.

"Oh, full on flashcard memory of everything. And I don't just mean Apple Day. The lot." Anna sagged a little. "She's in there alright."

The silence rolled a little between them.

"We have to get her out," Emz said at last.

"You mean exorcise Roz Woodhill." Charlie made it sound as though there was a practical approach to the situation. The other two looked at her.

"Exorcise. Yes, I suppose that's it," Anna nodded. "I've been thinking about how to do it. Trying to remember if there was anything at any time that Grandma Hettie taught us that might cover this."

There was another long silence. Charlie's mind blinked with the image of Roz and the toffee apple from her dream.

"The toffee apple," Charlie said. "The apples. We've got bait. Surely?"

"We use the apples. Somehow," Emz began. "She's weaker, you could feel that."

"If we offer up another power source, more fuel. Maybe there's a way to overload her," Charlie suggested.

"Use the negative energy against her. Weaponise it." Anna was filtering and sifting her thoughts.

"Are we going to have to poison someone to do it? Poison us perhaps?" Emz was tentative. Anna shook her head.

"Halloween," she said. "That power. That's what we must use."

There was a moment of silence. Charlie nodded and reached

an arm around Anna, another around Emz, and pulled them in close. They stood like that for a few moments.

"Home," Anna said as they pulled apart a little, Charlie linking Anna's arm on one side, Emz on the other.

In the shadow of the castle walls a ghost in a black waxed raincoat watched them break up and walk onwards, towards Old Castle Road.

THERE WAS hot chocolate and toast on the table at Cob Cottage as the Witch Ways planned.

"So. Trap her."

"Where?" Charlie was crestfallen. She hadn't thought that far ahead. "Do we bring her to the wood?"

Anna shook her head, doubtful.

"It doesn't feel right. We can't hem her in. Too many ways out."

"Hartfield then. Winn will let us," Emz said as she reached for some toast.

"No. Anna's right." Charlie spread jam over her toast, concentrating. "What we need is a fortress." She crunched her toast.

Anna looked up.

"We've got one," she said.

"Cob Cottage?" Emz looked alarmed. Anna shook her head and grinned.

"The castle."

39

I PIN YOU

Anna had a busy day ahead with prep for the booked-out Halloween Party at the Castle Inn. The kitchen resembled a proper fairy-tale with pumpkins rolling around every surface.

"Lella overdid the order," Casey explained as they picked their way through the bumper orange crop. Anna took in a deep breath. Her heart was fluttering, thoughts were shifting and altering inside her, the darkness of her grief trying to sweep forward. She pushed it back and focused on the task that lay ahead, dealing with Mrs Fyfe.

Anna moved quickly to the work surface; as she picked up her knife it made a sound like a sword. The peel on the first onion crackled, the scent rising, raw but savoury, and Anna breathed it in deep.

One year. One entire, whole, complete year. She had come this far. As the morning and the chores wore on Anna's thoughts deepened. At first she focused her attention on the chopping and slicing, on the frying and roasting and boiling, but the plan to exorcise Roz Woodhill and defeat Mrs Fyfe bubbled and boiled and in her head the deep well of memory began to ripple a little.

CHARLIE SEARED a path through the brewery that morning. The water splashing into the mash tun sounded alive and energised. The scents of barley and malt, of hops, all seemed to make her breathe deeper, to imbue her with more energy.

As the afternoon drew on Charlie could be found decanting more Blackberry Ferment, this time into an earthenware flagon she had picked up this morning from under the sink at Cob Cottage. The crackles in the brown glaze had seemed, to her, to show a map of Woodcastle, one that was old and slightly skewed and showing the Castle itself at the centre. Where, in the last few weeks she had felt lost and afraid, now Charlie felt that she knew the way, knew what must be done, and, more important than anything, had the skills to do it.

AT PRICKLES, Emz Way was in charge of the small school group, all the children dressed in mini high-vis vests with the school logo on the back. They had collected leaves and oak galls and beech-nuts, pheasant feathers and caterpillar cocoons.

At a particular turn in the path as they headed to the hide at Cooper's Pond a spider web stretched between the branches of the birch trees. The autumnal sunlight caught the rain in it so that it glittered like diamonds for just a moment before the clouds scudded over once more. Emz stopped. A fierce memory of Grandma Hettie,

"And a warp of web for winding..." her tongue just peeking out of the corner of her mouth as she twisted the thread of it, wound the spider web around her finger, around, around, a gossamer skein. Her wink as she put it into her pocket. Her black waxed coat pockets usually filled with feathers and pebbles, pine cones and seed heads. Emz felt in the pockets. Nothing. She took a step off the path and with care wound the web onto the spool of her fingers. It settled into the corner of her pocket.

In the kitchen behind reception there was a quantity of black smoke and Winn was struggling to wrench a singed crumpet from the aged toaster.

"You might as well trot off early, Emz," Winn suggested, knife rattling in the toaster's innards. "Usual Halloween rules and all that." She looked up at Emz with a sympathetic gaze. "I imagine your family have something quiet planned." Emz took in a deep breath at the notion of what Halloween might hold for them. She looked into Winn's face and was not surprised to see that the only face she could see was Winn's true and real one. The apple-cheeked girl looked concerned. Emz nodded assent.

"I will see you tomorrow," Winn said firmly. Emz saw the apple-cheeked girl reach up and touch a small brown leather pouch that was strung around her neck. Emz could not help but stare until the image blurred away and left the here-and-now Winn behind. "You look like you've seen a ghost," Winn barked. "Mind you, I suppose tonight is the night for it."

EMZ TOOK her leave and walked the wood, made a circuit of Cooper's Pond itself, aware that the scent of the water was strong, that it carried an earthy coolness inside it that she breathed in deep and that gave her a bright energy. This bright energy she carried with her, all the way through Leap Woods to the manicured edge of lawn and the rambling flower borders of Hartfield Hall.

The back door had been blown open and as Emz entered a squirrel shot out from the dresser at the far side of the room and bolted out through the cracked pane in the window. The Witch Ways had talked over their intentions and where, earlier in the day, Emz had felt rattled and uncertain, she now felt sure. The kitchen at Hartfield felt empty, there was no lingering sense of Mrs Fyfe, except for the sickly scent that now crept under the larder door. It was an odd aroma, Emz thought, as she stepped into the small cool storage space. There was a hint of something tasty and appealing and then a thicker layer of repulsion and disgust. As she picked up the basket of apples from the marble countertop this thicker scent wafted like a cloud. She saw too how the apples had grown darker red still. As she lifted the basket handle the apples felt suddenly leaden and heavy, the basket's weave screeling itself against the marble. These apples, Emz understood, did not want to be taken. Security measures were clearly in place.

"No." Emz spoke the word quietly, it caught on the air. She put both hands onto the handle of the basket and held tight. In her mind she recalled her first encounter with Mrs Fyfe, when Winn had been up the ladder. She took Winn out of the memory and focused on Mrs Fyfe's real face, angular, stretched. As she did so the face, thinner and more stretched, loomed into her mind, challenging, the eyes intense but tired looking. Before she could speak Emz pushed herself mentally forwards with a sudden burst.

"BOO." As the word rang off the cracked cheese dish in the larder so Mrs Fyfe's face vanished from Emz's mind with a look of startled horror and the basket of apples was suddenly the correct poundage. Emz hefted it onto her arm and, kicking the larder door shut behind her, headed out. At the edge of the courtyard she put the basket through the gap in the wall of the walled garden and followed after it. Night was falling fast and here and there across town fireworks were being let off. Emz seemed tuned to every bang and boom, as if the saltpetre and the gunpowder were her own weapons, topping her mental energy up and each step she took bringing her nearer and nearer, she knew, to the safe haven that was Havoc Wood.

AT THE CASTLE BARBARA BENTLEY, custodian, took the heavy iron key and locked the main gate. After she had done that she moved to the small riveted door and opened the latch, stepped out onto the gantry beyond. She turned and with another less heavy iron key she locked up. This was the favourite part of her commute, the short walk along the gantry with the keys clanking in her pocket.

The Witch Ways did not care whether the castle was closed or not. Already Anna was walking up through the Cromwellian siege tunnel that the fox had so carefully led them to and which now she imbued with extra meaning. This tunnel was a useful bit of knowledge to have. It felt as if the castle belonged to them, linked it closer to Havoc.

She emerged into the castle yard and took a few strides up to the highest rise of the greensward. She was carrying with her nine pieces of wood that she had gathered from the nine checkpoints in Havoc Wood that she and her sisters had beaten the bounds of in the last week or so since the Crimson Ball. They were all different: oak, ash, elm, beech, elder, alder, holly, rowan, and hawthorn. She had walked up to the wood after work, taking a long route up to the very top of Old Castle Road. Here was a narrow-hedged lane that, when followed, would bring her out at Thorn Thicket and as she reached the spot she saw at once where the slim branch of the hawthorn had been chewed at by deer and was broken almost clean away. True to her Grandma Hettie's grandparenting Anna never left home without her small pocket knife and now she hooked the blade open and sawed the deer damaged limb free.

At each and every point the chosen bough, branch, or switch was visible; at Thinthrough the thickened out and ancient holly snagged at her sleeve and as she pulled free so a long whipping bough came with her, the leaves looking like spiked shields; at Quill's Gate the elder leaning, uprooted by wind, a branch trailing across her path, so that, by the time she was down at Birch Stripes she felt the wood had given her these tools, and, in the giving, fed her Strength.

On the greensward Anna put the nine branches on the grass and took in a deep breath. She understood the significance that each of the switches and branches held but, if she was being honest, she did not have a real idea of how they were going to tackle this situation. The only clear thoughts she had were simple and were bait and trap. Her well of memory sounded a note as if a stone had dropped into it and she felt its cold darkness. Weaponise it. She would know how. She was trusting in her instincts.

It was only a few minutes before Charlie and Emz emerged from the tunnel together, Charlie carrying the last flagon of Blackberry Ferment and Emz the basket of apples. At the sight of the apples Anna shuddered. Fear tried to take a small step in her direction and she blocked it.

"What are we going to do?" Charlie asked the question. "We seem to have all the pieces but no instructions."

They looked at the items before them so that they didn't have to look at the fear in each other's faces.

"There's got to be something here to jog our memories." Charlie was thinking aloud. With a sudden small squawking sound, she lifted the flagon of Blackberry Ferment and unstoppered it. "First things first..." She swigged from the flagon and then offered it to Anna.

"No. I think we need to be..."

Charlie pushed the flagon at her.

"This is how we do it. Like a fairytale. We drink this and we..." her gaze ranged around the collection of objects. Emz came to her rescue.

"We don't eat the apples."

"Agreed." Anna nodded, already the edges of her mind were beginning to fold in and out on themselves and create memory shapes, Grandma Hettie in her black raincoat, as always, a step ahead. Charlie gave another squeak.

"And we make a house with the sticks," she said and grabbed for the first on the pile. "Oh my God... that's it... that's it..." she took the switch and with a step forward she jabbed it into the ground. The second she did this the memory clicked in both Emz and Anna.

The den. Always nine sticks.

"Now... I have a bit of business to take care of. You three wait inside 'til I get back."

How many afternoons, when Grandma Hettie had had what she termed 'a bit of business' to attend to, had she made them a den of switches? They had played or read or snoozed in those dens and, above all, they saw it now, they had been kept safe from whatever 'bit of business' Grandma Hettie had dealt with.

They arranged the nine tree limbs in a circle, each one staked into the ground.

"There's something else. Something missing." Anna walked the circle; a piece of memory nagged at her but would not tug free. Charlie walked around too, Emz strolling afterwards, her hand trailing along the staves. She gave a short laugh and stopped, her left hand reaching into her pocket. Anna and Charlie watched as she began to unspool some thread from a small, slightly scruffy ball. There was, it transpired, exactly the correct length of thread.

"Spider web," Emz smiled at them. "Remember?" At once Charlie recalled her Grandmother informing her of the strength of spider web and Anna remembered the fact that the Romans used spider webs in wound dressings. The sisters turned to check out their handiwork.

"It looks very..." Charlie cast her glance around the circle, was becoming transfixed by the long thin shadows that the switches and branches were casting, each dark line standing sentinel beside.

"Magical," Emz decided. "Very magical. Shouldn't we be standing inside it?"

Charlie reached for the flagon of Blackberry Ferment and ducked under the thin thread of spider web into the den. Emz and Anna were swift to follow. Charlie unstoppered the flagon, began to trail the ferment around the boundary of the circle. The Witch Ways took in a deep breath. Blackberries. Havoc Wood.

Anna looked up at the sky as fear scuttled about in her head.

"Of all the checkpoints we've patrolled…" Anna began, "which is your favourite?" she asked her sisters.

"What?" Charlie asked, stoppering up the last of the Blackberry Ferment and holding the flagon to her chest.

"Thinthrough," Emz answered at once. "I like Thinthrough the best."

"Hazzard's Pass," Anna said. The two sisters looked at Charlie. Her face was looking rather pinched and tired.

"I'm scared."

"Good. It's fuel. It attracts her and powers us." Anna was matter of fact. "What's your favourite checkpoint in Hav…?"

"Top Hundred," Charlie blurted. "Always."

Anna nodded.

"That's yours, Charlie. Over there, Emz." She pointed out two switches on opposing sides of the circle. "Mine's thataway." Anna's branch was at the top of the circle and, if anyone above had taken a compass and a pencil they could have drawn a strong, true triangle between the three points in the circle. The three sisters took up their positions.

"What now?" Charlie asked and looked at Anna and Emz. Emz also looked at Anna. Anna's gaze was making a circuit of the walls, and then drifting down to the standing staves.

"Invite her in," Anna said in a stony voice.

AT VILLIERS HOUSE Roz Woodhill was not cooking. She had not cooked since the night of the Crimson Ball and Matt was very worried about her. She was not doing anything much. Not talking. Not smiling. Not being very loving. There was something wrong with her ankle.

"You need to go and see someone about your ankle," he had

fussed, growing anxious."You need to leave me alone." Her voice was hoarse and small and not like her voice.

"Why don't you ring up? You've been hobbling about, you need to get it X-rayed."

Roz turned her tin glazed eyes upon him and, for just a second, they flashed black.

"Leave me alone."

Shaking and afraid Matt stepped away from his wife. He did not understand what was going on. He had thoughts, but they were stupid scared thoughts that were influenced by too many horror films.

In the evenings she slumped in the chair in front of the television. At night she slept like the dead.

And, most worrying of all, Matt dreamt each night that a woman, a thin, white-faced woman, was standing beside the bed and each night drifts of black smoke would lift from himself and Roz and the thin white-faced woman would inhale this smoke like marijuana.

He was beginning to be afraid to go to sleep.

He had poured out his woes to Gary at work over a mug of tea. He was not used to talking about personal stuff at work; usually it was the football or rugby or cricket in summer. Gary was sympathetic.

"Get her out of herself. Out of the house," he said when they had been talking for over two hours. "Why not take her to Jakey's Halloween Party?"

MATT HAD THOUGHT Roz might not want to come but she had been keen.

"A party? There will be people? How many?" The tinny eyes were greedy looking. Matt thought he might cry.

Usually they threw their own big Halloween party and indeed last year's had begun to get a little out of hand; naked people in the garden and black candles setting fire to the blind in the conservatory. Matt was a knot of fear and worry and, as he sat in the living room, Roz was staring at him.

"Penny for them?" she asked. He did not like the sound of her voice, it was off somehow and the way she looked at him was like a cat looking at a mouse. Gary's advice was exactly right. They needed to get out of the house.

"Nothing. Look, let's go. Yeah? Have a drink and a laugh." He got up from the sofa, struggled against the idea of running out of the room to escape that gaze. "It's Halloween." At mention of the word, Roz fetched her coat.

They walked down through town.

"I'm tired," Roz complained. Matt squeezed her hand. He was not surprised considering how much she was hobbling on that dodgy ankle. He wanted to lift her into his arms and carry her. Take her away from here.

"We're nearly there." They turned up Carter's Stretch and they could already see Jake's front garden where a small group of smokers had gathered dressed as rubber werewolves, bedsheet ghosts, slutty witches looking solemn and subdued.

"This is great," Matt said, squeezing Roz's hand again. "This is really great." He was convincing no one. Roz stopped dead in her tracks, her head turning slowly towards the castle.

"What is it?" Matt looked out into the night. A small group of trick-or-treating children were using the pelican road crossing, the sound beeping briefly into the night quiet.

As he turned back Roz was right in his face, her breath sour and smelling of rotting brown apples.

"I will take what you have," she said, her hand reaching for his frightened face. There was a flash of black between them, Matt suffering an odd, painful sensation like a blood vessel bursting in his eye. Roz's eyes widened, the tin glaze flared and vanished from her eyes and she crumpled. Matt half stumbled, diving to catch her before she hit the floor, his arms folding around her and with a sudden scared cry, Roz's arms folded tight around him. She was pulling herself into him, her fingers clawing at him.

"Matt. Matt. Matt," she whispered as if she'd just fallen into a life raft. "Oh... Oh..." her body shuddering and juddering and, at last, tears, Matt's fingers wiping them from her face.

"I'm here. I'm here." He held her tight, shifted to the floor, lifted her up into his lap and closed himself around her. "I'm here. I'm not going anywhere."

MRS FYFE WAS WORN thin and dry as a blade of summer grass. Now, with the burst of black from the stupid man and the last skein of black from the occult dabbling Roz woman she had enough, just enough, to get her there. She heard them. She saw them. Three fools waiting in their own trap.

The effort of spinning herself into the wind seeped at her energy but as she landed on the greensward on the other side of the Castle's curtain wall, she knew that this game was worth the candle.

EVEN FROM WITHIN the standing staves from Havoc Wood, the magic force from Mrs Fyfe crackled into the Ways.

"Look at her ankle," Charlie whispered. The sisters looked. Mrs Fyfe's left ankle in its snarled black boot was twisted back on itself, swollen out purple where the bone was broken.

"At last. The Witch Ways." This thought amused Mrs Fyfe. "What a miserable legacy Hettie Way has left," she sneered. There was a short silence during which the three sisters stared, unblinking, at Mrs Fyfe. She was not amused.

"Come far?" Charlie asked, her voice sounding strong as it echoed around the castle walls. Charlie had not known what she would do, the words had bubbled up unbidden and Charlie was trying not to reveal her own surprise at this phenomenon. Mrs

Fyfe was even less amused and pinched her lips together. She gave an ugly jerk forward as if pushed and there were sounds trapped inside her. Anna, Charlie, and Emz could hear them, like a distant voice, many voices in fact, crying to be let out.

"Going further." Emz now, taking in a breath, knowing where the words were and how it had to be said, her voice echoing into the stone. There was a soft and deep ringing tone in the air.

"Trespasser," Anna declared at which Mrs Fyfe was not amused at all. She rallied herself, swallowing down the voices and with her mouth still pinched shut she took a limping step and began a circuit of the staves. The Witch Ways watched her progress, their hearts beating hard, so hard in fact that Charlie knew she could hear her own beat vibrating in the stave from Top Hundred that she stood beside. As the wooden thrum of it blended with the soft ringing from the stones Charlie suddenly knew what to do.

She took three steps forward to where the basket lay and picked up an apple. For a second Mrs Fyfe's face glinted with anticipation but instead of taking a bite Charlie moved to the nearest wooden stave and finding an appropriately sharp branch she impaled the apple upon it. The fruit browned and withered almost at once.

"You are fools. All three," Mrs Fyfe smirked, but she had stopped walking. Charlie took another apple and impaled it. Emz and Anna joined the task. The effect on Mrs Fyfe was clear, the tiredness pulling at her, beginning to round out her shoulders. The ankle swelled a little larger, the foot caved in a little more and still Mrs Fyfe managed a low laugh, unpleasant and rumbling.

"I wonder what weapon you think will wound me?" the laugh rattled at them. Charlie began to struggle to move towards the next stave, and the apple in her hand was sending out a sour scent that was reaching right inside her. Holding her breath did not stop the smell invading her; instead it intensified, she must breathe so that she could breathe this horror out and yet each breath inwards turned up her fear, her doubt. The emotion wafted from her in a stench. She could see Mrs Fyfe inhaling it, breathing it in, as refreshing to her as oxygen. Emz gave a terrified gasp, clutched at the black smoke that was spooling out of her. They were fighting it but Charlie was crying, her hands swiping at her eyes.

"This isn't working... why isn't this working?" Charlie sobbed, watching as Mrs Fyfe's dodgy ankle realigned itself, as her thin, stretched face took on a little more flesh. "I can't... fight." She broke down, the tears pouring from her, all her grief and doubt. She reached out for her stave, her fingers closing around it.

"Strength. Find. Our. Strength." Emz choked out the words. She stood now facing her stave, both hands holding it like a staff, her mind filled with the memory of the little knitted hat. Grief like a knife through her. Logan's arm on hers, *I'm sorry*" and the jealousy was sour and vivid green.

Anna stood by her stave and felt the heavy black velvet of her sorrow fold around her. She was not afraid. She knew what she had to do. She took three strides to the basket and picked up the last apple. Charlie looked at the fruit, at her sister, and nothing could come from her except a thin whine of sorrow. Emz fell to her knees, sobbing into the grass.

Listen to your instinct, Anna. Red skin. White flesh.

Anna Way bit into the last poison apple.

At once she felt it, the raw uncooked venom of it and it tasted sour and sharp. It was not her mouth that puckered and dried, it was her mind. All the darkness rushed in and in that darkness Anna Way might have been lost.

Might have been.

Mrs Fyfe felt the rush of energy. The sorrow, the lament. It was like a piece of bloodied beef to her energy, more vital than all of the town together. It seethed and rolled in a heavy iron rich tide.

Might have been.

Except, that within this darkness, Anna Way knew where she was going. To a small, much darker corner, cooled by the stone and weed scent of the deep deep well of memory and here, in the darkness, the well water bubbled.

There would be no bounding or banishing now; Mrs Fyfe was beyond their reach. The Witch Ways offered her a main course, a high dark fear, crunchy and marrow filled. She was powering up, drinking in more than she had drunk in centuries. She felt her blood thicken and darken in her veins.

All that might have been. All that was. The well water roiled upwards, mental stones shifted with a rumbling grind.

All that might have been.

All that was.

Calum in his armour on that first day. Calum on any other day. Calum laughing. Calum grumpy. Calum shouting. Calum sleeping.

Calum gone.

The empty chair. The empty bed. The bare place, here, where Ethan slept.

Calum is gone. Ethan is gone.

The darkness curved in on itself and the thunder rumbled onwards, tears falling like a rainstorm, salt and sorrow, lashing, and here in her heart, the weapon of it at last unsheathed.

Black. Bitter. Grief.

But, more powerful still, the white burning lightning.

Love.

WITHIN THE STANDING staves a searing light cast the shadows of the branches outwards catching Mrs Fyfe in their black lines, her body and mind overdosing on the energy of Anna's emotions, the black heart of her grief pounding at Mrs Fyfe's corporeal form. Hammering, hammering, hammering until with the flash of lightning Mrs Fyfe exploded like a supernova, black star particles that vaporised into the stones of the castle and were gone.

40

A WHEEL, A KNIFE, A PIECE OF WOOD

The week after Halloween was quiet in Woodcastle. The entire town had begun to recover properly from the Apple Day events and was, consequently, feeling a bit hungover and sorry for itself. Plus, it was now November and therefore nearly Christmas and that was dragging along its own tinselly kind of depression.

Anna was working at the Castle Inn today and so her sisters and her mother had arranged to meet and eat there. They were coming in for the market day. Charlie was on the Drawbridge Breweries pop-up once again and Emz was finishing a day of revision sessions for her upcoming mock exams before dropping into town.

Vanessa had not been to the market for a number of years. She tended to pop into the big-name supermarket on the edge of Castlebury because it was two minutes' drive from the DeQuincy Langport Research Centre. Today, the supermarket did not carry what she needed and so she had walked into Woodcastle bringing with her the rather ancient basket that had once belonged to her mother.

"I'd like a small wheel of the Hartfield Hard please..." Vanessa asked the cheesemonger, a middle-aged woman in dungarees and an old-fashioned linen pinny matched with a pair of wooden clogs.

"Of course… want to try our new blue?" The woman offered a cheese knife with a small nub of the blue cheese on it and Vanessa tasted. It was brightly tangy and intensely creamy, and Vanessa savoured it, holding the flavours in her mouth as she looked through the stalls to where she could just see the edge of High Market Place and a glimpse of the black and white construction of the Moot Hall. Word had reached her of the Crimson Ball.

"It's good isn't it?" The woman smiled at Vanessa.

"Yes. Yes, it is."

Vanessa took the wheel of cheese which had been wrapped in waxed paper and placed it carefully in the bottom of the basket.

Yolanda Gill was wearing an all in one blue overall and was sitting at the rear of her stall weaving a scarf on a peg loom. The wool was spun from her own sheep, a small flock of Jacobs visible from Vanessa's house, grazing as they did in the top field. Vanessa made her selection from the ready woven items, a scarf in lichen greens. It was folded and put into the basket.

At the woodcarver stall she bought a chopping board made from sycamore.

"It was from a tree felled in Leap Woods…" the stall holder assured her. Vanessa knew, there was no chopping board made from wood felled in Havoc. The board, long and slightly curved to the grain of the beautiful wood was wrapped in paper and put into the basket.

The knifesmith had a small forge going at the back of her stall and looked heated in her t-shirt, jeans and leather apron.

"This one?" the knifesmith held up the large carving knife from the display rack, the handle a simple twisted design, the blade wide and sharp. She looked as though she were brandishing a miniature sword.

"Yes, please," Vanessa nodded and began to pull the notes out of her purse. The knifesmith was delighted at the sale, hurrying to place the knife in a black gift box and making sure she put in a business card.

The knife was placed into the basket. Vanessa checked her possessions: basket, cheese, knife, board, scarf. Her list was complete. She walked once around the market again winding in and around the stalls and then walking with some purpose along the lanes and streets, roads and avenues of the centre of Woodcastle. From Laundry Lane up to Riggs Row, Vanessa walked, turning in at last at Barbican Steep and heading into the castle where Barbara Bentley nodded as she passed the gate and flashed her Friends of Woodcastle Castle pass. Vanessa climbed the steps in the East Keep and walked out onto the curtain wall. She took a moment to look out over the town, over at Leap Woods and at Havoc Wood, her gaze resting for a moment each on Yarl Hill and Ridge Hill and Horse Hill before she walked the circuit of the wall and back down via the steps at the other side of the gate.

By then, it was time to stroll towards the Castle Inn and meet her daughters.

THE WAYS HAD the dining room to themselves this afternoon. Anna had prepared the lunch and they sat at the round table with the white damask cloth laden with their finished plates and half-drunk glasses of wine. The white wine had seemed particularly sparkly and the Way sisters appeared in a cheery and giggling mood. There was much loud laughter but Vanessa Way, with her scientific eye, observed each of them. Anna with a new glow to her skin, moon pale as always but brighter than she had been for the last year. Emz looking edgy, could that be exam nerves? Charlie was laughing too hard and smiling too much which never boded well. Now she was pouring them all more wine, the liquid making a musical sound in the tall and elegant glasses.

"A toast. A toast." Charlie was boisterous. "Let's have a toast."

They all raised their glasses.

"What are we toasting?" Emz asked. Anna raised her glass a little higher.

"The Witch Ways."

The glasses chinkled with a sound that, to Vanessa Way, sounded like ice.

AT HAVOC WOOD THE WAY SISTERS' daily patrols had proved quiet. They had established a system of individual routes through the wood.

"But we can't get too set," Charlie warned. "We need to mix it up, not always tread the same path," she advised.

"Or we leave a trail." Anna nodded. They were beginning to understand the wood and to pull forward more and more days spent with Grandma Hettie. They had all begun to sleep better in Cob Cottage and the sleep brought the memories which refreshed their knowledge. They had all remembered, for instance, Grandma Hettie's idea of Pocket Walks and it was these shorter routes that they revisited individually in the day whenever they had time.

"We need to do three routes in the evenings when we can." They might have been poring over a map together but instead they were looking at a splather of green lentils and each pushing their fingers through the legumes to make differing swirls and dunes.

To Charlie the lentil mess was an aerial view of Havoc Wood complete with all the checkpoints that before they had taken for granted and which now, after their adventures with Ailith and Mrs Fyfe, she valued as lodestones and markers to the territory.

"Tonight I'll take this eastern side from the back end of the lake up towards town." Charlie's finger pushed her route through, the lentils rustling like leaves. She needed to be out, pounding the paths and racing ahead of her thoughts.

"I'll take the western end then and up towards Old Castle and the edge of Ridge Hill…" Anna trailed her finger through the tumbled mass.

To Anna the green lentils made a sound like the edge of Pike Lake. She liked the feel of the wood of the old table beneath her fingertip, the gnarls and grain of it, and felt connected. If she didn't turn her head she could see, in the very corner of her vision, Grandma Hettie at the sink washing out a white jug that she always kept flowers in; the flowers were waiting on the draining board, some hogweed from beside the flat stone at the edge of the lake. The flowers delicate, the sap dangerous. There was a reminder in that for Anna.

"I'll take the last third then… keep an eye on the edge of Leap Woods too," Emz pointed and poked, a couple of lentils pinging like tiddlywinks as she did so. For Emz the green lentils showed her the quick trails of a deer through Havoc, twisting and looping. The trail drew her eye, drew her heart. She thought of the small shard of metal like an arrowhead that she had once taken from an injured deer at Prickles, the silvered glint of metal in the crooked daylight of Havoc.

They readied themselves for the patrol. Charlie keenest, tugging on her jacket and knotting her scarf and almost out of the door before Anna could stop her.

"Lantern," Anna reminded her. Charlie with a too energetic movement lifted her lantern from the hooks on the porch. Anna was next unhooking her lantern and turning to Emz who pulled on their grandmother's black waxed raincoat. The door to Cob Cottage closed behind them with a soft oaken thump.

LATER, an owl flew low over the trees, mapping its route by the three winking lanterns below, casting a web of light showing the Ways that wandered through Havoc Wood.

Proof

Made in the USA
Columbia, SC
14 August 2018